HOME

LEILA S. CHUDORI spent six years researching this groundbreaking novel, interviewing exiles and their families in Paris and Jakarta, basing her characters on these real individuals, trapped in the tides of history. The novel's central character, Dimas Suryo, abroad in 1965 and unable to return to Indonesia after Suharto's rise to power, winds up in Paris, where he helps found a restaurant, based on the real Restaurant Indonesia, a place to join and celebrate their longed-for home culture through food, dance, and song, while suffering a lifetime of homelessness away from Indonesia. In another narrative strand of the novel, Lintang Utara, Suryo's daughter with a Frenchwoman, arrives in Jakarta in 1998 for her thesis in film studies just as the student protests that bring down Suharto get underway. Father and daughter each become central characters in the history of Indonesia's tragic 20th century, marking the rise and fall of a brutal dictatorship.

HOME

—

Leila S. Chudori

TRANSLATED FROM THE INDONESIAN BY
JOHN H. McGLYNN

DEEP VELLUM PUBLISHING
DALLAS, TEXAS

Deep Vellum Publishing
2919 Commerce St. #159, Dallas, Texas 75226
deepvellum.org · @deepvellum

Deep Vellum Publishing is a 501c3
nonprofit literary arts organization founded in 2013.

First published in Indonesian in 2012 under the title *Pulang*
by Kepustakaan Populer Gramedia (KPG) of Jakarta.
Indonesian language copyright © 2012 Leila S. Chudori
English language copyright © 2015 John H. McGlynn.
First North American edition, 2015.

First English-language edition published in 2015
as part of the Modern Library of Indonesia by the Lontar Foundation,
founded in 1987 to promote Indonesian literature and culture
through the translation of Indonesian literary works.
The Lontar Foundation · www lontar.org

ISBN: 978-1-941920-10-7 (paperback) · 978-1-941920-11-4 (ebook)
LIBRARY OF CONGRESS CONTROL NUMBER: 2015946454

—

Publication of this book was made possible, in part,
with the generous assistance of the Ministry of Education and Culture
of the Republic of Indonesia

—

Cover design & typesetting by Anna Zylicz · annazylicz.com

Text set in Bembo, a typeface modeled on typefaces cut by Francesco Griffo
for Aldo Manuzio's printing of *De Aetna* in 1495 in Venice.

Distributed by Consortium Book Sales & Distribution.
Printed in the United States of America on acid-free paper.

Contents

To my parents, Willy and Mohammad Chudori,
and my daughter, Rain Chudori-Soerjoatmodjo

PROLOGUE
ON JALAN SABANG, JAKARTA, APRIL 1968

NIGHT HAD FALLEN, WITHOUT COMPLAINT, WITHOUT PRETEXT. Like a black net enclosing the city, ink from a monster squid spreading across Jakarta's entire landscape—the color of my uncertain future.

Inside the darkroom, I know not the sun, the moon, or even my wristwatch. But the darkness that envelopes this room is imbrued with the scent of chemicals and anxiety.

Three years ago, the Nusantara News Agency where I worked was cleansed of lice and germs like myself. The army was the disinfectant and we, the lice and the germs, were eradicated from the face of the earth, with no trace left. Yet, somehow, this particular louse had survived and was now eking out a living at Tjahaja Photo Studio on the corner of Jalan Sabang in central Jakarta.

I switched on the red light to inspect the strips of negatives hanging on the drying-line overhead. It must have been around 6 p.m. because I could hear the muzzled sound of the muezzin drifting in to the darkroom through the grate in the door, summoning the faithful for evening prayer. I imagined the scene on Jalan Sabang outside: the quarrelsome cackling of motorized pedicabs; the huffing and puffing of slow-moving opelets searching for passengers; the creaking of human-driven pedicabs in need of an oil job; the cring-cring sound of hand bells on bicycles as their riders wove their way through the busy intersection; and the cries of the bread seller on his three-wheel contraption with its large box and clear glass windows. I could even see the early evening wind bearing the smoke and smell rising from skewers of goat satay being grilled on the brazier at Pak Heri's itinerant but immensely popular food stall located smack dab at the intersection of Sabang and Asem Lama. I could see him using his well-worn pestle to grind fried peanuts and thinly sliced shallots on an oversized mortar, then drizzling sweet soy sauce over the mix. And then I imagined my good friend, Dimas Suryo, studiously observing Pak Heri and discussing with him his choice of peanuts with the same kind of intensity that he might employ when dissecting a poem by Rivai Apin.

Almost every evening, like clockwork, all other sounds from the outside were drowned out by the long shrill whistle from the steamer on Soehardi's food cart as our regular vendor of steamed *putu*—a favorite treat of mine, those steamed rice-flour balls with their grated coconut on the outside and melted cane sugar inside—pulled up outside the photo studio. But other than the smell of Pak Heri's goat satay, that sound was about the only thing—that shrieking sound—that was able to make its way into the darkroom. The deadly darkness of the developing room seemed to smother almost every sound. But the screak of the *putu* steamer and the smell of the cakes always served as a rap on the doors and windows of the photo studio. It was a sign the time had come for me to leave this room that knew no such a thing as time.

Today, I don't know why, I felt reluctant to go outside. Maybe because I could picture the world outside the room and how depressing it seemed to me: neon lights casting their harsh glow on the studio's white tiled floor and glass display cases; Suhardjo and Liang tending to customers who were there waiting to pick up prints from rolls of film they had left at the store a week before or to have their pictures taken for the formal photographs they now needed for identification purposes. For the past two years, income from the latter had been the largest source of revenue for the studio. Every day, at least ten to fifteen people came to have passport-size photographs taken to attach to government-issued letters of certification that they were not a communist, had never participated in any activity sponsored by the Indonesian Communist Party, and had not been involved in the so-called attempt to overthrow the Indonesian government now known as Gestapu, the September 30 Movement.

The banshee-like shriek of the steam whistle from the *putu* cart resounded again and again, as if calling out to me. But still I didn't move. Mixed with the whistle of the *putu* cart, I thought I could hear the sound of a human whistle as well. Listening more carefully, I heard the ringing of the bell that hung from the top of the door to the studio and then the tromping of heavy footsteps as they crossed the tiled space between the doorway and the sales counter in the back of the studio. Now I didn't know which was louder: the whistling of the *putu* cart or the beating of my heart.

My ear now to the door, I heard a stranger growl: "Hello."

"Evening! May I help you," came the reply of a familiar voice, that of Adi Tjahjono, owner of Tjahaja Photographic Studio.

"I'm looking for Pak Hananto."

I couldn't hear Adi's reply but I imagined him being immediately on guard. I guessed that in addition to the stranger whose voice I'd heard, there were two or three other men as well.

"May I ask who you are?"

A different voice answered—"His cousin, from Central Java"—in a tone more educated and refined.

I waited for Adi to answer but heard no answer. Even if the man speaking was not my "cousin from Central Java," because of the man's politesse and refined tone of voice, Adi could do nothing but to demonstrate a similar level of courtesy. Yet I heard him say nothing. I'm sure he was pondering how to respond.

Now I heard another voice, this one brisker and heavier in tone. "Ha-nan-to Pra-wi-ro, that would be his full name," the speaker stressed, as if to warn Adi that he was ready to throttle him if Adi persisted in stalling or pretending not to remember.

In the darkroom, I stood, motionless, unable to think of what to do. I could still hear the wail-like whistle of the *putu* cart which, for some odd reason, now reminded me of Ravel's "Miroirs." Why wasn't I hearing "Bolero," I mused. Maybe because "Miroirs" helped to dampen my sense of sentimentality?

The darkroom had no window to the outside, meaning that if I were to try to slip out and run away, I would still have to pass through the door, which was adjacent to the sales counter and which further meant that no matter how fast my feet might carry me, the visitors would easily be able to stop me in my tracks. But, that said, right there and then I made up my mind that I no longer wanted to live on the run—not because of the discomfort and poverty such a life entailed, and not because I had lost the will to resist or to fight for my life, but because of the news I'd recently heard: Surti and the children had been moved from the detention center on Jalan Guntur to the one on Budi Kemuliaan. The point had come where I had to stop, not because I no longer believed in the struggle, but because I wanted Surti and our three children to be able to live in safety. I owed them at least that for their years of deprivation during the time I was living on the run.

The door to the darkroom creaked—why was it I never

remembered to oil the hinges?—and then I heard Adi calling to me, announcing the visit of my "cousin from Central Java" which was immediately drowned out by another long shriek from the *putu* cart. I couldn't quite make myself hear what was said after that but I knew the intent: I had to surrender.

Opening the doorway to the darkroom, I saw my friend. We stared at each other. I could see tears welling in Adi's eyes. I knew he was powerless. I nodded then took my jacket from the hook on the back of the door. It was April 6, 1968. I looked at my wrist, somehow forgetting for that instant I had lent my watch to Dimas Suryo, three years previously. Dimas, Nugroho, and Risjaf were now living in exile in Peking, I'd heard. Maybe my 17-jewel Titoni was helping him to keep better time. Strange, I thought, even after three years I could still detect a lighter band of color on the skin of my wrist.

As I emerged from the darkroom, the four "visitors from Central Java" immediately rose from the wooden bench in front of the till and stepped towards me, each with one hand inside his jacket, as I came out from behind the counter. More accurately, they surrounded me and were obviously prepared to shoot me in case I tried to escape. One of the four—the leader, I suppose—stepped closer towards me and smiled.

"Bapak Hananto, I am First Lieutenant Mukidjo." His tone was polite, with the same level of refinement I had noted earlier. His eyes sparkled and his smile was one of great satisfaction. I caught a glint of gold as his smile widened. He must have been feeling intensely pleased; I was the last link in the chain the military had been seeking. Ever since the hunt for me began three years earlier, they had captured hundreds of friends and associates.

"Please come with us…"

First Lieutenant Mukidjo was acting in a truly civilized way—though I myself was mentally prepared to be kicked and beaten. From news I'd picked up from friends, the military detectives who had been assigned to track me down had dubbed me "the Shadow," so frustrated they were in trying to find me. I nodded to the officer, then calmly walked towards the front door of the store as he and his three companions, who were dressed in civilian clothing, took their leave of Adi Tjahjono.

Night had fallen, without complaint and without pretext.

Flanked by two men, at both my front and back, I went with them to the two vehicles that were parked in front of Tjahaja Foto: a Nissan patrol truck and a canvas-roofed Toyota jeep. First Lieutenant Mukidjo with the gold-filled teeth told me to get in the back of the jeep. I saw in my mind the faces of Surti, Kenanga, Bulan, and Alam, and then those of my friends who were now so distant. I don't know why, but of all of them, it was only Dimas Suryo who stared back at me. As the truck's engine roared, I cast my eyes down Jalan Sabang to see Soehardi's steamed-*putu* cart, Pak Heri's satay stall, and, finally, for the last time, the slowly, seemingly sadly flashing neon lights of Tjahaja Photo Studio.

I

DIMAS SURYO

SHE EMERGED LIKE AN UNFINISHED LINE OF POETRY.
Among the thousands of other Sorbonne students milling around, it was only her I noticed, standing beneath the bronze statue of Victor Hugo at the Sorbonne campus. Her thick and wavy brunette hair defied the wind's direction, but several unruly strands flittered about her face, obscuring her features. But, even with those strands flitting here and there, I glimpsed a pair of green eyes whose gleam was able to pierce my gloom-filled heart. For a moment she looked in my direction—one second, maybe two—but then went back to what she was doing: assigning marching orders to the other students around her. I was almost sure that she was concealing a smile.

Is the wind not attempting
to touch those perfect lips…

The May breeze continued to mangle her hair. The spring sun jockeyed with the brisk end-of-season Parisian wind. As if irritated, she brushed her unruly hair aside—not with the graceful motion of a dancer nor with the kind of a toss a coquette might use to attract a man's attention. Hers was the motion of a woman made impatient by a minor disturbance. Her posture was stolid, her eyes unwavering.

Separating herself from her fellow students, she looked back to observe them from a distance. Her eyes held a smile, yet her lips remained even. Occasionally, she'd bite her lower lip, then check the watch on her wrist. A few minutes later, she placed her hands on her hips and turned around, her back to me.

A man approached with two bottles of 1644 beer in hand, one of which he gave to her. He wore eyeglasses and had curly hair. If he weren't so scraggly-looking, the French might have considered him handsome; but, from the look of him, I suspected he hadn't seen the inside of a bathtub in at least a week—much like the thousands of other students who were there on the Sorbonne campus demonstrating against the arrest of students from the University of Paris in Nanterre and who had opposed the government's shut-down of their campus.

The May air was suffused with the rank odor of rarely-washed bodies and the bad breath of mouths unfamiliar with toothpaste but partial to cheap booze which, in their coalescence, elicited an incomparable scent of resistance.

I felt envious.

I was jealous.

The battle lines in the struggle that was taking place in Paris at that moment were clear. Both the plaintiff and the accused were known to all. The struggle was one between students and workers against the De Gaulle government. In Indonesia, we were well acquainted with confusion and chaos, but were never quite sure which people were our friends and which ones were our opponents. We weren't even truly sure about the goals of the various combative parties—with the exception of "power," that is. Everyone wanted power. How messy things were there, so very dark!

I had two letters tucked in my jacket pocket. Since the

beginning of the year anyone who was thought to have been a member of the PKI—or had family and friends, or colleagues and neighbors, in the Indonesian Communist Party—had been hunted down, detained, and interrogated. My brother Aji had frightening stories to tell about how many people had disappeared and how many more had died.

One of the two letters was from him, my brother Aji, who forbade me to come home. In previous posts he had told me of neighbors and acquaintances who had been swept up by the military. But this most recent letter contained news I never wanted to receive. My constant hope was that Mas Hananto would remain out of the military's reach. But now, the bad news had come: Mas Hananto, my friend, colleague, and boss; Surti's husband and father of Kenanga, Bulan, and Alam; and my inveterate sounding board, had been captured one month previously at the place where he'd been surreptitiously working on Jalan Sabang.

In an instant, a cloud fell over Paris. My heart darkened. I didn't want to open the second letter, which was from Kenanga, Mas Hananto's oldest child, because I knew that it would further paralyze my emotions.

It was ironic. It should have been me the military arrested in Jakarta that night, yet I was here, in Paris, amidst thousands of French students on the march. In their yells and cries, I somehow caught a whiff of stench from Jakarta's gutters mixed with the sweet smell of clove-laden *kretek* cigarettes and steaming black coffee. The bright gleam in the eyes of the French students reminded me of former friends in Jakarta whose fates I didn't know. With sparkling eyes and effervescent spirits, they demanded in loud voices a more just society (though, to be sure, some of those same idealistic students would one day become part of the same power structure they vowed to tear down).

That same spirit emanated from the eyes of the brunette woman whose attention remained fixed on the unwashed man with curly hair and eyeglasses. Staring at him, her emerald eyes seemed to protrude from their sockets. As if agitated by the woman's penetrating gaze, the slovenly man left the woman's side. Gulping what was left of the beer in the bottle in his hand, he tossed the bottle into a trash can in such a flippantly dismissive manner that he seemed to be speaking of his feelings for the beautiful woman next to him.

I wanted to approach her. The color of her eyes was the green of unripe grapes mixed with the blue of the Indian Ocean. I wished to shelter in their color. Their green was the carpet of grass under my feet; their blue, the stretch of sky over my head. I wanted to rest on that carpet and dangle my feet from that sky. What painter could possibly have created the blue-green color of her eyes? What sculptor could have carved the fluidly sensuous form of her perfect body? My eyes went to her, my body was drawn towards her, yet my legs remained fixed in place, my feet those of a criminal, shackled in steel chains, awaiting execution. The blustering wind of the Parisian spring mocked my hesitation, making me stare down at my miserable earthbound feet.

But then, into my view, came another pair of legs, with faded jeans and a pair of dark blue tennis shoes. Slowly, I raised my eyes to see the blue-green eyes very close to my own.

"Ça va?"

Her blue-green eyes could smile.

She came to me like a line of poetry perfectly complete, restoring my breath which had suddenly ceased.

"Ça va…"

Vivienne Deveraux and I were soon to become two dots which, when melding together, formed a line that traced the pores of the body of Paris. Only a few weeks after our first brief meeting that evening on the Sorbonne campus, nature brought us together again on the Rive Gauche, on the southern bank of the Seine. I was at a kiosk there, studying a display of posters in various artistic styles and formats. Their sight took me back to Indonesia, some of them reminding me of Indonesian painters I knew of who used a garish palette of colors in their work: bright yellow, steaming pink, and vivid purple. But there was also the work of artists reminiscent of the woodblock prints of several Eastern European artists. The posters seemed to shout out at me—though I first had to search my mind for the meaning of their words: "*Toute la Presse est Toxique*," "*La Lutte Continue…*"

"The struggle continues…"

Ah, that voice! It was she, again: Vivienne, the woman with the green eyes and the pair of lips whose only imperfection was that they were not locked with mine. She was standing next to me.

She smiled and pointed at the poster I was viewing with its image of six people in silhouette, whose ages, apparel, and accoutrements showed them to be a mix of workers and students, all with their right arms thrust in the air, in which was written, in jagged letters, the words *La Lutte Continue.*

"That means 'the struggle continues,'" she said again in English.

"So, the artist is saying that the spirit of the students and the workers are one, is that it?"

"It is the spirit of the entire French people," she said emphatically.

I nodded but knew that she could see the skeptical look on my face.

Vivienne invited me to join her at an outdoor café nearby,

where she immediately ordered coffee for us, not bothering to first ask what I might want. As in almost every other café I had visited in Paris, the coffee was served in a demitasse, whose size was, to my Indonesian mind, much more appropriate for playing house than for serving a proper cup of coffee. The first time I was served a cup of coffee in Paris, it was so strong and thick and had such an incredibly oily taste that I'd almost had a heart attack. My God, what would they have to put in their coffee to make it more palateable, I wondered, a bucket of sugar and a gallon of cream? And now again, for the umpteenth time, with my first sip, the instant the thick and oil-like liquid touched my tongue, my body recoiled in shock.

Vivienne noticed my reaction and the difficulty I was having in swallowing the coffee. "Don't you like it?"

"You should try Indonesian coffee," I said hurriedly, trying to cover my social faux pas. "We have hundreds, even thousands of kinds," I exaggerated, hoping to impress her with my country of origin. I was sure that she, like most other French people I'd met, knew very little about *l'Indonésie*. I mentioned some of the kinds of coffee that Indonesia produced—Toraja, Mandailing, *luwak*, and so on—and explained how in Indonesia coffee was usually prepared using an infusion method, with boiling hot water poured on finely powdered coffee.

As I rambled on, Vivienne smiled patiently, even after I went into detail how *luwak* is produced. *Luwak* coffee, I told her, is one of the few benefits of the forced cultivation system implemented by the Dutch in the nineteenth century. The Dutch colonial rulers had prohibited native farmers from picking coffee for their own use, I explained. They didn't realize that the civet cats which inhabited the coffee groves would eat the coffee berries and later,

7

because they couldn't digest the actual beans, would defecate them along with their feces on the ground. The natives would then collect the droppings, soak them in water to separate the beans, then roast, grind and them turn them into coffee.

The look on Vivienne's face was a mixture of humor and incredulity. I could see in her green eyes the question of how a method of production as foul as the one I had described could, as if by magic, produce a cup of coffee which I proceeded to liken to an aphrodisiac. I even went so far as to say that the first sip of *luwak* coffee could cause a premature ejaculation, so wonderful is its taste.

At this point, Vivienne started to laugh and couldn't stop. Her laughter came in rolls, causing her to hold her sides and tears to stream from her eyes. Finally she regained control of herself. "Phew! Oh my God. What a story! Thank you for making me laugh so much. For a moment I was able to forget what a fucked up state this country is in!"

I delighted in hearing her laughter. "France, fucked up?"

Suddenly, her laughter stopped. "Yes! The police attacked my friends," she said. "The campus has been shut down and the politicians don't know what to do."

She wasn't complaining. She was stating things matter-of-factly.

I watched Vivienne's lips as she spoke. To myself, I thought that when it came to the state of a nation, she had no idea what "fucked up" meant. Indonesia was rarely covered in the press, not even in leading news media such as *Le Monde* and *Le Figaro*. What the typical French person might know is that Indonesia is a country located somewhere in Southeast Asia not too far from Vietnam. (The only Asian countries the French seemed to know were China and North and South Vietnam.)

For Vivienne and her equally agitated friends to whom she had just referred, the futility of the Vietnam conflict served as tinder for the anti-government protest movements that had begun to erupt in Europe and the United States. They wouldn't have heard the names of Indonesia's political activists who long predated theirs—such as Sukarno, Hatta, Sjahrir, and Tan Malaka. Given that, what could they possibly know about the bloodbath that had taken place in Indonesia in the months and years that followed the events of September 30, 1965? Most of the people I had met, Vivienne included, would probably have had to open an atlas just to find out where Indonesia was.

Vivienne started to tell me about the roots of unrest among the students at Nanterre, which had grown and transformed into a mass movement joined by the workers. I was growing impatient. I knew for sure that if Vivienne knew about what had happened and what was still happening in Indonesia, she wouldn't continue to prattle. But I didn't want to tell her about the bloodbath in my homeland—or at least not yet. But how was I to get her to stop chattering?

I moved from where I was seated to a spot on the bench beside her and touched her beautiful chin. The effect was immediate: she stopped speaking and her green eyes opened wide. Seeing in them a desire that matched my own, I pressed my lips to hers. As if wanting to drink each other, we could not stop kissing and even without a cup of *luwak* coffee experienced an orgasmic sensation like no other.

Over the next few months, Vivienne and I were two *flâneurs*, a pair of adventurers, always together, taking in the sights and sounds of Paris. The revolution of May 1968 was out of sight and out of mind, as if it had never happened. France was again a flamboyant place, though one where civility and courtesy reigned.

During this period, Vivienne refrained from forcing me to open up and talk about my past. Whether because of a certain reticence on her part or because of my lock-lipped response to her initial exploratory questions about my life, she didn't ask—or, more precisely, stopped herself from asking—about certain aspects of my life history. Fair or not, I came to know much more about her than she about me.

Vivienne was the younger of the two children of Laurence and Marianne Deveraux, who lived in Lyon. Her brother Jean worked for the International Red Cross and had, for several years already, been stationed in countries in Africa. She had two first cousins, Marie-Claire and Mathilde, who were also students at the Sorbonne. The difference between the two cousins was that while Marie-Claire was an Earth-mother type, given to hugging everyone she met, Mathilde was much more reserved and looked on people with a suspicious eye. Regardless of any dissimilarity, this trio of stunning brunettes were closely bound by familial ties and friendship and spent much of their free time together, including those days of demonstrations in May when their voices could be heard loud and clear among the crowd.

Vivienne was a very intelligent woman, whose natural curiosity had been nurtured by the intellectual environment of her middle-class family, who placed high stress on academic achievement. But in France, or in the rest of Europe for that matter, intelligence was not very difficult to find.

What distinguished Vivienne from her two cousins was her keen sensitivity. She rapidly grasped that her openness about herself would not automatically elicit a similar frankness on my part about my life history. She knew that my move to Paris had not been the result of my being from a bourgeois family given to quoting

Albert Camus as a sign of their academic acumen. She could infer from my reluctance to speak of the past—or maybe it was from the way I carefully counted my franc notes, or maybe from the amount of time I could spend in a used bookstore without buying anything—that it was not of my own volition that I was living in Paris. Something else had brought me here and forced me to stop and stay in Europe.

Intuitively, it seems, Vivienne knew that she could not force me to give an encyclopedic version of my life without alienating me in the process. So it was that she allowed me to gradually feed her drops from the bottle of my memory at my own pace and in my own time.

As a relatively new arrival in Paris, I did not know the city well and, if truth be told, was only familiar with the Metro system in the area where my rundown apartment was located, an arrondissement in which there were several Vietnamese restaurants, whose food, to my great delight, more resembled that of China and Indonesia than European food, which I found to be bland and terribly short on spices.

Vivienne introduced me to the Bibliothèque Nationale in the Palais Mazarin. Using her membership card the first time we went there, she checked out for me several books on literature and politics. The library was so immense as to be awe-inspiring and I was almost afraid to explore the various floors. I promised myself that I would come back alone, one day, which I did soon afterwards.

Vivienne also took me to stores and places in Paris where prices weren't so hard on the pocketbook of a wayfarer like myself. (I still didn't know what to call myself. What was I? A refugee? A traveler? An exile? Or maybe something with a little more cachet: a writer or an independent journalist?) Frequently, three friends of mine—Nugroho Dewantoro, Tjai Sin Soe, and Risjaf, who were fellow Indonesians also living off the good graces of the French government—would join the two of us.

Vivienne took me and my three loud-mouthed friends to see the Grand Palais and Notre Dame Cathedral. With her, we explored Île Saint-Louis. We Indonesians were a quartet of gay and carefree ramblers ready to drop the names of locations in Paris in our (as yet unborn) poems and novels—or at least we acted that way, when in fact we were just a band of political exiles acting like thrifty tourists. But maybe it was by being able to laugh at ourselves that we were able to survive. I can't say.

Exploring the arteries of Paris with Vivienne was enlightening for me. Perhaps because of his talent as a writer, Ernest Hemingway was able to vividly invoke in his writing the special affection he held for Paris, as he did in *A Moveable Feast*; but Vivienne, as a woman, seemed to better understand the city's corpus.

I couldn't say that Paris was for us the "moveable feast" that Hemingway described; but it definitely was *"terre d'asile"*—our place of exile. Second to that, Paris was the remarkable River Seine, which divided the city into its left and right banks but whose thirty-seven bridges sewed the two halves together. It was also Shakespeare & Co., the celebrated bookstore on Rue de la Bûcherie; and of course it was a park bench on Île Saint-Louis, the site of Vivienne's and my first unexpected but marvelously prolonged kiss. As our land of exile, Paris was first and foremost for us the roof over our heads and the source of our next meal but it was the sights and sounds of Paris, the city's intangible delights, which provided sustenance for our souls.

Before meeting Vivienne, and as is true with most tourists and new visitors to Paris, I and my three friends—Mas Nugroho,

Tjai, and Risjaf—spent much time strolling the Rive Droite, the right bank of the Seine, in the northern section of Paris where the Champs-Élysées and other prominent sites are located.So impressed were we by the elegance of the northern arrondissements, we promised ourselves that we would explore every one of them before our return home—whenever that might be. But Vivienne, to her great credit, was the one who pointed out the more prosaic but no less interesting sites that were to be found on the left bank of the Seine, the Rive Gauche, where used bookstalls were plentiful. At one of them she introduced me to its proprietor, Monsieur Antoine Martin, a retired policeman who loved literature so much he was content to sit at his stall all day long and read aloud favorite passages from the novels of Alain Robbe-Grillet and Marguerite Duras or poems by René Char. The man's mini-performances always attracted the attention of passersby, who invariably ended up purchasing the book he was reading from, at a low price too.

The days we passed as *flâneurs* in Paris helped much to enrich my French vocabulary. At first, the only words I knew were *oui*, *non*, and *ça va*; but because Vivienne forced me to add ten new words to my vocabulary every day, I began to study the language more seriously. Even so, it wasn't her tutorial skills that made me attach myself to her. It was her eyes, definitely her eyes. I wanted to dive into those deep green eyes and remain buried within them forever. And her lips as well…Vivienne's lips were the lyrics of an unfinished poem. I was convinced that only when her lips were engaged with mine could the poem be completed.

Jakarta, August 1968

Mas Dimas,

Bad news…In April Mas Hananto was arrested by four intelligence agents. Adi Tjahjono, the owner of the photo studio
where he was working, told me about it. He couldn't tell me
where they took him, but probably to the detention center on
Jalan Guntur or to the one on Gunung Sahari. Nobody has
heard anything from him directly.

Maybe you didn't know this but Mbak Surti, who has been
interrogated by the military on a regular basis ever since '65,
was at that time in prison. And because she didn't want to be
separated from her children, when she was first called in to the
detention center on Jalan Budi Kemuliaan, she took them with
her and they ended up being imprisoned as well. Kenanga, who
is now fourteen, has seen things that no girl her age should ever
witness. And what must it be like for Bulan and Alam, who
are only six and three? I simply can't imagine. (I'm enclosing a letter for you from Kenanga. She told me she wanted to
write to you, because her father had said to her that you were
a second father for them. I could barely make myself read what
she wrote.)

Mother tells me to stress again the need for you to stay in
Europe. Now that we've moved from Solo and are living in
Jakarta, things feel a bit calmer—but the military's pursuit of
anyone and everyone with any link to the Communist Party
has only gotten worse. Now they're not just picking up people
suspected of being party members or sympathizers. They're
bringing in families and children too.

Mother and I consider ourselves lucky to have been called to
report to Jalan Guntur "only" a few times and to be permitted

to go home after a day of answering their same old questions. Most of them have to do with your activities and what we knew about Mas Hananto, Mas Nug, Tjai, and Risjaf. They asked us if we knew what you were doing in Peking when you were there. I don't know where they got the information, but they knew it was Mas Hananto and not you who was supposed to have gone on that tour to Santiago, Havana, and Peking in September '65.

When I was being questioned, I could hear the screams of people being tortured. Their shrieks of pain were so loud they penetrated the walls. I can only pray that their cries reached God's ears and not just my own. But the things that Kenanga has witnessed are much more horrifying than anything I have seen. Read her letter and get back to me soon.

Jakarta is hell. Pray for us.

Your brother,
Aji Suryo

One night, when Vivienne and I were out for a walk on Île Saint-Louis, I suddenly found that I could take my self-inflicted silence no longer. With the moon hiding in a narrow lane on the island, a lone bright eye staring at me, I put my hand to Vivienne's chin.

She looked at me. "You're upset. What is it?"

"I got some news from Jakarta."

Vivienne took my hand and pulled me to a park bench—the same park bench that had such historical importance for me.

"Can you talk to me? Do you trust me enough to tell me what it is?"

She'd finally asked the question. She was ready to learn of my past and I was ready to share with her the blood-filled history of my homeland.

"*Peut-être…*" I answered, now anxious that her body, now so close to my own, should ever leave my side.

I kissed her softly and saw a flash in her eyes. She put her arms around me, held me tightly, and returned my kiss with a passion I had never felt before. She infused my pores, my heart, and my soul with her warmth and emotion. I was silent, still hesitating, but I knew that that Vivienne could smell the bile in my blood and phlegm. And at that moment, I knew that I wanted, that I was willing, and that if ever I could hope for Vivienne to love me as much as I loved her, then I had to open the dark curtain concealing my past.

I took from my pocket the letter I'd received from Kenanga— from Kenanga Prawiro, the oldest daughter of my friend and colleague, Mas Hananto—and I read the letter aloud, translating it into French as best as I could.

Jakarta, August 1968

Dear Om Dimas,

Not too long ago, when I was given the chance to see my grandmother, she told me that if I wanted to write to you, she would give my letter to Om Aji to send. He could include it with a letter that he was going to send to you. So that's what I'm doing now.

All of us here are sad but trying to hold up. In April, they arrested my father and nobody has seen him since. We don't know where they're holding him. That's why, when they took Mother in, she took us with her. She said she couldn't bear to be separated from us. And we didn't want to be separated from her either. Bulan doesn't seem to know that we're actually in a detention center. And Alam doesn't know anything at all. Some of the soldiers are nice to him, acting like uncles and giving him toys to play with.

First we were taken from home to an office of sorts whose name I don't know because it was some kind of abbreviation but it was in Jalan Budi Kemuliaan. I knew that because one time when my parents took us to see the National Monument where it was being constructed, we passed that way.

They keep asking Mother questions, day in and day out, until she doesn't know what to say. It's worn her out. Her eyes are swollen and she has this gloomy look on her face all the time. When they're doing that, they put me to work cleaning the place. They've given me a number of rooms to clean every day.

At first I didn't know what these rooms were for and usually it was just cigarette butts and ashes I had to sweep up. But then, one day I found the floor in one of the rooms covered with dried blood, which I had to wipe up. That's when I knew what the rooms were being used for. That's when I knew that all the cries I'd been hearing—from so many different men and women—were coming from those rooms.

About a month ago I found in one of the rooms the tail of a sting ray all matted with flesh and blood. It gave me such a shock I started to shake and cry until I couldn't stop. I don't know how I finally managed to calm myself down. But this is something I've never told even Mother about because she's worn out from having had to suffer for so long. I find it hard to eat anymore. The sight of food makes me want to vomit.

I've seen men of about my father's age being herded down

the hallways in this place with their faces covered with blood.

Why are they doing this, Om Dimas? Why are these people being tortured? And why do they keep interrogating Mother, asking her questions she cannot answer? I hear them shouting at her, asking over and over whether she knew what Bapak was up to. They're always shouting, always angry. They can't seem to speak in a normal tone of voice. Why do they have to shout?

I'm so sad and so afraid. Bulan is so young that all she can do is to follow me around wherever I go. And Alam is just a baby. Once they let Mother feed him but then, right afterwards, called her back into the room for more questions and to be shouted at again.

I hope that you are all right. Bapak once told me that if anything ever happened, I was to contact you.

Yours,
Kenanga Prawiro

Vivienne looked at me, her eyes glistening, and for a long time afterwards all we could do was to hold each other wordlessly.

ON ONE VERY MUGGY SUMMER EVENING, VIVIENNE AND I lolled on the floor of her apartment, trying our best to do nothing. Her apartment wasn't especially large but as my eyes scanned its contents—books, books, and more books—I felt immediately at home. Works by Simone de Beauvoir and other French authors were mixed with titles by British, Irish, Japanese, Chinese, and Indian authors. My eyes paused for a moment on two of Joyce's works: *A Portrait of the Artist as a Young Man* and *Ulysses*. I noted that titles generally viewed as mandatory reading on Marxist political thought occupied a special shelf of their own. On another shelf, I saw Ayn Rand's semi-autobiographical work, *We the Living*, and her controversial novel, *The Fountainhead*. Judging from Vivienne's taste in books, I could see that she was, very much like me, a literary traveler. Like me, too, she apparently liked to study the various kinds of thought that marked important periods of time, without being forced to stop at or become trapped by a particular intellectual current. Hmm… My attraction to her increased exponentially. At that moment, I wanted to take her in my arms and never let her go.

Vivienne got up and opened the windows of her apartment as wide as possible. She was wearing a sleeveless T-shirt, and the delicate film of perspiration on her elegant neck excited me.

She took two bottles of cold Alsace beer from her small refrigerator and handed one to me. She drank her beer straight from the
bottle, gulping the amber liquid as if it were an elixir. I watched
the bluish vein on her neck pulsate as she swallowed the beer
flowing down her throat. A thin stream of liquid seeped from the
side of her mouth and trickled down her chin and neck. The beer
mixed with her sweat made me want to lap the salty mix from
her neck with my tongue.

Vivienne stopped drinking and smiled at me, a challenge in
her piercing eyes. She knew what I was thinking. "Tell me about
Indonesia…"

Not knowing how to begin to tell her about my home country,
I paused. Where should I start? With my family? With the country in tumult? Or back to early 1960s when President Sukarno's
shifting political alliances led the country—and me as well—to
the point we are today? My mind flashed back to Jakarta. What
had Sukarno been up to? Did he actually side with his friends on
the left? What had he wanted or hoped to achieve with his policy
of "Nasakom," his odd promulgation of nationalism, religion, and
communism? And as the chronology of the night of September
30 emerged, why had he fled the presidential palace and gone to
Halim Perdanakusuma Naval Air Base? This was a question that
had nagged my friends in Jakarta and continued to nag me.

How could I ever explain or even begin to unravel this messy
bundle of thread for Vivienne? Maybe it would be best to begin
somewhere else—with *wayang* tales, for instance, stories from the
Javanese shadow theater that were my secret obsession. Better that,
perhaps, than opening the doors to my country's warehouse of
history to cast light on its cluttered contents.

Vivienne took another gulp of beer from her bottle but didn't swallow. Instead, she lowered her body to straddle my lap and then kissed me, the cool beer emptying from her mouth into mine. The sensation quickened the flow of my blood, making it dance wildly through my veins, and inflamed my joints. Any attempt to prevent Vivienne from feeling my body's reaction to the blood coursing through my veins to my extremities would have been futile. How could it not be? Her midsection was pressed into my crotch.

As I became more excited, my blood raced more swiftly through me. Unable to restrain myself, I began to lick her neck and chest, which were slick with sweat and beer. With her torso positioned directly in front of my eyes, her breasts seemed ready to burst from the seams of her clinging T-shirt. And in my darting eyes, her long legs seemed to be begging for me to remove the skimpy blue jeans encasing them.

Vivienne rarely wore a bra during the summer. At times, I protested, not because I was prudish but because of the very evident physical reaction that occurred in me at the sight of her nipples beneath her T-shirt. At times it was almost painful. How could she torture me like that? Wasn't I supposed to be concentrating on my future life in Paris? I couldn't help myself. I couldn't think of anything except what was under that damned T-shirt of hers.

Once I begged her to wear a bra to prevent me from becoming so flustered. And her answer...?

"Do you know how uncomfortable it is to wear a bra on a day as hot as this? Here!" She took a brightly colored red bra and shoved it in front of my nose. "You try wearing it."

My mouth turned dry. I couldn't speak. I didn't know if Vivienne realized how excited it made me to see her nipples protruding from under her T-shirt. How can women be so cruel? But, in the end, I decided to give thanks to nature for its wisdom in making the summer in Paris so hot that Vivienne refused to wear a bra—because it made what happened next all that much easier. Not having to couch our feelings in lines of poetry from one of the books we were reading, Vivienne and I both raced to remove our clothing. Then we attacked each other, wrestling with each other on the floor. Paris was hot, but we were burning. After just a few minutes we lay exhausted and naked on the floor, staring at the ceiling of the apartment. The August evening was so stuffy and humid our bodies were drenched with sweat. But in our desire for one another, we thought nothing of the discomfort and made passionate love, again and again. What time it was I didn't know, but I suddenly felt the urge to smoke. "Have you ever smoked *kretek*?" I asked Vivienne, whose head was nestled on my chest. "No, but I've heard about them from Mathilde, who bought some in Amsterdam. She says they're amazing." I scrounged in the pocket of my shirt on the floor. "Ah, I still have some." There were still a few sticks left in a badly crumpled packet. I lit one and then took turns smoking the cigarette with Vivienne. Vivienne smacked her lips. "They have a sweet taste. What is it?" "Cloves," I said, "desiccated cloves," while trying to suppress the feeling of longing aroused by the scent of that spice and everything else that smelled of Indonesia. "It would be perfect if we had a cup of *luwak* coffee." There, I had said it, that dangerous word. Poor and stranded as I was in the middle of Europe, giving voice to a longing for something as exotic as *luwak* coffee was the same as sticking a knife in my heart. If I wanted to go on living, I had to—at least for now—bury and conceal Indonesia and anything connected with it. I felt my mind return to the Jakarta where I lived four years previously.

•

JAKARTA, DECEMBER 1964

A *kretek* was like a symbol for us. After a long discussion and sometimes heated debate about politics and the nation's state of affairs at the office, we would often end the discussion with a cup of thick black coffee and a *kretek* cigarette at Senen Market. At that time, in late 1964, Jakarta was a city that was neither calm nor comfortable.

The office of Nusantara News on Jalan Asem Lama seemed to have running through it some kind of demarcation line separating members of political camps. On one side were members of the Communist Party; people who sympathized with Party goals; members of LEKRA, a cultural organization with close links to the Party; and even people who simply liked to spend time with the artists who belonged to this organization, the League of People's Culture. On the other side and at the opposite end of the political spectrum were staff members who shunned anything that might be labeled leftist. Among them was my friend, Bang Amir, who was pro-Masyumi, the Islamic political party founded by Natsir, whose pan-Islamic philosophy was antithetical to leftist thought. As for me, I was a bit on the fence. I supported Marxist ideals and enjoyed reading all the books that Mas Hananto gave me on the subject; I enthusiastically listened to political discussions between Mas Hananto and other colleagues in the editorial room, and it wasn't rare to find me tagging along with them as they continued their debate over coffee at Kadir's stall in Senen Market. Even so, I also liked, and found much comfort in, talking to Bang Amir about things of a more religious or spiritual nature.

But that sense of wonder stopped at my body, not my soul.

Both Mas Hananto and Mas Nugroho strongly believed in the virtues of socialism, but I saw numerous weak points in their theories and, even in the face of Mas Hananto's derision, I continued to stand by my view that while there are some things that the government should ultimately be responsible for—public health and services, to name two—there are other things that are far better left entrusted to the private sector.

Lately, I had felt the political temperature in Jakarta rise precipitously, nearing the boiling point. At the top of my mind was the ever more strident war between LEKRA artists, who clung to the notion that art only has value if it serves to promote awareness of social issues, and artists who did not belong to the League and upheld the principles of individuality and humanitarianism. I then thought of literature. A literary work was, for me at least, a matter of the heart. Just because its theme or story line involved the struggle of farmers or laborers didn't mean it would have an enlightening effect. That power came from the ability of the work to touch the heart of its reader. In this matter, in particular, I was greatly at odds with Mas Hananto's point of view.

Hananto Prawiro... He was not just my superior; he was also my friend. I called him "Mas," after all, the Javanese term of address for a man older than oneself with whom one is a friend. But he was also my guru and my mentor. Mas Hananto, head of the foreign desk at Nusantara News, was constantly lending me books he thought might help to expand my world view—which he deemed to be excessively tainted by bourgeois thought and opinion. Novels like *Madame Bovary*, for instance; plays like *Waiting for Godot*; and all of Joyce's work, for that matter, he criticized as being self-indulgent.

"They're playing with their belly buttons!" he said of such

writers one day as he was flipping through *A Portrait of the Artist as a Young Man*. "They're not concerned with this world; they ignore class differences and poverty."

"But Joyce, through his alter ego, Stephen Dedalus, is trying to find himself through religion and art. I feel the process to be entirely rational," I argued, trying to explain myself in a manner not even entirely convincing to myself. I had read the novel several times and never found myself bored by it. Dedalus is both a tragic and humorous figure. Sure, he might be a tad too serious about himself at times, but was Mas Hananto unable to see the bitter humor underlying such a work?

Mas Hananto had the most annoying habit of often repeating his views and opinions, so much so, I swear, that if my ears could have replied they would have screamed that he was merely sputtering clichés. Among Marxist followers in Indonesia, social-realist jargon was sacred. And anyone who wanted to curry favor with the editor-in-chief, a man who happened to be close to Communist Party leaders, had only to drop such terms or quote a few lines from *The Mother* and then act as if he had read the entire book to gain access to the editor-in-chief's inner circle of colleagues.

For me, Gorky's novel, which had been translated into Indonesian by Pramoedya Ananta Toer, was boring beyond belief. All its focus was on social issues with no concern for style or literary execution. My thought was that if the only thing a writer is concerned with is social issues, then he had better not write novels or poetry; he'd best stick to writing speeches or propaganda essays instead.

Mas Hananto once referred to me as a "Wibisono," the younger brother of the ogre king Rahwana in the *Ramayana*, who allied himself with Rama, his brother's foe. But in Indonesian politics,

I didn't know who was Rahwana and who was Rama. What I did know was that Mas Hananto didn't quite know what to make of my views; they weren't straight forward like his. And, frankly, if I were going to be called by the name of any character from the legendary Javanese pantheon, it probably would be Bima, who, among the five Pandawa brothers, was the one with the softest heart. Even though Bima fell head over heels in love with Drupadi, when his older brother Arjuna made known his desire to have her, Bima willing stepped aside. Oh, and by the way, this reference to Bima has no relation to past Indonesian politics, but everything to do with my former love life.

Mas Hananto knew that the way to deal with me was not through a battle of wills or disputation of my tastes. He knew I had little regard for the novels that he praised for their defense of the masses. I once rebuked him by asking if it wasn't the case that we were supposed to be defending all of humanity, not just the proletariat. Why couldn't we inculcate the concept of embracing the humanity that is found in all of us? Mas Hananto guffawed at my comment. But, unlike Mas Nugroho, whose hackles would rise because of my argumentative manner, Mas Hananto seemed to take on the role of a patient older brother trying to educate his whining younger sibling. That was why, even with the demarcation line running through the office, dividing friends and foes of the Communist Party, I seemed to reside in a kind of Swiss neutral zone, and was able to move from one side to another and to engage with Bang Amir and his friends.

I called Amir "Bang," a term of address that derives from *abang* or "older brother," because he was indeed like an older brother for me. Also a journalist at the Nusantara News, Bang Amir was highly critical of "Bung" or "Comrade" Sukarno, judging the president guilty of too closely embracing the Communist Party leadership and also of having imprisoned Mohammad Natsir, the former prime minister and one of the country's top religious leaders, on charges of treason.

What with the constant wrangling between the two camps in the office and especially because the editor-in-chief had allied himself with Mas Hananto and Mas Nugroho, who were committed leftists, my in-between position was sometimes an uncomfortable one. Yes, Bang Amir was vocal in his opinions, but he was also a top-notch journalist, and when he was abruptly moved to the marketing and advertising division, I thought the move not only surprising but an insult both to him and to our profession. Regardless of the fact that "marketing and advertising" is essential to the success of a company or institution, Bang Amir was our best reporter. With his easy-going manner, he was able to get along with and, in fact, had become close to the leaders of all the political parties—except for the Communist Party, that is, whose leadership Mas Hananto claimed as *his* key source. Furthermore, as a writer, Bang Amir was both fast and effective, the very characteristics a news agency needs in a journalist.

"Why do you mean, an 'insult'?" Mas Hananto asked me in a shrill voice when I criticized the editor-in-chief's decision to transfer Bang Amir.

"Because it's idiotic, transferring Bang Amir like that. It was obviously done for political reasons. Isn't that so?" I asked Mas Hananto in turn. "And if that's the case, it's a bad decision."

Mas Hananto looked at me sourly but he didn't refute my accusation. "And where is there not politics in life?" he asked instead—another habit that infuriated me, always answering a question with one of his own. Just because he was my superior, my mentor, and better than me in many respects, it didn't mean he was always right. Sure, everything was political, but to have "exiled" Bang Amir for *any* reason—and this was for sheer political reasons—wasn't the right thing to do. And not only was it not right; it wasn't fair.

"In every struggle, we have to be ready for times that require sacrifice," Mas Hananto told me.

God, I thought, now he's sounding like Bung Karno. What was the connection between the so-called struggle and Bang Amir's transfer?

The scowl on my face appeared to make Mas Hananto uneasy, but I was angry and I wanted him to know it. Apparently sensing this and also knowing that if he tried to counter me our argument would only grow worse, he wisely turned and walked away.

That evening I decided to visit Bang Amir at his home, which was just a *becak*-ride from Nusantara News, on a small and shady side street off Salemba Boulevard. His wife Saidah—a woman with wonderfully long wavy hair and the tender voice of a mother who never seemed angry or impatient—answered my knock on the door. She invited me in and ushered me to the living room.

"Bang Amir is praying. He won't be long. I'll make some coffee," she said as she retreated to the kitchen in the back.

I nodded. Looking down at the coffee table in front of my chair, I saw *Capita Selecta*, one of Natsir's works, and several other titles as well along with a notebook and a fountain pen with its cap on. I knew that Bang Amir was a Masyumi follower, of course; and though I hardly knew Natsir himself and had scant knowledge of the ideology behind his Masyumi Party, the man struck me as being courteous and sincere. One day, in a conversation with Bang Amir at the office, he started talking about Natsir and told me how he hoped that Natsir would soon be released from the prison in Malang where he was being held. Unfortunately, because of a news deadline, we were never able to finish this conversation.

"Dimas Suryo…"

Bang Amir had a low and deep voice, like that of the popular bass vocalist, Rahmat Kartolo. Sometimes I found myself talking to him just to hear the rhythmic cadence of his sultry voice. But I was interested in what he had to say—and not just his criticism of the editor-in-chief, whose management style seemed to derive from herd instinct; I was interested in his other thoughts and ideas as well.

I stood to greet Bang Amir and we warmly shook hands. I stopped myself from blurting out how shocked I was not to see him in the editorial room, but I guessed he was able to intuit the reason for my visit, namely a sense of solidarity with him as a fellow journalist and editor. I'm sure he also guessed that I strongly disagreed with the editor-in-chief's decision to transfer him to another section. Whatever the case, we jumped into ready conversation, talking about this and that, while drinking *tubruk* coffee and smoking *kretek*, completely skirting the subject that was on each other's mind.

During the course of our conversation, Bang Amir revealed how he had come to meet his wife Saidah. Their first meeting was at the wedding of a friend, he told me, and when they looked at each other, they had immediately fallen in love. Amir stressed that as long as Saidah was beside him, he would be able to overcome whatever peril might befall him. "Even a transfer to the marketing division," he added sardonically, finally entering that taboo domain. "When I pray, I always thank God for having given me Saidah to stand beside me. Without her, I would be a boat adrift. With her, I am able to maintain my balance and feel calm."

As if having said enough about the sensitive issue, Bang Amir immediately segued into commentary of a more spiritual nature. "I believe that Allah shows the blessings He has bestowed on me by providing, inside myself, a small and private space, a little vacuum as it were, which only He and I occupy. And it is in there I go, Dimas, whenever I am trying to understand what is happening.

I wasn't quite sure what Amir meant by this "private space" or that "little vacuum" but I was charmed by the imagery and dissolved in it like cocoa power in hot water. Whether it was because of his mellifluous voice or as a result of what he'd said, I said nothing in reply.

He took another sip of coffee and then asked out of the blue, "So, why don't you want to get married and settle down?" yanking me back to the profane world.

I smiled. Suddenly, the image of Surti flashed before me. Bright. Shining. A kitchen smelling of turmeric. A kiss that overwhelmed my senses. I was startled. Why had her face appeared just now, when I was annoyed with Mas Hananto?

"That look on your face tells me you have someone already," Amir said. "Is she pretty? Who is she?"

I smiled and shook my head. "It's no one. I'm still single. But maybe one day…"

He smiled knowingly, like an elder brother. "Don't worry. One day you'll meet your Saidah."

I was unnerved by Bang Amir's sincerity. Shortly afterwards, when I stood to take my leave, I hugged him warmly. And as I walked away from the house to hunt for a *becak*, my heart felt like it was strapped in irons.

One night we finished writing up the news sooner than usual. It wasn't even ten o'clock. At first I thought I'd find a bite to eat and go home, but then Mas Hananto signaled for me to come with him. When I asked where we were going, he just smiled and kept driving his beloved Nissan patrol jeep. On the way to wherever it was we were going, he mentioned that he and Mas Nugroho were in frequent correspondence with people close to Andrés Pascal Allende.

"You mean, as in the nephew of Salvador Allende?" I asked in awe, like some country hick when hearing the name of a celebrity.

"Yes," he smiled, "and the founder of that country's leftist party, the Movimiento de Izquierda Revolucionaria."

I said nothing, leery of knowing (or not wanting to know) what their correspondence was about.

At the corner of Jalan Tjidurian in Menteng, Mas Hananto turned left. I said nothing. Now I knew that we were heading to LEKRA's headquarters. From a distance, I saw, sitting on the terrace of the large house being used as LEKRA's office, a number of people engaged in casual conversation.

"I don't know about this…" I whispered to my friend.

"Take it easy. I just want you to meet some of my friends. Plus, I have a book in there I want you to read."

I sat down among the nine or ten people who were there and soon found myself falling into easy conversation with them. Almost unaware of the passing time, we stayed at the office until almost midnight, drinking coffee and smoking cigarettes. Afterwards, Mas Hananto gave me a lift to my boarding house.

As I was getting out of the jeep, he handed me a copy of the Indonesian-language edition of John Steinbeck's novel *Of Mice and Men*. "Pramoedya translated it," Mas Hananto said to me, as if this gave the book official imprimatur. "The book is mine but you can have it."

I said nothing but nodded my thanks.

"After you have read it, I want you to tell me if you still think social realism is not interesting."

•

"What happened to Hananto and his family?" Vivienne's voice broke the spell and yanked me back to Paris in 1968. I couldn't give her an immediate answer. She seemed to acknowledge this and to understand that there were other chapters in my life's story that should, in their telling, precede what had happened to Mas Hananto.

I stared into her green eyes and stroked her face. I stood and was shocked, suddenly aware of my naked body. I looked down at Vivienne who smiled as her eyes traced my body's shape, moving upwards from my legs to my chest.

"His wife Surti and their three children are still in detention," I said flatly.

"Kenanga?"

"Yes, that's their oldest"

"Such a pretty name."

"It's a kind of flower. I'm not sure what it is in French. The name of Bulan, their second child, means *la lune* and Alam means *la nature*. He's the youngest, just three." I said, chattering and looking away as I put on my trousers. I didn't want Vivienne to know that those name were ones that I had once chosen when we were daydreaming. And by "we" I meant Surti and I.

"But what about Hananto?" Vivienne asked.

I was reluctant to say. The smoke rose from our cigarette,

twirling in the air, taking me to a world of fog.

"Mas Hananto was the last link in the chain to be captured. Most of the other members of the editorial board at Nusantara News had already been swept up. The only ones not arrested were members of either Islamic or anti-communist organizations. Of course, they were close to the military as well."

I sat down on the floor, silent in thought, counting the rising rings of smoke.

"There were these conferences for journalists in Santiago and Peking…" I finally began, attempting to give my gradually emerging story more historical context. "And Mas Hananto should have been the one to go to them with Mas Nugroho. He was more senior and much better than I in those kinds of networking jobs…" I stopped, searching for the words to continue. Vivienne stared at me, anxious to hear the rest. "But Mas Hananto couldn't go. He had a ton of work to do, or so he said, and some pressing personal matters to settle as well. So I replaced him and went with Mas Nug instead. Neither was against my going or taking Mas Hananto's place. Both thought I would learn a lot and gain some valuable experience besides."

Vivienne brushed her fingers over my hair.

"If he had gone, he wouldn't have been captured," I said, suddenly feeling a chill in my bones. I put on my shirt but still felt myself shaking.

Vivienne frowned. "Not necessarily!"

"Why not?"

"Because that's not the way life works. If Hananto had gone, then everything else that happened would have been different. We don't know what would have happened. Maybe you'd have been taken in or maybe not."

"I'd feel better if I was the one who had been captured. I don't have a family."

"You have your mother and your brother."

I didn't reply. I knew Vivienne was trying to comfort me. She had a good heart, a gentle soul, but there was no way I was going to feel consoled when I thought of what had happened to Surti and her children. My cigarette was a stub in my fingers.

Vivienne lit a new *kretek*. She took a drag then handed it to me.

•

THE TRIVELI AREA OF JAKARTA;
SEPTEMBER 5, 1965

I was on my fifth cigarette already and Mas Hananto was still getting it off with that woman in her house. I looked at my watch. Two o'clock in the morning! I swore that if he didn't settle his business and show his face before I finished the cigarette, I was going to leave him. I didn't care if he groused at me the next day at work. And what was he doing in there anyway? He had a beautiful wife: Surti, who was perfect in almost every way. He had no reason to betray her. I couldn't understand the man's behavior but, as I was his friend, I also couldn't remain oblivious to his proclivity for extramarital affairs.

This was the third time Mas Hananto had forced me to go with him when he went to see Marni. He needed me along to provide an alibi in case Surti asked where or with whom he had been.

Hearing a sound, I looked around to see Mas Hananto finally coming out of Marni's place. As he approached me, I could see that he was sweating but also beaming with satisfaction. With a big shit-eating grin on his face, he came over to where I was standing beside the cigarette vendor's kiosk near where he had parked his car.

Son of a bitch!

"What is it?" he asked while lighting a cigarette.

"What do you mean 'what is it'?"

"Why that hang-dog look on your face?"

"This is the last time I'm coming here with you!"

"Why?"

"Because I'm not your lackey, that's why, and I don't want to have to lie to Surti."

Mas Hananto's face was expressionless. He had always been very good at concealing his emotions. He just smoked his cigarette. We walked towards the car not speaking. The Jakarta sky was absent of stars, a mirror of my heart. I liked Mas Hananto. And I liked women, too; but for me, supposing I had a wife, especially one as lovely and faithful as Surti, that would mean I had made my choice in life. That would mean there would be no more playing around.

"What's special about Marni anyway?" I asked, breaking the silence.

Mas Hananto smiled. He knew that I couldn't stay mad at him for too long. "She makes all the cells in my body seem to come alive," he said with a glow in his eyes.

"Do you love her?"

He gave me a funny sideways look, and the kind of smirk that always made my blood rush to my temples because of the over-confident way he spoke. He was always so sure that nothing he did could possibly create problems for other people.

"Surti is my wife, my life's companion. But with Marni, I feel the passionate excitement of the proletarian class."

Pow!

Mas Hananto suddenly toppled over. I was amazed, because I hadn't thought the fist of my right hand could move so fast to strike his jaw.

•

"*Attends!*" Once again, Vivienne's voice suddenly tore away the scrim from my past, startling me. She raised her brows inquisitively. "Why were you so angry?"

Vivienne deserved an answer, but my voice was caught in my throat. How was I to explain to Vivienne who Surti was to me? The stem of jasmine that never wilted.

"You were angry because you were in love with her!"

Now I was the one knocked over—or, more precisely, dumb-founded by the ability of this Frenchwoman to read my heart.

I had spoken volumes to Vivienne about Jakarta and the political situation there, and never once had she interrupted me. But now, this one time, she instantly knew I was leaving something out and she cut off my story. Hmm…

I coughed to clear my throat. "Surti and I once were close…"

"You were in love with her," Vivienne said, correcting me, "and you were angry because Hananto was two-timing the woman you once loved." Vivienne stared at me to assess whether her assumption was correct. "Or, possibly," she added, "because you were still in love with her."

I hastened to explain. "What I was feeling at that time was only that Mas Hananto was squandering the affection of a woman who loved him—the same woman who had given him Kenanga and Bulan," I said honestly, though still avoiding her question.

Vivienne continued to stare at me, a small smile tugging on her lips.

"That was then, Vivienne. We all have a past," I said sincerely, hoping that the light in her beautiful green eyes would not fade. "I'm serious. And now I care for and respect Surti as I would a sister. She is—or was, rather—my best friend's wife."

Vivienne still looked unsure. I myself was unsure. I knew that whenever I mentioned Surti's name, my heart felt a jolt of pain. And hearing the names of Kenanga, Bulan, and even Alam, the youngest whom I had never known, still made my heart leap. I was the one who dreamt up their names. I don't know if Mas Hananto ever knew that.

In a firm voice, Vivienne now asked me to continue my story.

•

THE TRIVELI AREA OF JAKARTA;
SEPTEMBER 5, 1965

Mas Hananto rubbed his rub his jaw in pain. Inside the cigarette kiosk, the vendor snored, unaware of the disturbance outside.

"Mas Han…"

Hananto turned away, avoiding the look in my eye. "You still haven't gotten over her, have you?"

I didn't answer. It would have been a waste of time, what with the anger boiling in each of us.

"What time is it anyway?" I mumbled, suddenly feeling my body begin to wilt. My knees seemed to have lost their caps.

"Three," Mas Hananto said brusquely, looking at his watch, a 17-jewel Titoni which was like a second heart for him and never free from his wrist. "That's why I keep telling you to go to Senen Market and buy yourself a watch. You're always having to ask other people the time."

His tone was rough, but I could tell he was no longer angry. His jaw must have been hurting him, though.

I sat down beside him on the bumper of his jeep. "This will be the last time I interfere in your personal affairs," I told him, "but

I need to tell you that the way you live your life, with your family here and you going off to see Marni or some other woman there, shows that you are not consistent."

Mas Hananto helped himself to a pack of cigarettes from the kiosk, placed a bill to cover the cost beside the still-sleeping vendor, opened the packet, and then offered a stick to me. He signaled for me to get into the jeep.

The streets in Jakarta were silent. Silence and smoke suffused the jeep's interior.

In what seemed just a moment, we found ourselves already driving by the construction site of the unfinished National Monument in the park facing the presidential palace. From the disarray of the site, it was hard to guess when construction would be completed.

"So, you don't think I'm consistent?" Mas Hananto suddenly muttered.

A strange question, I thought, coming from a man like Mas Hananto, who was so sure of the political ideology he had chosen to follow and the woman he had selected to be a helpmate in his life.

"I say that," I told him, "because you have a family. A family requires stability and consistency. If you can't control yourself and are always giving in to impulse, then you shouldn't have gotten married. All you're going to do is to make other people suffer."

Mas Hananto glanced at me. "You're not saying this because of Surti?"

"You know this has nothing to do with her," I said unequivocally.

He gave me a serious look. "So I'm the one who's inconsistent and you are sure your position is the right one? Tell me, are you consistent? Do you know what you want? Either in politics or your personal life?"

I said nothing, certain that he was being rhetorical.

"You don't belong to a political party. You're not a member of any of the mass organizations. You always refuse to take sides. You malign LEKRA but then turn around and criticize signatories of the Cultural Manifesto."

"Yes, and so?" I stared at Mas Hananto, waiting for him to continue his critique.

"Well what is you want, Dimas? Take a look at your personal life. You don't seem to know what you want. Is it because you haven't been able to move on from the past or is it that you just like being single?"

Now I didn't understand. Was he irritated with me because I didn't want to take sides or because he thought I still had feelings for Surti? Why must a person take sides and join one group or another, I asked myself. Was it merely to prove one's convictions? And were convictions entirely unitary in nature? Socialism, communism, capitalism, and all the other isms… Must we choose one and then swallow it whole without any sense of doubt? Without any possibility for criticism?

I looked at Mas Hananto but kept my questions to myself. He had one hand on the steering wheel and was rubbing his jaw with the other. That night we said nothing more, at least not until Mas Hananto's jeep stopped in front of my boarding house, but how the conversation ended, I frankly no longer recall.

What I do remember is that the next day and for the entire week thereafter, we didn't speak to each other. At the office, Mas Hananto said only what was essential, hardly bothering to look at me when he spoke. His jaw and cheek were swollen and blue.

One day at the office, after about a week of us of not speaking, I watched from a distance as Mas Hananto laughed and spoke in whispers with Mas Nugroho and the editor-in-chief. I gave no thought to their little intrigue. I had no idea that their conversation that day would determine the course of my life, my fate, and my future as an exile, stranded in Paris. But then Mas Nug looked over in my direction and waved his hand, signaling for me to come to his desk.

•

"So, they had decided to send you to Europe?"

"No, they had decided to send me to one conference in Santiago and then on to another in Peking."

"So you went to Santiago, Chile, and then after that flew on to China?"

"My journey in life has been a long one, Vivienne. Before going to China, I went to Cuba first, and it was only after some time in China that I came to Europe."

I looked outside the window. To compare Paris and Jakarta would be like comparing coconut milk with gutter water.

•

A COFFEE STALL ON JALAN TJIDURIAN, JAKARTA;
SEPTEMBER 12, 1965

"I don't know anything about the I.O.J. or its conference in Santiago," I said to Mas Hananto after tracking him to an itinerant coffee stall near the corner of Jalan Tjidurian. I tossed the large manila envelope on the stall's rickety table. This was the first long sentence I had spoken to Mas Hananto since we'd stopped talking to each other. Inside the envelope was an invitation to attend a conference of journalists in Chile.

Mas Hananto, who was sitting slovenly with one arm on the table and one leg propped up on the bench, stared at his glass of hot coffee as if pretending to be deaf. He lowered his lips to the edge of the glass and started slurping—a sound that disgusted me. I knew he was doing this to annoy me.

Feeling both surprise and the desire to smack him in the jaw again, I finally decided to sit down beside him. "This invitation is for you," I said. "Why do you want me to go?"

Saying nothing, Mas Hananto lowered his head, looking into his glass of coffee again.

"I can't speak Spanish. I've never engaged in any kind of journalistic activity at the international level. I wouldn't know what to say at such a conference," I sputtered, angry with him that he could so flippantly assign me a task without even consulting me beforehand.

"It's the Chief's decision," Mas Hananto mumbled. "You have to go with Nug."

A glass of coffee suddenly appeared before me.

Mas Hananto said, "The name of the organization is the 'International Organization of Journalists,' which is English, right, so the language of the conference is going to be English, which you speak perfectly well. It's an annual conference for heads of media institutions from around the world. The delegates of each of the countries represented have been given a topic to discuss. You and Nug have one too."

Still not looking me in the eye, Mas Hananto took another sip of coffee. "Listen, it will be a good experience for you. Guys from *Harian Rakjat* are also going," Mas Hananto continued, as if to bolster the reason for me to go. "And we're sending Risjaf to Havana to represent Indonesia at the Asia-Africa Organization."

I didn't reply. In a normal situation, I would have made a joke about Risjaf trying out every Cuban cigar he came across or something on that order, but this situation was different; there was something Mas Hananto was not telling me.

"Why aren't you going?" I finally asked point blank.

"The Chief has decided that Nug will represent our office and that you will accompany him."

Mas Hananto, still avoiding my eyes, was staring so closely at his glass of coffee, you'd have thought there was a miniature Maya reclining on its rim.

"We also have the situation here to deal with. Word has been going around about intrigues among the Communist Party elite and military high officials. The Chief feels that it would be best for me to be here in Jakarta."

I didn't know what to say. This was the first time Mas Hananto had ever told me something that sounded so very "internal" in nature. Even so, I still felt that he was leaving out something.

"After the conference in Santiago, you and Nug will join up with Risjaf in Havana and then go on to Peking for the Asia-Africa Journalists Conference there," said Mas Hananto, offering further explanation.

I didn't want to react. And I didn't want to drink the coffee that had been placed in front of me.

Mas Hananto glanced at me. He knew that I wouldn't give in to his bidding before he divulged the full details.

"Whenever you sulk, you stick out your lower lip so far you could hang a frying pan off it," he said with a smirk.

I waited for Mas Hananto to say more but his attention was now on the stream of smoke rising from his cigarette. Shit! I stood to go, leaving the glass of coffee untouched and the envelope with the invitation and air tickets to Santiago on the table top. I had just turned and started to walk away when Mas Hananto called my name in a loud and broken voice.

I sat down, my lower lip still hanging.

Mas Hananto looked both irritated and sad. I had no idea what had come over him. "I can't go, Dimas. I have to stay here, in Jakarta."

I swallowed. This was the first time I had ever seen tears in Mas Hananto's eyes.

"Surti is taking the girls to her parents' home," he said hoarsely.

I said nothing. I knew how very much he loved Kenanga and Bulan and how much they loved him.

"Why?"

Mas Hananto didn't answer.

"Because of Marni?"

Mas Hananto took a deep breath. "I'm trying to persuade Surti not to leave me. That's why I can't leave town, much less the country, at this time. I have to take care of family business. If need be, I'll stay at home and won't go into the office until Surti has changed her mind and is ready to try again."

Wordlessly, I picked up the manila envelope and then patted Mas Hananto on the shoulder, as if to reassure him that everything would work out.

Mas Hananto unstrapped his beloved watch. "During the conference, you have to be on time," he said handing the watch to me.

I knew I couldn't refuse his offer, not that night, so I took the watch and put it on my wrist.

"I'm sure that by the time I get back, you two will be just fine," I said, trying to cheer him. "Surti is never going to leave you. She's just mad at you, is all. Trust me…"

Mas Hananto nodded. I nodded in return and then looked at him for what would be the last time.

FOR PARISIAN WOMEN, A CHANGE IN SEASON MEANS A CHANGE in fashion—perhaps just a light scarf with a floral design wound around the neck to complement maroon-colored flats or to contrast with a beret of checkered motif, or maybe just a simple but elegant white long-sleeved satin blouse. For men like me who pay little attention to fashion—except insofar that clothes are needed to ward off the cold—Paris is in any season the largest open-air catwalk in the world. There's no obvious planning here. And we're not talking about the designer or model crowd. Normal Parisian women act and look like models. Parisians are a special breed whose lives are filled with style. In my mind, the term *haute couture* is little more than a ruse of the clothing industry which has conspired with designers to increase their profits. Nothing more. But, whatever the truth may be, it doesn't matter, because whatever the season, Parisians are very fashion-minded and pay utmost attention to appearances. Even so, with all the city's apparent luxury and despite being known as "The City of Light," two things are missing here: orchids and jasmine flowers.

Tanah Air Restaurant on Rue de Vaugirard is a small and separate island in a Paris full of flair and color. It's tiny compared to Café de Flore in Saint-Germain-des-Prés which, since the nineteenth century, has been the meeting place for the world's literary figures and intellectuals who wish to engage in high-minded discussions while sipping soup and drinking coffee. Tanah Air Restaurant—"Tanah Air" meaning "Homeland" in Indonesian—serves authentic Indonesian food, meticulously prepared with ingredients and spices from Indonesia: shallots, turmeric, cloves, ginger, lemon grass, and galingale. But maybe all of this is just the Café de Flore for us political exiles, who spend our lives cooking food for customers and reciting poetry into the night, as we think of the homeland we knew prior to 1965.

Here, in this restaurant, I am sitting with them now. There's Risjaf, the most handsome and masculine of our lot, with wavy hair and an earnest and honest heart; Nugroho Dewantoro, originally from Yogyakarta, who sports a Clark Gable mustache and has an effervescent personality but a heart of steel; and Tjai Sin Soe (who sometimes goes by the Indonesianized name Tjahjadi Sukarna), an action man and fast thinker with a calculator in his left hand, which he seems to value more than life itself.

As always, at the end of each night of service, after our customers have paid and gone home, Tjai takes out his calculator, counts the money that has come in, and divides up the tips among us all. Mas Nugroho makes sure all the perishable foodstuffs have been properly sealed and stored in the refrigerator; Risjaf cleans the tables and chairs and removes the posters from the windows for the event that took place that evening. Meanwhile, my helpers, Bahrum and Yazir, wash and dry the dishes, glasses, pots, pans, and utensils.

Risjaf has just turned the television station to CNN, which proceeds to air a few seconds of the news that today, in the 1997 presidential elections in Indonesia, President Soeharto was chosen in an uncontested election to serve a seventh five-year term. We are not surprised by the news; just bored. The news is like the sound of mosquitoes at twilight in Solo: ever constant, never changing. Much more interesting for us is the additional bit of news that in the wake of the elections, student demonstrators have taken to the streets throughout the country, and that even the traditionally cowed news media have begun to express public disgruntlement about the fact that the president's new cabinet is filled with his cronies. Even his eldest daughter, Siti Hardiyanti Rukmana, was awarded the position of Minister for Social Affairs. We look around at one another. Risjaf turns off the television.

Together and without a word—perhaps all of us feeling the need to think of happy times and be consoled by the memories of younger days when we were naïve and full of love—we go from the lower floor of the restaurant to its ground floor and there stretch out on the chairs and listen to the song "Als de Orchideeën Bloeien," which Risjaf plays on his harmonica. The song stirs and pierces the heart.

As the chords of "The Orchids Are Now in Bloom" float through the open window of the restaurant into the spring air, all of us there are thinking of another orchid, one who went by the name of Rukmini. Rukmini, the orchid… Sipping on small glasses of rum to warm the body, our minds travel back in time to a place forty-five years ago.

•

JAKARTA, JANUARY–OCTOBER 1952

Three flowers, three young and beautiful women, transformed Jakarta into a garden of delight. Ningsih was a red rose of arresting beauty who made every man's heart beat faster; Rukmini, a purple orchid whose color never faded with the passing of the seasons; and Surti Anandari, a white jasmine who left her lingering fragrance wherever she went. Men who fell in love with her could almost not function when she was not in their sight.

These three young women were members of the freshman class in the Faculty of Letters and Philosophy at the University of Indonesia in Jakarta. Risjaf, Tjai, and I, being junior classmen, felt ourselves to be much more knowledgeable and superior, and we liked to tease them. The three women rented rooms at a boarding house on Jalan Cik di Tiro. My friends and I lived, as we had for the past three years, in a boarding house for men on Jalan Solo just a few hundred meters away. Across the street from our lodgings was the home of a Mr. Bustami who rented out his *paviliun*—a semi-detached annex of his home—to Mas Nugroho and Mas Hananto, older friends of ours who had recently begun to work at the Nusantara News office.

For Tjai, Risjaf, and me, the *paviliun* across the road became our place of recreation. Compared to our own small rooms, the *paviliun* was quite spacious, with a separate living room, where we could lounge about or play chess on the comfortable but louse-infested sofa. Mas Nugroho and Mas Hananto, who seemed much more mature than the three of us, frequently lent us their books—anything from anthologies of European poetry to titillating titles with pictures of men and women engaged in a myriad variety of sexual acts. Risjaf's eyes would open widely in surprise when he flipped through the pages of these books, as if incapable of believing that that women could wrap their bodies in such positions. Mas Nug even made it a point to lend such books to Risjaf, because he got such a kick from seeing this younger and more naïve man's reactions. Although Risjaf was the best-looking man among us, when it came to women, he was the most inexperienced.

At first I wasn't too interested in pursuing these three new freshman girls, not as girlfriends, anyway. To my mind, they seemed excessively cheerful and sweet-natured. Further, with all their fine clothes and makeup, they looked to me like privileged daughters of aristocrats who had never known hardship. One day as I was passing by their boarding house, I saw a man I guessed to be Surti's father pull up to the curb in front of the house in a white Fiat 1100, a car that only a member of the upper economic class could aspire to own. As I came closer and was able to see the man more clearly, my suspicion was confirmed: Surti was the daughter of Dr. Sastrowidjojo, "the" Dr. Sastrowidjojo who lived on Jalan Papandayan in an elite and leafy residential area in Bogor, south of Jakarta. Not only was he famous, he was the son and grandson of equally famous doctors, members of the crème de la crème in pre-independent Indonesia. Surti's father was known to have played a leading role in the founding of Jakarta's central hospital, the Centraal Burgerlijke Ziekenhuis. The fact that Surti had not followed her father's footsteps and gone into medicine suggested that there might be something special about her; but later, when I heard Mas Nug and Mas Hananto talk about her family back-ground, my interest in knowing her better dwindled. I could neither afford nor be bothered with all the things that having a girlfriend from her social and economic class entailed.

The problem was that Risjaf was attracted to Rukmini, she with the luscious red lips and very sharp tongue. Yet the more caustic her words, the more infatuated Risjaf became. In the end, it was for Risjaf—who swore that if he could go out with Rukmini just once he would be happy to die and go to heaven, and who often woke me when he talked about her in his sleep—that I decided to approach these three lovely women and invite them on a group date with my friends.

At first, the three girls paid no attention to my advances, pretty much ignoring me altogether. They were too busy flirting with the male students in the Faculty of Law, who were given to citing legal statutes. (And what for? What was sexy about citations from law books, which were still in Dutch no less? Wouldn't they find our skill in reciting poetry more interesting?) But I knew from the way they pretended to ignore me that they noticed me. At least Surti, for one, sometimes smiled. Once, I even caught her staring at me, her eyes like stars shining their light on me; but when she saw me staring back, she immediately turned her head. At that instant, I knew that she was the jasmine flower I wanted to pluck and store in my heart.

One day, as she was going into class, I slipped into her fingers a verse from the poem "She Walks in Beauty" by Lord Byron— "She walks in beauty, like the night / of cloudless climes and starry skies…"—but when she opened her mouth to speak, I immediately walked away, worried that she wouldn't like the poem. The next day, however, she was the one who slipped a note to me: two lines from the poem "Elegy" by Rivai Apin: "what is it that we feel, yet have no need to express / what is it that we think, yet have no need to speak…" I almost swooned—not only from the sentiment of the poem but from the paper on which it was written, with its fragrant smell of jasmine.

For a few days thereafter, we communicated almost only through lines of verse, with very few words spoken. One time I copied in longhand a romantic section from *Romeo and Juliet* and gave that to her. She replied with a quote from the poem "Bright Star" by Keats: "Bright star, would I were steadfast as thou art / Not in lone splendor hung aloft the night."

Surti Anandari was a stem of jasmine; she was a bright star in the midnight sky.

One day I waited for Surti outside her classroom. As usual when she saw me, she opened her hand to receive from me a slip of paper on which was written a romantic verse or scene. I smiled and when she raised her hand towards me, I took it and clasped it tightly. Startled, she instantly stopped walking, and looked at me in question. Lowering my lips to her ear, I whispered, "I want to be with you. Forever."

During the first few months of my relationship with Surti, things went along pretty much the way they usually did among young men and women at that time: politely, guilelessly, and chastely. Any time our breaths began to join as one, we'd suddenly hear Risjaf or Tjai cough, causing us to draw apart from each other again. Sometimes, Surti and her friends would come to our boarding house with Rukmini and Ningsih, "just to bring us cookies they had made" or something on that order; but, usually, after the brief-est of conversations, they would immediately take their leave. "It's not proper for an unmarried woman to be seen visiting a man," Surti reminded me.

And whenever this trio of young ladies did stop by, all of a sudden our older and more dashing neighbors, Mas Nugroho and Mas Hananto, would also appear, "just to borrow some glasses or a platter" (which I knew they'd never use) or to help me cook up some fried rice. Even though my fried rice was famous among the students who boarded on Jalan Solo, it was obvious that our neighbors were coming not to dine but to feast on the sight of the three young women. Crafty devils that they were, they'd pretend to help by grinding chilies or preparing the seasoning by mixing shrimp paste with oil, but all the while they would be shuttling back and forth between the kitchen and the living room where the three girls were seated, a farce that would end with the batch of them giggling together. Meanwhile, Risjaf and Tjai would find themselves staring, hopelessly frustrated by the sight. The three of us were just college students, whereas Mas Nugroho and Mas Hananto were grown men with mustaches they could shape like that of Clark Gable.

Through their gambit of borrowing things and "giving Dimas a hand" at our boarding house, Mas Nug and Mas Hananto succeeded in persuading the three women to visit their den of iniquity. Mas Nug, who had a much larger expendable income than we as students had, owned a hi-fidelity player and would play records for the three womem. For that reason, the trio willingly spent what I thought was an inordinate amount of time at the *paviliun* listening to the songs of Sam Saimun and others. Mas Nug, who couldn't carry a tune to save his life, would always start singing along, disrupting the glorious sound of Saimun's voice. Mas Hananto owned a radio and sometimes we'd hear the girls laughing at the comic repartee of Bing Slamet and Adi Karso on their show at Radio Republic Indonesia.

Initially, I thought that Mas Hananto was attracted to Rukmini with the ruby red lips. I knew that Risjaf was almost epileptic about this but was trying not to show his jealousy. Only later I realized that Mas Hananto was in fact helping to win over Rukmini for Mas Nugroho. As the competition between Risjaf and Mas Nug to capture Rukmini's affections heated up, I of course stood by Risjaf. As his friend, I was bound to support him.

One day I found Risjaf rummaging through books on my work table.

"I want to borrow some of your poetry books," he said. His eyes emitted a deep light of sincerity.

What? Here was this tall and very handsome man from Riau with thick wavy hair— a living and breathing testimony to masculinity—looking for books of poetry. A man with his build and temperament didn't need poetry to conquer a woman's heart.

I took Risjaf firmly by the shoulders and turned him around until he was facing me. "Listen to me, Sjaf! Rukmini likes you. She's always liked you. There's no need to woo her with poetry. Just ask her for a date."

Risjaf stared at me, wide-eyed. "That's easy for you to say, Dimas. You're good with words. But whenever I see Rukmini, my heart stops beating, and I don't know what to say."

Oh, Risjaf… I told my friend to sit down and take a deep breath. Obediently he sat down on the edge of the bed. His thick wavy hair was disheveled and big drops of sweat rolled from his forehead and down his cheeks. Risjaf, this Malay man with such a fine heart, was completely unaware of his own charm.

"Risjaf, just look into Rukmini's eyes and tell her that you want to ask her out."

Risjaf's mouth dropped open. "Where?"

Good God! How could such a handsome face exhibit a mien of such stupidity?

"Out! On a date!" I almost yelled. "Take her to see *Solo by Night* at the Metropole; invite her to dinner at Tan Goei; treat her to a milkshake at Baltic Ice Cream; or, if you really want to save your money, go for a walk with her at Zandvoort."

"Zandvoort…Zandvoort…" With his mouth still agape, Risjaf repeated the word over and over.

"In Cilincing, stupid!" I half shouted at him.

"You talk to her first, will you, please?" Now he was pleading with me.

My God.

For two long and painful hours I mentored this man who was so handsome but so naïve about women. Risjaf nodded at my instructions and wrote down all the places he might take Rukmini. After that, he quickly bathed and then changed into a blue dress shirt. He glossed his hair with pomade and combed it neatly. He folded the notes he had made during my primer course and put them in his trouser pocket—as if they were some kind of amulet that would help him to speak fluently.

With Surti spending the weekend at her parents' home in Bogor, I myself was "on vacation" that night, so I gave my blessings to Risjaf, wished him the best, and made ready for a night of reading. Risjaf strode from the house with an almost confident air.

No more than a half hour later, I heard a weak knock on my door. Who could that be, I wondered. Opening the door, I found Risjaf, who came into my room with his head drooping like a limp dish rag. He let his body fall onto my bed. His eyes stared blankly at the ceiling overhead.

I looked down at him. "What is it, Sjaf?"

"I went to her place…"

"And so?"

"So she wasn't there."

"Then you can go back another time."

"She'd gone out with another man!" Risjaf cried.

I was silent, not knowing what to say. My heart poured out for him.

Risjaf stared at me, his eyes reddened with anger or perhaps pain.

He spoke slowly and in a low voice, but the sound in my ears was like the ticking of a bomb.

"The lady at the boarding house told me that Rukmini had gone out with a man named Nugroho."

That night I let Risjaf sprawl on my bed as he played the same song repeatedly on his harmonica, the Dutch tune "Als de Orchideeën Bloeien." After about the fifth time, I was ready to wrest the harmonica from his hand and throttle him with it, but the tears welling in his eyes made me feel sorry for him. And after midnight, when the orchid still hadn't bloomed, Risjaf, in his now-crumpled blue shirt, finally fell asleep and began to snore. I stretched out on the floor and stared at the ceiling, unable to fall asleep. There were still many things about women that I, too, did not understand.

In the weeks that followed, I was Risjaf's shadow, going with him wherever he went: to campus, the library, Senen Market, Metropole Cinema, most everywhere, just to make sure he didn't wind up standing atop a tall bridge or on the edge of a deep well. His demeanor and manner were those of a man without hope. I also shadowed him when he walked across the street to stand motionless on the sidewalk outside Mas Nugroho's *paviliun*. He had held the phlegm in his throat for so long, I knew he was now ready, that he had to spit it out. *Splat!* At least he had spat on the walk and not into Mas Nugroho's face, I thought. But that would not have been my friend Risjaf, who was not the kind of man given to open displays of anger. I knew he realized that he had no claim on Rukmini. Therefore, what right did he have to be angry? Even so, I could not allow the situation to continue indefinitely.

From my point of view, the problem rested with Mas Nugroho, who was completely insensitive to Risjaf's feelings. He didn't seem to realize that Risjaf was suffering from a broken heart—even though I thought it was apparent to everyone else. Whenever we saw Rukmini stop by at the *paviliun* across the road, even if it was only for a moment, Risjaf would immediately scurry into his room, hide behind a pile of homework, and not come out again.

One Sunday, I finally spoke about the situation with Surti, who gave me a look of complete surprise. "What? Risjaf likes Rukmini?"

"Yes. Didn't you know?" In the mortar, I used my pestle to attack the sliced shallots and garlic and chunk of peeled turmeric root, as if they were to blame for keeping Rukmini and Risjaf apart.

Risjaf was still in the throes of misery, and I had promised myself that on Sunday I would cook up a pot of *ikan pindang serani* as a means to soothe his heart. Originally an Indo-Portuguese dish, the recipe for this spicy and sour milkfish soup was from my mother, and the taste of the fish which had been simmered slowly in turmeric sauce never failed to cheer me or my brother Aji when my father, who often had to travel for work, was not at home. I hoped that the dish would turn its magic on Risjaf, permitting him to recover and cast his attention on another woman.

As it was now Tjai's turn to shadow Risjaf, who had gone to borrow lecture notes from a friend, I had some time to spend alone with Surti, even if I was cooking.

The cuts of milkfish, sliced shallots, green tomatoes, and citrus leaves were in their respective piles on the countertop and I was now grinding the turmeric with red chilies and garlic. The skin on my hands had turned yellow from the turmeric, and the paste of spice mixture began to splatter as I ground.

Surti, who was standing next to me, placed her right hand on mine, causing me to stop what I was doing.

"How was Rukmini supposed to know?" she asked, now stroking my hand. "Whenever Risjaf is around her, he's as stiff as a statue, like he's in electric shock." She smiled gently and looked me in the eye. "I'm very sure that Rukmini is unaware of Risjaf's feelings towards her."

I stopped torturing the spice mixture and wiped my forehead with the back of my arm.

She was probably right. "Does Rukmini like Mas Nug?" I asked.

"It would appear so," she said evenly. Adding another slice of turmeric to the paste, she began to move the pestle. By the way she crushed the root—gently, wordlessly—she seemed to be coaxing the spices to surrender themselves to their individual destruction in order to create a more perfect union of taste, one more pleasing to the tongue. I stared, fixating on her as she slowly turned the wooden pestle in the mortar as if massaging the spicy mixture. I swallowed. My body tensed. I hardly knew what was happening and I was unable to comprehend why her actions excited me so.

"What's clear," Surti said as she continued to grind the spices (which in turn made me more tense and less able to speak), "Mas Nug is willing to express his feelings. As is Mas Hananto. They are men who know what they want."

She was right, of course. Damn the two of them, both of them older and more mature! Both had good jobs, though neither held a college degree. After graduation from high school, Mas Nug had enrolled in Chinese studies at the University of Indonesia but had never completed his degree. For several years, Mas Hananto had been a student in the Faculty of Law, but hadn't finished his studies either. Even so, regardless of their educational deficit, the two of them were definitely more experienced in dealing with women. I felt chagrin. It wasn't fair that we—Risjaf and I—were being compared to the two of them. And, for that matter, it wasn't right that those two guys were going after college co-eds.

But wait a minute, I then thought. "You said Mas Hananto. He's going after Rukmini, too?" I asked.

Surti looked at me clear-eyed, not bothering to offer an answer. A speck of the spice mixture—turmeric and chilies—was on her cheek. She looked away and then busied herself grinding the spices again. My God!

"Mas Hananto asked you out!?"

Surti squeezed my hand. "I turned him down. Doesn't my heart belong to you?"

"Surti…"

"Don't worry, Dimas, and don't ask again about Mas Hananto. I'm here with you, aren't I?"

I nestled my body close to hers. Her body emitted a scent of turmeric. I wiped the yellow speck from her cheek.

"I want you to be the father of my children," she said in a voice of certainty.

My God. She had never spoken with such assuredness before. I tried to follow suit and said lightly, "If you have a girl, we'll give her the name Kenanga."

"And if the child's a boy?" she responded in kind.

"Then we'll call him Alam."

There was still a bit of yellow color on her cheek and I licked it to wipe it away. Almost unable to resist my growing excitement, I held her chin in my hand and pressed my lips to hers, which were soft, velvety, and luscious, like the taste of Baltic Ice Cream. I used my tongue to explore her bodily curves: the nape of her neck, the cavity between her breasts, her erect nipples. When Surti released a suppressed moan, I knew that I would not, that I could not stop myself from further exploration. If Risjaf came back and demanded his promised dish of milkfish soup, I would cite *force majeure*: an earthquake had destroyed the kitchen. I lifted Surti and set her down on the kitchen table. As my body entered hers, I knew the feeling that I experienced would last forever. Forever and always.

I often use the word "forever." "Always" is a favorite of mine as well—especially when I'm naked. One should always remember not to say anything when making love, because ecstasy makes us forget the ground we're standing on and even our ideals. People who know me well tend to portray me as the antithesis of all that is certain and constant. There was some truth in Mas Hananto's accusation—that I wasn't willing to take sides, either in politics or in love. I was a ship never tethered to one port for long. Soon after calling into one harbor, I would be anxious to raise the anchor again.

After that love-making session, which raised havoc with the kitchen, I knew for certain what Surti would expect from me: one day, and sooner rather than later, I would have to fasten the knot of my love to something certain. But did that mean I had to stop my voyage now, I asked myself. Were there not more voyages to undertake, more ports to explore, more books to read? The ocean is vast. Even on such a long journey as ours, was it necessary to stop or take a break? When writing, I didn't like to use periods. I preferred to use commas instead. Don't tell me to stop. I would drown in stagnation. Don't.

I sensed that Surti was aware of my anxiety. At the very least, she knew that with the end of my formal education ahead of me, I was preoccupied with my review of lecture notes and literary texts as I prepared for final examinations.

Many of the books I used, I borrowed from Mas Hananto's personal library. I remember him once lending me works of Leo Tolstoy—books which the wife of a Dutch friend had given him. The wife had been crazy about him, he told me. And he was still friends with the both of them, he said; but then, with a glint in his eye, he added, "and their daughter, who is going to college in Amsterdam, is a real knockout." Why I had suddenly thought of that incident, I didn't know. There was no reason for me to get worked up thinking about Mas Hananto's fecklessness or his amorous adventures with his friend's wife or daughter.

At any rate, even though I had buried myself in books and notes, I shouldn't have been surprised when one day Surti stopped by my boarding house to see me.

"Dimas…" she began, with a serious look on her face and a bright glow in her eyes. "My parents are hosting a dinner for some relatives, a few of my aunts and uncles. And there will be a friend of the family from the Netherlands as well, Dr. Bram Janssen, who is in the country at the moment. I want you to meet them."

What?

What was this?

Why?

Was this necessary? Now? Her parents? At their home in Bogor? Her aunts and uncles? Dr. Bram Janssen? My throat suddenly felt scratchy. I understood the implication of her invitation, but there were still so many books, so many ideas, and oceans and continents to explore. Did I have to meet her parents now? Did I have to set anchor?

I looked at Surti. In my heart, I spoke out in protest, but my lips were sealed. Surti, Surti… Who was I to be introduced to your family with all its doctors and degrees? I could see myself, squeezed in among them in their elegant living room, with a glass of wine in my hand, as they chatted about the state of the nation and how it was never going to advance. What was I to say to her father and mother and to her aunts and uncles? All of these questions whirled around in my heart. Surti now knew me well enough to read my thoughts. Tears brimmed in her eyes. She turned away from me and left my boarding house.

After that unspoken conversation and the dinner invitation I didn't accept, it became ever more difficult for me to see Surti. Not only was I very busy preparing for my final examinations, she herself seemed to be doing her best to avoid running into me on campus. Frankly, I didn't try extra hard to meet up with her either. I had decided that, for the time being at least, I needed to concentrate on my studies. After final examinations and graduation, I would go to see her.

One day I went to Mas Hananto's *paviliun* across the road to borrow a dictionary. As was usual, the door to the *paviliun* was open. I stuck my head in and called out to Mas Hananto and Mas Nug. No answer. The door to Mas Hananto's bedroom was closed. A surprise. I knocked. No answer. I opened it. I didn't know why, but my heart was beating wildly. And there I saw Mas Hananto standing with his arms around a woman who was seated with her back to him at his desk. I couldn't see the woman's face, shielded as it was by Mas Hananto's form, but I could smell the scent of jasmine. I quickly pulled the door shut, causing it to slam. My heart pounded faster and faster. My breathing came in spurts. I fled the *paviliun* with its louse-infested couch.

I cursed and swore to myself that I would never again set foot in the home of that traitor.

Prone on my bed, I stared at the ceiling as Risjaf repeatedly played "Als de Orchideeën Bloeien" on his harmonica.

After some time, he stopped and then I heard him say. "Hey, Dimas..."

"What...?"

"How about if we burn down that *paviliun* across the road?"

I turned my head towards him and smiled weakly, somewhat consoled by Risjaf's display of solidarity and brotherhood.

"No need for that," I said as Risjaf lifted his harmonica to play again. "Better to murder those two fuckers instead."

Suddenly, we both burst into laughter, delighted by this black fantasy.

It wasn't easy for me to expunge the name of Surti from my life. Not only because I liked to cook and the kitchen was a constant and painful reminder of my feelings towards her. For the first few weeks after that incident I was forever seeing Surti standing next to the cooker and her reflection on plates and in pots. But where I saw her most often was on the handle of my knife, perched there, looking at me, as I prepared spices for grinding: shallots, onions, and turmeric.

Just as other men with broken hearts would do, I tried to forget my feelings for Surti in the most clichéd of ways: by sleeping around with other women. After each of these sessions, however, I always felt foolish and sick to my stomach. By coincidence, with political and social tensions on the rise in Jakarta at that time, we rarely saw Mas Nugroho or Mas Hananto. They were busy with their work at Nusantara News and both had been assigned to cover the incident of October 17, 1952, when a group of army officers staged a failed coup attempt to force the dissolution of Parliament and install President Sukarno as the country's supreme leader. If I had been on speaking terms with them at the time, no doubt I would have been dogging their tracks, hoping to learn more about the political situation. To become a journalist, I had begun to discover, was a career path I could not resist. Journalism uses the power of words in the same way that a chef uses the strength of spices in the dishes he creates.

So it was that for a few months our small community of friends broke down and dispersed. Neither our moods nor our schedules permitted any form of reconciliation. Mas Nugroho and Mas Hananto were busy with their work; Risjaf had his books; and I was busy with women, exams, and grinding spices in the kitchen as I thought about concepts of love between men and women as depicted in the *Mahabharata*.

Drupadi.

Drupadi had taken all five of the Pandawa brothers as husbands. But it was the brother Bima who always tried to protect her and had thwarted Kicaka's and Dursasana's advances when they tried to rape her. Tragically for Bima, Drupadi loved his brother, Arjuna, much more. I don't really know and actually never tried to find out whether Surti loved Mas Hananto more than me. What I did know is that she had made a choice.

I'm even more uncertain about why it is that, even after meeting the lovely Vivienne and marrying her, up until this very day my soul still stirs whenever I think of Surti. Perhaps I truly did give my heart to her. Forever and for always.

And forty-five years later in Paris, that same song from Risjaf's harmonica still softly suffuses the springtime air: "Als de Orchideeën Bloeien."

TERRE D'ASILE

don't come home comma wait till
calm here stop mother and I well
comma only been called in for
information stop aji suryo

PARIS, SEPTEMBER, 1965

"ONLY BEEN CALLED IN FOR INFORMATION..." Those were the words in the telegram my brother Aji sent to me two weeks after the storm that occurred in late September 1965. Mas Nugroho and I were two among the many Indonesian journalists who had been invited to attend the conference of the International Organization of Journalists in Santiago, Chile, earlier that month. Even though Jakarta was heating up and full of the smoke from rumors about a "Council of Generals" which had resulted in infighting among the ranks of the military elite, we had left the country with no apprehension or premonition about things to come. At least I had no inkling that anything out of the ordinary was going to occur, not in the days before our departure. We were going off on an ordinary assignment and, as such, said our goodbyes with little fanfare.

If I did feel any apprehension at that time, it was about the state of my friendship with Mas Hananto. A few weeks prior to my departure, we'd had an argument and I had punched him in the face because I was repulsed by the way he was treating Surti, taking her completely for granted. He accused me of still being in love with her—which was, I must admit, something I'd never been able to ascertain, even to myself. It was clear, though, that it

63

was because of Surti I had decided to go to Santiago.

Mas Hananto was the one who should have gone with Mas Nugroho to Santiago, but he had chosen instead to remain in Jakarta in order to resolve his marital crisis—a situation for which he was entirely to blame, he being given to chasing any skirt that passed by. Initially, I had been reluctant to go because of recent political developments in several Latin American countries. Mas Hananto and Mas Nug, in fact, were in correspondence with people close to Andrés Pascal Allende, Salvador Allende's nephew. I was aware of this, but I never really felt like I was in the same spectrum they were in. I was a free cell. What reason did I have to go to Santiago? But when Mas Hananto told me that Surti had threatened to leave him and take their three children with her, I immediately changed my mind. I felt Surti's unexpressed anger and pain suddenly overpower me. Her silent suffering became a strong voice speaking to me. I knew that the problem was not simply a question of Mas Hananto's womanizing; it was because she felt betrayed by her husband and shunned by her helpmate. I recalled the crude comparison Mas Hananto had drawn between Surti and his mistress, Marni: "Surti is my wife, my life's companion. But with Marni, I can feel the passionate excitement of the proletarian class."

Mas Hananto would never have said such a thing to his wife; but I knew Surti well, from the way she breathed down to her very pores. Being a woman who was highly sensitive to the behavior and demeanor of the man she loved, there was no way she could not have known about her husband's shenanigans. Maybe not in specific detail but she would have known, nonetheless. As I saw it, the problem with Mas Hananto was that there was something about Surti—maybe her deep sense of honor or her innate elegance and natural beauty—which he viewed as "aristocratic" and therefore something that he, a self-styled proletarian, could never truly possess. There was something about Surti so sublime that, in Mas Hananto's way of thinking, it could only be classified as "bourgeois," which made him reject it out of hand and engage in sexual escapades with women in Triveli.

I truly did not want to see the couple separate, which is why I bowed to Mas Hananto's wishes so that he could stay home and resolve his marital issues. In my departure from Jakarta, I never dreamed that I would not return.

●

It was during the middle of the conference in Santiago that Jose Ximenez, the chairman, made a special announcement in a plenary session about what the English-language press was calling the "September 30 Movement" which had taken place in Jakarta. (We later learned that the Indonesian phrase, "Gerakan September Tigapuluh," had quickly been changed by the country's new military rulers into the more ominous sounding acronym, "Gestapu.") We were shocked. High-level military officers kidnapped and killed? We couldn't imagine who might have perpetuated such an act. I repeatedly pressed Mas Nugroho to try to find out more from Ximenez about what had happened.

For a few tense nights, amidst all this uncertainty, we could neither eat nor sleep. Even as we marinated our minds with bottles of wine generously provided by our host as a sign of sympathy or solidarity, we constantly endeavored to contact our families and friends. Because of its leftist reputation, we were all but certain that the Nusantara News office had been raided, looted, or vandalized. Presumably, the military would have assumed that the agency was holding on to a trove of important documents. But that was the Indonesian military, for whom an ant might seem to be a raging tiger. Mas Nug assured me that there was nothing damning in our office: just books, piles of paper, and typewriters. We learned that most of the editorial staff had been called in for interrogation. No one seemed to know where the editor-in-chief had been taken.

It was only after twelve nerve-wracking days that I received the telegram from my mother and Aji. And although they sought to assuage my fears with the words that they had "only been called in for information," at that time, in 1965, the phrase had a sinister meaning. While it may have only meant "interrogation," it might very well have meant "torture." Indonesia's history during that time—even if it's not been completely written—reveals that in the three years following the events of September 30, 1965, the country went through numerous stages of inhumanity: the hunt for people, the naming of names, raids, capture, torture, killing, and slaughter. Given that fact, I was forced to see the phrase "only called in for information" as a kind of blessing. I had no doubt that my mother and Aji had been systematically and thoroughly interrogated. I was also certain that our home in Solo had been raided. I was sure that my late father's personal library—or, rather, the books in it that I had been unable to bring with me to Jakarta because my lodgings there on Jalan Solo were too small—had been ransacked and possibly burned. I could see soldiers' boots stamping on photographs of my father. I could imagine all sorts of things—all the things that Aji hadn't been willing to share with me.

Very disturbing for me was the news that Mas Hananto had disappeared and was now on the military's most-wanted list. I shouldn't have been too surprised, therefore, to learn that Surti and their children had been taken to the military detention center on Jalan Guntur. According to Aji, Surti had been permitted to go home following her initial interrogation, but then had been ordered to return the following day. When she returned, she took the children with her and that's where she and they were held for several months.

Three years went by; and because the military had yet to find Mas Hananto, horror returned to the Hananto family household. Surti and her children were taken to another detention center, this one on Jalan Budi Kemuliaan. And because her interrogators were convinced that she knew where her husband was hiding, that is where she and the children remained until he was captured.

Aji was a good and loyal brother. Unlike me in school, Aji had been a mild-mannered student, obedient to the rules of the system and averse to causing any difficulty for our parents. He was so good-hearted that he always tried to make it appear that his assignments, which were in fact very challenging, were actually very simple, just so that our mother didn't fret. He was a peacemaker, good at resolving strife. I was grateful that he and his equally kindhearted wife, Retno, were there to stand by and support our mother. Aji knew that I was in exile abroad not because I had fled misfortune, but because of a strange and unaccountable twist of circumstances. (I intentionally do not use the word "fate.") He knew that I would think nothing of the peril that I might bring on myself were I to return to Indonesia. He knew that I would want to come back to Jakarta or to Solo, regardless if it meant that I might be taken in. That is the reason he sent me the telegram, a simple but courageous act in the days after September 30. Ignoring the suspicion that he would have drawn to himself by this action, he sent me that telegram precisely at a time when suspicion was enough to have a person jailed or worse. Like many large towns in Java at the time, Solo was divided into two strongly opposing camps: those who supported the leftist-oriented "Revolutionary Council," which had the city mayor's backing, and those who supported a militarized order as expounded by the "Council of Generals." That had been the case for quite some time, or so Aji had reported even prior to my departure for Santiago. According to a colleague at the Nusantara News branch office in Solo, the war of ideologies going on at that time was reflected in a multitude of jargon-filled posters plastered on walls throughout the city.

I may have been worried about my family in Indonesia but, at the very least, I'd been in contact with them. Such was not the case with Mas Nugroho, who had lost all contact with Rukmini and their one-year-old son. Optimist that he was, he constantly tried to convince himself that no harm had come to them. He guessed that they had moved to the home of Rukmini's parents or her older brother and had not attempted to contact him for safety reasons.

In the second week of October, just after the arrival of Aji's telegram, Mas Nug and I decided to stick with our original plan and go on to Havana to meet Risjaf who was now stranded there. Our onward flight was one of increased foreboding; and in Havana, where life is supposedly meant to be lived like a festival, we drowned our depression in glasses of rum.

Although our hosts in Havana were busy organizing a conference for the solidarity of Asian and African peoples, to be held in early 1966, they gave us a warm and hearty welcome. Risjaf was Indonesia's representative on the organization's steering committee for the conference, which is why he had come to Havana.

It was in Havana that we heard of the death—or killings,

rather—of a number of senior officials in the Indonesian Communist Party, including the party's chief, D.N. Aidit. Mas Hananto had apparently succeeded in finding a hiding place somewhere, because his name was not among the list of the people whose deaths were mentioned.

From day to day, even almost every few hours it seemed, we would learn additional bits of bad news. A wide-scale hunt was on for Communist Party members, their families, and even Party sympathizers. These people weren't just being captured or detained; mass executions had begun to take place throughout much of Indonesia. Such items of news were like sketches drawn in blood. It was a time of unending insomnia; none of us were able to get a decent night's sleep. Even Risjaf, who could fall asleep on a sinking ship, remained wide awake all night long.

I tried to think of ways to contact my loved ones—my mother, Aji, Surti, and others—without putting them in additional danger, but our friends in Havana insisted that any form of contact would do just that, stirring up even greater attention from the military authorities.

Then the next bomb dropped: our passports were revoked and we became, in an instant, a band of stateless people with no fixed identity. So sudden and startling was this development, I didn't have even a moment to mentally prepare myself and think ahead of how I might live a life far from Jakarta or from Mother and Aji in Solo, distant from everything else in my life, both the good and bad. The sword of Damocles now hung over our heads, ready to fall. Every day our lives were filled with the pounding of our hearts, because we had no idea what our future held. To go home was impossible. To wander the world, unlikely—not without money or a passport.

We decided to go to Peking, where numerous other Indonesian exiles had congressed. We still had our air tickets and, with some help from our Cuban contacts, we were able to obtain temporary travel documents. We let ourselves be convinced that once we were in the People's Republic of China, things would somehow work out. Our friends there would help us solve the problems we faced.

•

Our friends in Peking were very accommodating and showed us extraordinary solidarity. They found us a place to stay. They fed us, and even entertained us, arranging all sorts of meetings for us, as well as visits to sites that often left us feeling exhausted. For the first few weeks in Peking, they put us up at the Friendship Hotel. Thereafter, they found a small house for us to live in. In just a month's time, Mas Nug, who had been a student of Chinese studies at the University of Indonesia in Jakarta, was able to find a job as a translator for the journal *Peking Review*. Risjaf and I, who couldn't speak a word of Chinese, were given work as assistants to the clerks in the same office. Frankly, we didn't care what kind of work we had to do; the important thing was to make a living. Between the time we arrived in October 1965 and the following year, we Indonesians in Peking were in constant contact with one another, everyone sharing and comparing the bits of information he had received.

By this point, I had been able to learn more details about what had happened to my mother and Aji and his family. Military personnel had visited them several times. They had been intimidated. Their homes had been searched and they had been called in for interrogation—several times, in fact—but they hadn't been detained or incarcerated. By good fortune, my uncle, my mother's brother, was a *kiai*, a respected religious leader in Solo, and his status in the community helped to shield my mother from harm. Because of him as well, Mother's neighbors and other people in the area where she lived offered her sympathy and comfort. In their eyes, she was just "a poor blameless woman who didn't know what her good-for-nothing son had been up to."

So be it. I didn't care what was said of me as long as my mother was safe.

By late 1966, we had received so much training in the concepts behind the Chinese Cultural Revolution that our throats were raw from screaming "Mao Zhu Xi Wan Sui"—Long Live Chairman Mao!—but we were also deemed sufficiently ready, it seems, to be "invited" to move into the Red Village, a commune on the outskirts of Peking where members of several Indonesian social organizations who had also been stranded in Peking were practicing *dong bei fang*, which can be literally translated as "Facing the Eastern Sea." Among the Indonesian exiles were other journalists, writers, teachers, and a number of Communist Party cadres. Through instruction in how to work together in a collective manner, we came to understand the kind of communal system the Chinese government sought to promote: a highly structured agricultural system where the members of the commune were obliged to turn over to the state a certain portion of what they produced. In observing this way of life, I became increasingly certain that Marxist theory, which I had once admired, had little more than theory to its credit. I longed to engage in a discussion about this with Mas Hananto—but he was now being hunted precisely because of this ideology and his belief in it.

The name of the village in which we lived was one that stood out for me. As this was the time of the Cultural Revolution, the word "red" in Chinese stood for "happiness" or "revolution." But as it was there, in the Red Village, that we Indonesians learned of what was happening at home, the word "red" for us symbolized the color of rivers in Java and elsewhere which were clogged with corpses.

So many deaths, whose number grew from hundreds to thousands and on up to a million or more. While some people were "only" interrogated, intimidated, or tortured, many more were killed straightaway—on roadways, in the forest, on river banks, and at the edge of ravines. We heard that in Solo, around the time of the September 30 Movement, some Communist Party members or sympathizers had killed a number of non-Communist youth activists and thrown their bodies into the Solo River. In East Java, the same thing had also happened, with the victims' bodies thrown into the Brantas River. So what happened was that after September 30, the region's strongly anti-communist military, paramilitary, and religious groups reclaimed the Solo River and turned it into their dumping grounds. According to the information that made its way among the Indonesian residents of the Red Village—news conveyed in whispers and hushed voices—so many corpses had been dumped into it that at bends in the river, where the corpses accumulated, one could walk atop the bodies from one bank to another. After hearing this news, and for weeks on end, the distance between the Red Village and Solo suddenly evaporated, and I could smell in the air the putrid scent of decomposing bodies.

When this mood came upon me, I grew furious, no longer caring about any threat to myself. Almost hysterical, I sent off a cable begging Aji to move Mother to Jakarta. I don't know why, but I felt Mother would be safer in Jakarta.

During our fourth week in the Red Village, friends in Peking brought word to Risjaf that most of our colleagues at Nusantara News had been detained. Miraculously, Mas Hananto was not among them. Somehow, he had managed to vanish without a trace.

"Probably disguised himself," Risjaf quipped in a low and mysterious-sounding voice.

"What as? A beggar?" I scoffed.

Mas Nugroho spoke firmly, optimistically: "Hananto can be slippery. I can see him being able to go most anywhere, without people catching his trail."

"I'm sure he's in disguise," Risjaf repeated.

I didn't have the will to rebut Risjaf's foolish notion. In the dark and depressing atmosphere of the Red Village, the only thing we had to bolster strength in one another was a sliver of hope and a gram of energy.

Mas Nug received news from his mother that Rukmini and Bimo had gone into hiding in Yogya a few weeks previously. He sent back the suggestion that they move back to Jakarta to live with his brother.

We received the welcome news that Tjai and his family had made it safely to Singapore. Although Tjai was the most apolitical person among us, he had two strikes against him: he was of Chinese descent and he worked at the Nusantara News office. Because of this, in the current conditions—even though he was not a senior staff member—the odds were not in his favor. Fortunately for Tjai, he had an uncle in Singapore where he and his family were able to find refuge.

There was always a two- or three-week lag in the news we received—sometimes even a month or more. In early April 1966, for instance, we received news dating from early March that was difficult to believe. On March 11, we were told, three army generals had gone to see President Sukarno at the presidential palace in Bogor, where he had taken refuge from demonstrations in Jakarta. There they asked him to sign a statement known as "Super Semar," an acronym for "The March 11 Letter of Command." The effect of this command was to transfer the power of the executive office to army commander Lieutenant-General Soeharto. That same letter authorized Soeharto to take whatever measures "he deemed necessary" to restore order to the nation. It was hard to get my head around what was happening in Indonesia. How was it possible for a cabinet meeting that Bung Karno was leading to be interrupted by a demonstration and why had our "Great Leader of the Revolution" felt forced to flee to safety in Bogor? What kind of pressure had those three army generals exerted to make the president sign such an important document, one with repercussions of such great magnitude for the fate of the nation? That day, that event, determined the course of all things to come. I was beginning to grow extremely tired of the political circus taking place at home.

●

After three years of life in Peking and having to constantly raise our fists in praise of Mao Tse Tung and calling out "Long Live Chairman Mao!" all the while studying agricultural production in a number of villages, I was fed up with the absolutism of the Cultural Revolution being crammed down the throats of the Chinese people. I was sure that Mas Nugroho, despite his unflagging optimism, and Risjaf, with his deep found sense of loyalty, felt the same kind of unease.

One night, after many nights of sleeplessness in the guest house where I was living in the Red Village, I finally came to a decision. I lit a match and began to rouse Risjaf, who was asleep on the upper bunk of the bunk bed we occupied. I patted him softly on the cheek so as not to startle him.

"Sjaf…Sjaf…Wake up, Sjaf…"

Risjaf moaned and rubbed his eyes, then sat up. "What time is it?"

"It's still dark outside. I want to go to Paris, Sjaf."

"Where?" he asked, his eyes still shut, in a voice as hoarse as a crow's.

"Paris, I want to go to Paris. Tjai has already said that he'd be willing to move to Paris or Amsterdam. We could meet him there."

Risjaf looked unsure as to whether he was dreaming or awake. He probably thought I was just the bedpost talking to him in his dreams. He mumbled "OK," then shut his eyes and lay down again, ready to go to sleep again.

I said nothing and started to count from one to ten as I waited for Risjaf to reach a normal level of consciousness. It worked. On the count of five, he swiftly rose and sat up again. His curly hair was a mess, his eyes red and open wide.

"Paris? As in Europe?" he shouted, still with a hoarse voice.

I put my hand over Risjaf's mouth, afraid that he would wake up other members of the commune.

His eyes shone brightly, a mixture of glee and fear. "But how?" he asked in a whisper.

"I don't know yet, but we'll figure something out. Tomorrow we can talk to Mas Nug about this. Tjai is ready to join us—but coming from Singapore that won't be hard. Getting out of here, however, I'm sure will mean lots of hoops to jump through and bureaucratic rigmarole."

Once I'd expressed this crazy idea of mine, neither I nor Risjaf was able to fall asleep. I kept staring at the metal cross braces on the bottom of Risjaf's bunk. Risjaf, meanwhile, kept turning on his side, to the left and to the right, trying to find a comfortable position, but causing the braces to creak.

"Calm down, Sjaf," I finally whispered.

"How am I going to calm down?" he whispered back. "You said 'Paris' and now the only thing in my mind is the beauty and the lights of that city."

I smiled.

●

I arrived in Paris in early January 1968, when winter's cold racked the bones. At first the four of us were separated. I was in France; Mas Nug in Switzerland; Risjaf in the Netherlands; and Tjai in Singapore. But after I arrived in Paris, I immediately hooked up with Tjai and his wife, Theresa, who had come to the city just before Christmas, a few weeks previously.

It was not long before Risjaf made his way to Paris and moved in with me in my small and shabby apartment. Mas Nug, who had fallen for a Swiss woman, delayed his arrival in Paris until April, when I finally got him on the phone and barked at him to come join us in Paris as we had planned. I reminded him that while he was in Switzerland thinking only of himself, Rukmini and Bimo were no doubt still living in fear as a result of the continued madness in Indonesia. Only then did he consent to break off his affair and join us.

Initially, the thought of moving to the Netherlands had seemed more attractive than France, what with the country's historical relations with Indonesia, as well as the ease of finding there most anything one wanted from Indonesia. But, in the end, we had chosen to gather in France because of the country's long history of providing a warm embrace to political exiles like ourselves. France was the *terre d'asile*, the land of asylum for exiles like us—the land of human rights: *le pays des droits de l'homme.* France. That didn't mean, of course, that the country offered easy citizenship. The process of becoming first a permanent resident and then a citizen required many complicated bureaucratic procedures and requirements that were time-consuming and difficult to fulfill. That said, we were able to obtain, without too much difficulty, a *titre de voyage,* which permitted us to travel anywhere in the world except Indonesia. A French government agency provided temporary financial assistance; but given the cost of living in Paris, the amount was hardly enough to survive.

We began to look for work almost immediately and took on odd jobs and part-time work to earn an income. After some self-promotion, Mas Nugroho, who had studied acupuncture in Peking, was soon attracting patients interested in trying his healing method—which is when I came to see why he had been reluctant to leave Switzerland: most of his "patients" were women.

Tjai, who held a degree in economics, had a much easier time finding a steady job than the rest of us, and began working as an independent accountant for several mom-and-pop stores on the city's edge. Risjaf and I were the unlucky ones, the two people least equipped to work abroad. In Indonesia, we had studied literature because we aspired to be members of the intellectual class. But in France, birthplace of so many writers and thinkers whose books had served as our compass, intellectuals, it seemed, were ten centimes a dozen. It's not surprising, therefore, that we were unable to find suitable work in our field and that every three or four months we'd be leaving one uninteresting job for yet another. From service work in restaurants, as bank tellers, up to assistant curators in small galleries whose only visitors were three or four pretentious people who called themselves artists, we did whatever we could.

Such was my life until an evening in May 1968 made boister- ous by student demands on the French government. That was the evening I met Vivienne Deveraux on the campus of the Sorbonne. She entered my life, then my body, and, finally, as she came to know my life history, my soul as well. With Vivienne, I tried to become reborn as a new man; but no matter how hard I tried, I continued to feel that some part of me had been left behind in Indonesia. Maybe it was my heart: my love for my mother and Aji; or my concern for Surti and her children. I didn't know. But a strained anxiety always affected me every time I received a letter from Aji, which inevitably contained more horrific stories about the slaughter going on in Java and elsewhere in the archipelago.

I remember one such letter from Aji in which he conveyed the shocking news about the hunt for communists in Solo, with the bodies of the hunted being thrown into the river.

Red. The river that had once nursed me had now turned blood red.

That is what Aji said. That is what our uncle Kiasno told Aji. And that is what finally convinced my mother to follow her brother's advice and move to Jakarta to live with Aji's family.

No one could comprehend what was happening. But we rec- ognized that—for a while, at least, although who knew for how long?—we would have to remain in exile. On cold nights, I stared at the Seine and tried to imagine what it would be like if its waters were red in color. I began to chastise myself for my perpetual waf- fling, for my inability to maintain a fixed opinion. I liked to sail in no certain direction: upstream, downstream, from the right bank to the left, pondering opinions without diving in to completely embrace a particular "ism." I now saw that, in the end, the effect of my wavering was that my family was thrown into a bottomless trench of trouble and travail.

Suddenly I needed that small space, that vacuum—the one Bang Amir said Allah had given to him. I didn't know whether I was His true servant but I knew I wanted that space, that small vacuum. I longed to see Bang Amir and talk to him again. Where was he now?

I posted numerous letters to my good-hearted friend, but had no proof they ever arrived safely in his, Bang Amir's, hands. In them, I asked about the meaning of that vacuum he once had mentioned, the one he said that could be found in every human heart. I desperately longed for something, but I didn't know what it was. Was it some kind of spiritual essence? When I wrote to Bang Amir, I wrote as if he were standing before me with that calm look of his on his face and speaking to me in the low voice of the popular Indonesian singer, Rahmat Kartolo.

I didn't know where to position myself in order to find that essence. If, in this tumultuous and transient world, the natural blue color of a river's waters could be changed to red, where was my station on this map of life to be?

I found no answer to my question.

•

In February 1969, the following year, Aji called me to convey the news that Mother had died in her sleep.

Was that the answer to my questions? To take Mother away from me? Away from Aji?

A rapid series of snapshots flashed before my eyes from our childhood in Solo with our parents. My father was a teacher of

English at the city's State Senior High School, a school with a reputation for its rigorous curriculum and the belief that Indonesian children had to learn to appreciate both Indonesian and Western literature. It was my father who instilled in me the importance of books as one of life's staples—just as important as food, drink, and sleep, he said (though he neglected to point out that sex was another necessary and natural part of life as well). When he told me this, my mother gave him a slight nudge. Though she was not particularly religious herself (unlike her brother, my uncle Kiasno), she did feel that some attention must be given to God and religion, that these things, too, were among life's needs.

It was Om Kiasno who first taught me and then, later, Aji, who was ten years younger than me, to recite the Quran. My father voiced no objection to this, just as he never protested when our uncle assertively reminded us to pray. Father was more concerned with matters of daily life and was apt to make much more of a fuss when Mother forgot to put her batik implements away after using them, because Aji would end up making them his playthings and leave them scattered around the house.

My mother, who was usually called Bu Giri—"Giri" being short for my father's full name, "Giri Suryo"—but who was also known by her own name, Pratiwi, had a creative hand and would, for nights on end, give herself completely to the transformation of a solid white length of cloth into a most remarkable thing of beauty.

After a day spent preparing meals—cooking was something Mother also enjoyed, a fondness for which she passed down to me—and tending to the needs of two overly active sons and a husband weary from teaching Solonese teenagers who he thought were growing up too fast, Mother would sit cross-legged on the floor for an hour or two with her *canting*, the small copper vessel with a spouted nib she had to frequently refill with melted beeswax, to create her batik designs. Ever since I was young, I likened Mother's work with wax to a poet's work with words—both of which processes produced something of beauty.

Perhaps my discovery of the joy of poetry began not with the fantastic verses of Chairil Anwar, but as the combined result of pressure from my father to speak Indonesian well and to mind my words, just as a body must mind its soul, and of my mother's love for the *canting* and melted beeswax.

After I had graduated from senior high school, my father sent me to Jakarta to live with his older brother, Om Muryanto, in order that I might obtain a better and more focused education than was possible in Solo at that time.

After adjusting to my new life as a student in Jakarta and learning my way around the city, I moved from my uncle's home into a boarding house with Risjaf, a fellow classmate. Thereafter, my visits home to Solo became rare, except for the Idul Fitri holidays, at the end of the fasting month. Patient man that he was, my father voiced no complaint about his wayward son's avoidance of home. He continued, to the best of his limited financial ability, to send me books of literature so that I would maintain and improve my Indonesian. Meanwhile, Mother would send me reminders from my uncle Kiasno to pray regularly so as "to fill myself with thanks for God's grace." Along with her missives of advice, Mother would also often send a newly made length of batik cloth—often one with a bird motif typical of Java's north coast. Mother knew I liked Cirebon-style batik.

After my father died in my sophomore year, Mother's letters to me would echo his reminder (to read and speak Indonesian well) and Om Kiasno's advice (to pray), before including her own personal counsel for me to eat nutritiously the food that I myself had prepared.

Throughout my sojourn, from Peking to Paris, the advice from my elders that I did follow was to read—how could I not? It was part of my oxygen—to cook my own food, and to eat well. Somehow, it slipped my mind to pray regularly.

I wondered whether when Mother died she was thinking about her wastrel son living so far away.

I couldn't speak for several weeks. I felt as if stones were lodged in my throat. Risjaf, Mas Nug, and Tjai tried various ways to console me, from the most profane of ways—with my favorite kinds of Chinese food that Theresa would cook for me, for instance—to the most spiritual, by arranging special prayer sessions on Mother's behalf. Nothing worked. Nothing could comfort me. No one could succeed in making me talk. Even a lovely stretch of batik, brown colored in background with green-colored birds, did not make me feel better or bring me calm. The fact was my mother had died and I was not there to kiss her forehead and to say a final goodbye. No voice escaped me.

After several weeks of virtual silence, I awoke one morning suddenly feeling both energetic and panicky, as if I were on some kind of stimulant. I went from one friend to another—to Mas Nug, Risjaf, Tjai and Theresa; to Vivienne and her family; to our neighbors; and to the offices of the French agency that arranged for us to obtain our asylum status—asking the same question: was it possible, with my exile status, for me to somehow enter Indonesia?

"Enter Indonesia? *Impossible!* You cannot enter Indonesia with a *titre de voyage*. And even if you were able to, there's a very good chance you'd never be able to leave that place again."

I didn't care. I had to pay my last respects to Mother.

I brushed off all attempts by Mas Nug and Vivienne to calm me down. I had to go home. I had to go home! I would find a ticket. Any kind of ticket. Plane, boat, whatever. The important thing was for me to go home.

In my apartment, Risjaf took me by my shoulders and tried to calm me down. I roughly pushed him aside as well. Finally, they were all silent.

That night Mas Nug handed me a telegram from my brother, which read:

DON'T COME HOME COMMA NOT SAFE STOP PRAY MOTHER IS AT PEACE COMMA WE PRAY FOR HER SOUL STOP

I crushed the telegram in my hand, threw it in the garbage can, and stomped out of our miserable apartment into a winter night whose chilled air seized my bones. I heard the voices of Risjaf and Mas Nug calling after me, but I picked up my pace and ran. The cold wind was a knife stabbing me in the face, but I didn't feel a thing. I ran and ran. When I finally stopped, I found myself standing on the bank of the Seine. The river was red in color. My face was hot with tears.

It was around that time, I guess, that Vivienne began to gradually turn Paris into a kind of resting place for me. Not a home, per se, but a place where I could stop for a while. Slowly, I came to see in her green eyes both assurance and a willingness to provide refuge for me, like a shade tree protecting a child from the blazing sun with its cool shadows.

Although Vivienne's curious cousins, Marie-Claire and Mathilde, asked numerous questions about my background—the French always seem to be interested in history—all in all, I felt that the Deveraux family was very accommodative to Vivienne's *Indonésien* lover, who as yet could speak to them only in broken French.

We married a year later in Lyon, at the vineyard of Vivienne's uncle, the father of Marie-Claire. That was the Deveraux family's ancestral home. Because all of her family's members were educated people who seemed to love to cook, I refrained from trying to impress them with my own culinary skills. As Indonesia has no enological history, Vivienne's father, Laurence, and her mother, Marianne, took it on themselves to give me some basic lessons about wine—ones I very much enjoyed. They taught me the difference between a sauvignon and a merlot; which kinds of wine were a good match for certain kinds of meat; what kinds of white wine were best served with fish. Marianne, who seemed to know how affected I still was by my mother's death, showed great forbearance with me, carefully listening to each word of French I spoke. Apparently hoping to instill in me a greater sense of confidence about my ability to speak that beautiful tongue, she was patient with my halting French and displayed no exasperation with my faulty grammar. On top of that, she was constantly offering me homemade petit fours—offers I never refused—or filling my glass with wine. Jean, Vivienne's brother, who was working for the Red Cross in Africa, came home for the wedding and he and I engaged in long discussions on politics and literature. With Vivienne's family embracing me so warmly, taking me into themselves, what more did I have to complain about?

•

Lintang Utara: "North Star." That's the name I chose for our daughter, born five years after we married. Everything about her showed her to be her mother's daughter, except for her wavy black hair, which came from the Suryo family. And I never tired of staring at that beautiful, living and breathing, little round creature with the wavy black hair. I never thought it would happen, but I had inexplicably found for myself a port—who knew for how long?—and put down an anchor in my life. If I ever needed a reason to stop my voyage, then this little creature by the name of Lintang Utara was the one. I couldn't stop watching her. I loved looking after her, caring for her, even changing her diapers. I sang to her the Indonesian lullabies my mother had sung to me— though more often than not I fell asleep before she did, and when I pulled myself awake would find her crawling around our small apartment.

Vivienne raised no objection to my giving our daughter such a non-French-sounding name. She agreed to my choice instantly, just as Surti had when I proposed the names Kenanga, Bulan, and Alam for the children we once dreamed of having together.

During the first few years of our marriage, I changed jobs several times. Vivienne, meanwhile, had much more steady employment: teaching in the Faculty of English Literature at the Sorbonne. Finally, however, after several years of seeing the look on Vivienne's face become one of increased annoyance as a result of the unsteady and uncertain nature of my financial contribution to our home— I was spending much of my time writing a newsletter, *Political Prisoner*, which I distributed to the Indonesian exile community in Europe—I finally committed myself to more permanent work and took a clerical job at the Ministry of Agriculture.

Even though I earned a decent enough salary, I was not at all happy with my desk job at the ministry. Instead of my work, my mind was either on the essays and poems that I intended to publish in the next issue of *Political Prisoner* or on interesting items of news that I received from friends who worked for the news media in Jakarta. One such piece of news was about the hullabaloo in 1972 when a foundation that had been established by President Soeharto's wife, Madam Tien, commenced work on an immense theme park called "Beautiful Indonesia in Miniature" or, more commonly in Indonesian, "Taman Mini." Not surprisingly, given the economic disparities in Indonesia at the time, some of the country's leading intellectuals objected to the project, including the well-known sociologist Arief Budiman, who damned it as a massive boondoggle; but what was surprising is that they actually voiced their objections in print and incited students to take to the streets. Another interesting but disturbing development in the political sphere was that Indonesia's political parties were coming to be dominated by businessmen and that Parliament was being transformed into an assemblage of clowns, convened only to rubberstamp anything and all that the executive branch of government proposed.

I wrote about these and other things in my newsletter as a means of keeping the exile community up to date on conditions in Indonesia. I offered the newsletter to fellow exiles, free of charge, but as it was fairly popular it sometimes did attract financial contributions from other exiles. Whenever enough money came in, I'd publish another edition, and with the help of Risjaf's design skills was able to produce something that was almost professional-looking, like a newspaper.

Gradually, after few years I grew so bored with my work at the Ministry of Agriculture, I knew I had to stop. I wanted to write a book. I wanted to publish a paper. I wanted a change.

So it was, one autumn night, I came home to our apartment bearing a bottle of wine and several cuts of choice beef. It was nine o'clock when I arrived home, and Lintang was already asleep.

"What's the celebration?" Vivienne asked, taking the bottle from me and pinching the meat. "This is expensive, Dimas. What's up?"

Vivienne's green eyes bore into me.

"Sit down," I told her.

She sat down beside me, a look of suspicion on her face. I took her hand and kissed her fingertips. It always excited her when I sucked on her fingers. I wanted her to understand the decision I had come to.

"You know I love you and Lintang," I began.

She nodded and frowned, a nervous look. "This isn't about another woman, is it?" she asked.

"What! Are you crazy?"

Vivienne laughed with relief. "You always forget how good-looking you are, Dimas. The grayer your hair, the more attractive you are for younger women. But never mind... What is it?"

I paused, wondering which younger women found me attractive. How unfortunate I did not even notice. "It's torture for me, Vivienne. I am so unhappy with..."

"You want to quit your job at the ministry, is that it?"

"*Oui.*"

She stared at me, a tree offering its shade. As long as the subject at hand was not another woman, Vivienne seemed to me to be the most understanding wife in the universe. Unlike some other French women I knew, who allowed their husbands to flit from the bed of one mistress to another, for Vivienne there were very clear rules in our marriage. She would tolerate everything except one: another woman. And I agreed.

"I knew."

I embraced her and held her tightly to me.

Once again, I asked myself, what did I have to complain about if I had around me a family that loved me? Why did I feel like a piece of me was still left behind in Indonesia?

That night, we poured ourselves a glass of wine and discussed what our future might bring once I resigned from my steady job at the ministry. In the course of our conversation, we were suddenly interrupted by a rapping sound. I opened the door to find Mas Nug, whose face was forlorn and whose appearance resembled a pile of dirty clothes. He was sweating, his shirt drenched. He held in his hand a brown manila envelope. He stared at me with tears in his eyes.

Vivienne quickly pull Mas Nug inside the apartment. "Come in, Nugroho, come in."

My heart beat faster. What had happened now?

Mas Nug's hands were shaking as he held the envelope.

Vivienne slowly took the envelope and gave it to me. I opened and read the document inside: a divorce request. Rukmini, his orchid in bloom, was asking Mas Nugroho with the Clark Gable mustache for a divorce.

I put my arms around Mas Nug and pulled him to me, hugging him tight. I knew how much he loved Rukmini, even if, like Mas Hananto, he too played around.

"I supposed I should have known why she refused to move here," Mas Nug said slowly, taking the glass of wine that Vivienne proffered.

"Why?" Vivienne asked.

"Because of her relationship with a military officer, the one who protected her during the hunt for communists in 1966 and 1967. This man, Lieutenant-Colonel Prakosa, I thought at first was just a friend of her father's who had in him a kind enough heart to help Rukmini."

I swallowed, imagining the faces of Lieutenant-Colonel Prakosa and Rukmini before me.

"So, you're saying that Rukmini is asking for a divorce in order to marry Lieutenant-Colonel Prakosa?"

Mas Nug lifted the wine glass to his lips and downed its contents in one gulp. He asked for his empty glass to be filled. Vivienne obediently granted his request.

Between tears and with the smell of wine on his breath, he ranted. "Tell Risjaf he was lucky never to have married her. Inside that orchid was a worm," Mas Nug spat with anger and hurt.

After emptying the rest of the bottle of cabernet sauvignon, Mas Nug picked up the letter of request for a divorce and flattened it on the dining table.

"Pen!" he shouted at me. Never before had I heard such a dictatorial tone in Mas Nug's voice.

I frantically searched for a pen but couldn't find one. Finally, Vivienne rummaged inside her purse and managed to come up with one.

Mas Nug scrawled his signature on each of the multiple copies of the letter of request. Silently, I hoped that he had managed to affix his signature to the right spot, because when he signed the papers he did so in anger and with a theatrical flourish.

When he had finished signing the papers, Mas Nug refolded them and gave them to me.

"Mail them for me, will you?" he asked, while putting his jacket back on, "I'll end up throwing them in the fireplace if I take them with me."

I nodded and said "sure" while signaling with my eyes to Vivienne. I would have to take Mas Nug home; he was already wobbling. Vivienne fetched my jacket for me and then walked us to the door.

"*Bonne nuit*, Vivienne, you're lucky to have Dimas. He's a loyal man. *Bonne nuit*, Dimas. And you're lucky to have married the very beautiful Vivienne. *Bonne nuit. Au revoir*, Rukmini. And fuck you, Lieutenant-Colonel Prakosa!"

I patted Mas Nug on the shoulder and motioned for him to follow me. As we walked towards the Metro station, crunching the red fallen leaves under our feet, Mas Nug looked up at the sky and screamed. The Parisian autumn heightened the sense of gloom.

THE FOUR PILLARS

A cook a pure artist
Who moves everyman
At a deeper level than Mozart...

W.H. AUDEN

90 RUE DE VAUGIRARD, PARIS; APRIL 1998
IN PARIS IN THE SPRING, THE DAYS GROW LONGER AND THE
nights begin only when one is ready to pound the mattress. I am
listening to a soft whistling sound, a tune of no certain pattern,
the song of someone who can neither read music nor keep a beat.
It is the song of my friend, Nugroho Dewantoro, who has come
to within hearing radius. I can detect the effort he puts into trying to sing like the remarkable Louis Armstrong or any one of
a number of the Indonesian *keroncong* crooners he so admires.
At any one time, he might be whistling Armstrong's "What a
Wonderful World;" at another, the traditional Indonesian song
"Stambul Baju Biru." It's always a guess. Only Mas Nug has the
verve and gaiety to not be affected by changes in weather. He's
the same, whether it's an incredibly hot summer day that burns the
flesh and causes skin to peal; the autumn, when the pollen count
is so high everyone is coughing and sneezing; the winter, when
freezing temperatures corrode our tropically pampered Malay
bones; or the spring, that fickle time of year when it's sometimes
cold and windy, sometimes warm and humid.

The only time I remember Mas Nug unable to beat back the
gloom was the time he received the letter-of-request for a divorce
from Rukmini. At all other times, he's always been the most

optimistic person in the world, ever capable of finding the silver lining in any disaster.

Even back in Jakarta, when there were the five of us, Mas Nug was a guy who could never say, "give up." That gang of ours on Jalan Solo was made up of five men, each of whom felt pretty sure about himself in one way or another. Look at Mas Nug, for instance, who, with his Clark Gable mustache, thought himself to be the best-looking chap in the world, but who nonetheless had to deal with as many failures as victories. Mas Hananto, Mas Nug, Tjai, Risjaf, and I once went through a period when we were competing for girlfriends, a time that ended with victory on the part of the senior members of our group: Mas Hananto won Surti's hand; Mas Nug tied the knot with Rukmini; and Tjai married Theresa Li. Risjaf and I, meanwhile, ended up as frustrated bachelors and didn't find our helpmates until after coming to Paris. But whatever the situation and regardless that we five often found ourselves at odds with one another, either because of women or ideology, we were always able to overcome any conflict that might arise between us. And one reason for this was Mas Nug's unflagging optimism.

Among the five of us, it was only Mas Nug who liked to whistle and sing, even though his was the worst of voices and he was unable to carry a tune. Whether he was aware of this himself is uncertain, because in gatherings at the Nusantara News office, he was always the most eager to join in the singing. Mas Hananto and Risjaf had some musical skills: Mas Han could pluck a guitar and Risjaf was pretty good on the harmonica and flute. Meanwhile, my bass voice wasn't too bad; but neither Tjai nor Mas Nug could carry a tune. The difference between those two was that Tjai recognized his shortcoming, whereas Mas Nug was blind to this imperfection and whenever there was a microphone present, he'd soon be clinging to it so fast you'd think it was a curvaceous woman.

So it was, blessed with this deep-seated sense of optimism, skilled at both massage and acupuncture (which he had studied and mastered during our time in Peking), and, with his Clark Gable mustache, very confident of his appearance, Mas Nugroho felt that he had all the capital in life he needed to get along. And it's true: among us, he was the one most capable of confronting the challenges that conspired against us. He was precisely the kind of person our band of stateless people needed to bear life's harsh realities.

And now I'm hearing Mas Nug's off-tune voice, happily yodeling as he makes his way towards the kitchen on the ground floor of Tanah Air Restaurant, which for the past fifteen years has been at once our home, our source of income, and a point of major pride.

Mas Nug comes into the kitchen carrying a few bags of cooking ingredients and other supplies I had ordered. I guessed that he had just come from shopping in Belleville, where it was possible to buy Asian spices, because the day before I had been grumbling about how low we were on many of the basic Indonesian spices: turmeric, ginger, red chilies, shallots, garlic, Javanese bay leaf, and citrus leaf. In Paris, some of the spices we needed were available in dried form; but, in Indonesian cuisine, there is no replacing fresh red chilies, shallots, and garlic, whose prices at the market were always much higher than we thought they should be. Bahrum was usually the one who purchased my kitchen supplies, but he was in the midst of cleaning the restaurant's wooden floor.

Still whistling, Mas Nug removes the purchases from their bags and plops them on the kitchen table I use for preparing spices.

I don't know whether it's because of his insufferable whistling or my irritation with him for throwing the purchases on the table where I am trying to work, but all of a sudden I feel nauseous, as if I am about to throw up. The fact is, for the past several weeks my stomach has been troubling me on and off, but, up until then, I have always been able to ignore it.

Mas Nug looks at me. "What's wrong with you?"

I don't answer him. Both he and Tjai are constantly ragging me about my health, like two parents angry with their teenage son for not wanting to study. Mas Nug thinks he can treat any illness with that bag of needles he takes wherever he goes. He is always going on and on about concepts of energy and acupuncture needles. Any time he starts to speak of such things, I immediately want to fall asleep. Who gives a hoot about "energy," "*chi*," and "New Age" treatments? Only Mas Nug!

I hate needles, especially Mas Nug's, whose efficacy I'm not at all sure of. But even though the hospital is a place that for me is identical with needles and all sorts of ghastly-looking machines, I do recognize that there are times when I am forced to surrender myself to a doctor for medical care. Like last week, for instance…

•

On that morning, last week, I suddenly collapsed outside the Metro station. I didn't feel anything, but everything turned black for a few moments, and the next thing I knew I was in a café near the kiosk at the entrance to the station where I usually bought the daily paper. Staring at me when I opened my eyes was Pierre, the newspaper vendor who never bathed, and André, the handsome blue-eyed waiter at the café who looked like he should be a Calvin Klein model instead of serving coffee. Speaking rapidly, in their nasalized Parisian French, they ordered me to drink water and kept asking me, over and over, if I was all right. When they said they were going to call an ambulance, I finally shook my head and asked them to call Risjaf instead.

What happened then was a nightmare: Tjai and Mas Nug, the two fussiest and most know-it-all people I know, came to the café. Tjai, with his low voice and calculated manner, grilled me about the quantity and frequency of my intake of alcohol. Mas Nug, meanwhile, began hectoring me about energy and similar nonsense. I wanted to disappear from their sight. There was no way they would let me refuse their demand that I go to the hospital for a physical examination. And the fact was, I was still in a bit of shock and too weak to do otherwise. I was suddenly an old codger in need of assistance from two creatures who were putting on airs of being much younger. As they led me out of the café to a taxi, I felt the ground move beneath my feet. When that happened, I knew I had to obey. There was something wrong with me.

The doctor in the emergency ward of the hospital where they took me ordered me to undergo a battery of tests. Afterwards, he prescribed some medicine. But I still haven't gotten around to picking up the results of the tests.

That same feeling of nausea and stomach cramps were now affecting me again. Mas Nug came over and put his hand on my cheek.

"Lie down in the office. I can take your place in the kitchen."

Hmm... I liked the taste of my cooking better, especially my *nasi kuning* or yellow rice with its side dishes of crispy tempeh, yellow fried chicken, and *urap*, spiced vegetables with grated coconut. And to make everything taste better was my fried hot pepper sauce, *sambal bajak*. I knew that my *nasi kuning*, along with my

Padang-style beef *rendang*, *gulai pakis*, fiddlestick ferns simmered in coconut sauce, and a Lampung-style curried chicken dish called *gulai anam*, were the most popular dishes on Tanah Air's menu, at least in terms of number of orders. Mas Nug's cooking was much too experimental for me. He was so busy coming up with fancy names for dishes, he often forgot about their taste.

"Dimas…"

I could tell from the tone of Mas Nug's voice that he didn't want to offend me. He knew that the restaurant's kitchen was my territory, a no-man's-land for anyone unable to follow my very explicit instructions. (Don't change the composition of spices. Don't touch my knives. Never use the onion knife for cutting meat. The work area must be absolutely clean, with no drops of water or coffee on it. And so on and so forth.) The Tanah Air kitchen was my throne from which I could not be unseated. Reign over other parts of the restaurant, I willingly relinquished to those friends who liked to show off their fine teeth on the stage.

But now Mas Nug was suggesting that he take my position as cook. I immediately thought of Mahmud Radjab, a Malaysian writer and friend of mine, who had booked a number of tables at the restaurant that night to celebrate the publication of his latest book with friends. He had written to me far in advance to tell me that he and several colleagues from Kuala Lumpur had been invited to come to the Sorbonne and that they hoped to celebrate at the restaurant. He sent me a menu, telling me exactly what kind of dishes he wanted to serve his friends. The kinds of dishes he mentioned were common enough in Kuala Lumpur, but not so in Paris. "Your cooking is extraordinary," he told me. "You have a gift with spices."

And now eighteen people, Radjab and his friends, were coming to the restaurant, expecting to be served a truly Malay-tasting meal.

I had been preparing the spice mixture since morning. All that was left to do in the afternoon was to mix them with the rice, prepare the chicken, and mix the vegetables with grated coconut for the *urap*. But I was feeling so nauseous, I thought I was going to regurgitate.

"OK, OK, I'll lie down for a bit, but don't put anything strange in my *nasi kuning*," I said in warning.

"Yeah, yeah..."

Mas Nug walked me to the office. Tjai, who was checking the tables that had been reserved for the event that evening, saw us and lowered his glasses and looked at me curiously. "What's wrong, Dimas?"

"It's nothing," I answered flippantly. "Nothing at all."

Mas Nug and Tjai looked at each other like parents trying to figure out how to get their unruly son to follow their orders.

Mas Nug now spoke in an authoritarian voice. "I'm not going to put up with any more of your excuses. Tomorrow, we're going to the hospital to pick up the results of your examination. If you don't, I swear, I'm going to mess with your spices and fiddle with your sacred recipes."

What an absolute shithead, I thought. Mas Nug knew I treated spices and other cooking ingredients like a painter treats colors on a canvas. I treated my blend of spices for the dishes I prepared like a poet treats words in a poem.

I don't know where I got the strength, but I whipped off the sarong I'd been using as a shawl and threw it at Mas Nug, and then grabbed him by the collar. "Don't you dare mess with my spices. Don't fiddle with anything. Don't mix any other spices with the turmeric paste for the *nasi kuning*. And don't even think of altering the recipes for the dishes on this restaurant's menu!"

I blew through my nose, my head spinning and my eyes watering. Mas Nug was startled, but whether this was because of my actions or because I had specifically mentioned "turmeric" and not "ginger," for instance, or maybe just because I looked very ill, I didn't know. After that, my head started to spin again and my stomach felt like it was being squeezed through the wringer of a washing machine. As I plopped into a chair, my stomach suddenly erupted. I can remember Mas Nug calling out for Tjai, Bahrum, and Risjaf but after that, not much more, except swallowing the medicine the doctor had prescribed for me.

The medicine must have contained some kind of sedative, because after that I began to feel much lighter and was able to lie down on the sofa without my stomach churning. The sofa... That white sofa had been a gift from Vivienne. She had been just as enthusiastic as the Indonesian exiles who joined the cooperative that we established to raise the funds to open the Tanah Air Restaurant. How many times had we re-covered that sofa? Yet every time, Vivienne always chose another shade of white. After we divorced, I covered the sofa with a length of Cirebon-style batik that Aji had sent me. Even though we were Solonese by birth, Aji knew I much preferred the more colorful batik designs of the north coast than the traditional brown and muted tones of the batik produced in our home town.

My lids grew heavy and I soon closed my eyes. Whatever was in the medicine seemed to produce a kind of hallucinatory effect. The dreams that ensued were wild and vivid, with all sorts of people popping into them from various periods of my life. Or maybe I wasn't sleeping at all; maybe I was awake and recalling memories of the past fifteen years, when the hands on the clock in

Paris determined my future: that we might be better able to make a mark not through politics or literature but, possibly and more effectively, through culinary arts. How very strange but how very delightful it had been to enter this strange new world.

With the weather being so hot and stuffy—which was when all I wanted to do was to take off my clothes and go nude in the apartment—it wasn't the best time to discuss plans for the future. Mas Nug, Risjaf, and Tjai were almost at each other's throats trying to figure out what would be the best way to build a more permanent support structure for Indonesian political exiles and their families. No indeed, Paris in summertime is definitely not the best time for discussing matters of import. Especially avoid all thought of financial problems and go bask on a beach somewhere in the south of France or take refuge in a corner of Shakespeare & Co.

Tjai had a very serious look on his face. The rest of us probably looked forlorn. None of us were happy with our jobs, and for the past several months we had been trying to find a solution to this problem: some kind of business venture where we could work together on something that was personally satisfying (as well as profitable) for everyone concerned. The work had to be enjoyable. My first thought was to publish an Indonesian literary journal much like *The Paris Review* with short stories, poetry, novellas, and critical essays about Indonesian literature and translations of foreign literature in Indonesian. I had hardly begun to explain this idea when Tjai said drolly, "Which will have to be distributed free of charge because the number of people who can read Indonesian and are interested in Indonesian literature in Paris is about thirty."

His answer was cynical, but he was right, of course. The literary landscape—both Indonesian and foreign—was littered with graveyards of dead journals and literary magazines. Even so, I loved the thought of us starting a serious literary journal. What an absolute delight that would be!

"I'm just trying to think of something we all like doing," I grumbled. "We're all writers, after all."

Tjai said nothing, but his small mouth became a sour pucker—which meant he was saying to me, "Try using that thing behind your forehead."

Tjai was the glue that held us together, the only one among us with no wacky side or affectations. He came from a Chinese family in Surabaya that believed completely in the value of hard work. His exile abroad, like that of many other Chinese-Indonesians, had very little to do with ideology and much more to do with race. Tjai was not in the least political; yet he knew, in the wake of events after September 30, 1965, that his family would be among the first to be arrested, because his brother Henry had active relations with Red Party officials in Peking.

Based on the history of race relations in Indonesia and the pogroms that had affected Chinese-Indonesians in the past, the decision of Tjai and Theresa to immediately flee to Singapore and then later join up with us in Paris was very pragmatic. Among us, Tjai was perhaps the only one whose personal life was free of melodrama. He was a straight arrow, honest to the core, good-hearted, and always on the right path. And it was because of this, his unerring record of shooting straight, that we trusted his unbiased and even cold-hearted analyses—even his assessment of the various ideas we had come up with for working together. Sure, I was sometimes rankled by his frankness, but I would be the first to admit that Tjai was almost always right.

Mas Nug threw in the idea of a political daily, to which, once again, Tjai rolled his eyes. "Look at that newsletter Dimas has been doing. The content is fine, but it depends on contributions to survive."

As a result of the butcher Tjai's rational way of thinking, our conversation quickly died. What could I say? He was our calculator.

Mas Nug sat next to the open window staring outside as he took a cigarette from a packet. After Lintang was born and Vivienne and I moved into a larger apartment, our home had become the place my friends usually gathered. It wasn't all that spacious, but it had a pleasant atmosphere, which was helped greatly by the numerous potted plants that Vivienne had hung around the rooms. But this was summer, and even with the plants, little could be done to lower the actual temperature of the non-air-conditioned room.

In the hours that followed, our discussion became more uncertain and even less directed. Mas Nug suggested that we buy Indonesian kretek cigarettes wholesale in the Netherlands and then sell them retail in Paris. Once again, Tjai again threw a damp rag on the idea: "You mean, set up a cigarette stand? Have you thought about taxes? And are you ready to compete with other brands? What research have you done? How many people in Paris smoke kretek besides you and Dimas?"

As we fell into silence, once again, I began to chuckle to myself.

Risjaf then began to say something but, frankly, I can't even remember what it was. The air was so hot, all I wanted to do was take off my clothes. It was a good thing that at that point Vivienne and Lintang came home, fresh from a swim at the public pool near our apartment. She immediately offered to make us some limeade. After the number of bottles of beers that we had consumed, limeade seemed like a good idea. Maybe that would help to clear our heads.

Vivienne signaled for me to follow her to the kitchen.

"Look at the time," she said. "Maybe you should make a snack, something to eat."

A brilliant idea, I thought. Indonesians can never think on an empty stomach. I was proud of Vivienne for being able to read the situation so quickly.

I searched the refrigerator and kitchen cupboard to see what was there: noodles, left-over chicken, some vegetables... Aha, I knew what to prepare. I nodded and looked at Vivienne who had read my mind and begun to assemble the things I would need: a wok, oil, and spices.

I stuck my head out of the kitchen and announced to my friends: "You guys go on without me. I'm going to whip up some fried noodles. Maybe in the meantime you can come up with a brilliant idea."

Having just said that, I already knew the discussion would falter further and that the only thing they would try to do is find a place in the room where there might be a bit of moving air.

I quickly sliced the shallots, garlic, and green vegetables, and then chopped the chicken into bite-sized pieces. I only asked Vivienne to help prepare the ingredients; she had learned long ago that I didn't like anyone touching my kitchen tools. Straight-away, she a put a finger's length of water in a pot and set it on the stove to boil. She raised her eyes when I took some oil from a can in which I kept used oil, but refrained from saying anything. I knew that for health reasons Vivienne didn't like me using this reused *jelantah* oil in my cooking, but I used only a little bit, just enough to add the flavor of the onions that had been fried in it, and that was the secret of my spice mixture. Maybe it wasn't the most healthy, but it was always delicious.

In just a few minutes, I had prepared the fried noodles and put the platter on the dining table for my friends to help themselves. Lintang was the first to dish up. Her eyes closed with pleasure as she began to eat. "*Un très bon plat!*" she announced, sticking her small right thumb in the air. Of course, given that my daughter was also my biggest fan there was an element of bias in the appraisal. Lintang, now seven years old, was the light of my life.

My three friends attacked the table like a trio of prisoners who'd been fed charred rice for a week. Tjai used chopsticks to eat the noodles, moving them so quickly and easily that his bowl of noodles was empty and slick in just a short time. Risjaf, on the other hand, picked slowly at his portion, savoring each mouthful as he ate. Lintang, meanwhile, helped herself to a second portion; the bowl she was using was a child's-size bowl. Vivienne smiled with satisfaction as we finished our bowls and then gave us permission to smoke.

While the rest of us stretched out on our chairs in the living room, staring at our embarrassingly protruding stomachs, Risjaf continued to eat his noodles slowly, not caring that the rest of us had already finished. With greasy lips, still slick from his noodles, he said offhandedly, "Why is it that you can't get fried noodles this good anywhere in Paris?"

Mas Nug suddenly looked at Risjaf and blinked, as if a light bulb had come on in his head.

"Yeah, just think," Risjaf went on, "how nice it would be if, whenever we pleased, we could eat fried noodles as good as Dimas makes. Or his fried rice smelling of shrimp paste. God, my mouth is beginning to water just thinking about it. Or his *nasi kuning*, like the kind he made for Lintang's birthday, with nice crispy slices of tempeh."

Suddenly, as if struck by what he was saying, Risjaf shrieked like a scientist who had just solved some kind of formula: "That's it, Dimas! I know what business we can do! I've got it!"

Mas Nug and Risjaf beamed at each other happily, like they wanted to hug each other. Oh, no, I thought. What would they have me do? Start up a catering business?

But then I looked at Tjai, whose eyes were shining brightly with a glow that permeated mine—a completely different reaction from the one earlier, when we had been discussing business ideas he dismissed as crazy.

He looked at me straight in the face. "That's it, Dimas. I think we've discovered our destiny. As a cook, you know, you are second to none."

I had never heard Tjai speak with such enthusiasm before. His eyes flashed. Mas Nug put his hands on my shoulders and called out to the heavens: "Dimas! We are going to open an Indonesian restaurant in Paris!"

•

Even though the Parisian summer was still so hot I thought my skin was going to blister, my heart felt cool now that a decision had been reached. The next night we gathered at Risjaf's apartment and, with no objections to slow down the course of conversation, we discussed our new plan. Mas Nug, twisting the ends of his Clark Gable mustache, usurped the role of manager and began to issue orders as to what each of our tasks would be.

"Obviously, Dimas will be the head cook and will choose the menu. We all know that he has a way of changing the simplest ingredients into a wonderful meal—no different from the words that slip from his pen to become a poem."

I guessed that Mas Nug's excessive praise was his way of consoling me because Tjai had not given his consent to the literary journal I wanted to produce.

"Tjai will look into a financial model. Once we've come up with a proposal, we can send it to possible funding sources: government and non-government agencies and the like as well as to our friends scattered throughout Europe, inviting them to contribute to the cause or to lend us the money we'll need. We have to weigh the alternatives and choose the best one. Tjai can also look into what kind of business our restaurant should be, a limited license corporation, for instance, or possibly a co-op…"

"A cooperative. Obviously, a cooperative!" Tjai said firmly.

"OK, a cooperative it is," said Mas Nug obediently, leaving me to wonder who in our group held the most authority.

"And in our proposal," Mas Nug said immediately, as if to reaffirm his position, "we must be very clear about the *raison d'être* for the business model we've chosen. It might be, for instance, for the purpose of strengthening solidarity. As a cooperative, this will mean that we have to schedule an annual *assemblée générale* and choose a slate of managers every two years."

I looked at Mas Nug with admiration. Any time we started to discuss how to run an organization, his brain worked as fast as lightning. Since Mas Hananto was no longer with us, it seems that the spirit of leadership had moved to him—even though it was at times expropriated by Tjai, who had a much greater faculty for finance and figures.

Risjaf stood like a soldier at attention, waiting for orders from his commander; but Mas Nug pretended not to notice. "Someone will have to undertake a survey of other restaurants—especially the Asian ones: Vietnamese, Indian, and Chinese—to see if we should focus on a place for fine dining, a casual eatery, or maybe a fast food place where people could take their meals home."

"It's not going to be fast food!" I answered quickly. "Indonesian food is fine for a casual restaurant and even for fine dining, but definitely not for fast food. And we're going to have a bar. This is Paris, after all. I'll get to work on coming up with a menu," I said with a growing sense of confidence.

Everyone listened attentively. Tjai diligently took notes.

I ran on, a dam now bursting inside me: "One thing for sure is that we should hold lots of kinds of events: book launches, for instance; discussions about developments in Indonesia; and literary readings, films, art exhibitions, and photography. We'll need a curator so that they run smoothly and so that the people who come to them will want to stay and eat at the restaurant or drink at the bar. That way, the place can become known not just as a good place to eat, but as a place where people can hang out and socialize."

My three friends clapped their hands happily, even Tjai who stood and raised his thumb when I mentioned the need for a bar.

"I can do the research. I can also curate the events!" Risjaf said, still standing in front of Mas Nug.

Mas Nug smiled, not wanting to dampen Risjaf's enthusiasm. "OK, but you can't do everything, you know. You'll wear yourself out. You plan the opening night and the nights that follow with a range of events. We can divide up the research on restaurants; there's a lot of them that we'll have to look at."

"And what are you going to do?" Tjai was heard to say flatly.

Mas Nug twisted the tip of his mustache. "I will explore the city of Paris and study the advertising section in *Le Figaro*. We need to find a location, don't we?"

Good God! Of course, Mas Nug was right, and that was something that had to be done right away.

Tjai nodded and made more notes. That night we each raised a glass of wine, except for Risjaf, that is, who held in his hand a ginger drink of *wedang jahé* instead. Clinking our glasses together, we said in unison, "To our restaurant."

We looked at each other.

"What should we call it?" Risjaf said to Mas Nug.

Mas Nug turned his head towards me. "Let's ask our resident poet!"

I looked at my friends, one by one. Someone was missing. There should have been five of us.

I took a deep breath and exhaled. "We, the four of us, are the pillars of Tanah Air Restaurant."

We again clinked our glasses together. Tanah Air. Homeland. The name immediately stole my heart.

PARIS, 1975

Tjai, Risjaf, and I shared an unspoken agreement: ever since Rukmini had asked Mas Nug for a divorce in order to marry Lieutenant-Colonel Prakosa, we had surrendered to him the authority to act as our leader. Though we all believed in equality and didn't think we actually needed a leader, Mas Nug seemed to need this kind of recognition, even if only temporarily. At least that's what we'd surmised. And it all started that accursed evening when, after receiving his wife's request for a divorce, he'd been shaken to the core and had tried to drown himself in alcohol. Nugroho Dewantoro, this man from Yogyakarta in the heart of Java, who always insisted on

speaking egalitarian Indonesian rather than status-marked Javanese, was a very sentimental man. In fact, I even suspected that
despite his frequent bouts of womanizing, he prized above all else
the warmth that only a family can bring. Unlike Mas Hananto,
whose relationship with Surti was complicated by perceptions of
class difference—which was a psychological barrier of sorts for
him—Mas Nug didn't think about such things. If he wanted a
woman, he wanted her, clear and simple. He became attracted to
Rukmini and despite the fact that his green-eared friend Risjaf
already had his sights set on her, he cast his net and succeeded in
winning the orchid for himself. He then went on to marry her, the
beautiful Rukmini with the sharp tongue. But because it became
apparent to Risjaf and I that Mas Nug truly did love Rukmini,
we long ago forgave him and joined in his happiness, especially so
when Bimo Nugroho, the son the couple had wished for, appeared
just nine months after their wedding.

What I always found difficult to understand about Mas Hananto
and Mas Nug is why, with all their political activities and respon-
sibilities as husbands and fathers, they felt such a compulsion to
sleep with other women. Mas Hananto said that he wanted to feel
the "passion of the proletarian woman in bed." As sorry and trite
as that class-based justification sounds, Mas Nug couldn't come up
with a reason even as good as that. Good-looking and hirsute, with
a thick mustache and a gilded tongue, Mas Nug easily attracted
women to him, proverbial moths to a flame. It wasn't surprising,
therefore, that even with his stateless status and lack of permanent
address either in Peking or in Zurich, he was able to easily win
women's favors and hearts. In the latter location, the crazy thing
was that his mistress there was one Mrs. Agnes Baumgartner, the
wife of a policeman and one of his acupuncture clients. Initially,

it was the husband who had come to Mas Nug, complaining of aches from rheumatism and arthritis; but then Mas Nug had gone on to use his therapeutic skills on Mrs. Baumgartner, who, as he described it, was especially achy and in need of his special touch. According to Mas Nug, the woman's thighs and midsection required special care and treatment.

When I called Mas Nug from Paris and then had to listen to him tell me of his sexual conquest in Zurich, my blood went straight to my brain. I barked at him to follow Tjai's suit and come to Paris immediately—not just so that our group could be together again or because of my concern for Rukmini and Bimo, but because of the stupid and dangerous position his sexual shenanigans were putting him in. Engaging in an affair with a married woman in a foreign country was not the same as keeping a mistress on the side in Jakarta or, for that matter, plucking an orchid in our more youthful days. The woman's husband was a police officer, for God's sake. And this wasn't Indonesia; it was the West, whose written and unwritten rules we could not yet pretend to be familiar with.

My vitriol apparently worked the trick and Mas Nug arrived in Paris a few weeks later, but with a very long face. Once again, I simply couldn't understand how it was possible for him to fall in love with a woman he'd only just met.

Seven years later a letter from Rukmini made its way from Jakarta to Paris and into Mas Nug's hand: a request for a divorce. That night, I supported Mas Nug's weight as he stumbled towards the Metro Station, all the while trying to persuade him to lower the volume of his increasingly shrill and incoherent voice. At the station, I remember clearly the severely wounded look on his face.

Half drunk, he spoke brokenly. "You know, Dimas…actually…

it was when I was in Zurich…I received a letter from Rukmini." His voice trembled and tears welled in his eyes. "In it she turned down my request for her to join me in Europe…but she didn't tell me why."

I said nothing, my mind for some reason still on his adventure with the policeman's wife.

"And Agnes, Mrs. Baumgartner, you know, was more than just a patient of mine."

"I know. You told me about your needles, her thighs."

"Yes, but I didn't tell you the real reason why." Mas Nug's voice grew hoarse and he shook his head violently.

I looked into his eyes, red and burning with pain.

"It was her name… I called her 'Baumgartner' but that wasn't her married name. It was her maiden name. But, you know, in German 'baumgartner' means someone who owns a garden…"

"So?"

"So, every time I made love with her, all I could imagine was a bed of orchids."

Tears streamed from his eyes.

What made this situation—Mas Nug's divorce from Rukmini—slightly more sensitive was that only a few months later, Risjaf announced that he had found his soul mate: a woman by the name of Amira, the sister of Mirza Syahrul, an Indonesian exile in Leiden, the Netherlands. An attractive woman with glasses, Amira was thirty-six years old and just finishing her doctorate in political science at Leiden University. She and Risjaf fell in love almost overnight and felt so comfortable with each other, they said, they decided to get married as soon as possible. They weren't that young after all. Risjaf was forty-five, the same age as me, having also been born in 1930.

"We're both adults and I'm long past my due-date as a bachelor," Risjaf joked.

I was pleased to see him so happy.

"So what are you going to do?" Tjai asked. "Commute between Paris and Leiden until Amira finishes her degree?" He seemed to be calculating the cost.

"Yes, we'll take turns," said Risjaf, eyes shining brightly.

"Have you already told Mas Nug?" I asked with a note of caution.

"No, but I'm going to go to his place and take Amira with me to introduce her…"

"Don't!" Tjai and I yelped at once.

Risjaf looked back and forth between us. People in the throes of happiness often forget about other people's pain. The look on Risjaf's handsome face was one of complete innocence.

"Why?" he asked simply.

Tjai and I looked at other, as if to agree on a more detailed answer. For Risjaf, with all his artlessness, we had to present a clear and detailed picture.

"Aren't you forgetting something?" I asked him. "Didn't Mas Nug just receive a request for divorce from Rukmini?"

Risjaf slapped himself on the forehead. "Oh my God, that's right! What was I thinking? So, do you think that maybe we shouldn't tell Mas Nug? It would be such a shame if…"

"What would be such a shame?"

Vivienne's and my apartment was much too small, not in the least ideal for trafficking in secrets. And as if to prove the point, Mas Nug had suddenly barged into the apartment, taking us completely by surprise.

Mas Nug looked at the three of us and then slapped Risjaf on the shoulder and laughed. "Hey, I heard you proposed to Mirza's sister. That great! And she's a looker, too! Congratulations!" He then threw his arms around Risjaf and gave him a big hug. Risjaf tentatively returned Mas Nug's embrace.

Mas Nug then plopped himself down on the floor in front of the couch and turned on the small old television, which aired only French-language shows. Regardless, he focused his attention on the screen, giving it his rapt attention. Risjaf scratched his head. Stillness, an unspoken tension, filled the air.

"Well, I guess I'll be going to Amira's uncle's place in the Marais," Risjaf finally quipped. "She and her father are staying there."

Mas Nug raised his thumb but his eyes remained on the television.

I sat down beside him. Tjai went into the kitchen to search the cupboard for coffee.

"It's OK. I'm doing just fine," Mas Nug said quietly to me as he watched the TV.

I nodded silently, still looking at Mas Nug whose eyes were pinned to the screen. Though he said nothing, I knew he appreciated my query-less presence. I could only imagine the sadness his heart must be feeling.

PARIS, OCTOBER 1982

All of that, of course, took place some fourteen years ago. I didn't know at the time whether Mas Nug had been able to bury the painful memory of his divorce beneath the lowest layer of his heart or whether his gaiety, which he showed by whistling out of tune, was his way of isolating the sadness.

One day at my apartment, our temporary meeting place, when I was working on the details of the menu that we intended to include in our funding proposal, Tjai announced he had already managed to secure a fairly substantial sum of money from the dozens of Indonesian exiles who were scattered throughout Europe. What I found touching was that not all those who had contributed to the restaurant fund were even political exiles like ourselves. Several businessmen, friends of Mas Nug, also pitched in; the same was true of friends of Tjai in Jakarta who anonymously contributed to the cause with no evident thought of return. Tjai maintained a detailed list of contributors and the amounts given, his idea being that if these donors ever came to the restaurant, they would be seated at a special "sponsors table" and given a special menu.

Mas Nug explored the city in search of the perfect location for the restaurant for what seemed a very long time, but found no place to be satisfactory. Either its location was too distant, the water system in the building was not up to standard, or the place would require major renovation. The list went on and on. I knew he was growing tired from the hunt, but he continued to undertake his task with unfeigned happiness—just as Risjaf did when preparing a report on his survey of restaurants that offered Asian cuisines in Paris. One of his more interesting observations was that very few restaurants offered both a place for dining and a venue for events. This fact made me even more excited about the possibility opening Tanah Air, which, as we intended, would highlight both Indonesian cuisine and culture.

Nonetheless, the problem of location still remained, and I was beginning to tire of all the meetings in my apartment. Of course, Risjaf had the perfect justification for our meetings there: they could try my dishes at the same time. But my friends were not proper culinary critics; they'd happily munch on a boiled table if they were hungry.

But then, one day, *Le Figaro* came to the rescue!

Buried inside the classified section was a small advertisement which didn't first catch our notice but became a game-changer in our quest. It was an advertisement for the sale of a family-owned restaurant located at 90 Rue de Vaugirard. We went to look at the place and to talk to its owners—a Vietnamese couple who had resided in Paris for almost twenty years. The restaurant occupied the ground and subterranean floors of a four-story early twentieth-century building. On the ground floor was the foyer, a cashier stand, and space enough for four to six tables. At the rear was the kitchen and a small office, beside which was a stairway leading to the lower floor, a much larger open space, with transom windows at the front and room enough for ten to twelve tables or more—a perfect place for private parties and special events.

Even as Tjai and Mas Nug were beginning their investigation of the restaurant's public spaces I immediately felt at home; but, of course, I needed to see the kitchen. When the older couple opened the door to the kitchen, I saw inside a wide rectangular space with white tiled walls, a checkered black and white floor, and a large work table in the center that apparently served as an island for food preparation. There was a large and clean professional oven, which had been properly maintained—I didn't see even a stray kernel of cooked rice. When I looked up to see hanging overhead a complete set of high-quality stainless steel pots, my heart was smitten. "Would you be willing to sell the cooking equipment as well?" I almost gasped.

The older man looked at his wife who smiled, showing the dimples in her cheeks. "We're all from Asia. We like you and if the price is right, you can have the kitchen equipment too."

I made a move to hug the woman, but Tjai, who had joined us by this time, immediately held me by the arm like an angry cat. I restrained myself as I allowed him to undertake his task of calculating the price, bargaining with the couple, negotiating the terms, and so on. The way he haggled with the owners reminded me of traders in Klewer, the traditional market in Solo: pretending not to be in need; feigning reluctance to buy; preparing to move to another stall because the same object there was far more attractive and much cheaper besides; but then, finally, smiling in assent when the seller agreed to his offer. The Vietnamese woman must have been smitten with us as well because she seemed uninterested in Tjai's Klewer-market game and rushed to have the deal settled, with little bargaining at all. She nodded and shook hands with Tjai. Only then did Tjai signal that I was allowed to hug the couple, which I immediately did with an immense feeling of gratitude. I adored their kitchen and its equipment, which included almost everything commonly used in an Indonesian kitchen: large woks, small woks, strainers, steamers, numerous kinds of knives, and a large flat stone mortar (though I could see I would still need to bring my small mortar to prepare individual servings of freshly ground chili *sambal*).

The cooperative was formed and the necessary capital secured from a variety of sources, including several French nonprofit orga-nizations. Risjaf contracted the services of carpenters, plumbers, electricians, and other skilled workers to repair what needed to be repaired, and while our Indonesian friends in Paris rolled up their sleeves to repaint the interior in white to give the restaurant a more spacious and airy feel Risjaf also designed and printed a flyer announcing the opening of Tanah Air Restaurant.

With free assistance and advice provided by two govern-ment-provided lawyers, Jean-Paul Bernard and Marie Thomas, Mas Nug and Tjai undertook all the steps that were necessary to establish our cooperative as a French legal entity. While they were doing this, I was busy training my two new assistants: Bahrum and Yazir, the sons of political exiles who liked to cook and shared the dream of going on to school at a culinary institute.

The four pillars of Tanah Air Restaurant decided to imitate the formula of the Dutch-Indonesian *rijsttafel,* with dishes on the menu from not just one but a variety of regions, each with its own culinary specialty—Padang, Palembang, Lampung, Solo, Yogya, Sunda, East Java, Makassar, Bali—combining the selections in packets based on the customer's desire and taste. In the West-ern manner—knowing very well that our European customers would demand it—we also arranged the menu so that the dishes could be served in three to five courses, from starters to desserts. We translated the Dutch *rijsttafel,* or "rice table" in English, into French, offering customers a *"table du riz,"* Risjaf and Tjai studied making aperitifs and digestifs from a friend of Jean-Paul, an expert mixologist, who volunteered to give them lessons for no cost at all.

We planned to open the restaurant in December, and the closer we came to the date, the busier I was in the kitchen, with Bahrum and Yazir, trying out recipes, playing with the selection of dishes, making various modifications for lunch and dinner service, as well as planning a number of special menus for private parties and cele-brations. Two weeks before the opening, our days and nights were spent trying the foods we'd cooked, looking for dishes that would make a lasting impression on visitors. We had yet to decide what dishes to feature on opening night, but we had purchased all the foodstuffs and spices we might possibly need, all the while keeping in mind Tjai's strict reminder to be conservative in the amount of supplies we had on hand during the trial period: "Asian spices are expensive, you know, because most have to be imported!" Tjai, with calculator in hand, like a soldier with his rifle, was completely obsessive. I made a secret promise to myself that one day I would throw that calculator of his into the Seine.

One afternoon, Mas Nug came into the kitchen and started rifling through my recipe cards while whistling off tune. Exactly like an Indonesian spook, I thought, who doesn't know the meaning of quality as he preens about his profession.

"Why are these names so boring?" He looked at the slate board on the kitchen wall. "'Palembang dishes,' 'Padang dishes,' 'Solo dishes'... God, put some creativity into those names!"

I lowered my eyeglasses and looked at him without commenting. What kind of louse was this, suddenly showing up in my kitchen?

"What would you suggest?" Bahrum asked politely.

Mas Nug smiled and looked at me. Like me, Mas Nug was a decent cook. Risjaf could eat just about anything, but in the kitchen could do little more than boil water and fry an egg. As for Tjai, he could help cut up onions but only after donning a face mask and eyeglasses.

Also like me, Mas Nug had a discerning tongue and was always curious to try different things. Tongues weren't just for discovering the inside of a woman's mouth; tongues were also able to recognize that certain kinds of meats could be matched with certain spices, with certain kinds of wine, and that vegetables tasted better if they hardly felt a fire's heat at all.

The difference between Mas Nug and me was pragmatism. Just as Mas Nug could imagine Agnes Baumgartner to be Rukmini, he could also see peanut butter as an adequate substitute for freshly ground peanuts, the basic ingredient for *gado-gado* and satay sauces. I, on the other hand, insisted on culinary authenticity: the peanut sauce for *gado-gado* or satay could only be made from peanuts that first had been fried with grilled cashew nuts and then hand ground together with red and green chili peppers and a dash of kaffir lime juice.

Neophytes that they were, Bahrum and Yazir were receptive to Mas Nug's suggestions: Bahrum stood ready with his pen and notepad in hand, Yazir with a stick of chalk beside the slate board.

Mas Nug coughed before speaking. "This is the thing… Instead of calling Kalasan-style fried chicken 'Fried Chicken from Central Java,' why not give it a more poetic name, 'Widuri Chicken,' for instance. People don't know what the word means and it doesn't matter, but it sounds more exotic and unique. You can still cut up and fry the chicken just as you would for Kalasan-style chicken, but you change the recipe a little—maybe with a *sambal* sauce made of shallots and— *Voila!*—you now have 'Widuri Chicken' instead. That's what will make Tanah Air Restaurant special. Or take our common everyday tofu dish that's been stuffed with white fish and use red sea perch instead and then change the name from 'Stuffed Tofu' to 'Rainbow Tofu,'" he suggested with a grin.

"Out, damned spot!" I screamed, banishing him from the kitchen.

Mas Nug burst into laughter and then turned to walk away, whistling off tune as he retreated from my domain.

Bahrum and Yazir looked at each other. Their fingers stopped writing.

"Good suggestions…" Bahrum started to say to me.

I stared hard at him. "I don't believe in pretentious packaging like that. I don't believe in formats. I don't believe that presentation will make a diner forget the meal's content. It's the tongue, not the eye, that decides. Ingredients and taste are everything."

Bahrum swallowed. "What do you mean by format?"

I sat down on the kitchen stool and ordered the two of them to sit down across from me. I leaned my head toward them. They leaned towards me.

"Do you two understand literature? Poetry, novels, short stories?"

"Well, I read," Yazir said, "but I can't create the kinds of work that all of you do here."

Yazir looked for all the world like I was about to present him with a treasure map.

"For my good friend Mas Nugroho, presentation and format are very important, which is why we left the 'look' of this restaurant to him. But for me, cooking is as serious as writing a poem. Letters jump from my pen to create a word; the words then twist and turn, maybe even running into one another, as they search for a harmonious match so as to create a sentence that is both meaningful and poetic. Every letter has a soul and a spirit; every letter chooses a life of its own."

Bahrum scribbled notes like a freshman college student. His ballpoint pen moved quickly, writing down what I said as if it were canon law. Yazir looked at me with a mixture of awe and surprise, no doubt wondering why I was talking about poetry in a kitchen that smelled of onions.

"And so it is with cooking!" I exclaimed, while lifting a shallot with the tips of my fingers. "This goes well with garlic, red chili, and shrimp paste. But this...?" I took a salmon fillet.

"Would this go well with shrimp paste?" I paused. "Frankly, I don't know. I haven't tried it yet. But what is certain is that they don't know each other and haven't yet learned how to be close to each other or to excite each other."

Yazir jumped straight into the world of metaphor. Now he looked at the pieces of chicken, salmon, and beef on the kitchen table as if they were living creatures looking for the spice of their life. Yazir picked the pieces up, one by one, as if having found a diamond amidst the booty. Meanwhile, Bahrum, a calculating young man but one with limited imagination—I had begun to suspect he was Tjai's offspring—looked at me the way he might look at an orangutan who needed to be put back in his cage.

"But there are traditional recipes for all these dishes, complete with measurements for spices, right?" he asked. "How are we supposed to know that, uh, this onion here might be attracted to this." He picked up a slice of fresh turmeric.

My heart skipped a beat. I took the turmeric and put it down in front of me, exactly in front of me.

"Turmeric is the spice that everyone competes for," I said, as if reciting a legal writ. "This is the flavor for all kinds of cuisines and a curative for all kinds of ills. Turmeric is the jewel in the crown of spices. Don't ever question its status or use."

"Use your feeling, your sense of taste, Bahrum," said Yazir, lifting his two hands as if suddenly imbued with the feeling that he could write a thousand poems of the same caliber as those of Chairil Anwar.

Bahrum rolled his eyes and took a knife. "I'm just more practical," he said to me. "Give me a recipe and I'll follow it." He threw up his hands and refused to join in the party of metaphors in the kitchen. "So," he said, trying to usher Yazir and me to reality, "are we going to put *ikan pindang serani* on the menu?" Bahrum pointed to the pile of turmeric in front of me.

I nodded. My Javanese spicy and sour milkfish soup was going to be the star of our menu, the restaurant's signature dish.

90 RUE DE VAUGIRARD, PARIS; DECEMBER 12, 1982

The poet Robert Frost once said that home is our destination, the place that will embrace us. Tanah Air Restaurant was our destination, the place that would embrace us, but she had to be able to demonstrate cheer upon our arrival.

Mas Nug looked at himself frequently in the mirror, studying his mustache—which he had kept from Jakarta to Peking, then on to Zurich and finally to Paris—practicing how to demonstrate that cheer. He practiced smiling in front of the mirror, repeating the question "*Ça va?*" and nodding his head in interest as he listened to the patter of his imaginary guests.

No one criticized or made fun of Mas Nug; each of the four pillars had his own way of standing strong in the face of mounting apprehension. Sometime before the opening day, Mas Nug and Risjaf asked me to hand-write an announcement, which they enlarged to create a large poster for display in the front window. I wrote: "*L'ouverture du Restaurant Tanah Air. Cuisine Indonésienne. Prix spécial pour la première semaine.* Grand opening of Tanah Air Restaurant. Indonesian cuisine. Special prices during the first week."

Risjaf paced the floor of the restaurant, righting the position of tables and chairs and checking on the attendants—students, most of whom would be working for us part-time—and teaching them how to pronounce "welcome" in Indonesian. "Se…la…mat ma…lam," he intoned. "Sa…la…ma' ma…laaaam," they replied; yet he was satisfied. They were better at the pronunciation of Indonesian than Indonesians were at trying to get their tongues around French.

Mas Nug hooked up loudspeakers outside the restaurant so that passing *flâneurs* could hear the alternating sounds of Javanese and Balinese gamelans. A few of our French friends, including Jean-Paul and Marie who had helped to set up the cooperative, arrived early to listen to the gamelan music, even though it was only coming from a cassette. Vivienne arrived shortly afterwards and engaged the two in conversation. She also tried to calm the four pillars, who at that tense moment in time did not in the least resemble strong or solid uprights.

To calm his nerves, Mas Nug stopped twisting his mustache and began sipping on a glass of wine in a corner of the room. Tjai and Risjaf took up posts outside the front door, waiting for our first customers to arrive. I remained at my place in the kitchen, while frequently glancing through the window of the door towards the ground floor dining area.

The hands of the clock pointed to six. The heavy beating of hearts, those of the four pillars, was almost audible to my ears. Even with the gamelan music playing, filling the room with its sound, I couldn't bear to view the emptiness of the dining room. I came out of the kitchen to join Jean-Paul, Marie, Vivienne, and Mas Nug, who was futilely attempting to the whistle to the tune of the gamelan's pentatonic scale. A sorry sound, indeed, but I didn't have the energy to tell him to stop. My eyes were glued on the front door.

"Stop staring at the door," Vivienne said in hopes of calming my nerves. "It's not going to look back."

I smiled, and I had just taken out a cigarette to smoke when the bell hanging from the top of the front door began to ring. I looked over to see a French couple enter. They stopped just inside to look around the room and study the shadow puppets and masks that decorated the wall.

Mas Nug and Risjaf immediately greeted them with a mixture of overwhelming good cheer and utter nervousness. I was just about to return to my domain of authority, when Risjaf called my name.

"Madame and Monsieur would like you to explain the menu and, perhaps, advise them what to eat," he said to me in front of the middle-aged pair.

Before advising anything, I first asked the two of them whether they preferred beef, fish, or chicken, or if they were vegetarian. I also asked whether they liked spicy food. Their answers would tell me what to recommend. Apparently, the couple were culinary adventurers and liked to try all sorts of food—which is why they had come to the restaurant. They had vacationed in India and Thailand and liked the foods they tried there. Now they wanted to sample Indonesian cuisine.

Based on their answers, I recommended that they try a complete Padang meal with an assortment of dishes from West Sumatra. So as not to put his practice in front of the mirror to waste, Mas Nug spoke with the couple in French and offered to bring them wine.

I had just turned to go to the kitchen when the bell on the door rang again. A group of six people came in, all of them French as well. Mas Nug called me over to speak with them. The first lesson learned on opening night was that customers liked this personal touch—the chef of the restaurant discussing with them what they would like to eat.

Then an Indonesian family came in, and then another group of French people. And then, and then, and then… All of a sudden, as if the flood gates had been opened, more and more people came in. Apparently, Risjaf had done a very good job of spreading the news about the opening of the restaurant. But I really did have to return to the kitchen in order to prove that Tanah Air could serve as a home away from home.

Vivienne and Risjaf took over my task of explaining to our curious but mostly unknowing French customers the various dishes on the menu. Watching and listening to Vivienne and Risjaf, our waiters and waitresses also learned about the food they were going to serve.

My hands, and those of Bahrum and Yazir as well, did not stop moving at the work counter. Through the kitchen window, we could observe the expression of customers' faces. The hits of the evening were grilled chicken; goat satay; *gulai anam* or Lampung-style chicken curry; *soto ayam*, spicy yellow chicken soup; and *nasi Padang*, with a medley of dishes special to Padang, West Sumatra. The waiters delivered hand-written notes from customers full of praise for their meals. I tacked them to the wall of the kitchen so that they would one day serve as a reminder of my first day as a poet in the world of Indonesian cuisine.

"The place is full. All tables are filled!" Bahrum announced when he returned from a survey of the two floors. They even had to get extra chairs out of the storeroom. "You should see how Pak Tjai is sweating!" he added with a wide grin.

"And the *pourboire!*" Yazir screamed. "Pak Tjai said there are several thousand francs in it." We had decided that any and all tips would go into a common tip box to be divided equally among the crew at the end of each evening.

I smiled to hear the good news—a delightful and unexpected surprise—but then went back to my cooking and preparing desserts. The most popular was *es cendol*, made from coconut milk, jelly noodles, shaved ice, and palm sugar, to which I added jack fruit (though, unfortunately, jackfruit from the can). Almost half of all the visitors that evening ordered an extra serving.

There had to be something right about all the work we had put into establishing the cooperative. There had to be something good in what we were doing as human beings. I didn't know whether the opening night's success was a matter of hard work or good luck; Paris, after all, has thousands of bistros, cafés, restaurants, and bars. But as I was slowly pouring the next order of *es cendol* into a glass, suddenly something, I don't know what, began to tug at my chest and made my eyes begin to water.

"Zir, could you help me here?" I said to Yazir as I put down the glass.

Yazir took the glass from me with a look of surprise. I quickly retreated to the corner of the kitchen, my back to my two assistant as I faced the wall. I lifted my apron to wipe my face, which was suddenly moist with perspiration. I didn't want my helpers to know that I was suddenly crying, for no explicable reason. But the more I rubbed my eyes, the faster my tears began to fall.

The door to the kitchen opened. *Shit.*

"Dimas…"

It was Mas Nug's voice. *Please leave me alone.*

But I heard his footsteps as he walked towards me. Then suddenly felt his hands on the back of my shoulders. This time he was not whistling or singing off key. From the trembling of his hands, I could tell that he, too, was silently crying.

●

Life as a political exile would not have been complete without a steady stream of trials: having our passports revoked; being forced to move from one country and from one city to another;

having to change professions; even having to change families—all with no obvious design or definite plan. All these things were happening while we were in the midst of a search for our identity, shapeless souls searching for a body to inhabit. The annoyances we faced—or the "challenges" as Mas Nug preferred to call them—were never-ending. For that reason, and despite the successful opening of the restaurant and the popularity of Tanah Air in the days and nights to come, we knew that our celebration would propel an opposing force.

This afternoon, for instance… I had just finished preparing spices and was enjoying a cool beer in the ground floor dining area next to the cash register where Tjai was working. The telephone rang and he answered it. I looked at him to see who was calling, but his face was flat and cold-looking. He frowned.

"Who was that, Tjai?"

"I don't know. Some crazy guy," he answered with a tone of unconcern as he went back to his calculator and notes. "Do you really have to use Bango soy sauce? Can't you use another brand?"

"No," I insisted. "Bango has a different sweetness."

"Well, OK," he said, but then turned to Mas Nug who was seated beside me. "If you're going to Amsterdam, pick up a bulk order there. It's much cheaper there."

"And while you're at it," I added, "you might pick up a bulk order of Jempol shrimp paste. And tempeh, too. And *kretek* cigarettes. Oh, and don't forget the turmeric, both powdered and fresh…"

"Yeah, yeah, yeah… You and your fresh turmeric. That's what's so expensive!" Mas Nug grumbled even as he wrote down all my orders.

"Up to you, but if you don't want the *pindang serani* tasting strange…"

The telephone suddenly rang again, clipping my commentary. Tjai picked up the receiver but then immediately put it down again. Mas Nug looked at Tjai in surprise.

"Who was that, Tjai? Your mistress calling?" he asked with a laugh.

"That's your department, not mine," Tjai said straightaway, not raising his face from the figures on the sheet in front of him.

"Yeah, yeah, but who was it? What if it's someone wanting to order catering?"

Tjai raised his head and motioned towards the clock. It was eleven o'clock. He then went back to work again, leaving Mas Nug's question hanging in the air.

Again the telephone rang and this time Mas Nug rushed to pick up the receiver. Tjai took a breath and crossed his arms, waiting to see how Mas Nug would respond to this mystery caller.

A startled look suddenly appeared on Mas Nug's face and he lowered the receiver slowly.

"How many times has that person called, Tjai?"

Tjai raised his shoulder. "I've lost count. Every day at eleven. He's crazy."

"Who is it?" I asked.

"Some thug, looking to shake us down," Tjai spat. "What, do you think Indonesia is the only country with shakedown artists?"

Mas Nug shook his head.

"How much is he asking?"

Tjai opened his eyes wide and quoted a figure that made me gulp. The swig of beer I'd just taken rushed into my nasal chamber. Damn!

There was no counting the number of *rendang* meals or skewers of satay that we would have to serve in order to come up with the baksheesh the man was asking for. For some reason, after Risjaf called Amnesty International to ask for their advice on what to do, the harassing phone calls stopped for a while. Maybe the people there had put in a call to the police or something—we didn't know—but we were sure that one day they would start again.

Then there was another kind of caller: the deep breather. Whenever that kind of call came in, Tjai, whose work area was right next to the telephone, would balance the receiver on his shoulder while going on with his calculations of income and expenditures. After a few minutes Tjai would put the receiver to his ear to see if the deep breather had already hung up. If he had, Tjai hung up our phone too.

One time a group of prominent Indonesian academics came to Paris to attend a conference at the Sorbonne. Among them was the sociologist Armantono Bayuaji, who was a strong critic of the Soeharto regime. He suggested a group dinner at Tanah Air. When they came to the restaurant and saw how busy it was, plus the slate of book discussions and photographic exhibitions that Risjaf had planned, he left the place truly impressed. A few weeks later, Armantono published an article about his trip in Indonesia's leading news magazine—almost two entire pages of praise for the work that we were doing and a not-so-veiled criticism of Indonesian government policies. Basically, the point of Armantono's article was that if the tens of thousands of political prisoners who had been incarcerated on Buru Island had already been released and allowed to return home—even though branded with a stigma—why was the government not doing something to encourage those political exiles who were still abroad to come back home? Armantono said that Tanah Air Restaurant was Indonesia's true cultural ambassador in Paris.

I don't know what happened in Jakarta after that, but I'm sure that Armantono's article must have caused quite a stir. Whatever the case, we continued to enjoy a steady stream of customers that surged daily at lunch time and early evening.

Then there was the day when a new form of harassment emerged. That day, Yazir burst into the kitchen like he had just seen a ghost.

"It's Snitch. Snitch is here."

I was startled.

"Snitch" was the sobriquet for a man we exiles viewed to be lower than a sewage drain. The man's real name was Sumarno Biantoro. He was a writer—a writer of some talent, I must admit—who had once been a friend. Many a night we'd spent together in friendly discussion with Mas Hananto and Mas Nug at Senen Market. Marno, as I called him then, was the son of the owner of a cigarette manufacturer in Central Java. He had been counted among the list of writers whose work before the fall of President Sukarno had garnered for him a fairly high measure of respect from leftist critics. His poems and plays were said to be "revolutionary."

Not surprisingly, therefore, after the September tragedy he was among the many artists, writers, and intellectuals who were arrested. It was said that he was tortured: that his teeth had been yanked from his mouth with pliers and his penis flattened beneath the leg of a chair. But it was also said that afterwards he had been allowed to go free and that he hadn't been sent to some unnamed detention center, much less to the penal colony on Buru Island. He got the name "Snitch" because when his interrogators presented him membership rolls for the many Indonesian arts organizations, he pointed out for them the names of leftists and left-leaning persons.

It was also said that the military finally succeeded in capturing Mas Hananto after his three years on the run because this man had learned where he was in hiding and had informed the military.

Tjai came into the kitchen, his face pallid, one of the few times I had ever seen him show such obvious emotion.

"He wants to talk to you, Dimas. Somehow, he knows that Mas Nug is in Amsterdam."

But would a rat be a rat if it were not quick on its feet and aware of the movements of its enemies? My body felt nailed to the floor. I was holding a long knife I used for cutting up chickens. Long and very sharp. My fingers trembled as I walked towards the door, the knife still in my hand.

I could see Sumarno seated alone at a table facing the front door. I noted that he had chosen not to descend and take a seat on the lower floor. I stopped walking. He was smoking, hadn't ordered anything. I sensed that he knew I was behind him. At my back were Tjai, Risjaf, Bahrum, and Yazir.

Sumarno turned and I don't know what it was that caused me to blink: the gleam from the pomade in his slicked-back hair or his gold teeth. Apparently, he'd replaced his former enamels with gold.

He rose and shook my hand. "Dimas Suryoooooooo." A strong and sure shake. He looked authoritative but also wily at the same time. He laughed, at what I didn't know and didn't care, and then motioned for me to sit down across from him, as if he were the owner of the restaurant who required a word with his cook.

I remained standing, the knife in my left hand.

"Busy cooking, are you? Come, sit down and talk to me."

I placed the knife on the table in front of me, removed my cooking smock, and then sat down face to face with the rat with the golden teeth. If he tried to lay a hand on me, I was ready to impale his hand to the dining table with my carving knife. I imagined Tjai worrying about damage to the table, but I didn't care.

I glanced at Risjaf and Tjai, who stood behind me like bodyguards, ready to act if anything untoward happened. My two assistants, who suddenly seemed to have forgotten that they still had more spices to grind, also stood in the background, waiting to see what would happen next.

"So, Marno, what's up?" I asked him. "Why are you here?"

"What, can't I be a customer here? Where is that European hospitality of yours?"

Sumarno looked beyond me and waved. "Sjaf, Tjai… Come here and join us. You know, Sjaf, I ran into your wife just this morning at the supermarket, uh, what's the name of the place…?"

Risjaf frowned and walked towards the table as if being pushed. Tjai came forward as well, but then went straight to his usual position at the cash register. I guessed that he wanted to be close to the telephone if that proved to be necessary.

But Sumarno was a rat, not a thug, and a coward besides, as sweet as sugar to your face but a backstabber when you turned around. The way he dealt out the information he possessed was yet another form of harassment of the most clichéd kind. In the course of our brief conversation, he quickly revealed that he knew the apartment building where Vivienne and I lived and the home addresses of Risjaf and Amira and Tjai and Theresa as well. Sniggering as he spoke, he also told me where Bahrum and Yazir lived. Although I knew he was a coward, unlikely to attack me physically, I kept turning the handle of the knife over and over in my hand.

"Nice set up you've got here," he said in Javanese, looking around. "You guys must be doing well."

"Would you like something to drink?" Risjaf asked.

"What do you have?" Sumarno looked in the direction of the bar to our right.

I couldn't bear this charade much longer. "Whatever poison suits you," I said. "Rat poison, perhaps?"

Sumarno burst out laughing, cachinnating like a gorilla. No one else saw the humor and everyone continued to stare at him.

For the next hour, without a drink and with no food on the table, Sumarno chattered nonstop about what was happening in Jakarta and what had become of the former political prisoners who had been released from Buru Island.

"It's too bad, though, they have a code affixed to their identification cards. You've heard of that, right? 'ET' for *eks-tapol*—former political prisoner. Remember Mas Warman and Mas Muryanto? They're working as journalists again but have to use pseudonyms; but I'm sure you knew that already. Warman writes under the name 'Sinar Mentari' and Muryanto goes by the name 'Gregorius.' Silly of them, really, to use names that are so obviously false. And you know, the children of former prisoners, those who are also working for the mass media, they're using pennames as well. I guess that's the trend these days, huh, to use fake names? Like father, like son, everyone hiding from one another."

As if there were something humorous about this situation, Sumarno giggled to himself and for so long that what came to my mind was a scene in the *Bharatayudha* where Bima uses his long, steel-like thumbnail to slice Sangkuni's mouth from off his face.

Risjaf knew what the grinding of my jaws meant. I clenched the knife in my hand so firmly that no one could take it from me. I felt myself grow hot then cold. The man in front of me not only took pleasure in causing the misfortune of others—people like Mas Hananto, for instance—but he was an opportunist as well.

Like a rat, he lived in darkness and filth.

Tjai came over from the counter with a cold look on his face to tell us that it was time for our weekly finance meeting, a lie of course but a good enough reason to bring this gavotte to an end before anyone got hurt.

The movement of Tjai and Risjaf to Sumarmo's sides forced the man to stand up. Still laughing, he said goodbye. But at the door to the restaurant, he stopped and turned around, then gave me a serious look. "You know, Dimas… If you apply for a visa again this year, feel free to mention my name. Maybe that will help you to enter Indonesia." He laughed again, then opened the door and disappeared.

Tjai and Risjaf took hold of each of my arms, knowing that I wanted to throw my knife into that bastard's heart.

After the rat slithered away, Yazir and Bahrum immediately wiped the table, chairs, and door handle—anything Sumarno had touched—with disinfectant, as if the man had been carrying a disease. This display of solidarity on the part of my two young assistants made me smile and breathe a sigh of relief.

"Go back to the kitchen," Tjai said to me as he locked the front door, "and use that knife on some beef or chicken." Lunch time was just one hour away.

I thought of Mas Hananto and of Surti and their children, and then of all the other friends whom Sumarno had put his finger on. I realized that Sumarno was not unique, but he was for me the personification of that mass of rats who prospered from misery. In life, it seemed to me, there are many people like Sumarno, all of whom easily breed to reproduce creatures of the same kind.

I suddenly felt sunshine attacking my eyes. What was happening? This was crazy. Why was I back in my apartment? I was confused about both time and space. I slowly rose, feeling completely disoriented and agitated. Amazingly, though, my head now felt clear. I no longer felt dizzy or like I wanted to throw up. In the living room, I found Mas Nug stretched out on the sofa.

The sound I made caused him to stir.

"Hey," he said, as he wiped his eyes and sat up. "Feeling better?"

"Much better. Who brought me home? And where is Sumarno?"

"Sumarno? What? You must have been dreaming."

Hmm… I said nothing. This was serious. What year was it anyway?

"Don't you remember getting sick last night? You took some medicine and fell asleep at the restaurant. I ended up cooking for those Malaysian friends of yours. And then Risjaf and I brought you home in a taxi."

I took two cups from the cupboard and began to prepare coffee.

"You shouldn't be drinking coffee or tea," Nug told me.

I ignored his ridiculous suggestion. How could I live without coffee?

"Listen, Dimas. While you were asleep, I put my magic needles in several of your pressure points. That's why you're feeling better now. And from the points I stuck, I could tell that something is wrong with your liver."

Mas Nug sounded more like a charlatan than a healer to me. After the coffee had brewed, I gave a cup to Nug and then poured one for myself. As I took a sip, I noticed that there were some used acupuncture needles in the waste basket. Good God, he wasn't kidding.

"Where did you stick those things in me?" I asked, darting my eyes at my arms and stomach.

"You don't need to know. The important thing is that you're feeling better now. You are, aren't you?"

I nodded. "That doesn't mean I'm going to let you stick those things in me again."

Mas Nug grinned and took a sip of coffee. "Before you go back to sleep, there are a couple of things that you should know."

Now what was he going on about? I waited for him to speak.

"The first is that in our conversation with those Malaysian friends of yours last night, the subject of political activism in Indonesia came up. They especially had a lot to say about one particular activist, a young man by the name of Pius Lustrilanang who had been kidnapped and tortured. Not that I found this information particularly surprising, but what did surprise me is not only that this Pius kid survived the torture but, as the Malaysians told it, he convened an international press conference and described in detail how he had been kidnapped and tortured and that he fully intended to find his captors and make them face justice."

I almost dropped my cup of coffee.

Wasn't that crazy to think of? Justice? In Indonesia? It was one of the most startling things I had heard in my thirty-two years in exile.

"What's happening there?"

Mas Nug shook his head. "I don't know; but now that one person has spoken up, it will only be a matter of time before other victims begin to speak out as well."

After mulling over this incident, I suddenly remembered something. "And what's the other piece of news?"

"Vivienne called this morning to say that the hospital had

contacted her because the results of your tests are still at the hospital, waiting to be picked up."

"The hospital called Vivienne?"

Mas Nug shrugged. "When we filled out the registration form at the hospital the time you fell, we put down Vivienne's name and number in case of emergency."

"What the hell? Damn you!"

Mas Nug shrieked like a monkey with a banana. He knew very well that Vivienne would now be on my tail about getting medical treatment. We may have divorced years ago, but she and I continued to maintain an amicable relationship.

"When I talked to Vivienne, she mentioned that she had told Lintang about you collapsing at the Metro station."

Merde! Now that Lintang knew, there would be no end to the matter.

Mas Nug finished his coffee and then packed his kit of needles. He needed to go home and take a bath and change his clothes, he said. Then he'd go to the restaurant to help in the kitchen and would come back to see me in this evening after the restaurant closed.

"We've all agreed that you need to rest. Go get the results of your test, and whatever they may be, follow the doctor's orders! If you don't, I'm going to come back here and stick you with a thousand needles," he said with a threatening tone.

"But the kitchen…"

"Let me and your two assistants take care of the kitchen. There's no bargaining this time," said my dictatorial friend, not permitting a reply.

As Mas Nug left my apartment, I listened as he began to sing "What a Wonderful World" in his terribly off-tune voice.

II

LINTANG UTARA

PARIS, APRIL 1998

FROM THE WINDOW OF THE METRO, I looked out on a gloomy Parisian spring. Dark and gray, thick with haze Where were the colors of cheerful times: bluish purple, golden yellow, and pastel pink? It was April. The air should be suffused with the scent of flowers and the aroma of a freshly baked croissant just dunked into a cup of sweet-smelling hot chocolate. And the people of Paris should be dressing up the city's body in preparation for a glorious summer ahead. But as the great poet T.S. Eliot said so effectively, *April is the cruelest month, breeding / Lilacs out of the dead land, mixing / memory and desire…*

Thus, it's not the fault of Paris, for this city is not a land of the dead that gives birth to putrid-smelling flowers. Nor is it the fault of spring, which should be festooned with flowers. April is an accursed month for the students at the Sorbonne, a time with no pause button for their lives. At this time, professors become gods, doling out assignments for tens of papers and examinations, even as they retire to cafés and bistros to drink glasses of wine and cackle with laughter.

Outside the Metro window, I could still see flashing, from one support beam to the next, the clouded look on Professor Didier Dupont's face—that same sour look that appeared on his face this morning when he watched the video footage I had produced over a period of several months on the subject of my final assignment: *Le Quartier Algérien à Paris*, the Algerian quarter in Paris.

The light from the small screen flickered on his face. I watched the images of the Algerian immigrants I had interviewed these past few months and whose stories I had methodically recorded. Occasionally, Professor Dupont would squint his eyes and sometimes purse his lips at footage of the adorable and wide-eyed Algerian children but, after ten tense minutes, the professor asked me to sit down in front of him.

For several minutes, my advisor allowed me to fidget nervously as he busily scribbled notes on a pad. Finally he took a breath and looked at me. "*Quelle est votre opinion? C'est un bon plan…*"

His voice was deep as he asked my own opinion of the footage and my future plans.

Professor Dupont was economic with his words and didn't continue his sentence. He took off his glasses, wiped the lenses with an old handkerchief, and then put them back on in a slow, almost stylized, movement.

I knew that he had more to add, but impatiently I raised my hands, palms up, as if to ask, "Well?" The man was getting old.

Professor Dupont tapped the keyboard of his computer, and on the monitor there suddenly appeared a list of final assignments previously undertaken by students of the Sorbonne on the subject of Algerians in Paris. As he scrolled, the list grew longer, with hundreds of titles. My heart suddenly skipped a beat. I knew, of course, that numerous Sorbonne alumni had made documentary films about the Algerians in Paris when they were students. But I was convinced the documentary film I planned to make would be different.

Before I had the chance to express my argument, Professor

Dupont turned the computer screen in my direction. "This is a subject that's been hashed and rehashed by students here. Your proposal isn't a bad one, Lintang. *Non*, not at all," he said, his blue eyes burrowing into mine. "But it's a good thing this is only a proposal… I strongly suggest you drop it at this stage."

I found myself forced to nod. I thought of all the footage I had already shot with Algerian immigrants. I had been sure that the professor would agree to my proposal for my final assignment.

"You have great potential, talent, and spirit, Mademoiselle. So, eh, why don't we try coming up with something a little more original?"

T.S. Eliot's poem immediately reverberated in my ears. No wonder the poet hated the month of April.

"I find the Algerian immigrant experience in Paris to be extremely interesting, Professor," I tried to say in a non-defensive tone. "They are French people who feel themselves to have two homelands."

Professor Dupont stared me in the eye. His blue eyes reminded me of the turquoise in a ring my mother owned. The stone seemed to be boring into my dulled brain.

"But aren't you forgetting, Lintang, that there is also something very interesting about you and your own background?"

My heart, which I thought had stopped functioning for the past few minutes, suddenly seemed to expand with a surge of new oxygen-giving blood.

"You, too, have two homelands: France and Indonesia. You were born in Paris, grew up in Paris. You know the place. But aren't you curious about that other side of your identity, the land of your father's birth?"

Professor Dupont took a copy of *Le Monde* from off his desk, which, given its crumpled state, he had apparently read. He opened the paper, folded it, and handed it to me. On page three, a headline read, "*Enlèvement: un Militant Indonésien Prend la Parole*," a short article about an Indonesian student activist who had been kidnapped but now was speaking out. On the Economics page opposite was a bigger headline and longer article about the monetary crisis now affecting the Asian region, Indonesia included.

I said nothing. I knew the direction Monsieur Dupont's conversation was taking. Indeed, I knew it very well. His question was one that had often disturbed my sleep. It was one that I had long ago stored away and buried deeply in my heart. I didn't want to arouse something that was now at peace, there in the deepest recesses of my heart.

"Your father is a part of an important period in Indonesian history," he said, refolding the paper and giving it to me. "Take it."

I took the paper but couldn't find a reply for Monsieur Dupont's suggestion. Staring down at my smudged sneakers now seemed to be much more interesting than looking into the man's blue eyes.

"The country where your father was born is in a state of unrest. Economics is the trigger, but the political situation is becoming increasingly unstable because of the country's one-man rule for so many decades."

So what if it was!? Wasn't this the case in almost all developing countries, which were constantly going through periods of unrest because of uncertain social and political situations? Many countries in Latin America, Africa, and Asia were led by corrupt authoritarian leaders.

"Don't you want to visit the place of your origins? Don't you want to understand what brought your father and his fellow exiles to a country that has almost no historical links to Indonesia?"

Obviously, I knew that my father had come to Paris not to admire the Eiffel Tower or to trace the steps of history at Notre Dame Cathedral. In fact, my father once told me that in all his life he had only twice set foot in the Eiffel Tower and those times had only been because a visiting Indonesian poet had forced him to go there. My father hated tourist sites.

I also knew that my father and his friends had not come to Paris with a briefcase of dreams or a suitcase of plans; there had been something darker, dangerous, and more covert. Even when I was too young to understand much about politics, I already knew that Indonesia—or rather, Soeharto's everlasting and seemingly invincible New Order government—would not make it easy for my father to return to his homeland. This was what Maman always told me. And this was a topic I always avoided, because whenever Ayah began to think of Indonesia, he would inevitably begin to cry, painful and bitter tears.

I pretended to clear my throat. "I've never been to Indonesia."

Monsieur Dupont pretended to be deaf. "What?"

"I know very little about Indonesia."

My first statement was true: in all of my twenty-three years I had never once set foot in Indonesia, because my father, regardless of how much he missed his homeland, could not take me there. But the second statement, I had to admit, was a lie. Of course I "knew" Indonesia, even if only in second-hand fashion—from Ayah, and his three friends, my three adoptive uncles, Om Nugroho, Om Tjahjadi, and Om Risjaf; from books and documentary films; and even from arguments my parents had. But also from certain incidents, both good and bad, which formed a source of tension between my father and myself to this very day.

"If you know so little, don't you want to know more? *Tu veux s'évader de l'histoire?* Do you wish to run from your history?"

Monsieur Dupont spoke with a flat tone, but I could hear him clearly. His questions were daggers and I could feel drops of fresh blood dripping from my heart. I'm sure he knew just what he was doing and what was happening inside me.

He took a calendar from his desk and counted off the amount of time that was left for me to find a topic for my final assignment to which he could agree. He muttered to himself as he took an empty form and then quickly wrote something on it in a hand that was fairly neat and even by European standards.

"You have six months to get to know Indonesia while undertaking research and taping your final assignment. *D'accord?*"

I took the form without replying, though my advisor's eyes demanded an answer.

"*D'accord,*" I was finally forced to agree.

"Surprise me. Come up with something brilliant. Come back to me when you have a clear plan."

Because the professor then stood, I, too, was forced to stand. He was not going to allow more room for debate, much less a chance for me to refuse.

"Don't be late, Lintang. You know the consequences if you're unable to finish your work on time."

The air in Professor Dupont's office suddenly felt stifling. April was indeed the cruelest month. At that moment, I heard the sound of the Metro, which seemed to be keeping time with the gusting wind.

From behind the Metro window, Paris looked gray and gloomy. Letters, words, posters, and photographs flashed past so quickly. Gray, black, white, gray...

•

My roots were in a foreign land. I was born in France, a country with a beautiful body and fragrant scent. But, according to my father, my blood came from another country, one far distant from the European land mass, a place that gave the world the scent of cloves and wasted sadness; a land of fecundity, rich with plants of myriad colors, shapes, and faiths, yet one that could crush its own citizens merely because of a difference in opinion.

Coursing through my veins was a kind of blood I did not know, but which was called Indonesia, and which melded with the other kind of blood in me called France. The flow of that foreign blood inside me always seemed to quicken and make my heart beat faster whenever I heard the sound of gamelan music in the biting cold of winter; when my father recounted tales from the shadow theater—about Ekalaya, for instance, the eternal outcast, or Bima, whose love went unrequited; or when Maman, in her halting Indonesian, would read to me Sitor Situmorang's poem about the prodigal son who, when finally returning home, still feels himself to be in a foreign land.

That blood in me felt at once foreign, pleasurable, and mysterious. All that was Indonesia and all that smelled of Indonesia was, for me, a site in a magical tale, one that existed only in dreams, like reading a novel set in a country I'd never visited.

Indonesia was for me a name on a map, little more than a concept. And the knowledge of that country, which supposedly flowed through my veins, had to make room for the French blood that was in me as well.

For the longest time, it seemed, I had forgotten about that foreign substance in myself.

A series of arguments between me and my father had taken their toll, and a long-simmering dispute between Maman and Ayah which had ended with their divorce had not made our relationship easier. A few months earlier the tension between us had peaked and we hadn't spoken to each other since that time—which meant, of course, that I had stopped going to Tanah Air Restaurant, which in turn meant I had long been separated from the restaurant's genial atmosphere, with its distinctive sound of gamelan music, and its interior walls decorated with shadow puppets, masks, and a map of Indonesia. Making things much more difficult for me was that I now rarely saw my father's friends: Om Nug, Om Risjaf, and Om Tjai, who were like true uncles for me. Yet another hardship was no longer being able to smell the scent of my father's goat curry, a dish that could compete with signature dishes of Europe's master chefs.

This estrangement between me and my father was thus, for me, hardly an ideal situation. But then having a father who was so complicated and filled with anger was not exactly easy either.

When the Metro came to a stop at Rue de Vaugirard station, I suddenly felt the need to leave the train and calm my thoughts. Professor Dupont's suggestion was a command I could not countermand. It meant that I somehow had to make a documentary film that was connected to my father or to Indonesia.

I-N-D-O-N-E-S-I-A.

On that spring morning, I felt myself being prodded to explore that foreign part of my body. I didn't want to do so, to thoroughly examine that region. There were things about Indonesia which for others would always seem to be exotic or unique—Java, Bali, Sumatra, the *Ramayana*, the *Mahabharata, Panji Semirang*, Srikandi, gamelan music, pink *kebaya*, the scent of *luwak* coffee, the spicy taste of beef *rendang*, and mouth-watering richness of goat curry—but for me, whatever cultural exoticism that Indonesia had to offer was concealed. Ever since I was a girl, I had always been haunted by a political upheaval that my peers knew nothing about, an event whose gory details had been expunged from Indonesia's official history books.

TANAH AIR RESTAURANT, 90 RUE DE VAUGIRARD, 1985

Winter in Paris. The smell of fried chili *sambal bajak* assails the nose. The ground red chilies and garlic that stimulate my olfactory nerves is a most pleasing torture. Om Nug is a great cook, but for me, my father is the best cook in the world.

There was a basic difference between my father's cooking and that of Om Nug. Om Nug was a modern-day cook who had only begun to study the wealth of Indonesian spices after the band of four decided to establish a cooperative and open an Indonesian restaurant. Om Nug emphasized efficiency. For example, he saw the preparation of spices for *rendang* as something simple; there was no need for the kind of elaborate ritual that made life difficult. All the spices could be put into a blender into which he'd pour coconut milk from a can that he bought in Belleville.

Ayah, on the other hand, loved ritual. He was both obsessive about and possessive of his stone mortar, which an aunt of his had sent him from Yogyakarta. With his faithful mortar in hand, Ayah kept the blender at a distance. He ground his spices slowly and carefully, mixing in the coconut milk, little by little, while complaining occasionally about having been forced to use coconut milk from the can. Whatever the case, I had to admit that the spicing of my father's *rendang* had a far more arresting taste than that of Om Nug, which he produced in a blender. I almost swooned whenever I tried my father's *rendang* or *gulai*, their taste was so good. But that meant that Ayah had had to lock himself inside the kitchen for much of the day in order to prepare his spices in the traditional way.

What's taking so long? It's seven o'clock and time to eat! But I could see a delicious meal ahead. *Le dîner sera délicieux!* On the menu that night was *nasi kuning* with side dishes of *tempe kering*, little sticks of tempeh soaked in brine and then fried until crispy; *sayur urap*, mixed steamed vegetables with spiced coconut; *empal*, seasoned slices of tenderized fried beef that melted in your mouth; and *sambal goreng udang*, a dish made with shrimp and chili sauce. Ayah always made two kinds of *sambal* or hot sauce to further spice up a meal: a *sambal bajak* which was not too hot—Ayah always removed the seeds of the red chilies and parboiled the chili's flesh before frying it—and thus more palatable for the tongues of French clientele, and a crushed peanut *sambal* into which he blended small green chilies that were so hot the *sambal* could be enjoyed by only the most tempered of tongues in Paris: those of Maman and me.

Maman was busy going back and forth from kitchen to dining room helping Ayah and Om Nug. In December the restaurant was always full. Over the years, dinner at Tanah Air seemed to have evolved into a kind of culinary picnic for French families wanting to celebrate the Christmas season. But Ayah had promised that tonight would be a family night and that no matter how busy the restaurant was, he would find time to sit with Maman and me so that we could enjoy together the meal he had prepared.

My eyes were on Maman. She was holding in her arms two large wide-necked glass containers filled with *kerupuk* shrimp crackers and was talking to Om Tjai and Ayah, who had just removed his white chef's smock, a sign that he was now free from duties and ready to eat. Come on! Why is it taking so long? Couldn't Maman and Ayah hear my stomach grumbling? Weren't they ever…

The door creaked. A cold winter's wind quickly swept into the dining room. And then I saw, *un*, *deux*, *trois*, *quatre*—four tall, hulking French men who filled the restaurant's foyer. They stood, not smiling, as if having no reason for coming to the restaurant except to cast their surly gazes.

"Police…" Maman whispered.

Police? The men weren't wearing the kind of uniform I usually saw policemen wearing on the streets.

I looked at Ayah. He seemed tense, with a fire suddenly flaring in his eyes, like the time I spilled a cup of *luwak* coffee on one of his books of poetry. I saw Om Nug and Om Tjai whisper something to him. Ayah bit his lips. I guessed they told him that it would be best for him not to do anything and let them deal with the police. But Ayah ignored them and immediately approached the four men. Together with Om Nug, he ushered the policemen to a quiet corner, away from the main dining area so that they wouldn't disturb the clientele. The restaurant was almost full.

"Lintang!" Maman called. She didn't like me sticking my nose into adult conversations.

I pretended to be deaf and watched the mini drama unfold as Ayah, Om Nug, and Om Tjai faced the unblinking policemen. I didn't want to miss a single thing. One of the policemen—I could see he had blue eyes—removed an identification card from his pocket.

I am Michel Durant," he said, showing the card to Ayah, who

gave it a cursory glance, "and this is my partner, Luc Blanchard."
He didn't introduce the other two men.

"May I help you?"

"We received a report from the Indonesian embassy that a subversive meeting is being held here; that you're planning a political
demonstration."

Ayah's features hardened, a look that was somewhere between
ghoulish humor and outright contempt. Om Nug, meanwhile,
broke out in laughter. Maman's cheeks turned bright pink, a sign
that she was angry. She immediately went up to the policemen
and started chattering at them in French.

"Meeting? A subversive meeting? This is too much. Can't you
see that we're busy preparing food for our customers?"

Maman's anger was evident from both the look on her face
and the tone of her voice. The two officers, Michel Durant and
Luc Blanchard, immediately stepped back as if being attacked by
a rabid dog. The other two officers behind them backed away
towards the door.

"The only thing we're doing here is cooking in the kitchen and
serving meals to our customers. There's nothing political going on
here," said Ayah in a much calmer voice than Maman's.

"Take a seat if you wish and you can see what we are doing,"
Maman said, putting her hands on her hips and turning away.
When Maman got this way, I'd bet that even Mitterrand wouldn't
want to take her on. Maman's bark caused Blue Eyes to fall back
a few steps.

I always cringed whenever Maman stared so hard that her eyeballs bulged from their sockets. Even Ayah would retreat when her
green eyes ballooned like that. Usually, he'd back down immediately or scamper off to another room. The four policemen—if

they really were policemen—looked nervous.

One of them, the thinnest and the youngest, plucked the courage to speak, "I'm sorry, Madame, but we're only carrying out orders."

Blue Eyes quickly added, "If all you're doing here is cooking and serving meals, then that is what we'll report."

At that moment Om Risjaf came out of the kitchen with a platter of *nasi kuning* and fried shrimp with chilies, the *sambal goreng udang* whose magic scent immediately suffused the air of the dining room. I watched as the policemen's nostrils flared and twitched.

"You'll pardon us," Luc Blanchard said as he held his hand out to Maman, though his eyes were fixed on the platter of *nasi kuning* in Om Risjaf's hand. Calmer now, Maman extended her own hand to the man.

"Oh, that smells good," said Blue Eyes pointing to the platter that Om Risjaf was carrying. "One day, I'll come back to try it."

"That's our homemade *nasi kuning* and *sambal goreng udang*— which are shrimp cooked in a chili sauce," Ayah said with a smile. "Please do come back."

"*Nasi kuning…*" The man suddenly seemed to have forgotten the reason for his visit as his eyes followed the platter to the table of the customer who'd ordered it. "With shrimp? *Ça sent bon!*" He swallowed. When his assistant coughed, he hurriedly took his leave, but added that he was definitely coming back to try the *nasi kuning.*

And Mr. Michel Durant was not joking. After that time, every month after receiving his pay check, he and his subordinates treated themselves to a meal at Tanah Air.

•

Although that incident took place when I was ten years old, I still remember it clearly—even the smells. I also remember feeling that there was something wrong with my family, or, to be more precise, that there was something that always made us feel like we were living in a state of uncertainty.

It was around that time I began to feel that there was another kind of life that was different from the one I had known as "normal" since childhood. My family was different from most French families. And I was different too. Not just because I was mixed-race, the product of an Indonesian and French marriage—in my class at school there were a number of mixed-race kids: French-Moroccan, French-Chinese, Anglo-French and so on—but because my classmates could talk about their parents' other home, whether it be Rabat, Beijing, or London. But not I.

My father came from Indonesia, a distant land I didn't know and could never get to know (for at least as long as the same government remained in power). Starting then, it slowly began to dawn on me that I would never be able to visit Indonesia, at least not with my father.

For the longest time I had realized, whether consciously or not, that the difference between my family and others did not end with my parents' mixed-race marriage. My father's background, full of political drama as it was, exceeded the absurdity of political events in Russian novels. In 1965 a blood-filled tragedy had taken place in Indonesia, yet Ayah spoke of the events that had occurred only in snippets and ever so sporadically. The older I became, the more stories I learned about that distant homeland of mine, invariably shown in documentary films as blue seas and waving palm trees.

Never, not even once, was I able to pry from my father the complete, comprehensive, and detailed story. I never really knew, for instance, how Ayah and his friends had been able to leave Indonesia to attend a conference in Santiago (followed by conferences in Havana and Peking) with only a metaphorical knapsack on their backs nor why they had never been able to return to their homeland. Wasn't that completely absurd? And why was it that Ayah left Indonesia to begin with? Nobody ever told me why.

At some point, I remember Maman telling me that in Indonesia anyone thought to be a member of the Communist Party, or a member of the family of a communist, had been hunted down, jailed, or made to disappear, just like that. Hearing these stories from Maman and Ayah, I didn't know which regime was more frightening: Indonesia, with its civilian-dressed dictator, or Latin America, with its generals.

So who was my father and who were his friends, my "uncles" Nugroho, Tjai, and Risjaf? Why couldn't they go home? Why were they on a wanted list? The story I got from Ayah and his three friends was piecemeal at best and often not even consistent. According to Professor Dupont, Ayah and his friends were a part of Indonesia's unwritten history. *Qu'est-ce que ça veut dire?*

What did he mean? And did I really have to make a record of this absurdity as my final assignment?

April is the cruelest month, breeding / Lilacs out of the dead land, mixing / memory and desire.

NARAYANA LAFEBVRE

"LIKE AN ANGEL, DESCENDED FROM HEAVEN..." That is what Gabriel Lafebvre said of his wife, Jayanti Ratmi. I was struck by the phrase. At the age of fifty-six, Gabriel was still a striking-looking man whose eyes were a seine for the sky. I've always believed that a man with stars in his eyes is likely to be a friendly man. And the amity I found in him, I came to see had been inherited by son, Narayana Lafebvre.

Narayana, whom everyone calls Nara, was given his name by his mother, Jayanti Ratmi, a Javanese dancer who loved the stories of the *Mahabharata*. She also gave him his adorable cleft chin.

That I spent most of my weekends with the Lafebvre family wasn't because of the similarity between Nara's family mine—his also being a mixed French-Indonesian family domiciled in Paris. That was pure coincidence. There was something else, something more significant, more magnetic about his family—something that I found calming when I was with them. I don't know what it was. Maybe it was their comfortable apartment, with a batik tablecloth here and a *wayang* puppet there—enough touches to show the Indonesian influence, but not like a craft store or a tourism bureau. It might also have been because of their dinners, whose light conversation invited intimacy, something I had rarely ever or possibly never felt again after my father left us.

I never tried to figure out why I was more comfortable lounging in the den at Nara's home than in my father's apartment.
Ayah's collection of books was, in fact, much larger and with
more interesting titles. I knew that I could easily spend hours
on end talking to Nara, because the both of us were drawn to
books of literature and philosophy. Nara had finished his studies
in English literature at the Sorbonne and intended to pursue a
master's degree in comparative cultural studies at Cambridge University in the autumn of this year. Meanwhile, I was still working
on my final assignment for my bachelor's in cinematography. But,
again, it was not just Nara that made me want to spend my free
time in his parents' apartment. His parents' living room and their
kitchen exuded a warm welcome and promise of comfort in
any season.

I preferred helping Tante Jayanti slice garlic, grind spices, and
grill meat to cooking at my parents' apartment in the Marais. Even
conversations about *wayang* characters, which I had engaged in
with my parents when I was small, transferred themselves to the
living room and terrace of the Lafebvre family apartment. Maybe
it was because I simply liked to see how happy and comfortable
this couple was with each other—or maybe because I was trying
to recapture something that I had lost. I didn't know.

I always imagined Jayanti Ratmi's marriage to Gabriel Lafebvre to
be just like that of the famed French photographer, Henri Cartier-
Bresson, with the Javanese dancer Ratna Mohini in decades past.
I often asked Gabriel to repeat the story of how he had come to
be entranced by his future wife when he saw her perform a *bedoyo*
court dance at an event sponsored by the Indonesian embassy in
Paris. (What I didn't ask was what the staff of the embassy was like
or how the Indonesian diplomats had treated them—those same

people who had no time for my father or his friends.)

Gabriel traded in exports and imports and had a wide circle of friends in the diplomatic community, including one who had worked at the Indonesian embassy. That night, his friend had invited Gabriel to try Indonesian food at an embassy reception being held in honor of Kartini Day. And it was there, at that celebration, that he met his "angel, descended from heaven."

Gabriel and Tante Jayanti seemed to like me, or at least to accept my presence in Nara's life. If they had their reservations, I could understand. Nara, their beloved and only son, was in a relationship with the daughter of an Indonesian political exile. They would have known full well that my father and his friends did not enjoy close links with the Indonesian embassy. But perhaps because I was the daughter she'd never had, Tante Jayanti like to share mother-daughter things with me. One of them was showing me her collection of *kebaya*. To me, a *kebaya* is the most demure piece of women's apparel there is. Long in the sleeve and long at the waist, this high-buttoned blouse completely covers a woman's upper body, yet there is no second guessing the wearer's shape.

And Tante Jayanti did have a wonderful collection. She owned all sorts of *kebaya*, in both short and long styles. She also had an Encim *kebaya*, my favorite kind, the style that Eurasian and Chinese-Indonesian women in Indonesia typically used to wear. All of them were very feminine with intricate lacework that was the equal of any piece of Dutch or Belgian embroidery.

I had never seen a woman as beautiful as Tante Jayanti in a *kebaya*. I was convinced that the *kebaya* had been created for angels like her, who had descended from heaven to earth.

"I'm not an angel," Tante Jayanti said to me, with a smile. "Our meeting—that of Gabriel and I—was simply a sign that we had to be together." Her voice was as soft as silk.

I was entranced. A sign?

•

"I bet you're talking to Jim Morrison!"

Oh, Nara... He knew that whenever something was on my mind, I would try to regain my composure at Père Lachaise Cemetery, the city's huge garden cemetery in the 20th arrondissement. There I could sit for an entire day, reading in front of the huge gravestone of Oscar Wilde, which was as flamboyant in its style as the author himself; or rest beside the tomb of Honoré de Balzac. But most often I spent my time in Division Six, sitting next to the simple grave of Jim Morrison as I intoned the lyrics of "Light My Fire. My father still owned several albums by The Doors, which he treasured as much as he did his Indonesian records and cassettes by Koes Plus, Bing Slamet, Nick Mamahit, and Jack Lemmers.

As it was still fairly early in the day, the throngs of autumn visitors had yet to flock to the place. Nara sat beside me as I stared at Jim Morrison's tombstone. My mother had introduced me to his music; and apart from his status as a musical legend he was, for me, a true and genuine songsman.

"'Light My Fire' is such an amazing song, a true work of poetry."

Nara knew me well, both my nature and my habits. If I wasn't ready to speak about something, I would choose a topic of conversation that had nothing to do with the subject at hand, which was, in this instance, my final assignment and Professor Dupont.

"Do you remember the first time we met?" I said to Nara, again avoiding the day's most important theme in hopes that he would not pressure me.

"Of course I do—at the Beaubourg library, when I caused you to drop that big stack of books you'd just borrowed."

Yes, that was Narayana: my savior angel who immediately and profusely apologized for knocking against me and then helped me to pick up the numerous heavy volumes I had borrowed. I remember the incident clearly. We were both freshman at the Sorbonne and still completely green behind the ears. How could I ever forget that event? But had there been a special sign, something telling us that we were fated to be together?

My father often said that "Light My Fire" by The Doors and the songs of Led Zeppelin were songs that always reminded him of the early days of his marriage to my mother, after the May Revolution in Paris.

"Your mother and Paris set me on fire," said my father, who was more than prone to romanticizing the past. What songs were playing when I first met Nara? I couldn't say for sure.

"What's up?" Nara asked, interrupting my daydream.

I shook my head but finally saw that it was time to enter the territory of Professor Dupont and my final assignment: Indonesia. I told Nara quickly what Dupont had advised, in just three short sentences. I didn't wish to rerun the entire embarrassing episode.

"Indonesia? He's suggesting that you make a documentary about Indonesian politics?"

"Not 'suggesting.' 'Commanding' is the word. He said that I have to make something related to Indonesia, that I need to explore my roots. Seek out what it is that has shaped me—or some kind of philosophical thing like that."

Nara frowned, but he didn't seem put off by the idea, not like I was. In fact, he seemed to be mulling over my professor's crazy suggestion.

"*Alors…*"

"*Alors, quoi?*"

"It's not actually a bad idea."

I looked at Nara's handsome face. He mostly took after the Lafebvre side of the family: blue eyes, brown hair, fair skin, and rosy lips. His aquiline nose divided his face symmetrically and his cleft chin made most female students want to make love with him. Everyone said that Nara's face belonged on a Hollywood billboard, pasted next to that of an equally attractive actress in some kind of fluffy romantic film comedy with an implausibly happy ending to its story. Justifiably, I suppose, Nara always got mad at me when I posed such a notion—linking his handsome appearance to something shallow and stupid. Being typically French, Nara was cynical about most things American. He had inherited a true French character. I saw almost no trace of Jayanti Ratmi in him, except for his fluency in Indonesian, and his academic interest in Asia.

"Didn't I once suggest that you make a documentary film about Indonesia—which you angrily dismissed?"

"*Oui*, I remember. But, Nara, this is about a country I have never even been to. The only way I know it is through the books my parents own, the literature I've read, and a few National Geographic documentary films. It's a country I know from the stories my father and his three friends have told me, whose first-hand knowledge of the country ended in 1965."

"That's more than enough for your final assignment. This is for your B.A., after all, not your master's or PhD. Your father and his friends are witnesses to history, Lintang."

I said nothing.

"You have the discipline. I know you can finish the work on time," said Nara with conviction in his voice.

What Nara should have understood is that this was not an academic problem. He'd already known me three years and was sensitive enough to know that this problem was far more complex for me than simply a matter of writing a scenario, filming interviews, and editing my film record.

Nara held my chin, then stroked it with his hand.

"It might be time for you to see your father."

"I went by the restaurant this morning, but couldn't make myself step inside."

I stood. Goodbye, Jim. I want to say hello to my friend Oscar.

Monsieur Oscar Wilde, please tell me if it's important for a person to look for her roots when she is already a tree, standing tall? You are an Irish poet, a tree who openly flaunted your sexual orientation in an age when such things were secret and not spoken of in polite society; the novelist who created Dorian Gray, a man of androgynous beauty immortalized in a painting that aroused its viewers. Tell me whether a tree, which stands upright and whose branches reach firmly for the sky, should bow in search of its roots for a name? For an identity?

Neither Oscar nor his bones offered a reply. The grandiosity of Wilde's tomb, with its sumptuously curved stonework, seemed to accurately reflect the nature of the man as described in his biographies: flamboyant and flirtatious. His lovely tombstone did not condescend to answer my question. But what I could see when I looked at it were images of my father at a much younger age walking among the tombstones of famous people, while holding the small hand of a girl seven years of age. I watched as he explained to the girl how even a warrior as great as Bhisma could fall in the battle of all battles; and how Bhisma could not die, even with his body pierced by hundreds of arrows from the bows of Srikandi and Arjuna, because he alone had been granted the boon to choose the time of his death.

"Bhisma chose to die the day after the war had ended," Ayah said to her, "and when he did die, his death was witnessed by the Pandawa brothers, their Kurawa cousins, and the gods."

I saw the seven-year-old girl pestering her father with innumerable questions. What a nagger she was! Tales from the *wayang* world, the land of the shadow theater, were as fascinating as they were baffling for her. How incredible that a person whose body was shot full of arrows could still choose his time of death.

Ayah then spoke to the young girl about the *wayang* characters who were closest to his own heart: Bima and Ekalaya.

It took a few moments for me to realize that the seven-year-old girl who was there, playing with her father, in Père Lachaise Cemetery, was I. How very odd it was, I thought, that when I was such a young age, my father had introduced to me the concept of death through stories from the *Mahabharata:* about Bhisma, who chose his time of death; about Bima, who was forced to agree to Krisna's plan to sacrifice Gatotkaca as bait to Karna in the duel against Arjuna; and about Ekalaya, the best bowman in the universe, who had even once defeated Arjuna.

But in those stories, Ayah also inserted his own hopes, whose tone was that of a person's final wishes: "Like Bhisma, I too would like to choose the place where I take my final rest," he said half to himself.

At first I thought Ayah wanted to be buried here, in Père Lachaise, among the writers, musicians, and philosophers he admired. I didn't know at the time that that would have been impossible. And it wasn't until later, when I was some years older, that I realized my father wanted to be buried in Indonesia. When Ayah introduced me to the poetry of Chairil Anwar, only then did I come to realize that, like the poet, he wanted to be buried in a Jakarta cemetery called Karet, a name that sounded so exotic to my ear.

Nara slowly approached and put his hand on my arm, a soothing feeling.

"This is an anxious spring," he said, looking at Oscar Wilde's tomb.

I could never be angry with Nara for long. Next to Maman, he most understood my heart. He knew there was inside me a space I didn't know, an odd and alien space called Indonesia. Although we were the same generation and both born in Paris to French and Indonesian parents, the difference between us was that Nara and his parents could go in and out of Indonesia freely, while Ayah and his three friends would always be repulsed by a force called the "September 30 Movement"— to which the Indonesian government had later come to affix the phrase "of the Indonesian Communist Party."

I tried to explain the meaning of this force for Nara. "The problem is, if I were to make such a documentary film, the subject could only be the testimony of Indonesian political exiles. I wouldn't be able to go to Indonesia to interview government officials. I wouldn't even be able to set foot in the Indonesian embassy to record their official stance on political exiles like my father, Om Nug, Om Tjai, and Om Risjaf. And…"

"Why can't you go to the embassy?" Nara interrupted. "If you really want to, I can introduce you to people there."

"No…"

"Why not? The embassy is always hosting one event or another.

Almost anyone can attend and they're always a good excuse for getting a good Indonesian meal. In fact, I have an invitation from the embassy to celebrate Kartini Day. What a brilliant idea!" Nara announced. "You really do have to see another side of Indonesian society—on the opposite side of the spectrum from the one at Tanah Air Restaurant."

I scratched my chin.

"Come on, what do you say?"

"But they might…"

"As you yourself implied, if you really want to be an observer or, in your case, a student with a research assignment, then you have to get to know the other side of things, the people who stand opposite your father and his friends. There's no need to be afraid. They're not going to chuck you out the door."

"But they might say something bad about my father in front of me."

"It's a celebration. Nobody's going to do anything to ruin the party. You can be my date. We can go there to study the enemy's movements."

"They're my enemies, not yours. Your family is on good terms with all of them."

"Whatever… But let's go. If you find yourself growing uncomfortable, we'll just leave and go home."

"*T'es fou!* You're crazy," I said.

"And you can wear a *kebaya*! It's Kartini Day, after all. All the women will be dressed up in beautiful *kebaya* and there will be lots of good food."

Hmmm, a *kebaya*… My heart began to waver. To waver because of *kebaya*… I had fallen in love with *kebaya* not because of Kartini Day—an annual celebration where Nara said women were expected to dress like Kartini, Indonesia's proto-feminist whose every image shows her dressed in a sarong and *kebaya* with her hair in a low chignon—but because of its sensuous shape which serves to accentuate a woman's beauty. The *kebaya* obeyed, did not oppose, the shape of a woman's body. And always complementing the *kebaya* was a *selendang*, a simple but elegant long scarf which became an extension of a woman hands, slicing the air when she danced.

Nara slowly rubbed his lips against mine. A second reason for me to waver. I loved his kisses. He was always able to excite me.

"Kartini Day? You know, I've never read her book of letters. Do you think I should…"

"Good lord. You can research Kartini later. I bet you could count on one hand the number of Indonesians who have actually read *From Darkness to Light*. This is a ceremonial event, OK?"

"Do you think I should wear a *kebaya*?"

"*Oui*. A *kebaya*, a *selendang*, and all the other garb."

Nara kissed me again. This time for a much longer time.

●

I first knew of *kebaya* from the photographs of my parents' wedding. The pictures held a promise of something for me in the future. In them, Maman looked beautiful. Ayah, too, looked dashing in his suit, and the two of them were full of smiles. Now they were divorced, but the image of my mother's beautiful white *kebaya*, a gift to her from my father's family, remained clear in my memory.

Earlier today, I rushed to the Beaubourg library to find a copy of *From Darkness to Light*, the English translation of *Door Duisternis tot Licht*, a collection of letters from the aristocratic young woman Kartini dating from the end of the nineteenth century to her early death in childbirth at the age of twenty-four in 1904.

When I was in high school, Ayah had told me about Kartini and her struggle against Javanese feudalism for the advancement of women's rights, but I had never read her letters. Fortunately, the Beaubourg library had a copy of the English translation and I was able to read about half of the book before I was forced to return home. Not too bad, I thought. At the very least, I wouldn't appear to be completely stupid if anyone asked me about Kartini at the embassy celebration. But more important for me was that the celebration gave me the opportunity to wear a *kebaya*. I chose to wear an Encim *kebaya*, a pink one my mother owned. From Nara's reaction, who said nothing except with his eyes, I knew I was right in my choice of this warm and cheerful color.

But Wisma Indonesia—the official Indonesian ambassador's residence—was, for me, far from warm. This was my first time to the ambassador's home, an immense, ostentatious building in Neully sur Seine, an elite area of Paris. Was Indonesia really a "developing country," I wondered when seeing the place.

Upon entering the gate to the residence, I could hear the lively sound of gamelan music playing somewhere in the distance. Balinese gamelan music, for sure, with its rapidly paced notes punctuated by a hammering sound. I was trying to remember where I had first heard Balinese gamelan music—was it from a cassette of my father's or one that Uncle Nug owned?—when a nudge of Nara's hand on my elbow signaled me to enter the outer grounds, an area already full of attractive and well-dressed guests.

Most of the Indonesian women wore their hair in a high bouffant style, ratted underneath and sleekly smoothed over. Each must have used an entire can of hairspray to make their hair stand so stiffly high and in place. Weren't they worried about being caught by a gust of wind? Or maybe they had birds resting inside their chignons, which resembled swallows' nests.

The men were inconsistent in their apparel. Some wore suits and ties, but many others wore long-sleeved batik shirts. I favored the batik, which I thought was Indonesia's most brilliant discovery. Ayah told me that his mother, my late grandmother, had been a skilled batik maker. To this day I am amazed at how a person with the use of just two fingers is able to create a painting so absolutely feminine on a stretch of cloth. When I was a little girl, Om Tjai once invited a batik artist to demonstrate her work at Tanah Air Restaurant. Every day after school, for the duration she was there, I would sit staring wide-eyed at the woman as she demonstrated her skills.

When Nara and I stepped into the portico of the residence where the ambassador and his wife were standing, we greeted the couple with a salaam, a quick rise of the hands, palms pressed together, our fingertips touching theirs. Because there were so many guests, I figured our hosts would not remember each and every one of the people they'd greeted. Inside the residence, we were greeted by a woman with a high bouffant who was dressed in a red *kebaya* and whose perfume was almost overpowering.

She motioned for us to proceed to the garden. "Go right in," the woman said to Nara. "You know your way to the buffet. But first tell me, who is this young woman with you? She's very lovely."

"Tante Sur, let me introduce you to Lintang," Nara said straight-away, quickly covering his gaffe in not having introduced me immediately.

"*Ayuneee.* Truly beautiful. New to Paris, is she? I must say you do have an eye for the girls," she said to Nara as if I had no ears. "Go in and help yourselves. There's goat satay, *gulai*, and lots of other food."

After saying that, this Tante Sur, who apparently was chair-woman or some such thing for the event's organizing committee, immediately rushed from our side to give orders to her various assistants and liveried servants. In the distance, through a set of double doors at the rear of the large hall, I could see a stage in the rear garden of the residence. Now I knew why the sound of the gamelan music was so clear. The music was live, coming from a complete gamelan orchestra, not from a cassette. On the stage was a dancer, performing a Balinese *pendet*, a ritual dance of welcome. I was just admiring the long buffet table heaped with enough food for at least a thousand guests, when two young men of about Nara's age came up to us. They shook Nara's hand and patted him on the shoulder. One of the two was looking at me so hard, I quickly pretended to be busy trying to choose what to drink from among the many choices. Did I want a lychee drink or *cendol* on shaved ice?

"Lintang, this is Yos," Nara said.

The man named Yos, who was dressed in a blue batik shirt, immediately shook my hand and broke into laughter. "No wonder you've never introduced us before. What a looker!" he said to Nara.

Yos continued to hold my hand as his eyes rolled upward in their sockets.

"And this handsome guy…"

"I'm Raditya," the man said, not giving Nara a chance to finish his introduction. "I'm single, not married, and don't have a girlfriend."

Raditya was the one who had been staring so intently at me. From his way of dressing—a suit coat and shirt but no tie—I guessed him to be a junior diplomat at the Indonesian embassy. My surprise and unease with the manners of Nara's two friends hadn't quite receded when three more of his male friends came up to us, all with broad smiles on their faces.

"Lintang, this is Hans. This good-looking guy is Iwan. And this big hunk of a man is Galih."

"Hans, why don't you get her something to drink?" This was Raditya giving orders. "What would you like?" he then asked me. "Orange juice? Or maybe *cendol* or a cold lychee drink?"

I didn't know how to react to this man's aggressive behavior. I looked to Nara for help, but he just rolled his eyes and smiled.

Hans then reappeared with a glass of cold orange juice and offered it to me.

"*Merci.*"

"*Tu es étudiante à la Sorbonne?*"

"*Oui*, I'm in my last year."

Yos stepped forward to nudge Hans aside.

"That's a very beautiful *kebaya*," he said, looking me up and down.

"Careful now, Yos," Nara cautioned, shaking his head. "It's my mother's; I don't have any of my own." I said with a smile to Nara, who I could see had begun to become irritated.

"Would you like to have some made? I know this seamstress, Bu Narni, who specializes in *kebaya*. She's the one behind most of the *kebaya* and *baju kurung* that the women here are wearing." Yos wasn't slowing down. "She's here tonight. Come on, I'll introduce you to her."

Hans now stepped in. "Don't listen to him, Lintang. He's married and has kids besides. But I'm still a bachelor and I promise always to be faithful."

Hans took my fingers and kissed the back of my hand. I turned to Nara who gave me a look of resignation, as if to say "What am I supposed to do?" It's true. It probably would have been useless for him to even try. For these friends of his, hitting on women was probably their only entertainment. Laughing loudly, they resembled a pack of male gorillas who'd never seen a female gorilla before.

It was at that moment that I realized something: this Kartini Day celebration had nothing whatsoever to do with Raden Ajeng Kartini or the ideals she expressed in her letters. Kartini Day was an excuse for people to get together and eat; for women to rat their hair and put on *kebaya*; and for men to show off their best batik shirts.

More than an hour had passed since we'd arrived at the residence, and not once in my conversation with other guests had anyone mentioned Kartini, that young woman from Jepara whose date of birth is one of Indonesia's most important days of commemoration. I began to ask myself if any of the other guests had even read Kartini's letters; her thoughts on the challenges to education for the native population in the colonial era were far advanced for the times.

Pretending to have to go to the ladies room, I placed my glass of orange juice on the table and left Nara's group of friends. As I was walking away, I let my eyes roam the garden. The *pendet* dancer had left the stage, and now there was being held a fashion show of sorts, with a number of very attractive Indonesian women showing off various kinds of *kebaya*. As fascinated as I was by the apparel, tonight I was far more interested in observing the guests—some of whom I could see were also studying me with a range of expressions on their faces. Some seemed to be trying to remember my face. Others stuck out their lower lips at my sight; but most gave me a friendly and welcoming smile, just as Nara's friends had done.

I was quite sure that most of the guests didn't recognize me and didn't know who I was. But I was also sure there were others who did and were whispering about me—that I was the daughter of Dimas Suryo, the Indonesian political exile who had found himself stranded in Paris and was never allowed to return home. When I went to take a glass of lychee and ice, I heard at my back a number of men engaged in a conversation about me. I kept my back to them and listened.

"Who the devil brought her here?"

"What does it matter? She's not her father."

"But have you forgotten government policy?"

"But that ban is for former political prisoners working as civil servants, or as teachers or journalists. What's the big deal about her coming to a party?"

"It's no big deal, but we did get that notice from Jakarta."

"What are you talking about?"

"That we're not to frequent Tanah Air Restaurant; that all the people there are communists."

"That's not what it said. It said…"

"What does it matter any way? What matters is the food and they have good *nasi kuning* and fried *sambal.*"

"The problem isn't about us going to Tanah Air Restaurant. The problem is that she's here and that, that she's…"

"That she's what?"

"That she's beautiful!"

At that point, I snuck away, distancing myself from the young diplomats busily debating my presence, unaware that I, the uninvited guest, was able to hear what they were saying. I safely returned to Nara's circle of friends, who were still razzing him.

Although I continued to find the behavior of Nara's friends

to be juvenile, after the conversation I had just overhead, I now enjoyed their japes and jibes. At the very least, they had accepted me into their presence without making an issue of my parentage. Furthermore, they didn't seem to care that my father was a political exile who was considered an enemy of the Indonesian government. But standing there, in the midst of all those people, I felt like there were hundreds of eyes staring at my back.

Across the garden I noticed a cluster of women with big hair and beautiful *kebaya* in conversation; they kept turning their heads to look in my direction. I felt incredibly thirsty. Not conscious of doing so, I had gulped down the entire contents of my glass of iced lychee. A few seconds later, Tante Sur with the red *kebaya* suddenly appeared and was standing beside Nara and taking his hand.

"Naraaaa," she said in a cooing tone. "Come with me, will you?" She then gave me a big smile. "I just need to borrow him for a second."

Ostensibly, Tante Sur wanted to talk to Nara about something in secret, but she only pulled him a couple meters from our circle and then spoke to him in a voice loud enough for the rest of us to hear.

"Where is your mother, Nara? Why didn't she come tonight?" Tante Sur pretended to whisper.

"She's with my father in Brussels, on business."

"Is that your girlfriend, Nara?"

"Yes, Tante, she is."

"Oh, not Sophie anymore?"

"Sophie…?"

I snuck a glance at Tante Sur. Her head was thrust towards Nara as if about to discuss a bank heist. "I was just talking to Om Marto, and he said your girlfriend is Dimas Suryo's daughter."

"That's right, Tante."

Restraining myself from turning to look at Nara and Tante Sur, I pretended to study the name cards Hans and Raditya had just given to me. Out of the corner of my eye, I saw Tante Sur do a double take.

"But, Nara," she said in the voice of a mother chastising her five-year-old son, "Om Marto mentioned the government's continued stress on the need for 'political hygiene.'"

Nara burst into laughter. I knew he was laughing at the euphemism the woman had used. The original Indonesian term, *bersih lingkungan*, could also be translated as "environmentally clean." The sound of his laughter was one of disgust.

"Excuse me, Tante Sur, but I really don't think that Om Marto or any of the other diplomats are going to be admonished because Lintang came to a *kebaya* fashion show held to commemorate Kartini Day. Enough said, Tante."

A few seconds later Nara was again at my side. He took the glass from my hand and put it on a side table, then took my arm and said that it was time to go home. I could see a look of anger on his face.

In the taxi on the way to my mother's apartment, where I was going to stay that night, Nara said almost nothing at all. When we arrived at my mother's apartment building and got out of the vehicle, we stopped and stood together on the sidewalk outside.

"Nara?"

He looked at me.

"That talk about '*bersih lingkungan*' and the need for political hygiene, is that some kind of rule set down in writing?"

Nara took a deep breath and shook his head. "I have no idea. What I do know is that it's the most discriminative regulation on earth."

Obviously, Nara was overstating the case. There were other regulations that were much more discriminatory—apartheid, for one—but Nara was angry, and his anger was natural, because someone had insulted his girlfriend.

As it had been some time since I had broken off communication with my father, I was not up to date either on developments in his life or in Indonesian political life. "I want to know for sure. I think I'll go to Beaubourg to find out."

"I doubt if you'll find much there," Nara said. "I'd be surprised if the Beaubourg had much stuff on regulations affecting former political prisoners or their families."

"Oh…" I didn't know what to say. I could feel my heart pounding.

Nara took my arm and walked me to the door.

"Coming in?" I asked.

"I'm sure your mother wants you to herself tonight. I'll just go home."

From the clutch bag I had also borrowed from mother, I removed two name cards and showed them to Nara.

"Hans and Raditya," I said with a laugh.

This time, Nara laughed along.

"They told me that if I wanted to go to Jakarta on a tourist visa that they'd be willing to help."

Nara smiled, now with a look of optimism on his face. "Not all the people at the embassy are cut from the same cloth. The younger ones, like those friends of mine, are very different in their thinking than the old-school diplomats."

I still hesitated to express my opinion on the subject of a "clean environment," the look on Tante Sur's face, and the opinions of the various diplomats and guests who were at the party. I was thinking of Professor Dupont's words about my father, and about history. That night I had been introduced to a part of Indonesia which was very different from the one I knew through Tanah Air Restaurant. Suddenly, having entered a long and dark tunnel into Indonesian history, I felt the need for a lighted candle. Just as suddenly, blood quickened in my veins. My chest pounded. The word "Indonesia"—I-N-D-O-N-E-S-I-A—suddenly became something of interest for me. I thought of Shakespeare and of Rumi.

How was I to pluck the meaning of Indonesia from the word "Indonesia"? The reaction of Tante Sur, she of the red *kebaya*, was one I had just come to know at a glance. What is the real Indonesia, I asked myself. Where is it? And where within it are my father, Om Tjai, Om Risjaf, and Om Nug?

I stroked Nara's chin and then kissed him on the lips. Delightfully surprised, he nestled his body closer to mine.

"What was that kiss for?" he asked.

"Because you are the angel who descended from heaven to save me."

And then I kissed him again.

L'IRRÉPARABLE

There once was what remained of a park
the place where we embraced.
("AFTERWORD," GOENAWAN MOHAMAD, 1973)

THE SOUND OF RAVEL'S "MIROIRS" was a constant in Lintang's apartment. Narayana knew very well that Ravel was always able to soothe Lintang's soul and heal her wounds. Nara took a video cassette and inserted it in the player As the video began to play, he saw the somewhat blurred image of a younger Dimas from ten or more years previously. Facing the lens, Dimas was giving instructions to the person holding the video camera.

"Don't come too close or you'll blur my face."

Dimas now stuck his head towards the lens to give instructions. The lens turned away from him. Only then Nara realized that the person who had been holding the camera was Lintang. Look at her, how young she is: only nine or ten years of age. But she was a beauty even then, this Eurasian girl with starry eyes.

"*Bonjour.* This camera is a gift from my *ayah*. Today is my birthday and I am, I am…"

"Ten years old!" came the sound of Dimas's voice, announcing his daughter's age.

Lintang giggled.

"Starting today, I am going to record…"

Lintang's small hands reached out to take the camera. Garbled images and sounds ensued as the camera moved hands. The next clear image was that of Vivienne sitting on a lawn chair beneath a tree. Her face had a weary look as she leaned against the back of the chair. Noticing the camera, she smiled and waved, but then she looked down, her lips stiff once more. Gloomy.

Narayana's forehead furrowed as he watched this fledgling documentary.

"It was around that time my parents began to argue a lot."

Lintang had suddenly appeared behind Narayana with two open bottles of beer in her hands. Nara grabbed one of the bottles and took a swig.

"Ayah bought a used video camera for me. A friend of his had several, and he bought one from him—but not all at once; he had to pay installments for months on end." Lintang sat down beside Nara on her threadbare sofa. As Nara pushed the pause button on the player, she stared at the image of her mother's face, frozen on the television screen. "Maman was not pleased with Ayah because their finances were so tight around that time."

"I'm sure she thought that you were too young," Nara quickly surmised.

For a moment, Lintang said nothing, then: "Later, of course, after she realized how much I loved film, she stopped complaining. But arguments between my parents always erupted whenever Ayah spent money on things Maman thought to be unnecessary."

Nara said nothing. And Lintang felt reluctant to talk about how a love as great as the one her parents shared could be riven by seemingly minor domestic issues. She thought of her father. How long had it now been since she had seen him?

As if reading her mind, Nara suggested, "You really should visit your father."

Perturbed by the thought, Lintang squeezed her eyes shut. "Nara,

Nara... Have you forgotten that dinner of ours together—that fucked up meal, the very worst dinner in my entire life?"

Nara laughed. "That was months ago! Besides, Lintang, it's in a father's nature to be protective of his daughter when he's introduced to the man she's now with."

Nara had already forgiven Lintang's father for his behavior the first time they'd met five months previously. It was Lintang who refused to compromise. The night of their first dinner together had been the breaker for her; she had decided then she would never again visit her father unless forced to.

BRUSSELS, OCTOBER 1994

When I first suggested to Nara that he meet my father, he immediately agreed and made arrangements for the three of us to meet over dinner at L'Amour, a favorite place of ours in Brussels where both food and art ruled. The first time we dined there was around the time we first began to date. If I had to list the five most unique restaurants I have ever visited, L'Amour would definitely be on the list. The restaurant resembled a cave, a real cavern, with walls constructed of what appeared to be mammoth stones and whose multi-colored tables and chairs—which had been imported from India and Egypt, we learned—also appeared to be made of stone. The menu was personal, planned and served according to a customer's wishes. The restaurant's lighting was minimal with almost no electric lights at all, except for a few small ones in the cave's recesses. Illumination was provided by candles, hundreds of them affixed to the walls of the cave throughout. Our first time there, I almost grew scared wondering if there was enough oxygen for us to breathe in that windowless place. But once that fear abated, we dissolved in the romantic atmosphere.

That said, and as much as I liked L'Amour, I didn't think it was the most appropriate place to invite Ayah to dinner or for the two of them to get to know each other—not because the restaurant was incredibly expensive, with a clientele made up primarily of well-heeled people from Brussels and Paris—but because I was sure that Ayah would find the place to be pretentious and a testimony to the class differences that had so marked his life. But Nara had chosen the place because that is where the Lafebvre family liked to celebrate special occasions—wedding anniversaries and birthdays, for instance—and that is where he had first kissed me.

I knew that for a man like my father, Dimas Suryo, who had come to France from a country in upheaval—a place called Indonesia which, for me, existed only in the imagination—L'Amour would come off as being no more than a primping room for members of the nouvelle bourgeoisie with an urgent need to show off their wealth, and pseudo-intellectuals with brains no bigger than peanuts.

I tried to explain all of this to my dearest Narayana as subtly as I could, but being both stubborn and naïve (at least in regard to my father), he resisted my suggestion and went ahead planning that first dinner with my father, full of love and attention. Meanwhile, I nervously wondered what my father's reaction would be.

The dress code at L'Amour required that male customers wear suit and tie—something my father never did unless absolutely forced to. That, I guessed would be a big problem. Then, too, I couldn't imagine him feeling comfortable beneath the fawning attention of the restaurant's beautiful waitresses or the haughty gaze of its handsome maître d'.

Remarkably, Ayah protested very little when I told him that he had to wear a suit. I knew that he was doing it for me.

That night, the two main men in my life looked handsome, a well-matched pair. My fingers were crossed that everything would work out all right. And I watched them intently as they adopted a polite attitude and began to engage each other in civilized conversation. It would be more accurate to say that Nara began the conversation. He began by telling Ayah of his visit to Jakarta the previous year. He spoke of the city's horrendous traffic conditions and how hot and humid the city felt. He talked about "Abimanyu Fallen," a dance-drama performance he had seen with his parents at the Jakarta Arts Building, and about developments in Indonesia's art world in general. More particularly, he talked about painting, whose popularity, he said, far surpassed that of other art forms.

Perhaps it was this talk about Jakarta, but Ayah suddenly seemed disinterested in Nara's explanation. He listened quietly, but offered almost no comment at all, as if unimpressed.

When the sommelier came to our table with the bottle of Saint-Émilion Bordeaux that Nara had ordered for our meal, Ayah accepted a glass and slowly took a sip.

"Expensive wine for a college student," he remarked.

Aha! The first of Ekalaya's arrows, shot straight at the target.

Nara smiled. "That's all right. This is a special occasion."

"What makes it special?"

Nara continued to smile and looked at me.

"Lintang is a very special woman."

Ayah stared at Nara like a tiger ready to pounce on a creature that had entered his domain.

"So, you're a student," Ayah said, "but do you also work part-time, like Lintang does at the library to earn enough money to cover her other expenses?"

The second arrow. But Narayana patiently continued to smile.

"No, sir. But during the summer two years ago I worked at my father's office."

"Must have been nice."

The third arrow, this one straight into the heart.

I stared at Ayah. What was he doing? Was it his goal to make the rest of my life miserable? Didn't he understand that Nara was the man I loved? The person who always put my happiness first?

Ayah grumbled about his tie and how it was strangling him. His eyes, a camera lens, panned the interior of the cave-like restaurant, scanning the reproductions of paintings around the room and the thick hanging plants suspended from the ceiling. What a mistake this was! Why had Nara invited him to Brussels, to this strange and expensive place?

"Why do we have to wear a suit in this cave? Why not costumes like on *The Flintstones?*"

Apparently thinking this was funny, Ayah chuckled to himself. I wanted to take the tub of butter the waiter had just set on the table and stuff it in my father's mouth.

Maybe because Nara did not react to his taunts, Ayah finally began to act more polite.

"So, Jakarta is chaotic, you say? I've heard all there is now are shopping malls. Is that true?" he asked as he cut his steak and broccoli.

"Yes, sir. But the thing is, there's no clear style of architecture. And not just the malls, but the toll roads that crisscross the city, which the children of the president own," Nara answered critically.

His answer appeared to appease Ayah somewhat. He looked at Nara and then at me with a friendlier light was in his eyes.

Nara might be from a wealthy family, but he wasn't stupid or ridiculous like many of the rich Indonesian kids I come to meet in Paris who drove Ferrari or Porsche cars to show off the fruits of their fathers' corruption.

"What with their fingers in businesses everywhere, I'd say Soeharto's children are the source of the problem," Ayah suggested.

"I was there in June last year, just at the time the government revoked the publishing licenses of those two news magazines and a newspaper. You heard about it, I'm sure. It really was quite the scene. People took their protests to Parliament and were demonstrating in the streets."

"I know, I follow the news," Ayah remarked. "It was an idiotic thing for the government to do. All it did was prove to everyone that the Soeharto regime continues to want absolute power."

I sensed Nara breathe a sigh of relief to see Ayah now acting in a more courteous manner. At the very least, he had smiled.

But, apparently, Ayah wasn't quite ready to give in so easily. His face grew serious again. Looking downward, as if to bury his face in the plate, he cut at his steak intensely. I knew the look on his face; it was the same one that appeared whenever Maman started to get on his back about their precarious financial situation.

I broached a different subject. "Nara likes to watch films."

"Of course he likes to watch films," Ayah snapped. "If you're a student of literature, you're going to be interested in theater, film, dance, and music as well. That's normal. It would be strange if he didn't," he added coldly.

I was getting the impression that the only reason my father had accepted Nara's invitation to come all the way to Brussels for this meal was to insult and hurt this rich kid's feelings. What he didn't seem to realize was that by hurting Nara, he was also hurting me, his own daughter.

The restaurant was getting busier and the music emanating from the piano and violins on the small stage in the corner of the cave made me want to cry.

"You're right, sir. A person has to choose the field he likes, but this is not a freedom all of our friends enjoy. Life makes its own choices." Nara continued to maintain a pleasant demeanor and friendly tone of voice. He must have wrapped his body in some kind of anti-bullet or anti-arrow armor. He seemed immune to all the negative energy being directed towards him, his body a shield that deflected the jousts aimed at him.

Ayah said nothing for a moment. Maybe it had begun to dawn on him that Nara was, in fact, an intelligent person.

"What films do you like?" he asked in a warmer tone of voice.

"Well, one of my all-time favorites is *Throne of Blood*. It's amazing how Kurosawa was able to reinterpret *Macbeth* the way he did. I had no idea that Shakespeare could be adapted to fit in with Japanese artistic traditions."

Ayah cut another piece of meat from his steak before answering, but then nodded. "*Throne of Blood* is a great film," he finally consented with a grunt.

"It's Kurosawa's interpretation of Lady Macbeth that really floored me," I said, joining the conversation. "The soliloquy she delivers while seated, with her eyes fixed straight ahead as she speaks her poisonous words... Just incredible!"

"But you like *Rashomon* and *Seven Samurai* better," Ayah stated as a truth before turning to Nara. "When Lintang was small, we used to go to film retrospectives in the park at the Domaine de Saint-Cloud," he added in an aside.

"I know that, sir. Lintang has told me about all the films she's seen," Nara said with a smile as he squeezed my hand in his.

Wrong move. I could see it in my father's eyes. His smile vanished.

The plates had been cleared away. Dessert arrived, but Ayah declined the offer and ordered coffee instead. I asked for mint tea. The waiter brought to the table several stems of mint arranged like a miniature tree in a pot. I had only to pick the leaves, rinse them in a small receptacle of water, and then submerge them in a cup of hot water. As he followed this process and the movement of my hands with his eyes, Ayah kept shaking his head. It was obvious that bringing such a cynical man as my father to this place had been a very bad idea.

I tried to bridge the looming silence. "Nara is one of the few men I know—aside from you, Ayah—who actually likes to read poetry," I said.

"Really?" Ayah asked with a tone of disbelief. Again his eyes scanned the interior of the restaurant with its hundreds of candles. "Whose works do you like?"

Nara wiped his lips with his napkin and slowly recited the lines of a poem: "When in disgrace with fortune and men's eyes / I all alone beweep my outcast state / and trouble deaf heaven with my bootless cries…"

"Shakespeare, huh?" Ayah took a breath. "But why did you choose 'Sonnet 29'?"

Nara said nothing. My heart beat faster.

Ayah set down his coffee cup on its saucer, then looked into Nara's eyes as if he were seeking some kind of truth. Ayah contended that a person's honesty could be seen in his eyes. Even the smallest of falsehoods could be detected in a person's downward glance or a timorous shade in his eyes. Ayah was confident of his ability to judge a person's character merely by the light in that person's eyes. He always frightened me by his ability to do so.

"When I think of that sonnet," Ayah said, "the picture that comes to my mind is of a young aristocrat who was born into wealth but is now depressed because he has fallen into poverty. He covets the things that other people own: 'Desiring this man's art and that man's scope…' The sonnet is well written, with a good choice of words, but its message is conveyed though the figure of a spoiled young man."

Ayah glanced at Nara as he said this.

This time Nara's reserve of patience seemed to be depleted. But he was not a person who easily angered, and he held his tongue.

"Nara likes Indonesian poetry too," I put in.

"Especially Subagio Sastrowardoyo," Nara said. "There's one collection of his that never fails to move me…"

Nara spoke softly, as if worried that he was about to be clapped like a mosquito. Ayah stopped drinking his coffee and stared at Nara, but didn't ask what book Nara was referring to.

Suddenly, they both said at once: "*And Death Grows More Intimate.*"

Although their chorus had been coincidental, I felt relieved. "I'll have to read it again!" I remarked enthusiastically, feeling that the shadow of a white flag had fallen between them.

"I'll bring the book for you tomorrow," Nara cheerfully told me.

I wondered if the source of his good cheer was my enthusiasm or the perception that he might have finally gotten an edge on my father; but then Ayah suddenly returned the conversation to enemy terrain.

"You can have my copy. It's on the bookshelf. Second rack down from the top, on the far left."

There was no sound of friendliness in Ayah's voice. Then he

immediately pushed back his chair and stood up, a sign that our dinner together was over. It was going to be a very long drive back to Paris.

•

The next day I went to Ayah's apartment for the sole purpose of berating him for his behavior the night before. His apartment, a small one in the Marais, with just one bedroom, a living room, and a tiny kitchen, was where he had lived since separating from Maman. His bedroom, though, was relatively large—at least compared to the living room. Apart from his bed, the room contained several free-standing shelves stuffed with books and a desk with a typewriter that faced the window.

The living room might better be described as a library, because all four walls were covered with bookshelves, and in its center was a sofa and two chairs, as if it were a reading room. Only a small bit of wall remained visible and that is where there hung two shadow puppets, Bima and Ekalaya, the two characters that had always served Ayah as his role models. On one of the shelves, in the middle of a row of books, were two sacred apothecary jars. The one jar was filled almost to the top with cloves. The other jar held turmeric powder. These two jars had been one of the reasons behind the argument that took place between Maman and Ayah on the night they separated.

"Hello. What's up?" Ayah said, looking at me over the top of his glasses as he came out of the bedroom.

I had already decided that I wasn't going to stay long, so I remained standing, my heart suddenly quivering with anger. "Ayah, Nara invited you to dinner to get to know you, not to be insulted," I told him straightaway.

Ayah took off his glasses and frowned with surprise. I couldn't believe it. He was surprised that I was angry? He told me to sit down, but I remained on my feet. I didn't want to get caught there.

"Insult Nara? Who insulted whom?"

"You had to find something wrong in everything he said and did: his choice of restaurant, his choice of films, even his choice of poems!"

"He's pretentious!" Ayah barked impatiently, as if he had forcibly refrained from expressing his true opinion about Nara the night before. "He's a rich bourgeois kid used to getting anything he wants without working for it, whether it's a car or eating in the most expensive bistro in Europe. If he wanted to meet me, why did we have to go all the way to Brussels? Wouldn't you call that pretentious?"

This was the first time I began to suspect the real reason why Maman had been unable to remain married to Ayah. How could she have endured living with a man who always had to criticize everything that was wrong in his eyes?

"I'm not faulting Nara for having the good fortune to be the son of a man who got his wealth from hard work. I'm just not interested in pretense. His choice to recite lines from 'Sonnet 29' was such a cliché." He paused before adding, "Sure he's good-looking and a smooth talker, too—but what is it you like about him?" Now he was being saracastic.

"I like being with him and his family. *Une famille harmonieuse!* They are kind and welcoming to everyone they meet. I feel comfortable when I am with them."

"What I asked you," Ayah stressed, "is what you like about him, not about his family."

Now Ayah had gone too far. "I don't want to be like you,"

I spat. "You're never happy. You're never thankful for the things you own. I don't want to be like you, always cynical about other people's happiness."

As these spiteful words spilled from my lips, tears fell from my eyes in a torrent. Ayah looked at me, speechless, as if not comprehending the meaning of my accusations.

"I don't want to be trapped by the past! And not just by your political past, Ayah, but by your personal life either."

Ayah seemed shocked by what I'd just said. But I left him standing there in silence. I saw the hurt that was in his eyes, but I didn't care. That night Paris was no longer the City of Light. Paris had turned into a dark and gloomy place, because that was the night I decided to break off communications with my father.

•

Lintang leaned her head against the arm of the sofa and lifted her legs to the cushion. Sometimes she didn't know where she was supposed to put her long legs and arms. By Indonesian standards, she was fairly tall, almost 170 centimeters. Her physique had clearly come from the Deveraux family. Anyone looking at her would immediately see her to be the spitting image of her mother—except for her black hair, that is, which came from her father, and the dark brown color of her eyes, which came from him as well. Otherwise, almost everyone said of Vivienne and Lintang that they looked like two very beautiful sisters, even when neither was wearing makeup. Lintang once told Nara that what made her different from her mother was that her mother was raised in a happy, normal, well-balanced family. Her mother had had a harmonious family life. Nara pointed out that another similarity between them was their amazing aptitude for languages.

Aside from French, Vivienne was fluent in English and Indonesian. And Lintang, even at an early age, was able to speak unaccented English and Indonesian with fluency and ease—a rare gift in France.

Nara pushed the play button, and the images Lintang had recorded in the past began to flash by again. He was now able to see that the images were a kind of record, not just of the times and places in Lintang's life, but of her progression in the mastery of film. He noted that over time the recorded images gained greater focus and cohesion: Canal St. Martin, Notre Dame, Musée Picasso, up to the Cimetière du Père Lachaise.

"And that's why finding you is so easy when you're down," Nara said with a fond smile. "You always end up at Père Lachaise Cemetery!"

"*Irréparable*," Lintang muttered.

Nara pressed the pause button and looked into Lintang's eyes. "What can't be fixed?"

On the screen was the image of Oscar Wilde's tomb: elegant and flamboyant, but nonetheless an attempt to eternalize something that was already gone.

"After months of me having to listen to Maman and Ayah's endless fights, Ayah finally left."

Though Lintang's eyes were fixed on the screen, her thoughts were in the past.

"What did you mean by your father's past personal life?" Nara asked cautiously.

"There's something I still haven't told you," said Lintang to him.

Nara stared at Lintang with no force in his eyes.

Lintang then told him about a time in the past when she had inadvertently discovered a letter her father had written but which he had never sent. She had read the letter, which was addressed to a woman by the name of Surti Anandari. Years on, she could still vividly recall the letter's intimate tone and how bewildered this had made her feel. She had given a stack of her father's letters to her mother and that was the start of an unending argument between her parents.

"That night, Ayah came into my room and gave me a big long hug. After that, he left taking with him just a small bag with just a knapsack on his back. For the longest time after that, I blamed myself for their divorce. If I hadn't found that letter, Ayah and Maman would still be together."

"It wasn't your fault, Lintang," Nara said, stroking hers cheek. "I'm sure they already had issues you knew nothing about. The letter was just a trigger."

Lintang remembered looking out the window to see her father's back as he walked away from the apartment building. Every evening thereafter, she still set three plates on the table at dinner time. She missed her father's fried rice with its scent of cooking oil laced with onions. But she always ended the night by returning his unused plate back to the cupboard.

Finally, after a few months, unable to bear her daughter setting three plates on the table for dinner, her mother could do nothing else but tell her daughter the truth.

"Your father's and my relationship is *irréparable*," she said. "Forgive me, Lintang."

Lintang continued to hold her father's blue plate. Staring wordlessly at her mother, she pressed the blue plate tightly against her chest. But once she was sure that her mother was not going to add anything more to her pronouncement, she put her father's plate on the table, as if nothing had happened.

She wiped away a tear drop that had fallen onto her father's plate. Vivienne said nothing.

Lintang looked at Nara. Only now, after all these years, did she finally realize what it was that was missing in her life: it was her father's past life, the part of his life she had never known.

The telephone rang and then rang again. Lintang was reluctant to pick up the receiver but finally did. Her mother.

"*Oui*, Maman…"

Nara noted the look of seriousness that suddenly appeared on Lintang's face. She talked to her mother for quite some time. Finally, after she had replaced the receiver, he asked, "What happened?"

"Ayah collapsed at the Metro station a few days ago. He was taken to the hospital and put through a series of tests."

"And what were the results?"

Lintang shook her head. "Ayah has yet to pick them up. That's why the hospital called Maman."

Lintang knew the time had come for her to put differences aside and go to see her father

EKALAYA

THERE WAS SOMETHING ABOUT MY FATHER and his relationship with Indonesia I had always wanted to know. It wasn't about the country's blood-filled history or the problems affecting the lives of Indonesian political exiles as they roamed the world in search of a country willing to receive them. There was something that made my father extra sensitive to rejection, which I became aware of, little by little, because of his obsession with the story of Ekalaya he often told to me.

Up until when I was ten years old, my parents and I had a ritual we always went through as summer approached. The sun in late May is a friendly creature, not the angry monster it can become in June or the months that follow. And every year, at that time, we would fall in love once more with the Parisian sky, which seemed close enough for us to touch.

Ayah and Maman would take me to Domaine National de Saint-Cloud, the large park on the outskirts of Paris. For our personal comfort, as we waited to watch the films shown there—*un cinéma en plein air*—we'd bring with us knapsacks filled with blankets and books and a hamper of food and canned refreshments. As Ayah and Maman had begun this tradition when I was just a baby, these outings became something I looked forward to each year. It wasn't until years later I came to realize that this custom hadn't evolved simply from the pleasure we found in watching film retrospectives in the open air, but also because this form of entertainment cost my parents almost nothing.

On the blanket that Maman spread out on the park lawn, we'd lie on our backs, staring at the sky above. Another hour to go before the film began. Would the film tonight be one by Federico Fellini or Akira Kurosawa? Or maybe Woody Allen? Even when I was in primary school, my parents had me watching the classics of cinema—which until today remain clearly in my head. But the most pleasurable time of those evenings was when we, the three of us, would let our imaginations fly. I can see our hands raised upward, our grasping fingers trying to clutch the sky as we imagined a throne room and other such things up there. And I can hear Ayah relating stories that he plucked from the *Mahabharata* and the *Ramayana*, the two sources of almost all stories in the shadow puppet theater. Looking back, I guess that had been his way of trying to familiarize me with all things Indonesian—though he did explain that most of the stories had originally come to Indonesia from India. Through his repeated tellings, a number of *wayang* characters came to hold a special place in my heart. Two of them were Srikandi from the *Mahabharata* and Candra Kirana from the story of *Panji Semirang.* My choice of favorite characters seemed to surprise my father.

"Why Srikandi?" he asked.

"It's like, in the story, she's searching for the right body for herself."

"And what about Panji Semirang?"

"He is looking for his identity."

I noted the surprised look my parents gave each other.

"It's interesting that you've chosen characters who change their gender," Ayah said, not judgmentally. He seemed curious as to why

I had chosen those two figures.

I was only ten years old at that time, and maybe my answers sounded too precocious, but it truly was because Srikandi and Panji Semirang were able to change their gender that they attracted me. For me, the rules of the game in the world of *wayang* were as complex as they were baffling: imagine being able to switch genders back and forth! Ayah said my choices might be an indication of the kind of person I would become.

That night, after we were home and as I was beginning to fall asleep, I overheard my parents talking about our conversation in the park. My father said that he felt guilty, that I had probably chosen characters who were in search of their identity because he himself suffered from an identity crisis. She must be asking: who am I, an Indonesian who has never been to Indonesia, or a French person who happens to be half Indonesian?

Maman placated Ayah by telling him that she was sure I liked those two female characters because they were strong and their stories were action-filled, something that children always liked.

I found Ayah's hunch to be the more interesting. He himself always said that his favorite *wayang* characters were Bima and Ekalaya from the *Mahabharata*. At first, I guessed that he liked Bima because the character was the epitome of masculinity: big and tall, strong and protective. But the fact was, he was attracted to Bima because of his faithfulness to Drupadi, the woman who—in the Indian version of the *Mahabharata,* at least—became the wife of all five Pandawa brothers. Bima's devotion to Drupadi was even greater than that of Yudhistira, the eldest of the five brothers. It was Bima who defended Drupadi's dignity when she was insulted by the Kurawa cousins at the time the Pandawa brothers had lost a bet with their cousins at a game of dice.

"It was Bima who protected Drupadi the many times that other men tried to force themselves on her during the twelve years the Pandawa brothers were forced to live in the forest," said Ayah, with his lively interpretation.

"So why Ekalaya?" I asked.

"Because only he was able to match Arjuna's skill with the bow—even without having studied under Resi Dorna.

According to Ayah, the lesson we find in the tale of Ekalaya is that a person is able to attain perfection of knowledge on his own accord, without having to study under someone. Ekalaya achieved his goal because of the strength of his commitment and will. Of course, the story actually begins with Ekalaya wanting to master the use of the bow and arrow beneath the tutorship of Resi Dorna. The arrow... What a unique and extraordinary weapon. So simple: just a rod, straight and thin, but with a sharpened tip capable of piercing the heart of its target. Arrows appear in some of my favorite stories; those from the *Mahabharata* and in films by Akira Kurosawa. But Ayah was frugal in sharing the story of Ekalaya with me. He waited for the right time.

I remember when I was little, Ayah received a package from his brother, my uncle Aji. In it were the two shadow puppets: Bima and Ekalaya. Ayah's eyes glistened with joy as he removed them from their box and found a place for them to hang them on the wall in the living room. He kept saying how difficult it was to find an Ekalaya puppet, because he was not one of the main characters in the Indonesian *Mahabharata*. Ayah guessed that Om Aji could only have found the puppet in some out-of-the-way and forgotten corner of Solo.

Often, while waiting for the Saturday evening film to start at Domaine de Saint-Cloud, we'd talk about stories from the shadow theater, mostly ones from the Indian-based *Ramayana* and *Mahabharata* but also ones from the Panji cycle, tales that were indigenous to Java. The sky overhead became a huge shadow screen. With his low but soft and velvety voice, Ayah became the *dalang,* the shadow master extemporaneously reciting a section from the *Mahabharata.* Ayah was very good at playing with his deep and heavy voice. If he had ever wanted to, I'm sure he could have been a *dalang* or a singer.

Except for a few brief demonstrations at Nara's home and at Tanah Air Restaurant, I've never seen a real *wayang orang* performance, where, in a reversal of what is normally the case in live theater, people play the roles of puppets and not the other way around; but when I was young I always enjoyed it when Ayah mimicked the basso profundo voice used by the character of Bima on the *wayang orang* stage. He often used that same technique to dissipate tension in the air when Maman was irritated with him. Like in the mornings, for instance, when he'd make fried rice. Almost every morning, before Maman left home to teach, Ayah would prepare a breakfast of fried rice for us—"special fried rice," he called it, because of the shredded omelet he always put on top. Maman always grumbled at the sight because, like most French people, she thought fried rice was much too heavy a morning meal. But Ayah always ignored her. Switching his voice back and forth, he'd make up a conversation between Bima and Ekalaya, as he tickled Maman's neck. No matter how hard she tried to maintain the scowl on her face, Maman would finally break into laughter and then join us in eating a plate of Ayah's fried rice: hot and tasty to the tongue and rich from the oil he'd used to fry the rice. Ayah always like to make his fried rice with *minyak jelantah,* oil which had already been used to fry something else, shallots and onions, for instance, so that their taste, too, was imparted in the rice.

That evening, I succeeded in coaxing Ayah to reveal Ekalaya's tale.

And so it was, one dark night that was blacker than a night, with no moon, Resi Dorna went into the forest pervasive with the scent of lotus. Suddenly, a young man of exceptionally dark skin appeared as if out nowhere, stopping the teacher in his tracks, and startling him with the light that shone from his eyes.

"Who are you, young man?" Resi Dorna asked.

The younger man was very tall and fit, his body all muscle and dark pliant skin. With a poised movement, he bowed deeply before the elderly man.

"Resi Dorna, teacher of all teachers, I am Ekalaya, the son of Hiranyadanush…" Impatiently interrupting the young man's introduction, which he expressed in a slow and measured pace, Resi Dorna said, "Go on, go on, young man. What is it?"

With his hands still raised in a sembah sign of obeisance, Ekalaya stated his desire to study under Resi Dorna, who was known throughout the universe for his mastery of the bow.

Not waiting even one second to answer, Resi Dorna said that it would be impossible for him to be his guru, because his teaching and mentorship skills were reserved exclusively for the sons of Kuru. What Dorna didn't say is that he wanted his favorite warrior pupil, Arjuna, to hold the title of best bowman in the world. But Ekalaya would not back down. Before him stood the master who he had long vowed would be his guru. He could not let Dorna leave him without obtaining from him some form of consent.

"Guru…"

"I am not your guru."

"For this humble servant, you will always be my guru. I beg of you to grant your servant's request."

Ekalaya bowed at Resi Dorna's feet. As he did this, his long and loosened hair fell forward, brushing the elderly man's toes and causing him to finally feel the sincerity of the young man's plea.

He stroked Ekalaya's head. "All right then, my son, I shall grant your wish."

Fireworks exploded in Ekalaya's eyes. His happiness was so real, he kissed Dorna's feet and then ran off shouting through the forest. He cried to all of nature that one day he would be the best bowman in the world.

Dorna watched the young man with a slight but distinct feeling of unease. What might transpire in the future, he wondered, as a result of his rashness in granting the wishes of a young man, a stranger to him, who had suddenly appeared before him in the forest?

"And then what happened?" I asked, because Ayah had paused for such a long time.

"Shush, the film is about to begin."

Ayah turned his head and pointed to the other film-goers who were preparing their blankets on the ground. As twilight fell on Domaine de Saint-Cloud, Akira Kurosawa's *Seven Samurai* began to play on the large outdoor screen. Usually, this was the time I had been waiting for, this shared time of easy intimacy with my parents as we snuggled together between blankets. Maman always brought an extra blanket with her to these viewings, because lying on the ground, close together in the open air, was something the Dimas Suryo family always did. We felt as one together. Warm and close.

To this day Kurosawa's *Seven Samurai* and *Rashomon* are for me two of the best films ever made. Between childhood and the time I enrolled at the Sorbonne, I must have watched *Rashomon* eight times, and at least four of those times with my parents. At each viewing, my father always said the same thing: "Everyone has his own version of history."

When I was older, I often fantasized about Akira Kurosawa being entrusted to adapt the *Mahabharata* to screen, as he had done with *King Lear* and *Macbeth*, transforming them into distinctly Japanese films. As an adolescent I also watched and came to love the works of Federico Fellini and Jean-Luc Godard; but for me their films could never compare with shadow tales from the *Mahabharata,* the *Ramayana,* and *Panji Semirang.* In *wayang* tales there are always unexpected surprises—which is why, when Ayah stopped telling me the story of Ekalaya before it was finished, I was unable to concentrate on watching *Seven Samurai.*

As soon as the film was over, we dug into the hamper Maman had brought along containing food Ayah had prepared: *nasi kuning,* tiny potato sticks seasoned with chili, and dried *rendang.* Usually after a film, it being late in the evening, I was so hungry that I wouldn't speak until I had gobbled all my food. But that night, even with my mouth full, I tried to force Ayah to finish the story of Ekalaya. He resisted my pleas, saying that he wouldn't tell me the rest until after he'd finished his meal. He chewed his rice slowly as if he had all the time in the world ahead of him. Meanwhile, I hurriedly finished my rice, expecting that Ayah would take notice and heed my wishes. And, after ever so long, he finally did…

Years passed, and after the five Pandawa brothers and their one hundred Kurawa cousins reached adulthood, the third brother,

Arjuna, came to be the best bowman in the entire universe, just as it had been foretold. No one could deny this; no one could challenge him. From every shooting contest, large or small, Arjuna always emerged victorious.

And so it was, one day, in a forest sprinkled with the color of lavender because of the many purple flowers growing there, Arjuna, Bima, and their group of hunters espied a deer in the distance. Arjuna was just preparing to shoot his arrow when, suddenly, a sharp series of sounds was heard—Whack! Whack! Whack! Whack! Whack!—that came in impossibly rapid succession.

At almost the same instant, five arrows impaled themselves into the heart of the unlucky deer, killing it immediately. It was not only Arjuna's courtiers who shook their heads in wonder; no one was more surprised or chagrined than Arjuna, the world's best bowman. He asked himself who could possibly kill a deer with such expertise and with no less than five arrows in the deer's heart. All the knights and jesters and, even more so, Arjuna, knew very well that a person who could shoot five arrows directly into the heart of a deer was someone to be reckoned with.

After calming his breathing, Bima finally asked his brother Arjuna the question on everyone's mind: "Who shot those arrows? Did Resi Dorna follow us? Might our guru be testing us?"

Bima's questions were meant to console Arjuna, who was now intensely disappointed to have discovered that there was in this world a better bowman than he. If that man were Resi Dorna, Arjuna reasoned, that would be acceptable, for Resi Dorna was their teacher, after all.

*The bushes moved. Without a smile widening his face,
Arjuna's mien looked long—as well as clouded and dark from
jealousy. He was sure the bowman was not Resi Dorna; his
guru would not have devised such a test. It had to be another
warrior.*

*Arjuna followed the rustling movement of the bushes. When
he parted the bush with his arms, he saw before him a towering man with a bow and arrows. The man's skin glistened in
the sunlight. Arjuna was again surprised and his heart flamed
hotter with jealousy. Who was this man with the dark and
gleaming skin? From whence had he gained his mastery with
the bow and arrow?*

*"Who are you?" asked Bima, who was now standing at
Arjuna's back.*

"I am Ekalaya from the clan of Hiranyadanush."

*Arjuna leaned forward, breathing in gusts: "And where did
you learn to shoot like that?"*

*With his eyes full of stars, Ekalaya answered, "From Resi
Dorna."*

All the trees in the forest shook with Arjuna's cries of anger.

Ayah stopped speaking.

"So, was Ekalaya lying?" I demanded to know.

"No, he was not. What he had done was this: he'd made an
effigy of Resi Dorna to which he bowed every day before his
practice. Even though he trained himself to shoot, he felt that
Dorna's spirit and soul had entered him through the effigy that he
had created; it was this that had made him succeed in becoming
a better bowman than Arjuna."

I stopped to think. I knew for sure that the story didn't end there, because in the *Mahabharata,* Arjuna was always referred to as the best bowman in the universe. What happened to Ekalaya?

"Arjuna whined and complained to Dorna. And Dorna, who was surprised to discover that someone had been able to learn from him at a distance, without ever having studied with him face to face, went to find Ekalaya. Dorna was astonished and proud, but then rankled, too, because he knew he had to do something to stop Arjuna from bellyaching like a spoiled brat."

Ayah's voice grew louder, as if he were angry. I wondered why.

"As was the custom, after a guru has transferred his knowledge to a student, there is a kind of handing-over ceremony called a *guru-dakshina.*"

"A *guru-dakshina*? What happens there?" I asked.

"During such a ceremony, the student must present to his teacher something the teacher has requested as a formal sign that his lessons are now complete."

"And did Resi Dorna ask for something from Ekalaya?" I asked, trying to guess what it was.

"Yes, he did," Ayah said with a tremble in his voice.

"What was it?" I then asked.

"Dorna asked Ekalaya to give him the thumb of his right hand."

For a few moments I said nothing; but then I was shocked when I realized that for a bowman a steady thumb is indispensible. And Ekalaya, obedient student that he was, willingly fulfilled Dorna's request and immediately cut off his thumb. Even though, thereafter, he could still use his bow with four fingers, he was never again the expert bowman that he had been. And Arjuna returned to the perch from which he had been removed, as the best bowman in the entire universe.

•

We liked to frequent a used book kiosk owned by Antoine Martin, a retired policeman, who was one of my parents' favorite book suppliers. Whenever we went there, we would scrounge around until we found one or two books of interest. They were extremely cheap, almost free. If we had a little extra money to spend, we might stop at Shakespeare & Co., which was one of my favorite haunts and that of many famous writers and artists as well. Every time we wandered into the store, my father—just like a tourist guide—would point out the chair in which Ernest Hemingway had always sat, where he would leaf through books, one after another, and then borrow some to take home from Sylvia Beach, the store's founder and owner.

"That's because Hemingway was poor, too. Just like me!" Ayah would say with a touch of pride. Then he'd show me that corner of the store where James Joyce and Ezra Pound often held discussions. When I was older, in my early teens, I came to realize that Ayah knew about these things from the photographs of writers that were scattered throughout the store in open spaces on the walls. By the time I was in high school, I had memorized which famous writers had left their mark in that small and cluttered but historic bookstore. Maybe because of all the history associated with the store, whenever Ayah had friends come to Paris—usually Indonesian exiles from Amsterdam, The Hague, Leiden, Berlin, and Bonn—he would invite them to visit the store. They were happy to do so, because Shakespeare & Co. was one of the few bookstores in Paris that sold English-language books, and also because there they could sit around in the store discussing how the city's intellectuals, journalists, and creative writers in the 1920s debated among themselves about the "Great War" that had just passed.

Maybe that was also why I grew up with a great feeling of respect for history.

So, when I was younger, the days I spent with my parents watching films and looking for books at Shakespeare & Co. were among the most pleasurable ones for me. Though I always wanted to fill an entire shopping bag with books when we went out exploring, my parents usually let me buy only one new book from Shakespeare & Co. and two used books from Antoine Martin's kiosk. In time, however, I found that even these conservative purchases could be a source of trouble.

I remember one bright Saturday morning very clearly when I heard Maman whisper to Ayah that we needn't go to any bookstore that day. And then Ayah whispering back that it was possible for us to visit a bookstore without buying anything at all. What's going on, I wondered. Didn't they have any money?

I passed that Saturday morning with feigned cheer. I put on a happy face but was anxious, nonetheless. Around midday, after Ayah had prepared fried noodles for us to take along to eat on the day's exploration tour—Ayah's fried noodles was another one of my favorite foods and more appealing to me than any normal French food—we headed off to Shakespeare & Co.

At the store, when Ayah was delving into books of poetry, I discovered a copy of *Le Petit Prince*, the book by Antoine de Saint-Exupéry I had long wanted to own. The book's colored illustrations—an elephant inside a snake, baobab trees, the Little Prince on a distant planet—were wonderful. And now having the book in my hand, I didn't want to let it go.

My cousin Marie-Claire, who was in my class, already owned the book and had told me all about it. But because the book was

new and in hard cover with color illustrations —which meant that
it was expensive and likely beyond my parents' means—Maman
told me to put the book back in its place on the shelf. I refused.

"Please, Maman. I've wanted it now for so long. I want to fly
like *Le Petit Prince*," I said, trying to keep from crying.

The next words she spoke were said in a loud and staccato
voice: "Lin-tang. *Remet-le.* Right now!"

Trying to hold back my tears as best I could, I returned the
book to its place on the shelf. But just as I was doing that, I caught
sight of another book, *The Mahabharata,* a condensed version of
the story by R.K. Narayan. *O, mon Dieu!* Excited by the find,
I hesitated, not knowing what to do. With a trembling hand, and
stealing a glance at my mother, who was standing near the front
door with an annoyed look on her face, I removed the book
from the shelf. As I quickly leafed through the book, the names
"Shrikand" and "Ekalavya" jumped out at me. Taking the book,
I then went to find Ayah in the poetry section. On the edge of tears,
I whispered to him how much I wanted to own the book. Afraid
that my tears might damage the book's cover, I hastily wiped my
cheeks with the sleeve of my blouse. No more than five seconds
passed before Ayah had taken the book from me and paid for it
at the cash register. Maman said nothing; she only blinked, but
I could guess what would happen later.

Throughout the walk home, the two of them trained their
eyes in opposite directions. I knew that no amount of fried rice
the next morning, no matter how good it tasted, would be able
to make them smile or to laugh at the silliness of their behavior.

There was something much deeper going on than just the issue
of Ayah's purchase of *The Mahabharata*, which I read from cover to
cover that very same night. Starting then, I realized that Ayah and

Maman were faced with a much larger problem, one that I would never know because, as Maman often said to me about friends of theirs: "It's useless to even try to pretend to know or understand what goes on between a husband and wife. Only they know what problems are affecting them."

When I read Ekalaya's story, at the moment he cut off his thumb to obey Dorna's wishes, I started to cry and couldn't stop. At my age of just ten years, I didn't know that I was crying because I sensed somehow that I was facing a loss as great as that of Ekalaya; or possibly that I suddenly had a premonition that my days of watching films with Ayah and Maman in the open air were coming to an end. A winter's wind was coming which, blowing between them, was turning everything cold as ice.

•

Only a few months after my parents separated, I began to sense that there was "something" between my father and Indonesia that could never be replaced by anything or anyone. It was around then that I also came to know that he had for years, on a routine annual basis, submitted an application to the Indonesian embassy for a visa to enter Indonesia. A tourist visa, of course. By this time, as a permanent political exile, Ayah—like his three friends—had obtained a French passport. But unlike Om Risjaf, who in some magic way managed to obtain a visa to enter Indonesia, my father's requests, and those of Om Nug and Om Tjai as well, were always rejected.

The officials at the Indonesian embassy never gave a reason for their rejection. Nor did they explain why Om Risjaf was being treated differently even though he, too, had been among those whose passports had been revoked when they were in Havana.

Every time he learned that his visa applications had been rejected, Ayah would take Ekalaya from his place on the wall and play with the puppet. He'd go off by himself, to sit alone in his room and read old letters, from whom I didn't know—a personal territory I did not want to know. When that happened, if it happened when I was spending the night at Ayah's, I would try, as best as I could, to open for him a space in myself in which to store his sadness.

It was later still that I came to understand that there was something in the character of Ekalaya that gave Ayah the strength to survive. After having at first been rejected by Dorna, Ekalaya had found his own way to study with the teacher. Every day, prior to his practice, this noble knight would bow before his teacher—even on that final day of instruction when the duplicitous Dorna asked Ekalaya for his thumb, which he willingly gave. Ekalaya knew that regardless of Dorna's rejection, the world of bowmen would accept him. He was, after all, the best bowman in the entire universe—even if in the *Mahabharata* Dorna had awarded this title to Arjuna, his personal favorite. Ayah knew that even if the Indonesian government rejected him, he was not being rejected by his country. It was not his homeland rejecting him. And that is the reason he stored a pile of cloves in the one large apothecary jar and several handfuls of turmeric in the other one that sat on the bookshelf in his living room. From them emitted the scent of Indonesia.

Around the time I was twelve, after all the visa rejections, the clove-smelling ceremonies, and Ayah's repeated reenactment of Ekalaya's tale, I had to conclude that Ayah was Ekalaya. He might be rejected, but he would survive even if his steps were marked by wounds and blood.

LE COUP DE FOUDRE...Who believes in *le coup de foudre*? Love at first sight is a romantic phrase held dear to the heart by those same people who think that Paris, City of Light, has a never-ending supply of *amour*.

I was born into the family of Laurence and Marianne Deveraux. My father is a man who believes in reason and that life ends when the heart stops beating and the oxygen tube for artificial resuscitation is removed. All those stories about life after death were, for my family, a romantic notion on the part of people who believe that humans are immortal beings. Such people want to extend life, something that is, by nature, finite. They don't want the thread of life to be broken or for it to end in uncertainty. I believed then, and I believe now, that life is transitory, that it will end one day. My family were deviants among the Deveraux clan, Roman Catholics mostly who spent their Sundays going to church and sharing a communal meal.

Given this way of thinking among my immediate family, people who lived and worked for the day, I obviously did not believe in *le coup de foudre*. How could you fall in love with a person you'd only just met? Or someone whose eyes you'd only just seen? Not likely. *Jamais!*

According to Indonesians I later came to meet, my attitude was *kualat.* This word, originally of Arabic derivation, was one with no direct equivalent in French. Dimas tried to explain its meaning to me, which was, approximately, that I was in some way doomed to a particular fate because of something I had done or spoken. Specifically as regards to me, the situation did not prove to be calamitous. I was *kualat* because my own words turned against me.

May 1968 was an important time not only because of the students and workers' revolution in Paris; it was also then that my arrogance was shattered and I was forced to believe in *le coup de foudre.*

It was the moment I saw him, that Asian man on the Sorbonne campus. I guessed he was from Indochina. With his brown skin, I thought he might be from Vietnam. But he was tall for an Asian man. And with his curly hair and aquiline nose he might even have been from the Middle East. From a distance, I caught him watching me; but when I looked at him he pretended to be busy puffing on his cigarette, as if that was going to help ward off the cold wind blowing that evening. He was standing at a distance, by himself, watching my fellow students who were huddled together against the cold and the government. I thought he might be a journalist who had ventured onto campus. There was no longer any artificial division between the students and citizens of Paris. Everyone mingled and mixed together. But no, he was alone, without a camera, watching history as it unfolded.

Some friends of mine and I had gathered beneath the statue of Victor Hugo and were waiting to hear Daniel Cohn-Bendit, a sociology student who was the student movement's most vocal leader. There were so many people, all of them pushing their way forward, excited to see what was going on. There must have been thousands of people who had gathered there. But then my desire to hear Cohn-Bendit's oration—and to glimpse his handsome face—suddenly withered, all because of him, that exotic-looking man, standing alone, undisturbed by both the mass of humanity and the brisk evening wind.

And then at that moment, for a second, and then two, our eyes met. And wow! How I managed to do it, I don't know, but slowly, going against the tide of students moving in the direction of Daniel Cohn-Bendit, I eased my way from the crowd to walk in the direction of that man. That Asian man. And then came an unexpected bolt of lightning.

Le coup de foudre.

His eyes bore into mine.

I greeted him: "*Ça va?*"

SAINT-GERMAIN-DES-PRÉS, PARIS, APRIL 1998
Vivienne picked up the receiver of the telephone screaming impatiently at her. "*Oui,*" she said while stuffing lesson materials for that day's courses into her large multi-pocketed leather bag. With the receiver clamped between her right cheek and shoulder, she filled the bag with books, folders, pens, a pocket diary, and a roll of mints. She grabbed her mug of coffee to take a sip but then suddenly stopped when she heard the name of the hospital the person on the other end of the line had just mentioned. Slowly, she placed her mug on the table.

"Dimas Suryo? *Oui,* that is my former husband. *Pourquoi?*"

"Your name is listed as his emergency contact," she heard the caller say.

Now was not the time for her to feel annoyed.

"Is there something wrong?"

"*Non, non*, Madame. It's just that we ran some tests on Monsieur Suryo two weeks ago and he still hasn't picked up the results. We've called him several times, but he never answers the phone, so…"

"OK, I will make sure he comes to pick them up." She took her pen and notepad. "Where in the hospital would that be?"

With that telephone call having ruined her morning, Vivienne lost her appetite for the mug of steeped *luwak* coffee she had just prepared. Steam from the cup rose and vanished in the air—like the story of her love for the man who had first introduced her to that wonderfully tasting coffee.

Vivienne picked up the receiver again, this time to dial Lintang's number. She took a breath to calm herself before speaking.

"Lintang, *c'est Maman*."

•

Love at first sight, a love that burns deep inside, and the wish to explore something new, foreign, and completely unknown are not, it turns out, enough to save a marriage. I realized that afterwards. As much as I loved Dimas and as great as my willingness was to give to him everything I had inside of me, to this day I don't know whether he ever loved me as much as I loved him—even though he did write me a poem, which he gave to me as a gift at our wedding. In Indonesia, he said, when a couple marries there is always a brideprice to pay. And the price he paid for me was a poem whose first lines were "*Benarkah angin tak sedang mencoba / Menyentuh bibirnya yang begitu sempurna…Is it true the wind's not trying / To touch such perfect lips…*"

He said the poem popped into his mind the first time he saw me, in May 1968, at the time of the student and workers' movement. But did he ever really love me completely? And forever?

My cousin Marie-Claire, an ever-cheerful person, always kind to everyone, told me that Dimas was an extraordinary man and would make a very suitable life partner. Mathilde, my other cousin, a much more skeptical sort, told me that Dimas was an exotic man who might be good for dating or as a lover, but not for marrying. Neither of my cousins quite understood that my attraction to and love for Dimas did not spring from some deep seated desire in me to explore a foreign territory that was exotic and unknown. Nor did it emerge from the urge to satisfy physical pleasure. Not at all. I sensed in Dimas a feeling of loss that I wanted to soothe and assuage. He had a sadness in his eyes I wanted to heal. And also, as I came to learn, he had an incredible ability to confront hardship and to survive, an ability to withstand and repulse life's vicissitudes. At times, as I later came to see, the survival mechanisms he employed seemed to border on the obsessive; but, perhaps, such is the case of all political exiles, in every country throughout the world: their will to survive makes them obsessive about proving themselves.

France would never be Dimas's home. I realized that from the moment our eyes first met. There was something that prevented him from being happy, from feeling completely at home. Was it the bloodbath that had occurred in his own homeland? Was it the country's political upheaval, which had not only eroded but also depleted all sense of humanity in Dimas and his friends, forcing them to pick up, here and there, whatever bits and pieces they could find in order to rebuild themselves into a new whole as human beings possessing a sense of dignity and pride?

Politics is never simple, and ideological struggle is but a pretense for the lust for power. All the books I've read on the subject have their own theories about what happened in Indonesia in September 1965. In my first few years of knowing Dimas and his friends—Nugroho, Tjai, and Risjaf—it wasn't easy for me to piece together their life stories, which they delivered in a piecemeal fashion. There were numerous common experiences they shared as wanderers, but they all had very different personalities and different reactions towards the tragedy that had occurred in their homeland. That said, they all wanted to go home and waited for the opportunity to see a better Indonesia. But thirty years had passed and "the Smiling General"—the country's long-reigning authoritarian leader, President Soeharto—was all the more strong and feared.

Maybe the overtly civilian style of government in Indonesia wasn't the same as the one adopted by military leaders in Latin American countries, but the Smiling General continued to retain a firm grip on his throne.

It's been a while now since I've seen Dimas, but I still look for the news about Indonesia that occasionally appears in the mass media, on the television and in the press. I'm sure that following the recent tumble in the value of the rupiah and the economic crisis that befell the region, President Soeharto felt the need to do something, the need to act. But what he did, according to the reports I've seen, was to install his own daughter in the government cabinet! Whether or not his political panic will escalate and one day cause him to fall, I don't know, but if he does fall, I am very sure that of the four pillars—Dimas and his three friends—Dimas will be the first to return in order to live out his old age in Indonesia. I'm also sure that if at all possible he will return home with a green Republic of Indonesia passport in his hand. If at all possible, that is, but likely it's not. Regardless, I'm very sure that he will try to return home.

Unlike Dimas, his three friends in exile seem to have long ago given up the obsession of spending the rest of their days in their home country. Nugroho seems to be comfortable, and long ago accepted the fact that he must consider Paris to be his second home. Tjai has said that he would like to go back to visit but not to stay permanently. Risjaf, meanwhile, somehow succeeded in getting a visa for Indonesia. But as long as he has Amira and their son Ardi at his side, he could feel complete and safe anywhere.

Dimas is in a different category altogether. He and his three friends are all Indonesian, and all of them come from Java with the exception of Risjaf, who comes from Riau, in Sumatra. Even so, after meeting friends of Dimas in Paris, Amsterdam, Leiden, The Hague, Berlin, and Cologne, I got the sense that there was something that set Dimas apart from his fellow political exiles. At first I thought of them as seagulls, flying from one continent to another as a flock and then setting down roots and establishing homes in the continent where they alighted (if only temporarily). But after meeting Dimas, marrying him, and raising a family, I came to see that Dimas was not, and had never been, in fact, an inseparable part of the flock. His camaraderie with his friends was deep and his loyalty to the group was not to be doubted, but Dimas still differed from the flock's other members. While the others tried to adapt and to build a home in another continent, Dimas's spirit remained in the nest where he had been born and raised. Differing from other gulls of the same generation, Dimas was a bird that always wanted to return to the land of his birth, never content to simply remain with the family he had formed in an alien land.

I was ready to follow Dimas in his desire to return to Indonesia one day—if that day were ever to come—which is why from the time Lintang was just a baby I began to prepare her as well, making sure that she could speak not just French, but also

Indonesian and English. Supposing, just supposing that miracle were to happen... But seeing the inexorable power of the Smiling General, I was never sure it would. And even in my dreams, I imagined that if one day Socharto were to die, his replacement would be a person cut from the very same cloth, of one mind and imagination—which is, in effect, to say, there would be no change in Indonesian government policy whatsoever and the wandering flock of birds would be left stranded in their foreign lands. Their names would be expunged from Indonesian history and the history of civilization as well, whereas the regime that oversaw their erasure would continue to live on, one generation after the other. I hoped I was wrong.

Every year Dimas did the same thing and experienced the same disappointment. My heart bled for him. Year in, year out, Dimas would submit an application to the Indonesian embassy for a visa to Indonesia, which was always rejected for reasons never given. If the embassy had summarily rejected the visa applications of all Indonesian political exiles, that might have helped to alleviate Dimas's frustration. But there were those among his friends—probably ones the Indonesian government deemed would make no noise—who were granted tourist visas: Risjaf was one; Mirza, in Leiden, another; and several of his friends in Germany. But it was after the protests and demonstration in Dresden two years ago, at the time of Soeharto's state visit, that I truly began to wonder how easy it would be for Indonesia to open the doors to its prodigal children abroad. Whatever the case, there were bureaucratic mountains and canyons to pass through in the Indonesian government's alleged open-door policy for exiles. That is why—just to try to get Dimas from forever feeling rejected like Ekalaya, that favorite puppet character of his—I once spoke my mind and suggested that he accept the possibility of not being able to spend his old age, and one day shut his eyes forever, in Indonesia.

Mon Dieu. You should have seen the hurt look in his eyes. My own words surprised me. I suddenly realized that sometimes stating the obvious, in a rational manner, can have calamitous consequences. I had extinguished the small light in a dark tunnel.

Dimas didn't say anything, didn't even express his distress. But that wouldn't have been Dimas's style. He just picked himself up from where he was and went out to the terrace to smoke. Because he didn't bother to close the door, cold winter air rushed into the apartment. I knew that I had said something wrong. But I was not wrong.

I followed Dimas to the terrace and attempted to defend my point of view without further upsetting him.

"Home is where your family lives."

"Home is the place where I feel I am at home," Dimas replied, his voice cold and flat. That conversation was not the point that determined our separation. That night was just one dot in a long line of dots that finally forced us to take our separate ways.

●

"*Bonjour.*"

"*Bonjour.* Vivienne?"

"*Oui.* Is that you, Nugroho? Is Dimas there?"

"Yes, Viv, I'm here, just keeping Dimas company. My word, how long has it been? How are you!? It's been such a while since you've been to Tanah Air. And how is Lintang?"

"Lintang is busy with examinations… Is Dimas there?"

Vivienne heard a long sigh.

"*Pourqoui?* What's wrong with Dimas?"

"He's not feeling well, is all."

"Nugroho...! This is me."

Vivienne waited for an answer.

Finally, one came: "He's sick but I don't know why. Maybe his appendix, maybe something intestinal, or it could be his liver. Last night he was throwing up..."

"Is he still drinking?"

"Yes, but how else are you going to keep warm in this freezing country?"

"And I suppose he's refusing to see a doctor. Is that right?"

Nugroho chuckled. "Oh, Viv, you know him better than anyone. What happened is that he collapsed at the Metro and we took him to the hospital. There they put him through a series of tests..."

"And he has yet to pick up the results..."

"Well, that's our Dimas."

"I know, but the hospital called me."

"Oh," Nugroho coughed. "Sorry about that, Viv. That was my fault. I'm the one who filled in the admissions form. I just figured that it was more likely that he'd listen to your advice than anything we said."

"It's OK. I called Lintang."

"Oh..."

"Where is Dimas now?"

"Still asleep. He had a bad stomach again last night, so I brought him home and stayed here with him."

"Thanks, Nug. OK, just tell Dimas that I called."

"Will do, Viv. Give Lintang a hug and tell her that all her uncles at Tanah Air miss seeing her."

"I know..." Vivienne answered, very slowly.

•

Just a week before the brouhaha about Dimas's health, Lintang had come to visit and to borrow my Encim *kebaya*. That night, I decided to cook one of her favorite dishes: spaghetti *alle vongole*. For our family, the Dimas Suryo family, food was always medicine for the sad soul. And even though I knew a number of Indonesian recipes, particularly the ones that Dimas used to make when we were still together, I still lacked the confidence to cook them on my own. Having a husband who was a good cook was, for me at least, a lucky thing. With him doing the cooking, all I had to do was choose the wine and music and then put my feet up and wait for the meal to be served. Dimas didn't like me interfering in the kitchen anyway; the kitchen was his kingdom and he didn't like anyone messing in it any more than I liked someone going through my office or library. As a result of this situation, with her father making all sorts of exotic dishes, Lintang grew to be a girl with a palate for a million tastes. Because she liked to tail her father in the kitchen and watch him when he was preparing his spices for whatever dish he was making, she always knew if a dish was lacking in spices and which ones were deficient.

That night, when she told me about her professor's comments and his suggestion for her final assignment, I immediately detected anxiety in her voice. I also heard notes of confusion and worry. To make a documentary film about her father's homeland and a part of its history that the Indonesian government had buried wouldn't just be difficult; it would be mentally taxing for even the soundest of minds. I didn't know where she would find all the materials she needed to properly research the subject of September 1965. From what little I knew, so much of the available literature contained as many questions as answers. And besides all that, my hardheaded former husband and my equally stubborn daughter were not even speaking to each other.

Just as I had suspected, when I went into the kitchen and returned to the dining table with the platter of spaghetti *alle vongole* I had made, a happy look instantly appeared on Lintang's face. She smiled as she inhaled the scent of clams cooked in white wine. I had thought of putting on Led Zeppelin music—that really would have made the evening complete—but I didn't, because I knew that Lintang would mock me for it and think that I couldn't let go of my memories with her father. Instead, I put on a CD of music by Ravel, her favorite.

Lintang closed her eyes when she tried a spoonful of the sauce. Good, she liked it. But Lintang would not have been Lintang had she not then dropped a bomb into the midst of calm.

"To do the project, I'll probably have to go to Indonesia…"

There it was: the first shell shock. It took my breath away. I stirred the spaghetti and handed Lintang a bottle of white wine for her to open.

While she uncorked the bottle and poured the wine into our glasses, I busied myself dressing the salad, without saying anything.

"Maman…"

"Does Professor *Dupont* know that this is what you want to do?"

"He was the one who suggested it, who said that I should look at my own history."

"But did he say anything about you having to fly off to Jakarta?"

Lintang ignored my question and dug into the spaghetti. Every bite she took seemed to make her more enthusiastic and she began to talk about what had happened at the Indonesian ambassador's residence earlier that evening.

"Just imagine it, Maman, when Nara and I first arrived at the reception, nobody paid much attention to me. There were so many people and so many kinds of food… Oh, the food was delicious! You should have tasted it. I bet if Ayah had had been there he would have praised the *pastel*, the beef tongue, and the iced lychee. I don't know where they managed to get it, but they even served iced young coconut."

"But then…?" I cut in. Lintang and her father definitely had at least one thing in common: whenever the subject of food came up in conversation, they immediately turned their attention to that until they lost the focus of their story.

"What is it that makes you feel the need to go to Indonesia now? What subject do you intend to address in your documentary?"

"I'm not sure, Maman. At first, when Professor Dupont suggested that I look into Ayah's history, I thought of focusing on the fate of the victims of 1965 here in Paris, the families of political exiles. But then, I went to that Kartini Day party at the Indonesian ambassador's residence and…"

"And you saw another side of Indonesia."

"Just a glimpse, *un petit aperçu*, but one so very different from the one I already know. It made me ask myself whether they, too, might be victims?"

"*Victims?*"

"Yes, victims of indoctrination! You've got to hear what happened to me," she said breathlessly. "All because of my presence at the reception, some of the people there started to panic, didn't know what to do. They were so nervous. I could see the questions running through their minds: How are we supposed to react to this daughter of Dimas Suryo? Are we supposed to be friendly, polite, engage her in small talk, or keep her at a distance? What would the Home Office say? The Home Office bans us from eating at Tanah Air Restaurant but it shouldn't be a problem for her to be here, should it? But wait a minute… What about the '*bersih lingkungan*' policy. What do such terms as 'a clean environment' and 'political hygiene,' even mean? Just imagine, Maman, for people like me who weren't even born at the time of the September 30 Movement and live far distant from Indonesia, they still require a prescription for what to think."

By now Lintang had wiped her plate clean. There was an excited look on her face, as if she had taken some kind of stimulant. Though I knew her animation didn't come from the alcohol, I circumspectly moved the bottle of wine to beyond her immediate reach.

"Maman," she said, drawing a breath, "I've decided it's not enough for me just to listen to stories from Ayah, Om Nug, Om Tjai, and Om Risjaf. It's not enough to interview people at the embassy either. There's a historical context I need to understand—how the absurdity of this part of Indonesian history even began."

This is the problem that comes from raising a child with books and a Sorbonne education.

"But…"

"And it's not enough, either, to go to the Netherlands or Germany to interview friends of Ayah there. I know that going elsewhere in Europe would be safer and less expensive, but am I going to find Indonesia there?"

Lintang's questions and her voice made her sound like her father.

"So, if you go to Indonesia, what will you record?"

"I'm not sure, Maman. I'm still tossing around ideas. But just that one hour at the Kartini Day party has set my mind abuzz and got me to thinking that there's something more I need to study than just the impact of that event here on people in Europe."

My daughter was both intelligent and mature, this I knew, but now she was making me worried. I didn't know whether to be proud or frightened. The thought of her going off on her own to Indonesia… Well, I just hoped the idea was merely an impulse.

"You know, Maman, how you're always telling me that the people of your generation liked to experiment and to explore all kinds of opportunities… Is that supposed to be true only for your generation?"

I shook my head. "Of course not. After you've done the research for your proposal, if it looks like you really have to go, then as long as you can get the funding, how could I object?"

"*Ne sois pas comme ça, Maman*," Lintang said in reprimand. "*Écoute, Maman*," she added, as she raised her glass of wine. "Whatever it is that we can pluck from I.N.D.O.N.E.S.I.A, that's what I want to do."

I stood and pressed my lips to her forehead. If she had started to quote Jalaluddin Rumi, what was I going to do?

"Listen, Lintang… If I were to be honest, I'd have to say that I would prefer for you to do your fieldwork here in Paris or somewhere else close by." Pausing for a moment, I then asked, "Have you spoken to your father?"

I had used my final weapon.

Lintang suddenly choked, but then quickly drank off the glass of wine like it was water.

"Not yet," she said after a cough.

"Thirsty, are you?" I remarked with a laugh. "You wouldn't go to Indonesia without speaking to him first, would you?"

"Of course not."

"Well have you thought about how you will enter the country?"

Lintang said nothing for a moment. "I'm not sure. But I met some younger diplomats earlier. Maybe I'll ask them. They might know the best way."

Apparently, Lintang had already come to a decision on part of her life's plan. Saying nothing more, I cleared the dishes from the table and took them into the kitchen. Lintang followed behind. As she loaded the dishwasher, I cut two pieces from the cherry tart I'd also made—another of Lintang's favorites—and put them on plates. Instead of returning to the dining room, we ate the tart there in the kitchen, savoring the taste of the cherries as we stood next to each other. It was moments like this I missed. Together with Lintang. Together with Dimas.

"Maman…"

"*Oui.*"

Lintang was using her fork to move a small piece of the tart around her plate—which meant she was trying to figure out the words for something sensitive she had to say.

"Do you think Ayah is an Ekalaya?"

I pulled the stopper off a half-empty bottle of wine on the counter and poured myself a glass. Red wine, this time.

"*Non.*"

"*Non?* Why not?"

"He's a Bima, always ready to protect the woman he loves."

•

"*Salut,* Dimas."

"Viv…"

"*Ça va?*"

Dimas cleared his throat.

"*Ça va bien.*"

"Dimas…"

"I'm sorry about the hospital calling you. Don't worry. I'll go and pick up the results."

"The call from the hospital didn't bother me, Dimas. I'm worried, is all. Have you thought about Lintang?"

"Of course I've thought about her."

"OK, so when are you going to pick up the results?"

The sound of Dimas snorting was that of a calf being led off to slaughter.

"You still need to rest. I can pick them up for you. …As long as I have a letter from you."

"No, no, no need," Dimas hurriedly said. "I'll go pick them up for sure. If I'm not up to it, Mas Nug or Risjaf can help."

"Promise?" I asked.

"I promise."

"Then I'll call you tomorrow. Lintang will be coming to see you."

"*Merci,* Vivienne."

SAINT-GERMAIN-DES-PRÉS, PARIS, 1988

In the living room of our apartment was an Indonesia that Dimas Suryo had recreated. Two *wayang* figures hung on the wall—Ekalaya and Bima—along with several masks, gifts that friends had brought back from Indonesia. There was a batik runner on the top of the bookshelf and a batik map of Indonesia in Lintang's room. But the most curious items were two apothecary jars, tucked between books on the shelf where Dimas had put them. One jar was filled with cloves; the other with turmeric powder. I never understood why Dimas stored these jars in the living room and not in the kitchen, or in the bedroom, for that matter.

Both Lintang and I had asked Dimas that question. He answered by taking from the one jar a handful of cloves and telling us to inhale their scent.

He then spoke in his story-telling voice: "Cloves have such an exotic aroma that many a sharp-nosed European sailor was able to smell them continents away. And these seamen competed to subjugate and control the spice-laden archipelago where clove trees grew. They even planted the name of their own country in that place and called it the Dutch Indies, making it a part of the land from whence they came."

"Then why turmeric, Ayah?" Lintang asked, wide-eyed as she stared at the yellow powder in the other jar.

That question, Dimas never answered; he just smiled and let Lintang inhale the sharp scent of the turmeric powder. Her nostrils twitched as she did this.

This scene took place time and again. Dimas replaced the contents of the jars annually, after the scent of the spices had begun to fade. Sometimes he received shipments of the spices from friends in the Netherlands; sometimes directly from Jakarta when friends brought them back as a souvenir from their trip. But there was one time when he was forced to pay an arm and a leg for them at the Asian food import store in Belleville. It happened only once, and only after multiple arguments between us because I didn't agree spending what little extra money we had just so that Dimas could savor the scent of memories.

Then one night, when Dimas was busy at the restaurant, Lintang came into my room with a pale face and teary eyes.

"Maman…"

She was holding sheets of paper in her hand. I didn't know what they were, but they were fluttering because of her trembling hand. Heavens! What was wrong?

Lintang handed me the sheets of paper, then left the room. The next thing I heard was the sound of her bedroom door closing. Just a soft click. Not a slam.

I looked at the top sheet. Handwritten, with well structured Indonesian in neat and regular penmanship. A letter for Dimas. I never read letters addressed to my husband, unless he specifically asked me to join him in reading them together. And I didn't want to read the letter, but Lintang… She had come across it. Where had she found it? I scanned the sheets of paper, one by one. All were letters from Surti Anandari, dating from the late 1960s, after the military had captured her husband. But wait, there were other letters too, dating from 1970, 1971, 1972, 1973, 1978, 1979, 1980, 1982…I looked at one.

Dearest Dimas,

I must thank you again for the assistance you sent to me through Aji. I never doubt the goodness of your heart or that of Vivienne, and Nug, Tjai, and Risjaf as well.

Congratulations on the opening of Tanah Air Restaurant! I am so happy that the four of you have been able to work together to make a go of it and overcome the challenges you've had to face there, in that distant land. I know that it couldn't have been easy for you to build something from nothing—and a restaurant, no less, a real business whose manner of operation you would have all had to study, like a child learning to crawl, then to walk, then to run, and to endure. But I have no doubt whatsoever that you will succeed, especially because you love the kitchen, with all its spices, and the culinary world, as much as you love the world of literature.

I can see you in the kitchen, enjoying every second you spend mixing your spices, treating them like living creatures, helping them to find their perfect mate so that they might commingle and then become one to produce a new taste altogether. Though I've never myself believed in destiny, the fact that the four of you have ended up establishing a restaurant together surely must be fate.

Kenanga, Bulan, and Alam are well. Kenanga is engaged to Fahri, Mas Amri's boy, and will be getting married soon. Bulan is a student in the Faculty of English Literature at the University of Indonesia, and Alam is waiting to see if he's been accepted for enrollment at either the Faculty of Law or the Faculty of Social and Political Sciences at U.I. The money from the four of you has made it much easier for them to get an education. Mas Hananto was so fortunate to have had loyal friends like the four of you.

And I, too, feel fortunate to have known a man as good as you, who respects and honors women. I will never forget your kindness and good-heartedness. I hold dear my memories of you and the gifts you have given to me; they are mine to keep forever and will never fade or be forgotten, because you are everywhere. Not just in the kitchen, or in the color of turmeric or the scent of cloves, but you flow everywhere. Everywhere and always.

Surti Anandari

At that moment I realized that I had never completely owned nor would ever completely own Dimas. At that instant I also knew why he continued to wish to return to the place that he so loved. Somewhere in the corner of his heart was Surti; there he owned her and there he could keep her along with all of his memories of her forever, eternalized in the spices found in those two apothecary jars. Surti was the scent of cloves and turmeric. All were one in Indonesia. That night I told Dimas I wanted to separate.

•

"Lintang…"

"Yes, Maman. I'm on the way to the Marais."

"OK. Let me know how it goes. Once it stops raining, I'll stop by to see Ayah, too."

"OK, Maman…"

"Lintang…"

"*Oui*…"

"Try not to argue, OK? Your father isn't well."

"*Oui*, Maman, I understand. And after seeing that other side of Indonesia at the reception the other day, I think I will always be able to understand Ayah."

AUX CHAMPS-ÉLYSÉES, PARIS, 1982

It was on the Avenue des Champs-Élysées, that I, too, once came across another part of Indonesia. Given the normal state of my pocketbook, the area was not one I often frequented. By chance, however, a friend of mine from out of town had come to visit and, to get to her hotel, I had to walk down Avenue Montaigne. On that street, which is known for its expensive boutiques, that "part" of Indonesia turned into a veritable party. In almost every store— Dior, Lacroix, Céline, and others—I saw groups of Indonesian women dressed in expensive clothing, with long flowing scarves and bouffant hairdos. Even from a distance I was able to catch the glitter of the diamond rings and the necklaces they wore. A few years earlier, the first time I'd seen this part of Indonesia, I had been astonished, because I had never before seen such obvious wealth displayed on a person's body. I had always tried to avoid interacting with this part of Indonesia, mostly because I worried that I would have nothing to say. But there on the Champs-Élysées, I came to see that this part of Indonesia was a comedic satire.

At another time and in another place, there was another part of Indonesia I came to see: this one dark, dirty, and foul-smelling. It happened a few weeks after the opening of Tanah Air Restaurant. That day, I was having a cup of coffee while correcting essays at L'Écritoire café on the Place de la Sorbonne. My eyes were looking down at my papers when there suddenly came into my view a pair of men's shoes. I then heard a man's shrill voice calling my name.

"Vivienne Deveraux! Or is it Vivienne Surrrrryoooo?"

I almost spilled my cup of coffee. An Indonesian man of middling height with slicked-back hair—he must have used a half a bottle of hair oil—was beaming at me. I immediately noticed his gold teeth. Who was he?

"May I?" the man asked, pointing at the empty seat across from me. What could I do but nod? The man extended his hand and said with a hiss in his voice: "I'm Sumarno. Back in the day, I was friends with Hananto, Dimas, Tjai, Nugroho, and Risjaf. Yeah, with all of them."

"Oh, you're a friend of Dimas?" I asked hesitantly.

"Yes, yes, of course," he nodded energetically. "We were all together in Jakarta, so I knew Dimas even before you knew him."

I nodded and invited this Sumarno to order something for himself when the waiter approached. He asked for a cup of coffee. But this was strange, I thought. If he was a friend of Dimas, Nug, Tjai, and Risjaf, then why had he sought me out here, and alone?

How did he know where I was? And, even more creepy for me, how did he know I was Dimas's wife? How did he pick me out from among the many Sorbonne students and teachers who were at the café?

"Have you been in Paris long?" I asked for lack of anything else to say. I had no idea who he was or what his reason was for suddenly appearing at the café during my break between classes.

"Not toooo long…" He seemed to have a habit of drawing out his speech. "Just a few days, or, well, almost a week now."

I took a sip of coffee to calm myself. I wanted to see Dimas, quickly. I had an uneasy feeling about the man. Who was he?

"I was juuuust at Tanah Air. I saw Dimas, Nugroho, Risjaf, and Tjai too. Amazing, amaaazing! Having been stranded in a foreign country like they were and then being able to make a go of it. Just ammaazzzing! And to be able to make a living from a restaurant that serves Indonesian food? That is quite something, really quite something!"

He then giggled for the longest while. I didn't know if what he'd just said was honest praise or pure cynicism. I began to gather my students' papers. He gulped his coffee as if he were in a hurry to go.

"I see you have to get back to your busy life as a teacher. Sorry if I've bothered you. But it's a good thing you have tenure at such a large and prestigious university. Imagine if you didn't—what with your husband changing jobs so many times and you having a daughter to raise. Hmm, what's her name… Lintang Utara. Such a beautiful girl."

I shivered as a chill ran down my spine, not because of the cold winter air but because I was sure this man had been someone evil and cruel in Dimas's past. Someone Dimas once knew, perhaps, but definitely not a friend. If he were a friend or even just a former acquaintance or colleague, he wouldn't have secretly sought me out and put on these airs of friendship and familiarity. God! What was he? An intelligence agent? Is that what Indonesian intelligence personnel were like? With gold teeth and a bucket of pomade on their hair, searching out the wives of their targets? I tried signaling for one of the waiters to bring me the bill, but they were all busy with other customers. Impatiently, I began to rummage through my bag, looking for my wallet.

"No, no, no, Vivienne! Please allow me," Sumarno said. "Chalk it up as returning the favor that Dimas once showed me. Yes, back in those days in Jakarta, when he was still thick with Surti, he'd often treat me to food or drink at places on Cikini or in Senen Market. I had so little at the time, there's no way I could ever have gone to Paris like he did."

My heart was pounding—and not because he had mentioned Surti's name, but because it was apparent that he was intentionally trying to terrorize me. I no longer had time for good manners. I stood, picked up my belongings, and walked away from the man to the cashier's counter. I paid for my coffee and the brioche I'd eaten, then walked back and past the table without saying anything. But then I stopped. I didn't like this. He had to know that I was not afraid of him. I turned, went back to the table and looked down on this man with the hair pomade and gold teeth, then looked him sharply in the eye.

"Listen to me, Sumarno, or whatever your real name is. I don't know who you are or what you want by coming to see me here. And, frankly, I don't care. But I know that you are no friend of my husband. And if you ever again dare to show your face here or to bother me or my family, I will call the police. And in this country, at least, the police do their jobs. Get it?!"

Sumarno looked at me in surprise, but then nodded slowly. I left him and walked back towards campus with the wind pushing me in the back.

That night, when I went to Rue de Vaugirard, I told Dimas, Nug, Risjaf, and Tjai what had happened. Hearing my story, these aging men suddenly turned into a gang of angry youth: clenching their fists, slamming a knife into the table, and doing all sorts of primeval "manly" things.

But my instincts were right. Though Sumarno had been an acquaintance of Dimas, he was now called "Snitch" for having pointed out to the military who should be picked up.

People like Snitch are everywhere in the world, of course. They might even be behind the door or the walls of our homes. They have ears everywhere and a thousand poisoned tongues. I knew Dimas and his friends did not want to expend energy uselessly on getting angry at a louse like Snitch. My experience in meeting him was just one part of the country of Indonesia. I was convinced that another part of Indonesia would yield for me an experience that was much more honorable and intimate.

"Are you OK?" Dimas asked, stroking the back of my hair worriedly as we walked towards the Metro station.

"*Oui*, I'm fine. People like Sumarno are everywhere. Don't worry.

Matters like these I can handle on my own," I said embracing
Dimas for a feeling of safety and closeness.

Dimas laughed. "I called him a rat. You called him a louse.
I don't know which description is more apt."

We continued walking, embracing tightly as we did. He whispered how much he loved my strength. And then I asked myself,
did he love me because I was strong and independent so that he
did not have to protect me as Bima protected Drupadi? Or did
he love me because he would not be able to breathe if ever I were
to leave him? Why could I not find the answer?

BLOOD-FILLED LETTERS

AS TWILIGHT SLOWLY SETTLED ON THE MARAIS, sadness also fell. Lintang could never understand why the area always evinced such a feeling of loneliness; the Marais was, after all, an area filled with cafés, galleries, and the homes of prominent French artists. Nara believed the Marais to be the hippest, most multicultural area of Paris. But Lintang could never decide whether the sadness of the place was caused by the colors of the twilight sky—thin strips of red, yellow, and orange—or because it always reminded her of her parents' divorce.

She once said to her father: "Your decision to live in the Marais must have had something to do with Victor Hugo, what with all his heart-wrenching works." Lintang preferred the morning because morning time brought with it the possibility of hope: maybe the possibility of doing something good that day or correcting a misdeed. Or maybe a reunion with her father after five months of evading him—which was something that made her feel guilty, of course, but angry as well. Even so, to feel riled by her father when she felt him to be judging her life choices was one thing but to be so put out as to shut down all avenues of communication was quite another, something she'd never before done, regardless of how irritated she was with this man whose attitude towards life she deemed to be warped and cynical.

Outside the door to her father's gloomy apartment, untouched by the warmth of spring, Lintang knocked on the door. No answer. She took the door key from her knapsack and opened the door. Entering the apartment, she took off her jacket and unwound the light woolen scarf from around her neck.

She scanned the length of the apartment where her father had lived all these years alone. Her heart began to crumble. Everything that had been upsetting her these past five months suddenly evaporated. The state of the apartment seemed to indicate that its owner was either very tired or ill. The living room and work space, separated one from the other by a wooden partition, looked like an untidy storeroom full of books. Usually the bookshelves in the room were neatly lined with their volumes arranged in alphabetical order by the author's name; but now the place was in such disarray it looked as if it were inhabited by a slovenly teenager.

On sections of the wall not covered with books hung glass paintings from Cirebon and photographs of Lintang and her father, many of the same ones that were displayed in the apartment she shared with her mother. The brown and green batik cloth with an avian motif that covered the coffee table—a gift from her grandmother, her father said—was wrinkled and faded, looking more like a rag for cleaning the kitchen counter. An array of LPs lay scattered about: Louis Armstrong, Branford Marsalis, Jack Lemmers, Bing Slamet, Koes Bersaudara, Édith Piaf, The Beatles, Pink Floyd, Led Zeppelin, and Creedence Clearwater Revival. In former days, whenever her father had played a Led Zeppelin record, he and her mother would compete in telling her about their meeting at the time of the May Revolution in Paris. "That was the year Led Zeppelin was born," her father declared proudly.

Lintang always felt that her parents forced the coincidence. In

1968, at the time of her parents' first meeting, didn't many other things happen in the world? But just as it was forbidden for her to criticize the works of Ernest Hemingway, George Orwell, and James Joyce, it was also forbidden to mock Led Zeppelin. Her father was in awe of their music.

Lintang now turned her gaze to the walls. Oh... The large shadow puppet of Bima, the strongest of the Pandawa brothers in the shadow theater pantheon, which usually stood erect as would befit such a mighty character, now hung aslant, as if forlorn and sad. At least the Ekalaya puppet remained upright.

On the coffee table, covered with a layer of ash, was an ashtray heaped with cigarette butts, a coffee cup in which only dreg were visible, and a hunk of half-eaten bread. She noticed the two apothecary jars with cloves and turmeric root standing neatly upright among the many books that were piled in disorderly stacks on the book shelf.

Suddenly, Lintang heard raised voices coming from her father's bedroom. A look of surprise washed over her face as she heard Nugroho trying to persuade her father to do something he obviously did not want to do. Her father was clearly rankled.

"It won't hurt; it's just a small needle. You don't even have to watch!" That was Nugroho speaking.

"No, Mas Nug, I don't want to," said her father.

"Come on, trust me. Just last night you had an acupuncture treatment, and you felt all right after that, didn't you?"

Lintang tiptoed towards her father's room, not wanting to interrupt the developing drama. She could guess what was happening: Om Nug was trying to treat her father with acupuncture and her father was loudly and staunchly refusing. She smiled; her big strong daddy was strangely afraid of needles.

Lintang peeked inside to see Nugroho opening a small bag of acupuncture needles. Her father blinked madly at their sight, as if he'd seen a witch. With what strength he had, he pulled himself up and then stumbled hurriedly towards the bathroom. Once inside, he slammed and locked the door behind him.

"Come on, Dimas..." Nugroho entreated.

"No! No!" her father shouted from behind the bathroom door.

Nugroho rose from the chair beside Dimas's desk and softly knocked on the bathroom door. "Please, Dimas. If we don't do it now, it will be too late."

"No! I'll sleep in here if I have to. I'm not coming out as long as you have that needle in your hand!"

Nugroho looked exasperated and ready to give up. Sitting down, he suddenly noticed that Lintang was now present in the room, watching him with a covert smile. Seeing her, he immediately gave a sigh of relief and jumped up to give her a warm hug.

"Lintang, Lintang, my girl... Why has it been so long since you've come to the restaurant? How are you?"

"I'm fine," she said, "just busy."

Nugroho looked at Lintang who so very much resembled her mother Vivienne, except for her hair and eyes which obviously came to her from Dimas.

Nugroho shot a glance at the bathroom door. "That father of yours... *Yo wis, wong ditambani kok wegah.* I'm just trying to help, but he won't let me."

Lintang smiled again and patted Nugroho on the shoulder. He had already begun to repack his set of needles.

"I'll try to talk to him," she said.

"Please do. Maybe if you talk to him, he'll listen." Now ready to go, Nugroho picked up his bag. "I have to get back to the restaurant. I hope we can catch up soon."

Lintang gave her kind uncle a peck on the cheek and then walked with him to the door. After Nugroho had gone, Lintang returned to the bedroom and rapped softly on the bathroom door. "Ayah…"

She heard her father angrily clear his throat and was surprised by the vehemence of its sound. He must have known the voice was hers.

"Ayah, it's me, Lintang…"

She heard the inside latch on the door release. The door cracked open and she saw her father's head appear. The stress in his features immediately vanished and his eyes glowed with happiness at the sight of his daughter. But wary that Nugroho and his needles might still be there, he hesitated before opening the door wider, first sticking his head further out and looking around.

"Is Om Nug still here?"

Lintang giggled, "He's gone, Ayah. Come out of there!"

Dimas emerged cautiously from the bathroom, his eyes still bright with suspicion, not trusting that Nugroho wasn't there, ready to attack again with his needles. Lintang shook her head in silent agreement with the view that over time the role of parent and child reverses itself, with the child acting as the parent when the parent is older.

Finally sure that Nugroho was no longer on the premises, Dimas breathed a sigh of relief. "Did you see the size of those needles?" he said, spreading his arms to the length of a broomstick.

"Yeah, yeah," Lintang muttered dismissively. Then noticing her father's unkempt bed, she immediately began to strip the sheets and take off the pillowcases.

Dimas observed the focused look on his daughter's face.

Throwing the used linen into a pile on the floor, Lintang looked up to see her father staring at her. She went to him and kissed him on the cheek.

"*Ça va?*"

"*Ça va bien.*" Dimas smiled and straightened his posture, then began to help Lintang, who had taken a clean set of sheets and pillowcases from the chest of drawers and was now putting the sheets on his bed.

"Your mother and Om Nug are making the problem bigger than it is," he said, then immediately changed the subject: "How are you and your studies?"

"My coursework is fine; all I have left is my final," she said. Then she brought the subject back to the matter at hand: "I was told you collapsed at the Metro station."

With her arms on her chest, Lintang looked like a mother speaking to her five-year-old son.

Dimas scratched his head and turned his attention to the pillowcases that Lintang had just changed. "Yes, yes… *Je suis fatigué.*" Dimas glanced at Lintang and again tried to change the topic of conversation: "You're looking thin. How long has it been since you've been here? Four months, five…?"

Lintang didn't answer the question. She was not going to feel guilty or take offense at her father's comments. Besides, he looked thinner too. And all those pills on the bookshelf? There were far too many of them.

"Did you pick up the results of the tests?" she asked.

"Om Nug said he'd pick them up for me tomorrow. But, you know, he's extra busy now at the restaurant now, covering for me."

Lintang began to straighten her father's bedside table, which was littered with ash. On it was an ashtray piled high with cigarette butts and matchsticks. At that moment, her father removed a cigarette from the pack in his shirt pocket and put it to his lips, but when he opened a matchbox and put a light to the cigarette, Lintang immediately yanked it from his mouth and stubbed it in the ash tray.

Dimas shrugged in surrender, not willing to risk an argument with his daughter, who had been boycotting his presence in her life for so long. He watched her as she slammed the contents of the ashtray into the wastebasket beside the bathroom door.

Lintang then began to check her father's medicine bottles, one by one, reading their instructions. "These pills, the ones that you're supposed to take in the morning and the afternoon, have you taken them?" she asked.

"This morning, I did. Haven't taken the ones for the afternoon."

Lintang went to the kitchen, filled a glass of water from the faucet in the sink and returned to her father's side with two kinds of pills in her other hand. "It says on the bottle: 'Take regularly until finished.'"

Her father downed the tablets obediently. As he looked on, Lintang went back to straightening his room After the bedroom was in reasonable order, Lintang shifted her attention to the living room. The sofa cover was rumpled and its upright cushions on the floor because Nugroho had slept there the night before; the books in their cases needed to be sorted and re-shelved; the dining table was a mess, and the wooden floor looked as if it hadn't been touched by a vacuum cleaner in at least a week.

"Come over here, Lintang. Sit with me. We can straighten up later."

"No, I'm not comfortable like this. It's like a pigsty in here!"

Just like your mother, Dimas muttered to himself, eyes closed.

He stretched out on the sofa as he watched his daughter straighten the living room.

"Stop, Lintang. We can do that later. I want to know what's happening with you. What's your final assignment?"

Lintang turned off the vacuum cleaner and set it aside. She knew it was time for her to stop this pretense. She had to drop the bomb and then convince her father that what she was doing was right, without getting into an argument. She sat down beside her father on the couch, then turned and looked at him directly in the face.

"I might have to go to Indonesia…" she began.

Her father immediately opened his eyes and blinked. "Why? What for? Your final assignment?"

Lintang took a deep breath and then told her father about her discussion with Didier Dupont and how he had nixed her proposal for a documentary on *Le Quartier Algérien à Paris*. She spoke of her visit to the Indonesian embassy for the Kartini Day banquet and the preliminary research she had conducted at the library to try to find the historical context of Indonesia during the crisis of 1965. She also told her father about the late nights she had spent discussing her project with several senior class members at the Sorbonne and even about her conversation with Narayana's father, who frequently traveled to Indonesia.

Dimas listened to Lintang carefully. Each question she raised seemed considered and well thought out. What had really happened in Indonesia on September 30, 1965? What was the impact of the events of 1965 on survivors and their families? What was the effect of New Order government policy on the years that followed? These were the questions of a future academician who was undertaking bibliographic research in a rational manner about the conflict in Indonesia's military elite at that time.

"While these are questions I very much feel need to be answered, I also want to find a more human side," Lintang said. "This is to be a documentary film, after all. I'd like to focus on the fates of people whose lives were affected by this political conflict—not just the bloodbath itself and the incredible number of deaths that occurred, but the ongoing political trauma and the extraordinary amount of indoctrination the Indonesian people have gone through in the period since 1965."

Dimas looked at his daughter with a mixture of surprise and admiration. Five months of her not talking to him had seemed to give her the time she needed to think about things. Or maybe this was the result of her Sorbonne education? Dimas didn't really know. And he also didn't know quite how to react to what seemed to him to be an impulsive desire on Lintang's part to go off to Indonesia, the homeland he had left so long ago and not set foot in since. He didn't want to sound discouraging or as if he doubted his daughter's abilities or intellectual acumen, but at the same time he didn't want her to be caught up in any kind of danger because of his political status, which the Indonesian government saw as subversive. Still waiting for her father to react to what she had just told him, Lintang continued: "But I still haven't found a clear focus. It's only going to be a sixty-minute documentary film, after all. So I have to be very selective in my choice of topic."

She paused, thinking her father might say something, but he said nothing. "For both practical and economic reasons, I think it would make more sense to make a documentary about the families of Indonesian political exiles who are now scattered about here in France and other countries of Europe…" Lintang glanced at her father. Still no reaction. "At the same time, I'm afraid it might be too personal, and I don't want to make something that turns out to be overly subjective. I do want to get to know Indonesia, however, even if it's only for a few weeks or a month. I want to find out what the country is now like, what with its blood-filled history, and whether its people…"

Dimas could only nod silently in response, his thoughts now untethered. He wanted to tell her that he had always wanted to be the one to take her and her mother to Indonesia and to introduce them to Jakarta, Bogor, Solo, Yogyakarta, Semarang, and the other cities he had known prior to 1965. He wanted to explain to her that there was something special about Indonesia, that the country held a special allure, but that even he didn't know what it was: whether it was the smell of the red clay earth after a tropical rainstorm; the exotic fruit—mangosteens, star fruit, jack fruit, rambutan—with their odd shapes and colors; the women of Central Java, particularly Solo, who spoke so slowly and rhythmically; or the dictatorial manner of pedicab drivers who thrust their index finger in the air when wanting to cross the road, causing all the motor vehicles to stop obediently. But what in fact did he know about his homeland now? His firsthand knowledge of the country had stopped after 1965; and Jakarta and Solo in 1998 were sure to be far different from what they had been thirty-three years previously. There probably weren't *becak* anymore dominating the streets of Jakarta and Solo. Elegant women who could sit silently composed for hours on end, with *canting* in hand, blowing through the hot wax dipper to miraculously change a stretch of plain white cotton cloth into a batik cloth of mind-boggling beauty and design, were probably a rarity. What about the fruit and the traditional cakes—*kelepon*, *nagasari*, *cucur*, *getuk lindri*, and the like—that were set out for him in the evening with a glass of strong hot tea into which he would drop chunks of rock sugar, after he and his brother Aji came home from Quranic study? Possibly gone too. But even if for most people such things had vanished with the advent of modern-day life, he was sure that he would find them somewhere, in what pockets of traditional life still remained, just to show them to Lintang. Dimas studied his daughter's face, which was at once so Indonesian and French as well. Her nose was aquiline but didn't dominate her small face. Her skin was fair but not the white, freckled kind. Hers was white and warm-looking, like a glass of heated milk, a mixture of his light chocolate flesh and Vivienne's white skin. Her eyes were dark brown, like his own. Her thick wavy black hair was his as well. But overall, her posture and bearing were that of her mother—which is why she was often taken for his former wife's young sister. Both were tall, slender, and beautiful. The only distinctive difference was Vivienne's eyes, that amazing color of green. Dimas tried to imagine Lintang in the midst of the busy metropolis that Jakarta had become, but could not get a clear picture. Both CNN and BBC television had begun to air news clips about demonstrations taking place in several Indonesian cities. This was worrisome for him. He was sure that Lintang must have participated in student demonstrations at the Sorbonne; but students in Europe and the situation in Europe were undoubtedly very different from that of Indonesia. Yet if he expressed his fears, Lintang was sure to be offended, and they would wind up in another argument.

"Aren't you going to say anything?" Lintang finally asked.

"Have you spoken about this with your mother?" Dimas took the safe route, hoping that Vivienne had used the "parent card" with her daughter, even though it no longer had much currency in France and especially not for Lintang, who was now twenty-three years old. She was an adult and could go wherever she wanted to go, with or without her parents' permission. That she talked to them at all about her plans was a sign that she cared for them and respected their opinions. But she wasn't asking for their blessing, much less their permission.

"I have, but she asked the same thing, whether I had spoken about this with you." Lintang seemed somewhat miffed.

"OK, then let me say this: first focus on Professor Dupont's requirements. What is it you want from your final assignment? What must you show in your documentary film? After that, given Indonesia's history and the events and impact of 1965 on the country, you have to be very judicious and use a macro lens in choosing your subject of focus. You have to be sharp and clear. The subject of 1965, with all its confusion and characters, all its victims and impacts, and the bloodbath that was perpetrated to achieve change in the country's power structure, is a vast one. And then, beyond that, there is the very sensitive matter that you will also have to face—"

"That I am the daughter of Dimas Suryo," Lintang cut in.

"That's right," her father answered. "You've spent your entire life in Paris, far from what happened over there. You were cut off from Indonesia. You don't know it. You've never experienced it, never met its people, never smelled its soil or heard the sound of leaves slapped by showers in the rainy season. You've never gotten to know your Indonesian relatives: your grandparents, your aunts and uncles, or your cousins. All that you know is what you've heard from me and what you've overheard at the restaurant. You still don't know the country firsthand."

Dimas took a breath, ignoring the ache he felt in his stomach. "In Indonesia, everything will be different. If you intend to interview the families of political prisoners, you have to know that there will always be someone watching and recording what you do—especially because of the family name you carry."

Lintang nodded.

"Have you thought about how you're going to get a visa to go to Indonesia? All the years that I've been here, I still haven't been able—"

Lintang interrupted her father, impatiently: "I met someone at the embassy, a junior diplomat who said that he would help."

Dimas looked at his daughter in surprise and silently praised her foresightedness. Wherever had she attained her planning skills?

"And you must always remember," Dimas continued, "that my crime—being part of the 'political fornication' engaged in by PKI, LEKRA, and whatever other groups you want to mention—is a permanent one that will extend beyond my generation. Like it or not, you have inherited my political sins and they are now your burden to bear." He looked at his daughter with affection. "Let us only pray they won't be a millstone for your future children as well."

"'Political fornication…'" Lintang mused. "I've never come across that term in any of the books on political theory that I have read. *Je dois me rappeler.* I must remember that one. You, my father, have a gift for words."

Dimas laughed and mussed his daughter's hair. "In the '60s, before I left Jakarta, the political situation was explosive. You were either on the left or the right. You were red, pink, green, or maybe even greenish. Jargon and catchphrases were an essential element of any kind of discussion or discourse. There were all kinds of accusations thrown around. Nouns instead of adjectives were used to describe you. You might be a 'Manipol,' a person who supported the 'Political Manifesto' that Sukarno espoused. Then too, you might be a 'Nekolim,' standing for a person bent on 'Neo-colonialism and Imperialism.' If not one of those, you might be a 'Revolusi' or a 'Kontra-Revolusi,' a person who either supported the goals of the revolution or was against them. These are just a few of the terms that were being thrown around, but there were hundreds of other epithets, atrocious acronyms, most of them not worth remembering, much less studied or researched. The point is, in that time, Indonesia had no neutral zone. There was no gray: you were black or white, either with 'us' or 'them.'"

Lintang listened to her father with rapt attention. She had never really discussed Indonesian political history with her father before.

"I was friends with everyone," he added, "with Om Hananto, Om Nug, and so on... Well, I wasn't completely of one mind with the editor-in-chief of Nusantara News Agency, where I worked at the time, but I was friends with Amir, or 'Bang Amir,' as I called him. Even so, I was seen to be in bed with leftists and had committed acts of political fornication with them. As such I was a Red, a Communist Party supporter. I won't dwell on this. That was the risk for anyone who did not want to choose. Not to choose was seen as the same thing as making a choice."

"Who's Bang Amir?" Lintang asked.

"Bang Amir was a member of the Masyumi Party. There were two political parties that Sukarno banned: the Socialist Party and Masyumi. ...You'll have to read up on Indonesian political party history to keep all the characters and factions straight." His eyes studied his shelves of books.

"Later, Ayah. I can look myself. But I'm curious about this Bang Amir."

"Amir is my friend, Mohamad Amir Jayadi. I don't know how it happened really, but for whatever reason, we were close and saw eye to eye on many things. A lot of the things he said seemed logi-cal to me. Maybe I couldn't always grasp Natsir's reasoning—that's Mohammad Natsir, chairman of the Masyumi political party and one of the country's leading Muslim thinkers at the time—but Bang Amir was able to make me think about spirituality without having to link it to organized religion." Dimas looked enlivened and leaned towards Lintang. She followed suit, leaning closer towards him. "Spirituality was something older and deeper than religion, something that was honorable and integral to the essence of man-kind. When I talked to Bang Amir, it was like two normal people talking, without all the trappings of color, symbols, parties, ide-ologies, or groups. We spoke together as friends, as two reporters curious about the relationship between man—that small and finite creature—and the greatness of nature."

Lintang felt that her father was entering an area completely foreign to her, but she savored it.

"Did he—Bang Amir, that is—share the view that you had committed political fornication?"

Dimas shook his head slowly. "No, he didn't."

Lintang could see that her father thought highly and fondly of this man, that he had not been her father's political enemy.

"He wasn't the kind of person given to sticking political labels on everyone. By the way, that term is one that I came up with after years of trying to figure out why I was never able to obtain per-mission to go back to Indonesia." Dimas took another breath, then exhaled. "And that's what you have to be ready for: that you too will be seen in the same light. They see it as an inherited sin. Will you be able to deal with that kind of small-minded prejudice? With having people shun you for the blood you carry in your veins?"

"I think I can. What with all the documentaries I've watched and with all the books I've read…"

Dimas raised his hand. "Watching and reading are very different from experiencing, my sweet." He then took her face in his hands. "It's a terrible thing to experience, one that could haunt you for the rest of your life."

Lintang knew her father was right. Ever since childhood, she had a capacious mind and a gift for detail. Past events were as clear for her today as when she had experienced them: the feel of the grass and the smoothness of gravestones at the Père Lachaise cemetery when she visited as a child; the pungent scent of spices in her parents' kitchen when her father prepared Indonesian food; the gaiety of discovering a secondhand book at Antoine Martin's bookstall; the titles of books that lined the shelves at Shakespeare & Co. She remembered everything very clearly. Not only could she remember all the events that had happened in her life, but she was able to remember their sensations and smells. Yes, indeed, her father was right. If anything bad were to happen to her, she would not be who she is if she could expunge that experience from her memory.

"I want you to be prepared," her father went on. "Your decision to make a documentary film will not be easy to carry out. Will you need permits? I cannot imagine the trouble you'd have if you were to seek official permission, especially with my name on the back of yours. You know, don't you, that most former political prisoners use pseudonyms when they write for the mass media and that their children don't use their father's name?"

Lintang nodded. "I know that, Ayah. I read about that; but, still, I've never felt more prepared than I do now."

"One more thing," Dimas added. "I know that you know—from articles in the paper and news on the television—that Indonesia is going through a very unstable period at this time."

"Yes, I know. President Soeharto installed his daughter as Minister for Social Affairs and packed the cabinet with his cronies! That stuff has been widely covered by the media."

"I know," Dimas agreed. "Ever since the Asian economic crisis at the end of last year, problems have been growing: economic, political, and social. Indonesia appears to be on the brink of chaos. In this situation, not only will it be difficult for you to focus on your work, but you yourself might be put in danger's way. You must be very careful."

"I will be," she promised.

"If your mind is made up and you are going to do this, Om Nug and I will send messages to friends and family members who will be able to help you locate sources. But before we can do this, you must clearly define what your film is to be about. Once you've done that, we will do everything we can to help."

Lintang leaned against her father's shoulder and smiled. "*Oui…Merci*, Ayah."

Dimas smiled. Beginning to feel the effect of the medicine he had taken and the drowsiness it induced, he yawned.

Lintang felt it was time to speak of something she had been avoiding for months. "About that argument of ours, Ayah, I…"

Dimas waved his hand, a sign that he'd already forgotten about it. He closed his eyes as he leaned against the arm of the sofa. "I'll just lie down. I'm not sleepy yet."

Lintang rose to give her father more room to rest. No sooner had he stretched out on the sofa than he fell asleep. Lintang covered her father with a blanket. He looked pale and tired. Lintang leaned down and kissed him on the cheek.

Because the sound of the vacuum cleaner would surely disturb her father's sleep, Lintang decided to put off cleaning the floors of the apartment. Instead, she concentrated on straightening the books on the shelf. After a half hour doing this, she then moved to her father's desk in his bedroom, the only territory that was in relatively good order. Apparently, during this time of recovery, her father had been unable to do much work. She pulled out the rolling office chair and sat down. Her eyes fell on a manuscript, one that her father had been working on for some time now, apparently with the view of having it published one day as a book. On the first page of the manuscript was its working title: "Testimony." She turned the first page to scan the table of contents. Chapter headings denoted that the manuscript contained life histories of people from various regions of Indonesia who had been hunted down by the military in the period 1965–1968. Subchapters were devoted to the fate of their families, their children, and the parents of the targets who were hunted down.

Lintang glanced at her father who was breathing slowly, his chest rising and falling like that of a baby. Near the desk were several large wooden chests apparently serving as file cabinets for her father's work. Opening the lid of one of the chests, she saw that it contained clippings from newspapers and magazines, as well as scholarly books by Western political analysts with various views and theories about the September 30 Movement—whether the Indonesian Communist Party had been behind the attempted coup or whether the alleged coup had been the result of fractures in the military that pitted leftist officers against the military elite. Based on her research into materials available at the Beaubourg library, Lintang could see that her father's collection was fairly comprehensive. It was also in neat order.

Closing the lid of the chest, Lintang's eyes moved to the next one. When she opened the cover, the sight of its contents made her heart beat faster. The letters inside were her father's personal domain, which could very well be out of bounds for her. She recalled a letter she'd come across years before, when she was thirteen years old. The letter was from Surti Anandari, the wife of Hananto Prawiro, her father's good friend. Lintang shivered to remember that night. The letter had led to an explosive argument between her parents, and that same night her father had left the family's apartment.

The letters in the second chest, it seems, were there because they related to her father's work. Lintang went through the stack, careful not to disturb their order. One that was dated August 1968 was from her uncle Aji, her father's younger brother. She perused its contents. In the letter Aji informed her father that his friend, Hananto Prawiro, had been arrested and that no one knew where he had been taken. He also mentioned that during the time Hananto was on the run, his wife Surti and their children, Kenanga, Bulan, and Alam, had been detained twice, first for a time at the detention center on Jalan Guntur and later, for a longer period, at the one on Budi Kemuliaan. The intelligence agents knew that it was Hananto who was supposed to have gone to Santiago. Why then, they asked, had Dimas Suryo had gone instead?

Lintang mused. If it had been Hananto and not her father who had gone to Santiago, her father would never have met her mother and she would not exist.

Lintang continued going through the stack of letters until she came to another one from her uncle Aji, but this was one that time had not served well. So faded its ink and so fragile the paper, her father had placed it in a protective plastic sleeve. In sections of the letter the ink had faded so much she found it almost impossible to decipher. It was written in "1968," but she couldn't read the month or date.

...1968

Dear Mas Dimas,

Now that we've moved to Jakarta, I finally can give you some detail on what happened in Solo. In Solo, I was much too paranoid to write at length about the hell that the city became after September 1965. Even now, three years after the tragedy, it seems like only yesterday the world was turned upside down. Imagine: three years later and we still live in fear! How did it all happen? How did our hometown come to be divided into two ever opposing camps—with one in support of the PKI and the other against the Party—when previous to that time differences in opinion were accepted and tolerated? I remember you telling me before you left for Santiago that the pro-PKI people had become ever more aggressive in their tactics and had begun to go after their opponents. Maybe that's why, after September 30, the table turned. But what I witnessed wasn't just a matter of anti-PKI people getting revenge for the past actions of PKI supporters. A concerted effort was made by the military to inflame the enmity of the one camp towards the other, so much so that the hunting down and slaughter of communists came to be seen as normal.

I remember in mid-October, two or three weeks after the events of September 30, military troops arriving at Balapan train station. They weren't brought in just to tear down anti-military posters or to help clean up the town; they were brought in to stir people up and drive them to burn and destroy all Communist Party offices, symbols, and equipment. By this time the PKI in Solo was completely paralyzed and powerless—at least that's what was reported in the news. With them now so weak, I thought the madness would end and the situation would be brought under control. In fact, it was allowed to spin further out of control.

One day when I left the house to send a telegram, I heard that the military had embarked on a coordinated roundup of senior PKI officials who were said to be hiding in the Sambeng area of Sidorejo. I wasn't sure if this was true, but I heard it from Om Kiasno.

Even after the Party leaders had been arrested, the hunt continued, but now they were bringing in anyone thought to be sympathetic to the communists: mothers, wives, and friends. That was what made me worried: thinking of Mother being hauled into the city square where people were being held. Fortunately, Om Kiasno had enough power and authority to prevent that from happening. It was only because of him that Mother and I weren't touched, though we were interrogated several times.

Now in Jakarta, even though we feel we still need a pair of eyes on our backs, we can at least pass the days a bit more calmly. It's not that Jakarta itself is any safer but, for us at least, there is now a distance between ourselves and the calamity that happened in Solo. For the time being, at least.

I hope you are well. As soon as I find more information about Surti and the children, I'll send you a cable.

Your loving brother,
 Aji Suryo

Lintang shivered to think of how awful it must have been to live through that period of time. It was lucky her two cousins, Uncle Aji's children, hadn't yet been born. Lintang then removed another letter from her uncle, this one relatively recent, having been written in 1994.

Jakarta, June 1994

Dear Mas Dimas,

I just watched a news program on television about an incident that's as shocking as it is disturbing. Last month the Indonesian government banned two news magazines, Tempo *and* Editor, *and a tabloid newspaper* Detik—*which, quite naturally, angered the students and political activists, who took to the streets and staged a demonstration outside the Department of Information building on Merdeka Barat, which is only a few hundred meters away from the presidential palace. Rendra was there, reading his poetry. The crowd held aloft banners protesting the ban. The military came and victims fell. They arrested Rendra (but later let him go) and beat the painter Semsar Siahaan so bad they broke the bones in his legs.*

I know that the New Order government has more power than ever before, but the ban of those magazines and newspaper indicates a level of arrogance that is beyond belief. They did it because they knew they could do it and get away with it without there being any impact whatsoever on their continuation in power. The students and activists can protest all they want, but the noise they make is little more than the buzzing of a mosquito waiting to be slapped. The (Western) world may grumble, but the Indonesian government could care the less; their ears are plugged and sealed. It's all so easy. Life goes on, "aman sentosa," as our Javanese president is prone to say, in a situation of safety and security.

What is the news of Lintang? She must be a high school senior now. Is her plan to go to the Sorbonne working out? I always pray for her success.

Andini is preparing for her final high school examinations and is experiencing a bit of stress. She hopes to get into the Faculty of Letters at the University of Indonesia. Rama meanwhile has just done something both startling and worrisome: he applied to and was accepted for employment at PT Cita Karya, one of the state-owned construction companies in Jakarta. Obviously, he didn't use the Suryo name on his application form. Ever since his acceptance into the firm, he's rarely been home to visit except at the time of the Idul Fitri holidays.

Retno sends her warm regards. If you know anyone coming to Jakarta, let me know and I'll find the cloves and other spices you want. And, of course, if there are any new books you want, tell me and I'll pick them up as well.

In closing, give my love to Vivienne, Mas Nug, Bung Risjaf, and Bung Tjai. And a big hug for Lintang!

Yours in Peace,
Aji Suryo

Lintang leaned back against the chair and thought of her uncle's family. She had never met her two first cousins, only seen their pictures. What she knew of them she had learned first from her father, when he would tell stories about his brother, and then, when she was older, from her own correspondence with Andini. She had met her uncle Aji just once, when he came to Europe for office-related work and took some extra days off to come to Paris to see his brother, whom he hadn't seen in the flesh in more than a couple decades. Even though she was only in primary school at the time, she would never forget how long the two brothers had embraced and how they had talked as they smoked and drank coffee through the night and into the morning. That was the only time her mother hadn't grumbled about the ashtray full of butts and the ashes scattered everywhere.

That visit was when Lintang learned a bit more about her two cousins, Rama and Andini, enough to make them more real for her. Rama was in senior high school; Andini was still in primary school, just like herself. Om Aji told her that Andini liked to read, just like her; so that same evening she begged her mother to take her to Shakespeare & Co. to buy some English-language children's books. Lintang willingly sacrificed her small allowance so that her cousin could read the books that she was then reading: *Little Women*; an English translation of *Le Petit Prince*; and an abridged English-language edition of *Les Misérables*.

Sometime after Om Aji returned to Jakarta, Lintang received a thank-you letter from Andini for the gift of books she'd sent. Thereafter, the two of them soon became pen pals. Lintang was especially pleased to have a cousin like Andini who, like herself, was a fanatic reader. Over time, and with the advent of the Internet and their subscription to e-mail accounts two years previously, the traditional snail-mail exchange of letters between the cousins had changed into a rapid exchange of ideas through the virtual world.

Lintang imagined meeting her cousin for the first time and how happy she would be. Having grown up as an only child, she had often wished for a sister or brother. She had some distant cousins from her mother's side of the family; but since her mother's brother, her Uncle Jean, had never married, she had no close cousins in France. She was excited and looking forward to meeting this sister-like cousin with whom she had corresponded for so many years.

Lintang's thoughts returned to her father's cache of correspondence. Looking through the stack, she found several more from Aji but then, when she saw one with a completely different kind of penmanship, her fingers stopped searching. She removed the letter from the pile. Surti Anandari. Her fingers trembled. The stationery had yellowed and the ink was somewhat faded, but she could still read the words clearly.

Jakarta, December 1968

Dear Dimas,

I don't know whether you will receive this letter or not. After having been detained for several months at the Budi Kemuliaan detention center, I am now home.

In the many times I was interrogated, I didn't know what to say and didn't know how to answer their questions whenever they asked me about Hananto, because I really didn't know where he was. I wasn't lying then and I never will lie. I never knew what Hananto was up to—either in matters of love or politics. But they didn't believe me. Or simply didn't want to believe me.

Since they captured Hananto last June, we've heard nothing from him directly. After he disappeared in October 1965, I only heard about—but didn't actually know—how he was able to move about, like a shadow in the mist, from one village to another, from one city to another. I only heard of his peregrinations through the wind. And more than that, through silence.

For the last three years, I have faced calamity, which was a risk I took on when I married Hananto. In each session, the interrogators threw at me the same set of questions from morning till night, with breaks of only a few minutes in duration. Sometimes the interrogators were polite. More often they shouted the same questions over and over like a cracked LP. Did I know about Hananto's activities, and what kind of activities his friends were engaged in? Did I know about the meetings that Hananto attended?

But if I had to choose between the two kinds of interrogators who questioned me, I would choose the one who shouted and screamed at me rather than the soft-spoken one, who asked in a mild-mannered tone what I and Hananto did in bed. One interrogator, a middle-aged man, was truly vile. The day it was his turn to find out where Hananto was hiding— Was he with some family member? Was he at their home?—he asked his questions with his left hand in his pants pocket all the while. As he slipped in questions about our marital relations, he slowly masturbated. I was so disgusted, I refused to answer his questions. But then he began to ask about Kenanga—how old she was and whether she had begun to menstruate. That, I tell you, Dimas, was the worst kind of mental terror that I experienced! I wasn't as concerned with Bulan and Alam, as they were still so young. Being just six, Bulan looked on everything happening as a kind of game. In fact some of the guards and interrogators even gave her and Alam toys to play with. Alam was still of the age that he liked to be cuddled by almost anyone. Alam is such a

good-looking boy, and with his fair skin and curly hair, many of
the inhabitants and detainees of Budi Kemuliaan took pity on
him and gave him rice water as a substitute for milk.

But Kenanga was almost a teenager. She knew that her
father was being pursued and that we were being held there
because of something he'd done.

If I wasn't careful, I feared they might do something to her.

One day, one of the interrogators politely asked if Kenanga
could be assigned to clean one of the rooms in the building.
I could say nothing but agree, even though it turns out that her
job was to mop up the dried blood on the floor of the torture
room. She once found a stingray tail in the room, matted
with dried blood—but this she didn't tell me until a month
afterwards. I had been down with a terrible fever for ever so
long and she didn't want to make anything harder for me. She
finally told me, crying all the while. She imagined her father
being captured and that happening to him as well. She's seen
too much. She's told me of the men she's seen, their bodies
covered with blood and staggering all the way, as they were
moved from one cell to another.

I write this to you, Dimas, only to share with you and at
once thank you for taking the time to send us assistance, even
though as an exile you are in difficult straits and don't know
what lies ahead.

Whatever difficulties we here might face, we know and
recognize that you are doing whatever you can to make our
lives easier. For that, I thank you from the bottom of my heart.
I know that you are a friend forever.

Surti Anandari

Lintang breathed in and out, trying to fathom how her father's friends and family had coped in such straits, even as she began to become aware of the difficulties that she herself might face after her arrival in Jakarta. The letters she was reading were old ones, written ten, twenty or more years previously, but the Indonesian government now in power was still one and the same.

Lintang fingered another letter, written with a deft hand on white paper. She studied the penmanship: so neat and written in evenly spaced lines, almost as if by a machine because of its uniformity. The thought occurred to her that Indonesian teachers of penmanship must be very patient. Most of the samples of writing by Indonesians she'd seen were very similar and very neat—far different from the way that she and her French schoolmates wrote, paying little attention to the uniformity of size and shape of the letters they put on papers, not controlling their fingers, and letting them moved as they pleased.

Jakarta, June 18, 1970

Om Dimas,

I feel like the sky in Jakarta has cracked apart and sharp pieces of dark metal are raining down on us.

There's no end to the problems affecting us. I don't know if this is the start or the end of our suffering. For the last month, ever since they executed Bapak, I haven't been able to function at all. All I've been able to do is stay in my room until, finally, it seemed that I became part of the room's features, no different from the bed or the floor. I felt more useless by the day.

Exactly a month ago, we were told to come to Salemba Prison in order to see Bapak for the last time. We were given two hours to talk to him before he was to be executed. What

were we supposed to say in those two hours when all we could
do is imagine him standing in front of a row of men with rifles
aimed at him?

My father held Alam on his lap where he giggled and played
with Bapak's fingers. Just five years old, of course he's going to
look at the sky and see rainbows. Bulan, who had just turned
eight, understood the meaning of "coming" and "going," All
she could do was cry and repeatedly ask if she was going to see
Bapak again. Mother tried to be strong. She held Bapak's hand
tightly and tried to stop herself from crying. Every once in
a while, she would whisper something to him I couldn't hear.

Trying to avoid the sadness, I sat as far away from Bapak
as possible. I wasn't strong. I didn't know what to do to make
my body sit up straight when all I really wanted to do was to
scream and wail. I didn't cry and I don't know why, but I was
actually proud not to leave a trail of tears in there. I didn't
want to look at my father's face, which, on that day, in those
two hours, looked so calm and wise. What could have been
going through his mind?

In the last thirty minutes, Bapak came to me, alone. He
kneeled beside me and took my hands in his own. "Kenanga,"
he said, "you are the tree that protects the entire family. You are
the heartbeat of us all…"

Still trying to avoid looking into his face, I stared down at
my shoes, a rundown pair of sneakers I'd been wearing for years,
and all I could think about at the time was to wonder where
Mother had bought them and what color they once had been.
Was it pink or orange? Their color had faded so much and the
shoes were so stained, the only way to describe their color was
a muddy brown.

But then, suddenly, I felt my father's hands holding mine in his own. He said "Kenanga…I beg your forgiveness for all the trouble I have caused. Because I now must take my leave, I can ask only that you remain strong—for Mother, for Bulan, and for Alam…"

I hate tears, I hate crying. Tears come and go as they please with no regard to me.

Kenanga Prawiro

Lintang felt all her energy exhausted by these blood-filled letters—not only because she was spent from trying to chase away her own tears, crying for the broken family she didn't know, but because she suddenly felt so close to them all. Reading these blood-filled letters had made her feel bloodied herself. She wanted to find a message that might lift her spirits. Within the pile was one written on light blue paper. The letter was short, the penmanship superb. Jumping to the bottom of the paper, she saw from the signature that it was from her father's friend, Bang Amir.

Jakarta, 1969

My brother Dimas,
Having received your message, I now write to you. I am sorry for the loss of your mother, Dimas. I kneel and pray to God that He has taken her to His side. I hope that you and our fellow countrymen there in that distant land are strong and in good health.

Do you remember our discussion that one time about the vacuum that each of us has inside, the one that only you and God can fill, to create a Union between you and God that can never be broken or disturbed by anything or anyone? This is the right time for you to look at that space inside yourself, alone. To converse with it if that is your bent, or to be silent if that is what you choose. Either way, He will listen to you.

He is always listening.

Your friend,
Moh. Amir Jayadi

Unconsciously, Lintang held her chest. That vacuum. That little space in her body. That conversation between us and Him? Was it in her as well?

FLÂNEURS

On ne voit bien qu'avec le coeur.

L'essentiel est invisible pour les yeux.

LE PETIT PRINCE,

Antoine de Saint-Exupéry

"YOU CAN SEE CLEARLY ONLY WITH THE HEART. The essence cannot be seen with the eyes." That's the sentence from *The Little Prince* Lintang remembered best, ever since the first time her father read Antoine de Saint-Exupéry's fantastic tale of a little boy whose plane crashes in the Sahara desert.

That night Lintang had one question. Or maybe she had a thousand questions—but one question, always starkly present, unendingly posing itself, was there in her heart. Would she have the clarity of mind to see and to decipher the complex problems that awaited her in Jakarta?

Lintang wasn't able to answer that question, at least not yet. But that night, and during the days and nights that followed, she typed almost nonstop, as if there were no tomorrow. Every so often she'd look at a book, a manuscript, a journal, a clipping, a paper, or an old photograph and then would begin to write again, to type again. Reading something more, using a yellow highlighter to underscore a phrase, she'd then write again. Countless cups of coffee filled her stomach, which was about to scream from high acid content, and Ravel's music filled her ears. Eyes open wide, she blinked as she studied the tens of pages in her proposal, checking its language for fluency and whether or not the sources that she quoted effectively bolstered her argument. In her proposal, Lintang explained the importance of revealing information that had too long been buried by official Indonesian history; how necessary it was to provide a space and a place for those historical actors whose voices had been silenced. Lintang had to produce a convincing argument for her need to conduct her work in Indonesia, and not, for instance, in Paris or Amsterdam. The names of the sources she quoted ranged from well-known players to persons whose voices time had almost forgotten.

Three days had passed and now on the morning of the fourth, she was sprawled on the sofa in her apartment, trying to get a little sleep before bathing and getting ready to see Professor Dupont to turn in her proposal. She slept so soundly that she definitely would have been late had not a kiss as gentle as cotton awakened her.

"Nara…"

Lintang rubbed her eyes. Her throat suddenly felt parched. What time was it? Where was she?

"I started to get worried when you didn't answer the telephone. I know your proposal is due today and that you should be leaving soon for campus."

Lintang jumped up from the sofa. As she did, the loose pages of her proposal flew into the air. Not bothering to first pick them up, she raced into the bathroom, slamming the door behind her. Nara smiled and shook his head as he picked up the sheets of paper and arranged them in their proper order. Then he poured orange juice into a glass and rolled up his sleeves to make breakfast. He assumed that Lintang had not been eating well and had probably consumed gallons of caffeine during the past several days.

"Yum, an omelet and sausages? And where did you find the croissants? I've haven't had a chance to shop this week. Did you hold up the *boulangerie* on the ground floor?"

Dressed in a kimono bathrobe, Lintang pounced on the breakfast Nara had arranged neatly on the table.

"Their first croissants of the day were just coming out of the oven when I arrived, so I scooped them up," Nara said.

"You are an angel," Lintang said as she kissed his lips. "That place is the only reason I can stand to live in this shit hole of an apartment. I love waking up to the smell of their freshly baked croissants."

"But this morning you woke up because of my kiss," Nara said as he repeatedly kissed her face. "Is there enough time for me to help relieve some of your tension?"

Lintang laughed, pulled the lobe of Nara's ear, and then went into her bedroom to change her clothes.

"I straightened up your proposal and put it in the green folder," Nara called after her.

"Did you read it?"

"Just skimmed it—I was fixing your breakfast, you know—but it looks to me to be pretty good, in content and in tone. I'm sure Monsieur Dupont will be impressed."

As Lintang dressed, Nara put her messy kitchen back in order. She came out from the room wearing black jeans and a white blouse. Hanging from her shoulders, and complementing her simple apparel, was an almost diaphanous batik scarf her mother owned.

Sitting down at the kitchen table, Lintang began to talk: "You know, all the stuff I've read these past few weeks, in my father's unpublished manuscripts and the letters that's he's received over the years, and all the documentary films I've seen—both the unprofessional and professional ones produced by Australian filmmakers and the BBC—reveal a blood-filled side of Indonesian history that has thus far been largely ignored."

Nara could only nod as he listened to Lintang speak.

Pausing to take a breath, Lintang then attacked the omelet and sausages before continuing: "The massacres that took place around Indonesia and the hunt for members of the Communist Party and their families served to bolster a strong and enduring power structure. And those concepts of 'political hygiene' and being 'environmentally clean'…*Merde!* What the hell are they anyway?!"

Still eating her omelet, Lintang spoke quickly, no pausing for commas, no stopping for periods, sometimes jabbing her fork in the air.

Afraid that Lintang was going to stick him in the eye with her fork, Nara took her hand and lowered it to the table. "Very good, darling, but it's time to get ready to go. I'll go with you as far as Monsieur Dupont's office; but after that, I must go see Professor Dubois."

"Oh, hmm…" Lintang suddenly felt guilty for not having paid sufficient attention to Nara or his own academic concerns. "Is he going to give you his recommendation?"

"It looks like it…but come on," Nara told her. "When all this is over, I am going to kidnap you and lock you in the bedroom for three days!" he added with a leer.

Nara grabbed Lintang's jacket and the two of them ran to the Metro station. At that moment, Lintang could not help but think how easy her life was. She would finish her final assignment. Nara would continue his schooling in London. Soon, it would be summer in Paris again. Life was neat and orderly, just as it should be.

●

Dimas put the oversized envelope containing the X-rays of his chest and abdomen into a large bag the hospital had provided. He was sorely tempted to throw the results of the examination into the trash container—Bam!—but he realized that would be overly dramatic and childish. He sat at the Metro station, staring at its subterranean walls and the array of announcements on them. They suddenly seemed to transform into a series of advertisements and health advisories about vaccines, skin diseases, breast cancer, and AIDS. He felt chafed. What a cliché it was: he would not die like Hananto, before a firing squad, or be thrown off a cliff or drowned in the Solo River. He would be slowly worn away by a fucking disease he could not even see.

It was such a cliché, so damned banal and mediocre that Dimas was relucant to talk or think about the topic, even to himself.

Dimas held his stomach, which had begun to feel queasy. He took the bottle of pills he had just paid for at the hospital. Opening the cap, he popped two tablets into his hand and then swallowed them straightaway.

Paris was preparing to welcome the beginning of summer. Dimas counted the number of summer days that he still might see.

•

Ever since the first time Lintang set foot on the campus of the Sorbonne as a freshman student, the wide corridors of the main hall held a special place in her memory. The Sorbonne was where she first met Narayana; where she first recorded autumn's falling leaves and winter's chilling winds; where she learned to wait patiently for the right moment, for those few seconds, when a flower opened in bloom; and where she had honed her editing skills by sifting through hours of film footage to find the most arresting images and most interesting quotes of the people she'd interviewed. But the most important thing, and what made the experience different from her primary years of education, was that the Sorbonne had made Lintang feel accepted, a natural part of academic life, where questions of a student's skin color or appearance were of no concern. She felt at the Sorbonne a life of freedom, one which she and her fellow classmates had been invited to explore, to plunge into the world of intellectual life. Nothing was more exciting and stimulating.

Professor Dupont's challenge for her to take a closer look at her own history had brought her here, to this corridor. Today, walking down one hallway and then another on the way to her advisor's office, Lintang felt that she had already embarked on a journey towards a foreign destination called Indonesia. The door was open. Lintang took a breath, gave the door a rap, and then stuck her head inside.

Seeing Lintang's face, Professor Dupont waved for her to come inside. "Lintang…"

"Professor…"

Dupont smiled widely. "Amazing!"

Lintang breathed a sigh of relief. "Hmm, *oui*?"

Dupont nodded and took Lintang's proposal from a stack of folders.

"The topic is interesting and unique. No other student has done such a thing before. You have a clear focus—even if you yourself might be seen to be a victim of the events of 1965 in Indonesia."

"*Attendez, Professeur.* I don't think I want to include myself as a victim."

Professor Dupont stared at Lintang with his blue eyes. His eyes smiled, though his lips revealed no emotion.

"I understand. But in the eyes of the viewer, the outsider, that is how you will be seen. Because you've never had the chance to know that part of yourself: your father's homeland."

Lintang said nothing.

"This could be an amazing documentary film—as long as you can bring it on time, that is, and are able to stay faithful to your focus."

"But Professor, about my final point...?"

"You mean, the need for you to do the work in Indonesia? I don't see a problem," the professor answered. "I'll give my recommendation to the dean. Some funding should be available, but you'll probably have to come up with some of your own as well."

Lintang had to resist throwing her arms around her advisor and giving him a big hug. But from the happy look she gave him, Professor Dupont could see in her eyes two gleaming stars.

"I'll send in my recommendation today. You'll need to wait a day or two for approval but, after that, we can meet again to discuss the technical details."

"*Merci*, professor."

Lintang took her advisor's hand and shook it happily.

"*De rien*, Lintang." He gave her a serious look. "Your documentary film is about the joys and sorrows of mankind, about life and life's history. *C'est la vie et l'histoire de la vie.* As such, you must not see your work merely as my final assignment for you. Your film must come from here." He pointed to his chest. "Not just from your brain alone."

On ne voit bien qu'avec le coeur. We can see clearly by using the heart.

"*D'accord, monsieur.*"

"You must be careful, Lintang. Indonesia is going through a period of unrest. Students and activists are taking to the streets. But you have to remain focused. Even more important, you must finish your work on time. If you are late, you will not graduate. *Tu comprends?*"

"*Je comprends. Merci, monsieur.*"

Lintang ran the entire length of the hallway. She felt that she was reaching for something. Reaching for something that had always been foreign inside her. Plucking something from I-N-D-O-N-E-S-I-A.

•

Nasi kuning, ayam goreng kremes, kering tempe, sambal bajak teri, urap tabur kelapa… My God. Yellow rice, coconut-battered fried chicken, tempeh sticks with peanuts and chili, fried hot pepper sauce with dried and salted white fish, steamed vegetables with grated coconut… It was unreal! Lintang was really going to Jakarta where she would be able to get those dishes any time she wanted. Even so, she still dug into her father's cooking like an inmate who had been fed on stale rice and salt for the past two years. She tried everything, ate everything, almost not even chewing before she swallowed.

"Just look at you, eating like that. That should teach you not to fight with your father." Nugroho was astonished to see Lintang wipe clean two whole plates of food.

Nara scratched his head; the rissole served as a starter had never tasted so good. When Dimas came out of the kitchen to check on them, he found that the *nasi kuning* and all the side dishes were gone, with only empty plates left on the table.

"Like something more?" he asked his daughter.

Lintang smiled widely.

"*O, mon Dieu.*" It was Nara who groaned.

Dimas laughed happily, then returned to the kitchen to fetch Lintang more food.

Shortly thereafter, three young men entered the restaurant. All were clean and good-looking in appearance, neatly dressed in suits and ties. Each carried a valise.

Risjaf, who was standing by the cash register, looked taken aback. He knew who the young men were and so he remained, standing there, unmoving and unsure what to do: whether to roll up his sleeves to fight or invite them to stay. They looked friendly, however, and even more than that, they looked hungry. Were they here for lunch? Nugroho lowered his glasses on the bridge of his nose and stared at them cautiously. Even Tjai forgot about his beloved calculator, he was so entranced.

It was Nara who spoke first, calling out to the three: "Raditya, Yos, Hans! Hi! Come on over here."

Still looking surprised, Risjaf showed the young men the way. His suspicion diminished when he saw the three warmly shake Nara's hand, and then vanished altogether when Lintang rose, moved two tables together, told them to sit down, and handed them menus that Yazir had brought to the table.

"Am I seeing right," Nugroho whispered to Risjaf. "It looks to me like those boys are from the embassy."

"I was just going to try to find out who they are," Risjaf answered.

"Good afternoon. May I be of assistance?"

Suddenly, Tjai was standing in front of their table. What the...? Nugroho and Risjaf stared quizzically at each other. Now, with Tjai exhibiting such authority over the situation, Yazir retreated in orderly fashion from the scene. Since when had Tjai shown interest in greeting customers and taking their orders? Tjai was a creature enamored with his calculator; so fixated was he on fiscal discipline that the restaurant's books were always neat and never showed red on the bottom line. What could possibly have caused Tjai to leave his calculator and come down from his perch at the cash register to approach the three men who were now sitting around their lovely young "niece"?

Lintang took control of the field: "The Padang set menu is good. How about if we all get *nasi Padang*? That way you'll get a variety of dishes to try. And you too, Nara? That way I can steal food from you."

"Four *nasi Padang*," she said to Tjai. "And do you want to try the iced jackfruit?" Lintang asked the three men. "It's like this," she said with her right thumb in the air.

The young men nodded like dullard cattle. Nara smiled, letting Lintang control the wheel. Tjai just stood there, not moving, not doing anything, just staring at these Indonesians who were strangers to the place.

Lintang quickly understood that these three men had to *kulo nuwun*, that being to offer their greetings to the restaurant owners.

"Oh, Om Tjai, this is Hans and Yos and Raditya."

The three men stood and politely shook hands with Tjai.

"And this is Om Nugroho and Om Risjaf. The other partner is my father, who is in the kitchen cooking. We call them the 'four pillars' of Tanah Air Restaurant."

The three nodded politely in the direction of Risjaf and Nugroho who stood somewhat at a distance, watching. Risjaf and Nugroho returned their nods.

Tjai wrote down their orders and then scuttled off towards the kitchen. Lintang imagined his gesticulations as he reported to her father that there were three young Indonesian diplomats sitting outside, in the restaurant, at a table with his daughter. Then she saw Om Nug and Om Risjaf disappear behind the kitchen door as well. She was tempted to sneak into the kitchen just to overhear the tittle-tattle of the four pillars, who had never seen any representatives of the New Order government set foot in the restaurant ever since it opened.

Hans looked around at the walls of the restaurant. Raditya left the table to study the guest book on a side table near the entrance. He looked at the signatures and read the supportive messages of famous people who had dined there: Indonesia's leading poet, Rendra; the famous sociologist, Arief Budiman; Abdurrahman Wahid, head of Indonesia's leading Islamic organization, and his wife, Nuriah; Danielle Mitterrand, wife of the French prime minister; and others.

Only a few minutes passed before, suddenly, Dimas Suryo—yes, Dimas Suryo, Lintang's father—appeared at the table carrying several plates of *nasi Padang*. Lintang was sure he had come out of the kitchen to make sure that his daughter was not being scalped or in any other way violated by these three young men. She repressed a smile as she helped her father serve the meals.

"I know you only ordered four servings," her father said to Lintang, "but I felt sorry for Nara. You're sure to eat most of his meal for him."

Lintang motioned towards the visitors. "Ayah, this is Raditya and Hans and Yos. They're friends of Nara."

The three young men rose instantly, like soldiers before a general.

Dimas shook their hands and then invited them to enjoy their meals. But he didn't make a move to leave the table where Lintang and the young men were seated. He stood, his hands now knitted together, watching them. No smile on his face.

"Ayah...?"

"Yes?" Dimas lifted his brow.

Just as is done in Indonesia, the younger men were apparently waiting for the most senior person to give them permission to eat. Nervously, Raditya raised his spoon and fork and stuttered: "Ehem, shall we start, Pak Dimas?"

As if coming out of a trance, Dimas quickly answered: "Oh, please, please, go ahead." He looked around to see his three friends standing, hands crossed, in front of the kitchen door. "If you'd like more, just ask Yazir," he said to Lintang, then turned and made his way back to the kitchen. But Lintang's three uncles remained outside, pretending to be busy, even as they kept their eyes on her.

"Sorry," Lintang said in English, shaking her head. "They're all very protective. They've never had anyone from the embassy come into the restaurant before."

"No problem," Yos said. "We understand." He then lowered his head and dug into his meal, as if not wanting to raise his head again. The succulent pieces of beef *rendang* seemed to melt on his tongue. He forgot his friends' presence and didn't notice that Raditya and Hans had also lost themselves in the plates of food before them.

The three young diplomats seemed to have forgotten where they were, so engrossed were they in eating the beef *rendang*, the chicken curry whose sauce nestled with the steaming hot rice, and the spiced cubes of fried calves liver with diced potatoes. On each plate was also a portion of Padang-style green chili sauce.

Not caring that they were in Paris and ignoring their spoons and forks, just as they would do at a Padang restaurant in Indonesia, they dug into their meals with their right hands. Dear God, this was heaven. Why were they forbidden to come here?

Lintang signaled for Yazir to fetch finger bowls.

"My father still likes to cook himself, especially when we have special visitors," Lintang said, opening the conversation. "And it's been so long since I've been here, Ayah insisted that he was going to cook."

The three young diplomats nodded, ignoring Lintang's explanation. Their attention was on the scrumptious *rendang* and curried chicken.

"Aren't you forbidden to eat here?" Lintang then asked, as if intentionally hoping to disturb the visitors' pleasure. "Wasn't there an official announcement to that effect from Jakarta?"

Risjaf, Tjai, and Nugroho, who were still standing within hearing distance, immediately pricked up their ears.

Hans reluctantly raised his head. "I don't give a damn!" he swore in English, his lips smeared with oil. "Who could turn down an offer of *rendang* as good as this?" he said and turned back to his plate.

Raditya and Yos said nothing at all, so busy were they with their portions of curried chicken.

Raditya had broken into a sweat from the spicy heat of the meal, and Lintang laughed to see him wriggle out of his suit jacket and struggle to remove it without staining the sleeve with his right hand, wet from oil and curry sauce.

Even though she had already eaten two plates of *nasi kuning* earlier, Lintang ate her own plate of *nasi Padang* enthusiastically.

"My God, Lintang, where do you put all that food?" Nara laughed, knowing how much Lintang had eaten that day.

All the plates were completely clean and the scent of cloves from *kretek* cigarettes now filled the air.

Yos leaned against the back of his chair and watched the smoke he had exhaled. "Oh, God," he moaned, "I really do not want to go back to the office."

Except for Lintang, who was nibbling on iced jackfruit, the diners were now smoking, slowly playing with their cigarettes as if they were on vacation, without a care in the world.

Finally, when his cigarette was just a stub, Hans took out a folder from his valise and removed a multiple-page form.

"This is a visa form. For your name, write 'Lintang Utara.' Don't use Suryo."

Lintang furrowed her forehead. "And this box, for the family name?"

"That's where you write 'Utara.' For all we care, that is your last name," said Yos in English with an airy tone. "The important thing is that you get to Jakarta, right?"

Lintang nodded and proceeded to fill in the form.

Risjaf and Nugroho seemed less nervous now. They had begun to move around the restaurant, taking care of other customers. And Tjai was once again buried in his figures.

"Weird," Lintang remarked as she intoned and wrote: "First name 'Lintang.' Family name 'Utara.'"

"Not to worry," Raditya said as he stubbed his cigarette. "With your French passport, the people at immigration aren't going to be extra wary anyway. And even if they do notice that you have an Indonesian name, they probably aren't going to give it any thought. Most Indonesians, especially the Javanese, rarely write down a family name. They don't have one. Like Hesti Handayani, who works at the embassy here, and Retno Sulistyowati, a classmate of mine: their names are their own and they don't put down another name to indicate who their mother or father might be. That's what appears on their I.D. cards and in their passports."

Lintang was astounded by this information. Could it really be that easy? But, at this point, she had neither the time nor the will to discuss the customary or, rather, "non-customary" use of family names in Indonesia. She completed the form, signed it, and affixed to it several regulation-size photographs of herself.

After the three men had finished eating a dessert of fried bananas, they began to say their goodbyes. Wanting to give her father the chance to thank the three men, she called for him to come out of the kitchen. But, still flummoxed about something, she spoke to them first: "Yos, Raditya, Hans… I want to thank you, but I also want to know why you're doing this, why you're helping me."

The three of them looked at Narayana, who nodded.

Raditya, who had already stood to leave, sat back down again. He saw that Nugroho, Risjaf, and Tjai had joined Lintang's father, and were also waiting for an answer to Lintang's question.

"I don't know, it's just…"

"Come on. Tell them the story."

"What story?"

"The whole story."

"OK." Raditya finally gathered will to speak. He looked at the older men flanking the table and then at Lintang. "What I was going to say is that it's just that times have changed and we have to change with them. For far too long now, we Indonesians have let ourselves be imprisoned by the politics of the past. Like you, Lintang, we're all from a new generation, born long after 1965. We have brains; we have our own minds. Why should we be told what to think?"

"What Raditya wants to say is this," Hans added impatiently: "Before their first posting abroad, all candidates to the diplomatic corps have to take written and oral examinations. In the written exam is a question: 'What would you do if a person you are speaking with tells you that he's a communist?'"

Lintang's eyes opened wide. Nara leaned forward. Risjaf, Tjai, and Nugroho raised their heads.

"What did you answer?" Lintang asked, impatient to hear this story being told in dribs and drabs.

Raditya glanced at his two colleagues and chuckled. "I wrote my answer in English: 'That would be none of my business. Everybody has the right to his own political beliefs.'"

Lintang clamped her mouth shut in surprise. Dimas and his three friends broke into laughter. Nugroho even shook Raditya's shoulders.

"Wow! And what did you answer?" Lintang said to Yos.

"I left it blank. I didn't answer."

"And I wrote, 'Nothing. So?'" Hans put in.

Again the room sounded with the men's laughter. Dimas laughed so hard he started to cry and held his stomach.

"So, what happened?" Nugroho asked. "Did they punish you?"

"Yes, they did," Raditya answered. "They didn't give us permission to leave that year—even though we were all set to go to our first posting; they delayed our departure for two years. Originally, I was supposed to go to England; Yos to Argentina; and Hans to Canada, but, instead, they gave us desk jobs in Jakarta, pushing pens and giving us trivial things to do. And we had to take a P-4 course, which is short for *Pedoman Penghayatan dan Pengalaman Pancasila*," Hans informed her, "the so-called 'Guidelines for Instilling and Implementing the Nation's Five Principles'—which was an exercise in boredom if there ever was one."

Raditya then revealed that he had studied political science at the University of Toronto, in Canada, when his father, a senior diplomat, was posted there. "Any serious student of economics or politics is required to read all the important works, including those of Marx and Engels as well as those of other leftist writers, and the more modern thinkers who followed them. I had to study the various kinds of political thought. And it was precisely because of my reading that I came to see why communism had failed in many countries." Raditya stood again and put on his suit jacket. "I think it's ridiculous for the government to ban the study of communism. It shows that they think the people are stupid and can't use their own brains to think. For years and years, the Indonesian people have been thought of and treated like idiots, unable to think for themselves."

Dimas now understood why these three junior diplomats had dared to come to Tanah Air Restaurant in defiance of the official ban from Jakarta. It wasn't a question of the succulence of his *rendang* or curried chicken. It was that they were members of a new generation who would not let their actions be dictated by rules they deemed to be irrational. They were a new and more intelligent generation, with the will and the ability to think independently.

Hans and Yos now stood as well.

"We've been following developments at home..." Nugroho said to Hans, trying to stall the young men's departure, "and there have been large demonstrations in some cities. Maybe you can tell me if I'm right, but it seems to me that their cause this time is not just a rise in the price of fuel but a whole series of things that have happened since last year when the rupiah was unhooked from the dollar and the president reshuffled his cabinet."

"It's all because of KKN," Risjaf interjected, citing the popular acronym. "That's what's wrong with the country: corruption, collusion, and nepotism."

"But Soeharto acts like everything is just fine," Dimas said in puzzlement. "The country's a mess and he's still planning to skip off to Cairo for that Islamic Nations Conference? Is that true?" he asked.

"It looks that way, sir," Hans said. "And you're right: the situation in Jakarta really is a mess." He then looked at Lintang. "Be careful when you get there. Please do take care."

"Thank you, Hans, and you, too, Raditya and Yos."

The three younger men shook hands with Lintang's father and his three colleagues. "I'm sure that one day things will change," Yos said to Dimas as he gave each of the young men a hug.

Once again, Lintang felt herself to have been blessed with so many favors amidst the absurdity of I-N-D-O-N-E-S-I-A.

●

Just one week later, Lintang's passport was returned to her with a tourist visa stamped inside. It was evening. Dimas and his two helpers were preparing food. Risjaf and Tjai were getting ready to greet the evening's customers. Lintang had just finished having coffee and boiled bananas with Vivienne and Nara. Nara looked at his watch, then drank the rest of the coffee in his cup.

"Where are you going?" Risjaf asked, surprised to see Nara pick up his knapsack. "Aren't you going to have dinner here tonight?"

"Can't. I'm getting ready to go to London and have lots of stuff to do. And tomorrow, I have meetings with three of my teachers."

"Where are you going? What university?" Risjaf asked.

"Cambridge."

Risjaf raised his right thumb.

Nara kissed Lintang on the cheek and then said goodbye to Vivienne.

After Nara had gone, Lintang whispered to her mother: "Did

Ayah tell you what was wrong? That it's nothing serious, just some kind of liver infection?"

"Yes, why?"

Lintang shrugged her shoulders. "I'm worried…"

Vivienne looked towards the kitchen door. Dimas's head could be seen through the door's window. She felt the same way. Dimas had not shown her the results of his examination. She felt that she didn't have the right to interfere with such matters anymore. She was not his wife, after all. But, at the same time…

"Wait here," Vivienne said to Lintang. "I'll try to find out more. Maybe this time he'll be more open, but I can't say for sure."

Vivienne stood and went towards the kitchen. After she'd disappeared behind the door, Lintang's three uncles immediately sat down around her, then waited for her to consume the last piece of boiled banana, one of her favorite treats.

"Here is the list of the names, addresses, and telephone numbers of your father's and our friends," said Tjai rapidly, exhibiting his natural sense of organization. "Some of them I've e-mailed; others I've had to contact by post."

Lintang read the list and noted the ones she had already contacted herself.

Nugroho handed her another sheet of paper. "And here is the list of restaurants that you should visit, if you have time. "One of the restaurants I've listed is Padang Roda. Try to find out if it's still there. And make sure you visit Senen Market. That's where we always used to drink coffee and gab."

"That place is a shambles now," remarked Risjaf who had been back and forth to Indonesia several times since getting permission to visit. "It's a very different place now."

"Most important is for you to visit the family of our late friend,

Om Hananto. Tante Surti…"

"Kenanga, Bulan, and Alam… All their names are written down," Lintang said, interrupting Nugroho, who was too busy looking for the addresses of other friends to notice the rising impatience in her voice.

Lintang still hadn't decided quite what she felt towards this hodgepodge family of hers. There was something odd and complex in the relationship between her father and the rest of them. What was it between him and his late friend Hananto and his wife, Surti? (What was she supposed to call her? Tante? Aunty?) What kind of weird *ménage à trois* was it anyway? Where did she and her mother fit in this strange configuration? And what about Kenanga, Bulan, and Alam? She didn't know them at all, yet they seemed so familiar. She had read their letters, after all. Why did her father feel more responsible for those three children, in particular, than, for example, the children of other former political prisoners?

Lintang was still studying the names and addresses Tjai and Nugroho had given to her when her parents came out of the kitchen. All eyes turned towards Dimas and Vivienne.

Nugroho couldn't resist goading this odd couple whom he knew still loved each other. "If you were still teenagers, I'd have a snide comment for you, like 'What were you doing in there?' or 'You sure were in there a long time!'"

Dimas waved his hand dismissively, signaling he couldn't be bothered to respond. "Vivienne came in to ask about the results of my medical checkup. She thinks I'm sick and hiding something from her," he groused. "I don't know why she simply can't accept that I, in my twilight years, can still be so fit and healthy and handsome!"

Vivienne shrugged and sat back down next to Lintang. "That

was a failure," she whispered.

Lintang smiled. "Let me try, Maman. Tomorrow we're having lunch together and then going to Antoine Martin's."

Vivienne nodded, but didn't expect her daughter to succeed where she hadn't.

Risjaf offered some words of advice: "I'd just like to say, Lintang, that whenever you meet someone connected with the Soeharto government, your first reaction shouldn't be antipathy. Many have actually helped us. Just like those three young diplomats. Some have even sent financial assistance or found jobs for the children of former political prisoners at their offices. So, what I'm saying is that as a student researcher, you had best adopt a neutral position."

Lintang nodded in reply.

"Your uncle Aji will explain it all to you." Dimas stroked his daughter's hair. "For the most part, the kids of friends of ours who work for the mass media don't go by their own names."

"What? Haven't you ever told Lintang about Rama, Aji's boy?" Nugroho asked, surprised.

Dimas scratched his chin, which wasn't at all itchy. "I'll let Aji explain. Lintang will be staying at his house."

The others said nothing. Lintang looked left and right, not knowing what had happened to her cousin.

Dimas immediately changed the subject. "So, now that your ticket and visa are in order, what about your equipment: cassettes, tape recorder, laptop, notes, pens, and so on?"

Lintang nodded. "All I have left to do is to pack."

"Before you pack," Nugroho started to say as he removed a thick brown envelope from his back pocket and handed it to Lintang, "this is from all of us here. It's still in francs but you can change it when you get to Jakarta."

"*Iki opo to?*" Dimas asked in Javanese, not knowing his friends' plan.

"It's not a lot," Risjaf said to Lintang, "but maybe it will help. For us here, you are our daughter too."

Lintang looked at her three uncles, from one face to another, with tears beginning to well in her eyes. Tjai nodded, reaffirming what Risjaf had said. This was crazy. Lintang knew very well that none of her uncles were rich, with money to give away.

"I got a stipend from my department," she said to them, "and I have some savings as well. I've been working part-time, and Maman…"

Nugroho, too, had tears in his eyes: "Listen, Lintang. We can't go to Jakarta. Only Risjaf has been able to go there. That's why you are going for us. You will be our eyes and ears."

Lintang felt her throat constrict. Suddenly unable to speak, she squeezed Nugroho's hand.

"Please, Lintang, go see my Bimo and tell him that I am just as healthy as I was when I left thirty-four years ago. And that I am just as handsome as I was when I saw him in Singapore fifteen years ago. We talk on the telephone, but I almost never get to see him. Who can afford the airfare? Please take as many photographs of him as you can."

Nugroho's voice grew hoarser as he spoke. Dimas's eyes glistened. Tjai and Risjaf pretended to be busy getting plates and glasses, trying not to be seen wiping away the damn tears that had come to their eyes.

Vivienne squeezed Nugroho's hand. "Lintang is sure to meet Bimo. He and Alam are good friends. I've heard that they are going to try to come to Europe next December for the International Conference on Human Rights in The Hague."

Always so rational-sounding, Vivienne was ever able to soothe a person's heart.

Wiping his tears, Nugroho nodded and laughed. "That's right. He told me that he'd be coming to The Hague with Alam and representatives from other non-governmental organizations on December 10. After the conference, he'll swing down here with Alam. I mark the calendar every day, counting how many months and days it will be before I meet my little boy again."

"He's not your little boy anymore," Risjaf said, patting Nugroho on the shoulder. "He's a young man now and better looking than his father."

Dimas squeezed Nugroho's shoulders, not saying anything.

"I will give you full report on Jakarta," Lintang promised Nugroho. "Thank you all for this," she said with the envelope in her hand.

Lintang hugged each of her uncles, those strong and steadfast pillars. If, when she arrived in Jakarta, she possessed even a shred of their strength, she knew that she would be ready to explore this foreign world that she called her homeland.

●

Dimas and Lintang walked among the rows of grand and beautiful tombstones. They looked at Édith Piaf's grave marker—black with a crucifix—contrasting in its simplicity with the others. Before the grave of Marcel Proust, it was as if they were *flâneurs* in the midst of enjoying the beauty of death eternalized in beautiful form. Death celebrated in poetry, flowers, and verdant trees that lent passersby their cooling shadows. Dimas hadn't thought to wonder why, on the day before his daughter's departure, they had ended up coming to this cemetery. What they had decided was to visit a number of places in Paris they both liked—with no clear plan, time schedule, or map. Earlier in the day, they had enjoyed a simple meal together at a small café on Île St-Louis. They spoke of the Tour d'Argent, one of the city's oldest and costliest restaurants, and laughed at the craziness of anyone willing to spend so much money there just on lunch or dinner.

"Why Balzac, Dumas, and other poets, even modern-day ones, have cited that place as a source of inspiration, I will never understand."

Dimas shook his head. They walked along the bank of the Seine until they came to Antoine Martin's bookstall. There, they engaged the owner in small talk and Lintang said her goodbyes, even as they rummaged through the place for used books and records.

"You're going so far away," Monsieur Martin said to Lintang through clenched teeth in which he held a cigarette as he scanned the shelves and piles of books. "I'm going to find something nice for you to read along the way."

Finally, he found what he was looking for and handed the slim volume to Lintang: *The Waste Land.* "This is free for you."

Lintang laughed. She already owned Eliot's collection of poems but she thanked Monsieur Martin enthusiastically. Maybe she would take it with her. The one she owned was a wreck, full of scribbling and loose pages.

After buying a few used books, they slowly traced the River Seine, their purchases in hand, marveling at how this river, which was constantly being groped and explored by tourists, photographers, and filmmakers, was able to hold so many stories in its rippling waters, including the arrival of Dimas and his friends in Paris, this large city, home to some of the best and most important writers, philosophers, filmmakers, designers, models, and architects in the world. But at the very least, the River Seine had not been violated in the same way the Solo River had. How mankind had betrayed nature by using the river as a place to dispose of corpses and, worse still, by doing so, had betrayed all sense of humankind.

"Ayah...?"

"Yes...?"

"Are you really OK—your health, that is?"

"Yes."

"What did the results of the tests show?"

"A problem with my liver, is all. Medicine will cure it. I'll go in for another check," Dimas answered, his eyes on the tourist boat coming up the Seine.

Typical. Lintang knew that when her father didn't want to talk about something, he would segue the conversation to a topic lighter in tone.

"Ayah..." Lintang stopped and took her father's hand. "I want you to be here to see me graduate, build a career and home, and have children."

Dimas placed his hand lovingly on his daughter's cheek. But there was something, some kind of clot that seemed to be stuck in his throat.

"I don't intend to miss any of those events, Lintang. I will be there, right at the front. And on your wedding day, when you marry Nara, your mother and I will be there to be a give you to him and his parents."

Lintang laughed and exclaimed. "Ayah! Who says I'm getting married to Nara? I don't know who I am going to marry. I don't know if I even want to get married. I know I want to have children but I can't picture myself in a marriage."

Lintang's statement caught Dimas by surprise. This information was new and foreign to him. What?

"But aren't you serious about Nara?" he asked. "Didn't you get mad at me and all defensive about him when you thought I was mocking him? And now...?"

"Stop!" Lintang suddenly demanded, seeing that her father had indeed succeeded in steering the conversation to another topic. "Don't try turning the conversation around. I was asking you about your health."

"Dear Lady, can you hear the wind blow, and did you know Your stairway lies on the whispering wind..."

Dear God... Lintang knew that she had to hold her tongue when her father went into his Led Zeppelin mode. If she were to dare to mock his taste in classic rock—a musical period she felt should be stored in a museum along with memories her parents shared, such as the time they went to London to see a Led Zeppelin concert—the result would be a three-hour course in its merits. Her father would lecture her about this legendary British band, which he deemed to be the most influential band in the world. He and her mother were just two of the band's billions of fans.

Her father was so good at changing the conversation and she was so irritated with him for his skill that she didn't even remember having immediately agreed with him when he suggested they go to the Père Lachaise cemetery. And so it was, without a plan, without a destination in mind, and without a fixed desire of something to do, they had found themselves in the cemetery grounds.

"Today, we really are *flâneurs*."

Dimas smiled. "Which doesn't necessarily mean this to be a meaningless journey."

Dimas felt calm and at peace in this place. Perhaps it was strange, but that is what he felt. So, too, Lintang—which is what, in the end, reunited them again: their shared memory of exploring the graveyard, studying the gravestones, and talking about the famous figures who were now nothing but bones beneath the cemetery ground. Lintang's first experience in using a camera as a girl had been here in this cemetery.

In Indonesia, cemeteries were generally not places for strolling, sitting, watching twilight, or creating poetry. Even in front of Chairil Anwar's grave, whose stele-like gravestone set it apart from all other graves around it, Dimas had never found the cemetery in which it sat to be an intriguing or comfortable place—not like the Cimetière du Père Lachaise. But, that said, there was something—a scent, a sense of ownership, or a sense of unity, perhaps—that united it with Karet cemetery where the great Indonesian poet was buried.

As they were passing Jim Morrison's grand tombstone, Dimas bent down and picked up a small clump of soil from the site. Smelling the soil, he shook his head. "It smells different."

Lintang followed her father's example and picked up another small clump of soil near the grave and smelled it too. A look of confusion appeared on her face. "What's the difference? Different from what soil."

"*In Karet, my future home,*" her father said, not bothering to cite the source of the quote, because he knew Lintang was familiar with Chairil Anwar's poetry.

As a child Lintang had never been comfortable when she heard her parents speak about death or plans for their final place of rest. Frankly, she still wasn't.

"Look at the gravestones here," Dimas said to Lintang. "Aren't they extraordinary? You get the feeling that they were erected not only as a result of the desire on the part of the living to continue their relationship with loved ones who have already crossed over to a world we do not know, but also with the intent of nurturing in the living a feeling of melancholy. But, whatever the case, I think I would be more comfortable and happy to be buried in Karet, Chairil Anwar's home."

Lintang immediately paraphrased one of the poet's more famous lines. "I want you to live for a thousand years more, Ayah. So stop talking about where you're going to be buried."

"OK," Dimas agreed. "There's one thing I want you to do for me," he said while removing the Titoni 17-jewel watch which, for decades, had gripped his wrist. "I want you to give this to Alam, Om Hananto's son. It's very old but it still runs well."

Lintang's heart trembled as she took the watch from her father. "This was Om Hananto's?"

Dimas nodded. "Yes. He gave it to me the last time I saw him, before I left Jakarta."

As if it were a precious gem and not an old timepiece, Lintang carefully wrapped the watch in the scarf she had been wearing.

"Ayah, one thing I've always wanted to know is what it is with this ménage of you, Om Hananto, and Tante Surti." Lintang felt relieved to have finally released the question that had haunted her for years.

A slight look of tension appeared on Dimas's face. Finally, he lowered his body and sat down beside Jim Morrison's gravestone. The sun was edging towards the horizon, but with summertime approaching, daylight would remain for some time to come.

"What can I tell you, Lintang? It's just the story of a student romance. I was friends with Om Hananto first, ever since I started college."

Lintang waited for the rest of the story, but her father appeared to be trying to figure out how to disentangle a snaggled skein and turn it into a smooth, straight, and simple thread that did not give rise to perturbing questions. But Dimas didn't know how to untangle this knotted ball of thread. Could he not just bury it with the bones in the ground of the Cimetière du Père Lachaise?

"And then…?" Lintang gently tried to stress the tone of demand in her question.

"I once…I once dated Surti when we were students, but, in the end, she married Hananto. That was it; nothing special about it. Just an old romance, now forgotten." The greater the undertone in his voice, the more unconvincing his words seemed to be.

Lintang studied her father's face and the soft flickering light in his eyes, which sapped her of the strong urge to know more and to ask him further questions.

"It was just like Om Risjaf and Tante Rukmini. He was interested in her but, in the end, she chose to marry Om Nug. They're just funny stories from our student days that are not important now and don't have…"

"The two stories differ," said Lintang, her curiosity renewed. "There were plenty of times I heard Om Risjaf and Om Nug talking and joking about the past, plus Om Risjaf never actually dated Tante Rukmini. That's different from your situation with Om Hananto and Tante Surti."

"Why is it important for you to know about this?" Dimas had begun to feel his daughter trespassing on personal territory—a domain he had never truly spoken of or freely explained, not even when Vivienne had demanded that he be honest with her about his feelings. "And what does this have to do with your final assignment?"

For a while, Lintang said nothing as she tried to understand her father's feelings. Yes, this was his personal space. But she had to know the entire context and background of her respondents, especially the Hananto Prawiro family.

"I will be meeting the Hananto family," she finally said, "and if there is some kind of special relationship between you and them, I think I need to be prepared. I am coming to them as a research student to document their life history, which is a dark spot on the history of your homeland, Ayah, and on my homeland too…"

Dimas looked at Lintang, his heart was touched when hearing her say "my homeland."

"You know, don't you, that the word '*flâneur*' has multiple meanings?"

Lintang nodded her head slowly.

"In the sixteenth century the word *flânerie* meant the custom of strolling the pathways, enjoying the twilight air or flowers blooming in the spring. The implication here is that it was an activity undertaken by aristocrats who had time to spare. More recently the word *flâneur* came to have a much more ambivalent meaning. In it was now an aspiration on the part of a person who is undertaking a journey to fulfill his curiosity and study the local culture. This is different from the previous '*flâneur*,' which meant a stroller or a wanderer who went from one place to another, without any certain destination. Witnessing a *flâneur* is like watching a motion picture of an urban life."

Lintang felt certain that her father had a reason for this lecture on the semantics of '*flâneur*.' She would try to be patient. At the very least, listening to a lecture on etymology would be much more beneficial than hearing him expound on the awesomeness of Led Zeppelin.

"But I am most in agreement with the explanation provided by Charles Baudelaire, who said that activity on a journey is the same as a home for the *flâneur*, like water for fish. Passion and work become one in the activity. A *flâneur* will forever be looking, and building his home in the flow and motion of movement. He might feel he has left his home, but in fact he built a home in his journey."

"Like a seagull," Lintang commented.

"Yes," Dimas said, turning his head, as if being drawn back to the real world after being submerged in a sea of thought and semiotics. "That's what your mother used to say: like a seagull."

In late spring, the Paris sun doesn't retire early from its duties. Père Lachaise Cemetery was still bright even though the hour showed it to be eventide. "I am still wandering, with or without a destination. I was still a *flâneur* when Surti asked me to throw down my anchor and seek port. I guess it was a logical risk. I shouldn't have been surprised when Surti chose for herself a man who was ready to stand beside her and was able to promise to protect her and their future children from anything the sky might cast down on them. That's all…"

Lintang nodded slowly, though her face was full of questions.

"And when you met Maman? Did you feel ready then? Or did you still feel yourself to be a *flâneur*?"

Dimas paused. He knew that his marriage to Vivienne had been based more on need and comfort than anything else, but he was also aware of how unfair that sounded. Certainly what he felt for Vivienne would always be pure and sincere. To this day, however, he did not know whether it was love or a comfortable sense of security. He so very much wanted to tell his daughter that settling in Paris, starting a family with her mother, and building a home in exile was not something he had ever wished or aspired to. But "exile" was not a word he ever would have said in front of Lintang's mother, because, for Vivienne, Paris was home. What he and his three friends had done—jumping from Santiago to Havana and then to Peking before finally landing in Paris—had not been a journey they had made out of choice. They were not epigones; nor were they members of the Beat generation who wandered about the United States because of choice—to breathe in the air of freedom and to experiment with sex and drugs. He and his friends were forever haunted by a feeling of being watched and hunted as a result of their political choices—or, in his case and that of Tjai, as a result of their not choosing.

"I love your mother and everything about her. I love her because she gave me the most beautiful gift in the world, which is you."

Finally, after having found the right formula for closing the topic of conversation, Dimas had provided an answer. But Lintang was a curious student, trained by both her parents and teachers not to accept at face value the answer given or what is written in a book.

"Kenanga, Bulan, and Alam… Are those names ones that you chose?"

Dimas almost fell over backward. He suddenly turned pale. Damn! Having such a bright daughter was as irritating as it was pleasing.

"Yes," Dimas answered with a long sigh. "Those were names that I came up with long before the children were born. They represent the dreams of a young couple in love. But it was Surti who chose to give the names to her children. What you might…"

"Ayah! Don't underestimate me," Lintang chastised with a smile. "Look at my name and look at theirs. They all have your finger-prints on them. Supposing I had a younger brother or sister, I'm sure you would have given them names like 'Button Flower' or 'Blue Sea.'"

Dimas broke out laughing. Just like Vivienne, Lintang had no space in herself for secrets or darkness. Everything had to be bright and glowing.

"Tell me, Ayah, once and for all, are you still a *flâneur*? Are you the inveterate wanderer who is always seeking, always traveling, never able to anchor?"

This time Dimas gave a sincere and honest answer: "I want to go home, Lintang. To a place that understands my odor, my physique, and my soul. I want to go home to Karet."

•

After saying goodbye to her father at the door to his apartment, Lintang went to meet Narayana at *Au Petit Fer à Cheval*, the classic bistro in the Marais. She was late by ten minutes, but Nara greeted her warmly, impatient to possess her for the three days and nights he had so often mentioned to her. As soon as Lintang arrived at the table, one they had to reserve far in advance because of the café's popularity, Nara gave in to the desire he had postponed for so long and immediately embraced her and gave her a passionate kiss. Lintang neither resisted Nara's embrace nor encouraged him to continue. Her head was still full of Indonesian names unsuited for a French vocabulary: Karet, Surti, Hananto, Kenanga, Bulan, Alam, Karet, Bimo Nugroho, Karet, Chairil Anwar, Karet...

"What is it, *ma chérie*..."

"My father kept talking about Karet."

"Karet?"

"A cemetery in Jakarta."

"Oh..."

"He said it's not as grand or beautiful as the cemeteries here, that it's just a normal cemetery. But still, he said, Karet is the place where he wants to go home!"

Why she had suddenly snapped at Nara and thrown this information in his face, Lintang didn't know; but sometimes, and for no apparent reason, Nara suddenly seemed to transform into a young aristocrat who had no idea that there were still places in the world where beggars existed and piles of shit littered the streets.

"I know of Karet, Lintang. I know it's a cemetery in Jakarta," Nara answered patiently, trying to understand what she was really saying. He had been to Jakarta often. Lintang knew that.

Hearing Nara's calm voice, Lintang suddenly felt guilty and started to cry. She hugged him, then took a sip of whatever it was he had been drinking.

"I'm so sorry, *mon chéri*. My father was in such a strange mood today."

"Maybe he's just sad because you're leaving."

"Leaving? I'm only going to be gone for a few weeks. At most a month and a half, if I have to extend. I have a deadline to meet."

"But you've just been reunited and now you're going away."

"Maybe you're right," Lintang said in agreement with Nara's theory. "Maybe that's it."

"I'm sure that's it. Your parents love you. And your relationship with them is not only that of parent and child; you are like a friend for them. But enough of this for now. It's getting late, my lovely. Let's get something to eat and then go home for dessert! I want to kidnap you now."

Nara stroked Lintang's neck.

Lintang smiled and her eyes were aglow. She lifted Nara's glass and drank the rest of its contents in one swallow. "How about if we forget about having dinner tonight? We can pick up a bottle of wine and go to my apartment now."

Nara grinned widely when he heard this brilliant idea.

"But you're going to be hungry," Nara noted soberly. "I know you're going to get hungry." He protested because he knew that if there was one thing that might get in the way of their lovemaking, it would be Lintang's empty stomach.

"After our kidnapping session, we can order Chinese," Lintang suggested. "Come on, let's go!"

Lintang straightened her bag and Nara quickly paid the bill. On the sidewalk, they held each other closely as they walked.

"One and a half months is too long, *ma chérie*. Please make it just three weeks. More than that and I'm going to come and get you!" Nara nibbled Lintang's ear. He was restless and the Metro seemed so far away and would take so long that he immediately hailed a taxi and they soon set off in the direction of Belleville.

"*D'accord!*"

For three smoldering hours—three days was not realistic—Nara succeeded in making Lintang forget the word "Karet." For three hours Lintang whispered a different vocabulary, an intimate one that further flamed Nara's passion. Weeks and weeks of delayed desire had to be allayed in that one night only. They turned up the music as loud as possible so that their neighbors, separated from them by only a thin wall, would not be bothered by the constant creaking of the bed and the high-pitched moans of its inhabitants. But after three boisterous and sweat-filled hours, when Nara was lying asleep and naked on the bed, Lintang opened her eyes to look at the ceiling. She got out of bed, wrapped herself in a sheet, and went into the kitchen. There, her father's words began to stir up her thoughts. She tried calming herself with a glass of water.

Through the large window in her apartment, Lintang could see the streetlights of Belleville washing the old buildings with their glow: spice stores, a *boulangerie,* and the old apartment building across the street from her own. Suddenly, the streetlights began to die, one after another, and in just a few seconds the buildings outside had turned into tombstones, standing in a neat and even line. Lintang squinted her eyes to see. Directly in the middle of the row of tombstones, she could see a mound of fresh red clay earth, not yet covered by stone or cement, where a plain wooden plank was planted. On it was printed the simple words: DIMAS SURYO, 1930–1998.

III

SEGARA ALAM

A DIORAMA

THEY'RE ALL STANDING, bodies bloodied, limbs injured—miniature statues that have been placed there, arranged just so, forever frozen in one position. Maybe a few facts can be gleaned from their assemblage; maybe the rest is just a series of poses.

The small figures behind the glass seem to be actors in some kind of play. One of them has been shot in a living room. Another one, tied to a chair, is being tortured. All kinds of cruelties have been carved into this extensive diorama which has served as the official history of this country for twenty-eight years.

I watch as a group of grade school students form a neat line behind their teacher and the museum guide, who proceeds to explain to the children how the communists abducted the generals and then hacked and slashed their bodies with swords and knives. Two of the boys press their foreheads to the glass, their eyes bulging as they take in the cruel sights they're seeing. Behind them is a group of junior high school girls, waiting to take their turn to look through the glass.

> *Ooh, yuck! Creepy! Those are bad guys.*
> *Is that blood or ketchup, ma'am?*
> *In the film, they were singing.*
> *Be orderly now, and write down what you see for a report...*

The first and second comments are from the grade school students and the third is from a junior high school student who is comparing the scene in the diorama to *The September 30 Movement: the Treachery of the Indonesian Communist Party*, a feature film that all students are obliged to watch annually around the time of the anniversary of the events depicted in the diorama.

This is history. Here, in this place, the powers that be have conflated a story capable of disrupting childhood memories, inserting in them scenes of defilement, corruption, and horror. Compared with the filmed enactment of the same events, which come across as highly theatrical if not outright melodramatic, the diorama is able to elicit a more powerful emotional reaction precisely because of its silence, which permits the mind greater room for a gory imagination. Who created this diorama? What was its original intent—a tool for information, education, propaganda, or entertainment? Or all of them together? Could the diorama's creator have known how effectively it would be used as an educational tale for the schoolchildren of this country, how this country's mentality would come to be shaped by wounds and paranoia?

If you open the encyclopedia and look up the name Louis-Jacques-Mandé Daguerre, you'll find that it was he who partnered with Charles Marie Bouton in 1822 to construct the first diorama in Paris. You will read that their creation was intended as a tool for entertainment and education—and not, as it were, a device to project a version of history that was supposed to be accepted as true.

I watch those two grade school students, their foreheads still pressed against the glass, entranced by the scenes of torture. And then I recall a time twenty years earlier, when Bimo and I were in fifth grade.

I remember the date very clearly: September 30, 1975, the tenth

anniversary of the events in 1965. I can see my class being herded
onto a bright yellow bus, each one of us carrying a knapsack
containing a notepad, pencils, a stuffed bun, and drinking water.
We're taken to far eastern Jakarta for a tour of the Sacred Pancasila
Monument. Arriving there, the lot of us are ordered out of the bus
and told to line up in straight and orderly fashion.

Just that one visit was enough for me to have the whole scene
memorized. The first thing I remember about the site is a kind
of suspended stage on which life-size bronze statues of the seven
military officers who were killed that night are standing. Posed in
heroic positions, they project an air of supreme authority.

We are told to gather around the woman guide and listen to
her as she repeats all the names and incidents we'd often been
told of before.

> *As is well known and recorded in history, the generals who
> are depicted here were abducted and tortured, and their bodies
> thrown into a well called Lubang Buaya, the infamous
> Crocodile Pit. The blame for this rests solely on the shoulders
> of the PKI, the Indonesian Communist Party...*

Unfortunately, that statement was not true. The blame didn't
rest *solely* on the shoulders of Communist Party members. It was
transferred to their friends and families as well, and even to their
children who hadn't yet been born in 1965. All were sinners; all
carried a permanent stain.

I became frightened and started to shake. Bimo, too, and we
didn't know why. Was it from hearing that scary story? Or from
the fear that the guide might know who our fathers were? Bimo
and I focused our attention on the white streaks in the guide's hair.
In trying to count the number of streaks, this little game made us

less nervous and the tour pass by more quickly.

Over the years, the voice of the woman guide grew more tremulous as she aged. I sometimes wondered if she was doing that job because she needed extra money for her family, or out of some kind of zealot-like dedication to the New Order government and its monument to history. In the end, I concluded that she was there just doing what she had been told to do, without any real understanding of what she was saying. I bet that if she were asked, she couldn't answer the question of who the real owner of history is.

What else did Bimo and I do when we were there? For one thing, we'd stand next to each other beside a support pillar and compare each other's height. Although Bimo is older than me, born the year before I was, for as long as we can remember, I've always been taller than him. For all the world, we looked just like those two grade school boys who have their foreheads pressed to the glass in front of the diorama at the museum that opened to the public this past year. In addition to the diorama, which extends the length of the main hall, the museum also contains, as illustrations of historic scenes, a number of reconstructed rooms, sites where various nefarious meetings were held and acts of torture were perpetrated. I stand there, staring and asking myself a question. Twenty-eight years ago, the question was a simple one: how much truth is reflected in the diorama?

To give my question a more academic or philosophical sound, I might ask instead who are history's owners? Indeed, who is it that determines who is a hero and who is a traitor? Who is it that determines the accuracy of events? Is it the historians who were hired and paid by the government to write the official history of September 1965? Or is it that far smaller number of historians and intellectuals who have dared to ask about issues not recorded in official history? I know several Indonesian historians who have long been itching to dig up, uncover, and refute the New Order's official version of history. I know of their grumbling—in academic terms, that is—about the twisting of history and the amplification of certain events so that particular individuals emerge as heroes.

One historian wrote in an academic journal I read that the political situation in 1965 was not nearly as black and white as might be inferred by the diorama at Lubang Buaya or as depicted in the state-produced film that we were obliged to view every year. I also know the views of friends of mine in the mass media who have long seen as problematic the government's version of history that has been shoved down the throats of school children for now going on thirty years.

My sister Kenanga has often said that history is owned by the holders of power, not just in Indonesia, but in all authoritarian regimes. Even countries in the West that are thought to be democratic tend to shape history as they perceive it to be. But at least their historians are able to be fairly independent-minded. Any overt distortion of historical facts would cause outrage in the academic quarter.

The way I see it, history is owned not just by the power holders but also by the materialistic middle class who cuddle up with them. I more often use the term "power grabbers" to describe the former because the people who have been in power in this country for these past few decades no longer have the right to govern. Meanwhile, the middle class, which emerged during this same period of time—and which does have the choice to be critical—remains incapable of questioning the legitimacy of the corrupt New Order government.

And now here I am, at the age of twenty-eight, and the

government is unfurling its flag further with the expansion of this "sacred" monument to include a Museum of the Treachery of the Indonesian Communist Party.

Maybe it's just easier for the middle class to act as a fan of or to play a role in the New Order government than to exercise their critical faculties. But the only possible way to do so is to pretend to be deaf and blind as the government continues to bury rotting corpses and to perch like vultures on victims' graves. The middle class has the education. Imagine if they actually had the nerve and integrity to speak up? I suppose that they, too, would end up like the signatories of the Petition of 50 after they protested against Soeharto's continued rule. If the president can silence Nasution, Ali Sadikin, Mohammad Natsir, and other influential people, what would he do to people less powerful?

Imagine!

Standing in this museum, I find myself being forced to expunge all traces of my father's memory.

•

Most of what I know about my father I know from stories told to me by my sisters, Kenanga and Bulan, and Om Aji. My own memory of my father is much more vague. I have just snippets of an image of him holding me, his youngest child and only son, in his arms and of me sitting in his lap.

I was three when the military arrested my father. He was imprisoned but never put on trial. He was executed when I was five. Even the memory of that time is a vague one, but somewhere inside of me I can see him and my mother with me on her lap, and Kenanga and Bulan crying.

I have a faded photograph which I carry with me in my wallet.

It's always been a source of strength for me, for both my body and soul. It's a picture of my parents and Om Dimas that Ibu said was taken some twenty-some years ago at the wedding of Om Aji and Tante Retno. The picture has yellowed, as if wasted by jaundice and revenge; but in the light that is visible in my father's eyes, I find assurance that even if we have nothing else in this life except goodness, we will survive.

In the picture, my father looks like a handsome and intelligent man, simple in his taste in clothing and appearance. Both my mother and Kenanga say that I look just like him. But I'm not all that sure about the comparison. To me, he looks much more self-assured, with a steady gaze capable of piercing the heart of anyone—even the person now holding this square of yellowed and cracked photographic paper. Whatever the case, that's also what other women I've once been close to have always said about me. I say "once" here because I've never had a long-lasting relationship with a woman. Kenanga says the fault is mine and that if I ever hope to have a long-term relationship I'm first going to have to learn to control my anger. Maybe she's right, but at least that hasn't put a dent on intimate relations. Matters of the body and the heart are two different things. The body is on earth, the heart is in heaven. My problem is that while I prefer to spend my time on earth, most women seem always to want to talk about a future heaven. When that happens it is, for me, the time to say goodbye.

Starting from around the time my father was executed, Om Aji and Tante Retno became frequent visitors to our home. For years I thought that they were somehow related to my family. It wasn't until I was in junior high school that I learned that "Uncle" Aji was no relative at all. He was my father's friend or, to be more exact, his older brother, Dimas Suryo, had been a close friend of my father.

It was Om Aji who told me about the relationship between my father and Om Dimas, Om Risjaf, Om Tjai, and Om Nugroho, all of whom had worked together at Nusantara News. They were at once colleagues and friends, he said, who liked to discuss the important issues of the day. But while the rest had gone abroad and never been allowed to return home, my father had stayed behind and was hunted down by the military. It all seemed so hard to believe, like the plot of a film.

Whenever Om Aji spoke to me about these things, he'd always get this bright look in his eyes. But then, afterwards, he'd hug my shoulders and tell me over and again that if my father were still alive, he would be proud to see my dedication to my work and my lack of concern for material standing or wealth. For me to have started an NGO during the New Order regime, especially with the stigma I carry as the son of an executed communist prisoner, was not a choice that many people in my position would have made.

I suppose Om Aji says such things to console me, but I always nod in agreement anyway. Supposing my father were still alive, I think the question I would most like to ask him is whether or not what has happened in this country is a case of historical malpractice. That's the term I devised for it: "historical malpractice." I didn't want to ask Om Aji, because I'm sure he'd just tell me not to get all worked up thinking about the so-called "foundations" of the New Order government. I understand. Om Aji just wants me to be more cautious and not to be so overt in exercising my critical and challenging approach.

For my family, Om Aji and Tante Retno are a large umbrella under which we sheltered in times of rain and storms and from the heat of the sun. Almost as far back as I can remember, Om Aji and Tante Retno were always coming to our house to check on our well-being, bringing with them a dish of baked macaroni; the fried chicken in soy sauce that Bulan likes so much; children's books by Soekanto S.A., Djokolelono, and Mark Twain; and magazines like *Si Kuntjung* and *Kawanku* that their kids had already read. At the end of each visit, I'd often catch sight of Om Aji slipping an envelope into my mother's hands. Ibu, who worked as a seamstress with the help of two assistants, rarely had extra funds to spare. She, the daughter of a renowned and wealthy doctor, had to make ends meet by working as a seamstress. Whether she ever received any assistance from her parents, my grandparents, I didn't know and din't care to find out. They live in Bogor, which isn't far from Jakarta, but it might as well be another world away from us. Om Aji, who was no blood relation at all, was more like family for us.

Many of the envelopes that Om Aji gave to Ibu came from those unknown uncles of mine in Paris—Om Dimas, Om Nug, Om Tjai, and Om Risjaf—who took turns sending funds her way; but it was Om Aji who gave Ibu the most assistance. Om Aji, with his degree in industrial technology from the Bandung Institute of Technology, was obviously very bright, but he was also highly practiced in the skill of not drawing attention to himself. The name on his identification card was simply "Samiaji S."—with "Suryo" having been shortened to just an initial. As head of the laboratory for material processing in the research and development division of one of the country's biggest tire manufacturers, Om Aji didn't have much need to come in contact with the nitty-gritty of the world outside. He didn't have to deal with the government, for instance, which, beginning in the 1980s, had been doing its best to implement its policy of "Environmental Cleanliness" and "Personal Hygiene." He had no occasion to deal with the mass media either. He was able to keep himself busy in his laboratory, and didn't have to mix so much with others, which helped guarantee for himself a safe if not stellar career. There had been no fast career track for him, but his had not been obstructed either.

I don't know why Om Aji felt so responsible for my family; but every time there was any kind of emergency—whether financial, political, or domestic—he'd fly in like a mother hawk to take her chicks under her wide wings. Once, when I was in junior high school, I was called to the principal's office for an infraction, and I probably would have been expelled for at least a week if Om Aji hadn't suddenly showed up at school to speak to the principal. I'll never forget that...

At my school there was a kid named Denny Hardianto, and it was he and his gang who controlled the school. But it wasn't because they themselves were naturally strong, not like a banyan tree with its roots spreading in every direction. That's not where their power came from. They were just rich kids whose hobby it was to heckle and harass anyone who would allow themselves to be stepped on. Maybe their target was a skinny little girl or a boy with acne covering his face. Or maybe a guy like me, who didn't like to talk much and whose only close friend was Bimo, who shared my enthusiasm for books and karate.

One day, when Bimo and I were together, Denny and his five flunkies surrounded us and started calling us the sons of traitors. That's when I lost it and completely forgot what Sempai Daniel, my karate teacher, had taught me: that karate is to be used only as a means of self-defense. But what was I supposed to do? How was I supposed to keep myself from punching Denny in the face when he kept calling my father a traitor? A traitor? What was that? I don't suppose Denny knew that I'd never really known my father and that he had been executed when I was five years old, yet he had the gall to call me the son of a coward and a traitor. That information could only have come to him from his parents, whispered in his ear when they told him the New Order government's version of Indonesian history. He was just repeating their words, shouting them just to rankle me.

What do I actually remember about my father except for those fleeting images? Ibu has always said that I have a good memory, a photographic memory. I know it's not the kind depicted in Hollywood films, where savant-like characters are able to conjure up an amazingly detailed picture of past events and places; but, even so, I can remember most everything I've read; most every picture I've ever seen; most every road and every place I've passed; and, for damn certain, any person who has ever rapped my knuckles. They're all recorded indelibly in my mind.

Maybe that gift, if that's what it is, is what diverted my teachers' attention from all the whispers about my father, the bloody events of 1965, my father's execution, and his position at Nusantara News Agency at the time of the September 30 Movement. Instead, what impressed them about me was my memory which, throughout my years in grade school, junior-high, and high school, served me and my schools well, yielding trophies from the events I participated in: inter-school quiz contests, forensic contests, speaking debates in English and Indonesian, and the like. The principals of my schools chose not to make an issue of my father's history because they were happier to acquire the gleaming trophies I helped to put in their schools' display cases. The only times I fell from their good graces were when my temper got the best of me—which is what happened whenever kids like Denny and his ilk, in all their myriad shapes and forms, made me lose control of my will not to get angry and lash out. And whenever that happened, it usually ended with a lecture from Om Aji and a bowl of my mother's kidney-bean soup.

Brenebon soup was my special comfort food, capable of soothing my soul, which Ibu always served whenever I got into a fight at school. This is how the scene played out: after one of my bouts, first Om Aji and Kenanga would lecture me on how "violence is never a solution" and then Tante Retno would chime in with stories of the prophets who were patient in the face of trials and travails. (Insolent kid that I was, I'd retort that I was no prophet and that was not the best way to encourage me to be patient.) Bulan, who made it her task to clean my wounds and put ointment on my bruises, offered a more realistic route: a true champion always waits for the best and most appropriate time to exact his revenge. Now isn't the time; you have to learn to wait. Such advice sounded much more reasonable to me. And then, after this hour of advice and healing had passed, Ibu would come out with a pot of steaming *brenebon* soup, the final element in my clan's push to calm me down. And, for a time it would work, or at least I would pretend to be calm and that all was right with the world—even as my brain was ticking with anticipation for the next outburst. No one had to tell me that after a certain amount of time had passed—maybe just a matter of weeks or months—when Denny and his gang started heckling me again, I was going to try to turn their pusses into pudding. The only thing that ever really stopped me from smashing them to a pulp was the threat of expulsion from school.

But what was I supposed to do? I could remember everything, the bad as well as the good, in vivid detail—which, I suppose, is the curse and not the blessing of a photographic memory.

One day, during lunch break, I found Bimo in the schoolyard tied to a pole and being pissed on by Denny and his friends. Of course, I had to do something. Denny, that fucker, had no right to feel that he could do anything he pleased just because he could get away with it. So I took on him and his five friends and thrashed them. I forgot my karate oath and Sempai Daniel's instructions and beat them all. For that, I was suspended from school for two weeks and then made to apologize to Denny and his lackeys. (I suppose I should mention that Denny suffered a brain concussion and had to be taken to the hospital after I slammed his head into a wall. And that Anton, one of the other guys, had to have a cast put on his arm from where I kicked him, and that Fred, the one who was pissing on Bimo's head when I found him, ended up with a very painful and bloodied penis.) But shit, to this day I don't feel bad for having beaten Denny and his friends. What kind of person would piss on another person's head?

I can picture that day when I was made to apologize to Denny and his gang in front of the principal and their parents. I can see them smiling victoriously. For the entire two weeks that I was suspended, Bimo didn't go to school. And Ibu, whom I'd never seen so angry before, railed at me for almost the entire time. But again, it was Om Aji and Tante Retno who came to spend time with me and Bimo and try to comfort us with their soothing advice.

I see Kenanga coming into my room with her hands on her hips. "Satisfied now?" she shouts at me. "Do you think you can settle everything with violence? Are you proud of your black belt now? Do you think your sempai is proud of you?"

Bimo, who is at my desk drawing something, wisely keeps his head down and doesn't say anything.

"It's history that's made me this way," I say, trying to sound philosophical so that Kenanga will turn down the volume of her voice. "And it's history that will determine what I do and how I will act in the future."

"Alam!" she screams back and then sticks her thumb and index finger at me with a tiny space between the two: "There's this much distance between you and permanent expulsion from school. One more fight and you are going to be expelled, permanently. Not those other kids. And it won't matter if you're the overall champion in quizzes or contests or whatever it is that makes your school proud. Those kids' daddies are big-shots. They're in government. They're in the military. They're in power. Not us, little brother! Not us by a long shot. We are at the other end, the far end. We can't afford to pretend to be rebels!" Still standing there with her hands on her hips, she stares at me, her eyeballs almost rolling in their sockets.

"So…?"

"So if you get expelled, the only thing you'll achieve is to make things more difficult for Ibu because she's not going to be able to find another school that will take you!"

That's what made me give in. For me, giving my mother a hard time was the greatest sin of all. Kenanga left my room, still grumbling. She was incredible; there was never an end to her complaints about me. I went over to Bimo, who was still drawing at my desk. On a white sheet of paper, his fingers moving with a skill only God could have given him, he had drawn a clenched fist plowing into two capitalized words—"HISTORICAL MALPRACTICE"—their shape distorted by the force of the blow.

When I got to university, I tried to look at history more objectively, not just as the son of my father, but there was a scant amount of available literature and the official history presented one side only. I truly did want to study the subject from a non-defensive point of view. From informal discussions with historians who quietly admitted that it was in the interests of the New Order government to entrench its hold on power, I came to conclude that the real source of the problem in 1965 was rivalry among the power elite. But what I couldn't figure out, and what no one could tell me, was whether my father and his friends had been highly placed enough to know the maneuvers that were taking place on both sides. The darkness surrounding September 30, 1965 ,had yet to be illuminated; the details of what really happened had yet to be revealed.

The impression I got from my study of that period in Indonesian history is that my father and his friends were, first and foremost, a group of young people enamored by leftist ideology. When I heard the stories that Ibu and Om Aji told me about Om Dimas—who seemed to hold a quite different opinion from that of my father—I could only conclude that they were little more than pawns on the chess board or, to say it differently, fans on the edge of the playing field who didn't quite know the rules of the game that was being played. If history can be likened to a puzzle, these pawns were not the ones putting the puzzle together. I wasn't sure if the puzzle that was Indonesian history could ever be put together completely, with every piece of it matched and put in the proper place. But that was the job of historians, at least those with any moral or academic integrity.

I enrolled in the Faculty of Law, which is somewhat ironic, because I couldn't help but laugh about the gaping chasm in Indonesia between the code of law and its implementation. Had I not kept my mind focused on Ibu, whose irritation with me and my obstinate behavior easily brought her to tears, I most likely would have chosen to drop out of school and spend my time in bed with the gorgeous assistant lecturer instead.

Not surprisingly, when I did finally graduate, Ibu looked to be the happiest person in the world. Om Aji, Tante Retno, and my two sisters joined her in shedding tears of happiness for my success. Good lord…

Ibu didn't particularly care how I was going to put my degree to use; she just wanted to see me graduate and was happy that I did. So it was that after interning at various places, from corporate law firms to institutions like the Center for Legal Aid, Ibu seemed to understand why it was I chose to establish Satu Bangsa or "One Nation," whose primary activity was advocacy for minority groups being treated unjustly. Even though the idea for the organization was mine, its "front man" is Gilang Suryana, who is only a couple years older than me but, more importantly, has nothing at all "suspicious" in his background.

Gilang, the son of an editor at *Harian Massa*, holds a dual master's degree in history and political science from Leiden University in the Netherlands and bears none of the burden of the past or that cargo of revenge that Bimo and I do. Our small office is in the annex of a house owned by a friend of Gilang's father, a man who prefers to keep his name anonymous. He is businessman and a member of the old rich class who admires our goals but can only help us on the sly. Though Gilang uses a light hand in running the office, he is a master of authority and planning—the very traits one needs in a leader.

My watch said eleven and my cell phone was yelping at me. The call was sure to be from Bimo, who was out of patience with me for my courtesy in waiting at the office for our "special visitor" to arrive. Ever since the day before, when Bimo's father called from France to ask that we give a hand to Om Dimas's daughter and watch over her while she was here, Bimo had been grumbling half to death. The situation in Jakarta was heating up; it was the wrong time and the wrong place for anyone to come here to play tourist.

"She's not playing tourist," I reminded Bimo. "She's here to finish her final assignment."

"Yeah, yeah…"

Despite Bimo's grumbling, he couldn't ignore his father's wishes. Bimo was always polite and respectful towards this man he hadn't even met until he was an adult and had gone abroad to meet him, once in Singapore and another time in Europe. That was because Om Nugroho, like Om Dimas and my father's other friends in Paris and Amsterdam, had never been able to come back to Indonesia. At any rate, when Om Nug called to say that Om Dimas's daughter was coming to Jakarta to undetake her final assignment, the real message was that he expected our help, which is why I was waiting there in the office while Bimo was out on the streets. And now he was calling for the umpteenth time.

When I punched the accept-call button, he started barking in my ear: "Where are you, fuckwit?"

"Take it easy. Gilang is out there now."

I immediately punched the off button, tired of hearing him complain. I knew that many of our fellow activists were already out there in the streets, showing their support for the Allied Student Movement. Salemba Boulevard and the streets leading to it in Central Jakarta were sure to be filled with a sea of people and protest banners, whose common theme was economic issues: the rise in the price of staple foods, electricity, and fuel. Even though the atmosphere was like a powder keg ready to explode, we'd heard that the government—President Soeharto, that is—was still intent on raising fuel prices. He probably thought the situation now, in 1998, was the same as it was in 1967 and 1968 when, after taking power, he had increased the price of fuel with no overt protest. I for one felt sure that this issue would lead to a change in cabinet and a special session of parliament. This waiting was frustrating, but because I'd already promised to meet this girl, I couldn't leave the office.

I was just about ready to leave the room when Ujang came in, bringing with him... *Wow! What the...?*

"Alam, this is Lintang," Ujang said with a huge grin on his face. "She said she has an appointment to see you," and then in undertone: "Sheesh, I thought she was a movie star."

So this is Lintang? *Hot damn!*

"Hello...Mas Alam? I'm Lintang, Dimas's daughter."

"Dimas Suryo... Oh, yeah, yeah, of course!" I said quickly, interrupting her to hide my sudden goofiness, and immediately shook her hand. From all accounts, I knew that Om Dimas was a good-looking man but, my God, what must her mother look like!?

Ujang was still standing at the side, looking left and right as if waiting for instructions.

"What's with you?" I asked him.

"Maybe she's thirsty...? She came here by motor-taxi. That's awfully gutsy," Ujang tittered as if something were funny. "Would you like a cup of coffee or tea, or maybe a bottle of cold tea?" he asked Lintang, eager to help. Usually by this time he would have forgotten the visitor and plopped himself in his chair outside and started to snore. Hmm...

"Oh, water will do, thank you."

So polite.

Ujang turned and walked toward the kitchen, giving a thumbs-up sign as he left. Asshole.

"Please, have a seat. Did you just come from Om Aji's? When did you get in?"

"Last night. Yes, I'm staying at Om Aji's house."

"And how is Om Nug? And your father? Is he in good shape?"

"Om Nug is fine. He misses Bimo and gave me a letter and package to give to him. My father, well, he's fine too. Om Tjai and Om Risjaf are also in good shape."

Ujang returned with a glass of water in his hand and a shit-eating grin on his face. Ujang was always the first to act up whenever I received a female visitor in our chaotic office. He pitied me because I was still single and was always giving me advice—and more attention than any woman would—about the importance of tying the knot of intention with a good and honorable woman, or some kind of bullshit like that.

Though Ujang could see that I had begun to lose my patience with him, he just stood there, rolling his eyes.

"So, how can I help you?" I asked Lintang while peeking at my watch. At that moment my cell phone started to ring and this time I was forced to answer because Bimo is one person who does not understand the emphatic use of the word "no."

"Yup...?"

"Where the hell are you?" Bimo demanded to know.

"Our visitor just arrived. Hold your horses, OK?" I glanced at Lintang and shut off my phone.

Lintang was seated directly in front of me.

Tall for a woman, almost the same height as me, but with fair skin and brown eyes, and a student at the Sorbonne. Daughter of Dimas Suryo, a political exile who had married… God, I'd suddenly forgotten her mother's name. Whatever. A Frenchwoman.

"I'm sorry, Mas Alam. I've caught you at a bad time. It looks like you have to go somewhere."

She seemed nervous as she rummaged through her knapsack, apparently looking for something.

"That's all right. And call me Alam, by the way, without the '*mas.*' So, you're here to work on your master's thesis?" I asked, trying to start the conversation in order to bring it more quickly to an end. Bimo was helpless sometimes, almost unable to function unless I was beside him.

"I'm making a documentary film, Mas…I'm sorry to bother you."

Now she looked frustrated.

"I really am sorry to bother you," she repeated, "but I'm here to interview a number of former political prisoners and their families. I could do it on my own, I know, but Om Nug insisted that I meet with you first."

Her head was still stuck in the knapsack as she looked through its contents.

Om Nug…Om Nug was up to something, I knew. Whenever he wrote or called Bimo, he always asked him about our girlfriends—as if we were a pair of boys too stupid to find girlfriends for ourselves.

"Ah, here it is!"

Lintang took out a folded sheet of paper which she opened to reveal a list of names of the former political prisoners and their family members she intended to interview. At a glance, I could see among them many whom I knew very well, even some whose names were rarely in the news. The selection was a good one, even and across the board. It wasn't only famous people she intended to interview.

"Those are the people I'd like interview but I need to be finished in three weeks or a month, at most."

What? God couldn't have created a perfect being. She was stunning, to be sure, but she was equally irritating to me for taking up my time. But I had to be patient, not because she was beautiful, but because she was the daughter of Om Dimas. And this was her first real day in Jakarta, after all, in the homeland she had never known and now would come to know only as an adult. That said, she seemed oblivious to the fact that she was visiting Indonesia at a time when it seemed that all hell could break loose.

"Why just a month?" I tried to smile.

She looked either confused or unprepared to answer my question. I looked at the list of names again. There were some who would be difficult to get an appointment to see, a number because they were very busy, but others because they would be reluctant to sit in front of a camera. I took a breath. I didn't want to sound argumentative, but this was going to be troublesome. All of us at the office were super busy—with meetings, with strategy and planning sessions, and with our supervisory work in the streets. The military leaders who had engaged in a dialogue with organizations affiliated with the Association of Youth Organizations the month before might feel content that they had done their duty, but our intention to engage in actions in their support had not at all diminished. Gilang and dozens of people in other NGOs had made plans for the establishment of free-speech platforms throughout the city. Because the situation was daily growing ever more difficult to fathom, Bimo and I often took turns sleeping at the office. But, once again, this was the only daughter of Om Dimas, the man who had been my family's umbrella.

"I assume you know that the names of the people you have here are on the government's watch list?"

Lintang nodded. "I know that, and I know that the topic is controversial, but the way I've calculated it, it shouldn't take more than three weeks, or at most four, to interview eight or nine of the former political prisoners and their families I have on my list."

I didn't know how to explain in so many words to this daughter of Om Dimas, who was completely foreign to Indonesia, that interviewing that number of former political prisoners and their families was not going to be the same as interviewing people on the street about the weather.

"I'm sure you've heard of the abductions, right? And that many of the people who have been abducted have not returned? It's only by chance Pius Lustrilanang survived—but after that press conference of his last week, he immediately left the country for Amsterdam."

"Yes, I know."

"Which means, or what I'm trying to say is, that the situation at present is very dangerous."

Lintang nodded. I said nothing. I didn't know whether she was naïve or full of herself, but she most definitely was a beautiful woman. Regardless, I could never be comfortable with a beautiful woman who was full of herself.

"Why the rush?" I then asked.

"Because I have a deadline."

"Well, if you have such a tight deadline why did you choose

such a difficult topic?" I didn't know why I was suddenly acting like an older brother trying to give advice to his innocent and over-confident younger sister. "With the political climate as it is, you'd not only be endangering your sources; you'd be putting yourself in danger."

I waited for Lintang to say something and began to become impatient for her to speak. She looked jumpy. Maybe she hadn't thought I would be so stern or acerbic. But I wasn't one to take pity on a woman just because of her gender. Having been born into a female household and raised by three women who were strong and self-reliant, I never gave in to whining or simpering. Lintang didn't look that way—like a whining and spoiled brat—but she did look fidgety.

I was impatient by nature, I knew that, but I still didn't want a person to become upset by something I'd said.

My cell phone started to scream again. This time it was Gilang calling, and I pressed the ignore button.

Lintang seemed to have overcome her apparent discomfort. "I know what's happening. I've been following developments in the papers, and on CNN and the BBC. Everybody knows: my parents and my uncles in Paris and my advisor as well have all told me to be cautious, that the situation is getting serious. But I've been in demonstrations before and…"

"There are no comparisons," I suddenly snapped. "From what I've seen, demonstrations in Europe are a polite affair—kind of like a meeting between future in-laws: enough to make your heart beat faster but, in the end, easy to control. Demonstrations in Europe are orderly and even when there is unrest, like what happened in Paris in May 1968, it's still not in the dangerous category. But here, in Indonesia, with so many factions involved whose motives are completely uncertain, anything can happen. A peaceful demonstration can turn into a riot. Indonesians lose their heads easily, and when the situation is heated they can be easily ordered to do things they would not normally do. Look at the brutality of September 1965. Look at the riots of January 1974.

"None of us want anything untoward to happen. All of us want the demonstrations to proceed safely and peacefully. But, at the same time, we have to be prepared, because even a safe situation can quickly turn violent."

"Don't worry. I won't disturb your work. If you can't help me, that's all right."

Shit. Now what?

"Please, don't get me wrong, Lintang. I'm just trying to explain the background to the situation here. You are Om Dimas's daughter. He's been like a father to us and if anything were to happen to you, I'd be the first to be blamed, not only by your father and your uncles at Tanah Air Restaurant, but also by my family."

Lintang didn't reply. She seemed not to have known that an entire welcome committee had been established for her visit and a red carpet rolled out for her arrival.

"I'm sorry, but I didn't come here to lie on the beach in Bali. I'm not a guest who needs to be cared for."

I held my breath and reminded myself again of her parentage.

"That's just it. Because you came here to make a documentary film, you can't just interview those people like some foreign journalist who comes and goes in search of the daily news."

Her eyes widened. "Excuse me. I know that. I'm not working for a college paper. This is serious work. I need to get to know my sources and their situation before any interview begins. And I will only record them if they agree and feel comfortable.

This is not my first documentary film."

"But with that approach and the number of people you want to interview, you're not going to be able to finish all your work in a month's time." I was getting tired of the conversation and began to say whatever I felt. "Two months would be the minimum—unless you're content to make something slipshod."

A flash appeared in Lintang's eyes as she yanked her head back and stared at me. "Do you think I would make something slipshod?"

She said "you" like it was a dirty word. How old was she, anyway: twenty-three, twenty-four? Now beginning to feel weary of this conversation, I leaned back in my chair. I wanted to get up and leave her sitting there, but I couldn't. I could see my mother calling to complain at me for my discourteous behavior. And Kenanga, pounding on the door of my place like she did last year when she was upset with me because I had broken off my relationship with Rianti, whose future presence in my life had, unbeknownst to me, been blessed by my contrarian family. It wasn't easy having been born into a family of vocal and strong-minded women. Every time I took a wrong step, I was blasted by criticism from all directions. And here I was, expected to sit and engage in a serious conversation with this Frenchwoman, but I was not able. It was getting towards noon; I was hungry; and I was sure that Bimo was angry with me for making him have to wait. The demonstration was sure to have started by this time.

"I'm sure that you do want to make a good and serious film," I told her, "which is why I would argue that you can't do it in a month. The topic is too difficult. Not too long ago, a crew from the BBC was here making a documentary about former political prisoners and they were here for several months."

"I already know some of the names on my list. If I am disciplined, I am sure that I can finish in three to four works."

I gave up, not wanting to debate with her any longer. Just like when Kenanga interrogated me: I'd give in purely out of boredom.

"OK, go ahead and contact those people. I'll ask my friends here in the office to help you with information from our database. But please remember, these people are not celebrities who like to preen in front of the camera. It's not easy for them to open their mouths or speak their minds."

"I apologize for having disturbed you. If you can't help me, that is perfectly fine." She stood and gathered her things. "Really, I can do this on my own. I'm quite used to it."

Oh, shit. What did I do now to make her angry?

She again started looking for something in her knapsack, lowering her head and sticking her hand into the bag. This time she quickly found what she was looking for.

"This is for you, from my father," she said in a crackly voice. "My father said that your father gave it to him the last night they saw each other. My father wants you to have it."

I was stunned to receive from her a classic old watch with Roman numerals on its face. A 17-jewel Titoni. The leather watchband was obviously new, but the watch seemed to still be running well. My heart stopped beating. Suddenly, Lintang had vanished. Flabbergasted by how fast this Frenchwoman could walk, I rushed to follow her.

"Hey, hey, slow down…"

Lintang was already on the sidewalk in front of our office. Did she know Jakarta or where she was?

"Lintang…"

She turned. Damn it! I'd made her cry. *What the hell…?*

"I apologize."

Lintang again looked for something in her knapsack, all the while saying "No need, no need," Finally, she found a packet of tissues and blew her nose. A whole gob of snot came out. So she really was crying. Maybe I had been insensitive, but I was serious. I really didn't know what I'd said that had upset her.

"Lintang..."

I put my hand on her arm. She said nothing, but didn't yank it away either. Suddenly, out of the blue, a crazy idea came into my head.

"Listen, Lintang, let me take you somewhere interesting for you to record. I promise that from there you will be able to find the context for the topic of your final assignment. Follow me!"

She stared at me curiously with her large and tear-filled eyes. "Where?"

Images of the statues in the diorama danced around in front of me like characters on a carousel. This blood-filled diorama continued to flash before me. And at that moment I knew: Lintang Utara would make a documentary film full of significance and heretofore silenced voices.

BIMO NUGROHO

MY CHILDHOOD HOME. A house filled with tension and disappointment. I never wanted to go back there again. But that is where my mother resides, still silently serving the man she calls her husband at a house in the Tebet area of Jakarta, where he took her along with the risk that she would bring me with her as well.

When my mother married Bapak Prakosa—whom I will never be able to call "Father"—I knew that my life would change. But even though my father, my real *bapak*, had disappeared from our lives long before, this didn't mean that I had to willingly accept this man's presence in my life. In our lives.

Bapak Prakosa was not an evil man—though his career in the military was not a profession that would immediately endear him to many. But he also wasn't a person who gladly or wholeheartedly accepted the burden that the woman he married brought with her. Bapak Prakosa viewed raising me as an unwanted but necessary duty, something he had to do for the beautiful woman he had taken for his wife. It was a risk he had to take.

I never tried to be the son he wanted. For him, a boy who liked to doodle and draw was fairly useless, not much of a male child at all. That my classmates at school often heckled me because my real father, Nugroho Dewantoro, was said to be a traitor to the state was not a subject I ever brought up at our meals together.

The bruises on my body and my puffed lips were always caused by "having fallen on the stairs at school" or "getting roughed up when playing soccer." (Since when did I ever play soccer?) All those incidents I remember well and have transformed them into comic-strips. Maybe someday I'll publish the collection.

One very determinant day in my life occurred when I was in junior high school. Ibu had gone somewhere and was not at home. Pak Prakosa called for me.

"Do you think I don't know that you're getting beat up by kids at school?" he stated more than asked.

I didn't answer. My eyes studied the ceramic tiles on the floor of my stepfather's home.

"Do you think I can't tell the difference between a bruise that comes from a fall and one from being beaten?"

The tiles looked expensive. Maybe that's what they call "marble"?

"I am your father. Listen to me!"

You are not my father.

Pak Prakosa came close and stared at me. A cold look. But also a gleam that spoke of his will to put some gumption into this soft stepson of his.

"Fight back! Don't take it. Beat them up!"

Now I stared at my shoes.

"Are you listening, Bimo?" He clenched my hand and shaped my fingers into a fist.

"This is how you do it, with a clenched fist. Come on!"

Listlessly, I clenched my fist.

"Do it right!"

He took a cigarette and lit it. "I don't want to see you get beat up again by other boys. Fight back! Do you get it?"

I nodded.

"Where's your voice?"

"Yes, sir."

His words of advice were useless, of course. Once, when I was in junior high, I was beaten by three classmates, big and burly guys they seemed to me. It was Alam who came to my rescue. But when Pak Prakosa saw me come home with bruises all over my body, he was so disgusted with me that he jabbed the lighted end of his cigarette into my arms and thighs. That was his usual choice of punishment, the one he meted out whenever he found something wrong in me.

It was around that time that I began to see my home as a hell hole, filled with tension and disappointment. My poor mother was too blind to see. Either that or she was too busy erasing all traces of my real father, the man whose child she had borne but who had disappeared from her life. There were no photographs of my real father on display in the house. No personal effects that he had ever owned. Not even any letters from him to me —at least not until one day when Alam came to the house to give me a letter that my father had sent to the Hananto family home. Somehow, my real father had at last figured out that if he wanted to communicate with me, it would have be through an intermediary. Thereafter, when he wanted to speak to me, he'd first call Om Aji's or Tante Surti's and tell them when and where he was going to call back. They would then call me and I would go and wait wherever it was he was going to call. I especially liked it when he called me at Om Aji's, because it gave me an excuse to see Andini, whom I was secretly fond of. I'd always borrow her books and pretend to forget to return them to her.

No one else in the world knew about what I was going through except Alam. Maybe Andini suspected. And I suppose Kenanga,

Bulan, and Tante Surti might have guessed as well, since Alam was always getting punished at school for standing up for me. That Tante Surti often invited me to stay overnight at their house was another indication that she knew something of my troubled relationship with my stepfather.

Once, when Alam and I were in senior high, this gang of boys beat me up, tied me to a pole, and took turns pissing on me. Alam came in like a superhero to save me and beat the shit out of those guys. Afterwards, when the principal called my mother to school, it was difficult for me to lie anymore about what was happening. I was just happy that on that particular day God showed mercy on me. Pak Prakosa happened to be on duty out of town, so I managed to escape punishment from him.

In 1982, after graduation from high school, I was accepted for admission to the Faculty of Social Science and Politics at the University of Indonesia. Alam got into the Faculty of Law. This was when I finally was able to say goodbye to the hell of living in my stepfather's home. Alam and I moved into a crappy boarding house near the campus in Rawamangun. Money was tight and food was whatever we could manage. Sometimes we ended up eating instant noodles for weeks on end. But that was OK. If we got too hungry or wanted some variation in our diet, we weren't at all embarrassed to go to Tante Surti's place, on Jalan Percetakan Negara. Alam's family home always felt more comfortable and pleasant than my own home ever had; and Tante Surti was always generous, ever ready to give us a simple but comforting meal. On weekend nights, when Alam was teaching karate to his students, I'd lounge about in his room drawing by myself. Sometimes I'd draw faces: my mother; my father as a young man with a thin mustache, just as he appeared in an old photograph; Andini; and others.

Sometimes I'd just scribble, producing images in shapes and forms as unclear and uncertain as my future.

On nights that he taught, Alam would usually come back around ten, always sweating but never tired of trying to persuade me to study the art of self-defense so that we could "beat the shit out of sons-of-bitches like Denny and all other species like him,"

Alam was like a brother to me, and I knew he felt the same. He wanted me to be as butch and masculine as he was, ready to face any challenge. But I wasn't born with his body of steel or sarcastic wit. He was always telling me that I had to build my own future, that I had to do something, anything at all, to make our country a better place. He sounded so heroic and full of fire, which I admired; but I knew I would never be like him. Even so, I truly did want to do something to make this country a better place, even if it was only through my drawings, because I had no idea whether the knowledge I gained in my studies at the university would ever help to make this country better.

And now here I am, back again at my childhood home, standing outside with the same feelings of tension and disappointment that plagued my childhood. Why had did I so readily agreed when Alam asked me to meet him here? I suppose it was because when he finally returned to the office at around sundown yesterday, he had in tow with him Om Dimas's daughter, Lintang. Sight for sore eyes that she was, I couldn't cuss him out in front of her. The demonstration to protest the rise in fuel prices and the corruption, collusion, and nepotism that were underming this country hadn't broken up until around the time for evening prayer, and all that ass could do when he finally appeared was to grin and smile. Gilang didn't seem at all put out, and gave Lintang an enthusiastic welcome.

So we didn't get much of a chance to speak. We just snapped at each other under our breath. The demonstration had gone off smoothly, I have to confess, without any untoward incidents and all pretty much according to plan. But Alam was gone the whole day! And the thing is, I'm sorry to admit, when Alam isn't around, I'm reluctant to act on my own. Gilang has hectored me about this, my "dependence" on Alam, saying that it's reached a "worrisome stage." Which is why, I suppose, he'd been very happy to see me flying solo that day.

"Where have you been?" I asked Alam.

"Long story."

"What do you mean?"

"I'll tell you later. Hey, how about if we meet at your mother's house tomorrow?"

"What for?"

"Don't argue. Let's meet there tomorrow, OK? Call it a history exercise."

Sometimes, Alam could be brilliant. He was always bubbling over with new and interesting ideas. But just as often, they seemed crazy to me. Why were we meeting at this hell house?

Eleven o'clock on the dot, the shithead appeared with Ms. Beautiful beside him. Hmm, with Lintang around, maybe Alam was going to be careful about bathing and start shaving regularly?

"Wow! Clean as a dolphin's backside!" I said in jest, because Alam often neglected to shave, even though he was a guy with a constant five o'clock shadow. Alam just smiled at the remark. No way! This was going to be trouble! Whenever Alam started seeing a girl, he'd usually be all hot and bothered about her for about two weeks max. If he passed the one-month mark in a relationship, it was an exception. And in such cases it was usually I who had to lend a shoulder to the woman whose heart he'd broken for her to cry on. …Which happened not too long ago when Andini and I were forced to console Rianti, who cried so much her eyes were swollen and puffy. She was just the latest in a string of girlfriends Alam had broken it off with because she had asked for assurances about their future. I felt sorry for Om Dimas's pretty daughter if Alam was going to take her for a ride.

"Hi, Bimo." Lintang smiled and placed her hand on my shoulder. "I didn't get a chance yesterday to give you the package your father sent with me." She took from her knapsack a small package and a white letter-sized envelope which she gave to me. My eyes were fixed on her bag. "He said he was sending some recent photographs so that you'll know he's still young and fit-looking," Lintang said with a laugh.

I thanked Lintang but put the package aside for opening later and then invited them to take a seat on the front terrace. Even though it was a Saturday and the office is closed that day, I was sure that Gilang would soon be calling everyone for us to gather that night or the next morning, because the government was supposed to announce an increase in fuel prices. There were no days off from the struggle.

Lintang and Alam sat beside each other on the rattan settee. When Lintang asked where the bathroom was, I pointed inside the house and to the left. Only then, after Alam and I were alone, did I get the chance to swear at him.

"Where the hell were you yesterday and what the fuck are you up to now?"

"Calm down, Bro. I took her to see Lubang Buaya yesterday."

"What for?"

"She's making a documentary on '65. I wanted to give her

some context and to make sure she understands that the history of Indonesia as it is depicted there is the only one the younger generation knows."

"And...?"

"She was mesmerized. She recorded everything: the monuments, the diorama."

I said nothing. I was beginning to understand the reason for Alam's disappearance.

"And how is she up here?" I asked, with my index finger on my forehead.

"Very bright. At first I thought she'd be the typical Westerner: all rational-minded and that kind of thing but then bowled over by exoticism and so on. But in fact she's not. She asks good questions, straight and to the point."

Alam smiled. *Ngehe!* Fucker! He's the one who's mesmerized.

"You watch yourself, buddy. This one isn't for the bedroom. You'll be tarred and feathered by all of Paris and Jakarta if you try. God, I can see your mother running after you with a machete and hacking you to pieces!" I chortled, imagining Alam's elegant mother crazed and with a machete in her hands.

"Don't worry. Not my type. The bright ones are always trouble in bed."

Alam took a cigarette and offered me one, too.

"Not now, Alam. My mother," I glanced inside the house.

Alam put his cigarette back in its packet and swished his tongue around the inside of his mouth as if to dissipate the urge to smoke.

"So why did you want to meet up here?"

Lintang returned to the terrace. She looked at Alam and then at me. "Bimo, I have a huge favor to ask of you."

"Name it."

"All the names on my list of potential respondents are victims. But I'm thinking…I'm thinking that I really need to interview the other side, too.

The other side? I shook my head in disbelief. *The man with the burning cigarette butts? You must be kidding.*

"I know this might be hard, Bro, but I think it's a good idea," Alam said to me. "Yesterday Lintang recorded Lubang Buaya but she needs more…"

"More context! Right, I got it," I cut him off impatiently. "But I don't think he'll agree to do it. The military has its own special bureaucracy and procedures. And even though he's retired, he'd still have to get permission and that could have consequences. Lintang would have to provide an official letter of request and then, even if her request for an interview was granted, which I doubt it would be, they'd probably appoint a public communications officer to talk with her, not my stepfather."

Alam looked at Lintang, who was trying to get her head around this bureaucratic tangle.

"Then how about this, Bimo… How about if I just try speaking to your stepfather and see what he says?"

I took a breath.

"OK, Lintang, but only if you can accept the risk in what you're doing. My stepfather is not the friendliest guy in the world."

Lintang nodded. The three of us then went into the house and walked through it to emerge at a rear terrace that faced a small garden. After my stepfather retired from the military with the rank of brigadier-general, he was appointed to serve on the board of commissioners of PT Maharani, the state-owned tin mining company. The job was neither pressing nor time-consuming and most weekends, Ibu told me, my stepfather usually spent at home, sitting there on the back terrace, viewing the garden as she prepared their midday meal. Afterwards, she said, they usually went to visit friends or, if they were in the mood for spending money, maybe go to one of the malls where Pak Prakosa might buy a new golf club and my mother a tube of expensive lipstick. I didn't know whether they had plans to go somewhere today or not. When I called my mother the night before, she didn't say if they had plans today but told me that she would tell my stepfather that I was coming to see him. "Pak…" My stepfather closed the newspaper he was reading and turned his head toward me. No change of face. No difference in expression. "Yes?"

"I want you to meet Lintang, a friend of mine. She's a student at the Sorbonne and would like to ask your help."

My stepfather looked at Lintang and nodded. Lintang extended her hand to him, which he shook, and then asked us all to sit down on the chairs facing him. My stepfather had never much liked Alam, whom he thought was a trouble-maker but also because his father was Hananto Prawiro. He scarcely acknowledged Alam's presence.

"So, Lintang, how can I be of assistance?" he asked.

"I'm sorry to bother you, sir, this being a weekend and all, but I came to Jakarta to finish my final assignment for my undergraduate degree."

"Good. Good for you," he nodded, without evident emotion. "What's it about? What's your field?"

"Cinematography. I'm hoping to make a documentary film."

My stepfather nodded again, his face still expressionless. He didn't seem to know who Lintang was, but I was sure that he was trying to guess right now.

"I want to make a one-hour documentary about Indonesian history."

"Well, that's awfully broad. What part of Indonesian history do you have in mind?"

"September 1965 and its impact on the families of victims."

Pak Prakosa straightened up and looked at Lintang more closely.

"What do you mean by 'victims'?"

"I mean the families of political prisoners, the ones who didn't know anything or weren't involved but then had to suffer for years afterwards, even up to this day."

The general's features immediately hardened. At that same moment, my mother came out of the house and onto the back terrace, no doubt to announce that lunch was ready to be served. Ibu didn't know that I was bringing others along to talk to her husband.

"Ibu, this is Lintang, a friend from Paris. From the Sorbonne."

"Oh…" Ibu shook Lintang's hand and nodded towards Alam. "Paris?"

"That's right, Bu Prakosa," Lintang answered in a polite tone of voice. Ibu studied Lintang's face, as if searching her memory for something she knew about the younger woman.

"Lintang, is it?"

"Yes, Lintang Utara Suryo."

Lintang seemed to be testing the waters. My mother's face immediately paled and she released Lintang's hand. "Oh…"

My stepfather immediately stood up and looked at her. "You're Dimas Suryo's daughter?" I could feel the tension in the air and stood, I don't know why.

"Yes, sir, I am," Lintang answered calmly, "but the documentary film is for my final assignment as a student at the Sorbonne."

Ibu quickly took control of the uncomfortable situation by doing what she always did: changing the subject and ignoring the matter at hand.

"Lunch is ready, Mas," she said to my stepfather. "Bimo, do your friends want to eat lunch here?"

Offering lunch was, of course, the only civil thing to do, but it was also a sign for us to go. I knew very well the look on my mother's face, which meant that I was to get out of the house now and to take with me these "friends" who were likely to give her husband a migraine.

"That's kind of you, Tante, but we have an invitation for lunch at a friend's house," Alam smoothly lied.

"Yes, thank you, but we must be going," Lintang interjected, no less politely. "I'm sorry if I've disturbed your weekend, Bapak and Ibu Prakosa."

"Lintang…" Pak Prakosa's voice caused Lintang to stop in her tracks.

"Yes, sir."

"Even though I'm retired, I am not allowed to give any kind of interview without permission. If you would like one, you'll have to go to the military headquarters with an official request from your university."

Lintang nodded. "All right, sir. Thank you, sir."

"But…" My stepfather was never satisfied until he had driven a thorn into the flesh. "Even if you are granted permission, I won't say anything to you."

He smiled. Coldly. As if he had won.

"We got to go," I said to my mother while taking Lintang's hand. "Goodbye, ma'am, sir."

"Bye…"

The three of us left the house, not breathing again it seemed until we had reached the front terrace. The nervous tension that Alam and Lintang felt was, I knew, very different from what I was feeling.

What I had felt during that brief time with my stepfather and mother was the endless torture of my childhood years, which suddenly returned to grip me.

"Are you all right?" Alam asked when he saw that my body was suddenly wet from sweat.

I nodded. Alam hailed a taxi. Lintang held my shoulders. In the taxi, none of us said anything.

•

In just twenty minutes we arrived at Jalan Diponegoro. Even though it was Saturday, our office was full of people. One could hardly see the office signboard, "Satu Bangsa," because of the many banners with protest slogans about the increase in the price of fuel, the need for reform, the abusive practices of corruption, collusion, and nepotism. People were lounging about the place, on floors and benches.

Lintang got out of the taxi with her large knapsack and the laptop she seemed to carry everywhere. The girl was a mobile library with everything on board she might possibly need. Even so, she refused my offer to help lighten her load.

Gilang, who seemed to have just bathed because his hair was still wet, was on the terrace smoking a cigarette. He smiled when he saw the three of us.

"Hi, Lintang. Where have you been? Have you eaten?"

Then, in front of us, Ujang appeared and asked, "Lintang, would you like to order something to eat?"

Alam shook his head to see the attention being paid to Lintang.

"Thank you, but not now. Maybe later, OK?"

"Come on, let's order something," Alam suggested. "If you don't, you're going to get hungry and then start to cry," he wisecracked.

"*Nasi Padang* for all of us," he said to Ujang. "Would you like *rendang* or chicken?" he then asked Lintang, very attentively. Whenever Alam went into such a supercilious mode, it usually meant he liked the woman he was with. If he wasn't interested in Lintang, he wouldn't be so fawning or showing her so much attention.

"Do they have grilled chicken?"

"Sure they do. Breast or thigh?" Ujang piped in. "And how about a cold fruit cocktail for desert?" Now he was going close to going overboard in showing off his hospitality skills.

Lintang laughed and nodded, then opened her wallet.

"Put that away!" Gilang said, shaking his finger to stop Lintang from giving money to Ujang. "I'll make you a deal. I'll treat you to a meal here and you can treat me in Paris!"

"Why don't you introduce Ms. Sorbonne to our other friends here," he said to me. "I need to talk to you," he said to Alam.

Alam looked at Lintang and pointed at his desk. "You can put your things over there, on my desk."

Lintang followed Alam's suggestion and then went with me as I began to show her around, but I could see that she was keeping a watch out of the corner of her eyes on Alam, who was now off with Gilang in a corner of the room discussing something.

"We have several advocacy divisions," I said to Lintang as I began to introduce her to other staff members. "This is Odi. He handles cases of discrimination towards the ethnic Chinese. Odi, this is Lintang. And that's Agam. He's in charge of land rights issues."

Lintang greeted our fellow activists, one by one, who were busy working at their desks. Then I led her into what we called our audio-visual room, a very simple affair. Lintang looked at the computer and our set of editing equipment, which was old and out of date.

"These antiques… I'm sure you don't have anything like them at the Sorbonne," I remarked.

Lintang looked with wonder at Mita, who was operating the editing equipment. "What's important is the result, not the equipment itself," she said with a smile.

"This is Mita. She rules this room. Mita handles the documentation of all our advocacy activities, both audio-visual and print material. Mita, this is Lintang. Lintang is making a documentary about September 30, 1965, and its impact on the families of victims. She might want to use this beautiful set of equipment one day."

"You'd be welcome," Mita said, "but you'll have to be patient. The equipment is mighty ancient."

"I'm used to it," Lintang commiserated. "The cameras and editing tools at my school are pretty old, too."

I was getting the impression that Lintang would quickly fit in with the other people in the office.

"And what do you and Alam do?"

Lintang asked at the end of our brief tour.

When I smiled at her she immediately guessed my answer: "Victims of 1965?"

"Yes, but we can't be too out in the open," I explained to her. "The other people handle advocacy issues; they are our public face. Meanwhile, we work in the background, collecting and documenting the treatment of families of the victims of 1965. We've collected a lot of material, but we're not yet at the point where we can take anything to court."

"But one day you will, Bimo. I'm sure of it," Lintang told me, with conviction in her voice. Not entertaining me, not trying to soothe me. Her sentence had the same kind of effect that Bulan's words had had on me when she treated my injuries after being beaten by Denny and his gang: "One day, don't you worry, they'll get their just desserts."

I don't know if what Bulan said is true but, at the very least, her words helped to assure me that my life still had meaning. I became increasingly sure that Lintang being here in Indonesia—even with all her French beauty and Sorbonne smarts—was like a fish just released in its own sea. I watched as she looked at the walls near my desk, which were covered with my sketches. There were a few of my father. There was one with a clenched fist and the words "Historical Malpractice."

Lintang gave me a smile as she pointed to that particular sketch. "Is that your work?"

"That's not 'work.' That's just doodling."

"No, it's better than that."

She shook her head and looked more closely at the images.

"Om Nug, your father, looks so young and handsome," she commented. "His mustache is still the same."

"That's a sketch of an old photograph. I've only met my father twice, you know. It's too expensive to go see him," I answered off the top of my head.

Lintang looked at me and then took my hand. "But now you can make some new sketches with the recent photographs I brought for you. You looked at them, didn't you? He's still handsome, isn't he?"

Lintang smiled as if wanting to draw me out from my sadness. I nodded. Sad and happy, the two feelings mixed together.

Lintang looked again at the sketch of the fist. "Historical Malpractice?"

"That's a term Alam made up," I answered.

"He does seem to like making up new terms."

I smiled. "That he does, Lintang. But I'd be careful; he's a ladies' man."

Lintang laughed. I led her back to Alam's desk.

"If you want to use Alam's desk or phone, go ahead. I'll be right over here."

Lintang quickly removed from her knapsack her notebook with its list of potential respondents and began to make telephone calls. Meanwhile, I busied myself answering e-mails. As I typed, I kept an eye on Lintang, and could see on her face growing frustration as she learned that this person was out of town, that one was down for an afternoon nap, this one would have to first check out Lintang's background, and that one hung up before she could speak.

At one point, Lintang leaned back against her chair and said out loud: "Now I can see why Alam said that three weeks would not be enough time." She turned to me. "I guess it's not easy for some families of former political prisoners to open up old wounds. Especially for people they don't know, like me."

"Be patient," I told her, having no real answer. "This is just your first day."

"I'm going to need your and Alam's help to open their doors for me," Lintang said.

"Later, we can look at that list of respondents and talk about them one by one. But to be honest with you, Alam would be the better person to help you."

After Alam and Gilang had finished whatever it was they were discussing, Alam came to our corner of the room with a stern and serious look on his face. Just as I started to ask what was happening, Ujang returned with our meals.

"What is it, Alam?"

"Food's on, Lintang."

"What is it? What's going on?"

Alam took his packet of rice and left Lintang's question hanging. Lintang seemed to understand that she couldn't force him to give her an answer.

The three of us ate our packets of rice with their Padang-style mix of side dishes while we talked about things that had nothing whatsoever to do with Alam's furrowed look or the irksome time with my stepfather. Lintang, who I noticed was good at eating with her fingers, talked about my father and his Clark Gable mustache and how he had chased down her father with his acupuncture needles. The way she described the scene had us laughing so much we were holding our sides and trying to keep from choking on our rice.

That evening, after our work for the day was over, Gilang came to Alam and spoke again in a whispered voice about plans for the coming Monday.

Only when the three of us were on the sidewalk, walking to find a taxi, did Alam tell us what Gilang had said: "Gilang said I had to be careful. He found out that those four activists who were abducted last March…"

Lintang and I furrowed our brows.

"What?"

"He found out they heard that I was to be the next O.T."

"O.T.?"

"Operation Target."

"Oh…"

"What? Does that mean you can't go anywhere?" Lintang asked.

"Are you supposed to keep your head down?" I asked.

Alam lit a cigarette, apparently to calm himself.

"Whatever…Gilang just wants me to keep a lower profile.

Not to be so vocal. He said that there have been some flies around this place."

"Flies?"

Ms. Sorbonne needed a translator. "Intelligence agents," I told her.

Alam smiled, which surprised me. Normally, he would have been angry. With beautiful Ms. Sorbonne around, he had become extraordinarily docile.

Lintang looked around at us, left and right. "Do you mean, like spies?"

"Don't worry, Lintang, our local brand of spy is easy to pick out, because they want to be seen," said Alam with a laugh.

That night, the three of us walked the length of Diponegoro down to Salemba even though the sidewalks, which smelled of urine, were definitely different from those of Paris, which had been built with the pedestrian in mind. But Lintang seemed to enjoy the contrast. She listened to us attentively, every once in a while needing a translation for a term she didn't know. Whenever that happened, she would try to find a synonym in French. "Intelligence," she said, but the way she pronounced it was "entelijongs," with a somewhat nasal sound. "When you say that word in French," I told her, "it sounds much too poetic for the dirty flies the term describes." We laughed at that and for the first time that day I was able to forget my childhood home of hell.

THE AJI SURYO FAMILY

AS THE SCENT OF TORAJA COFFEE infused the morning air, Aji Suryo wished to do nothing more than spend the weekend in pleasing solitude. After a full week at the office listening to noisy and oft-repeated conversations about the demonstrations that were disrupting traffic and causing everyone to be late to work, that is what his intention had been. These conversations had grown even more clamorous when, as the demonstrations spread, it became increasingly difficult for the staff even to leave the office building. There was little choice for Aji or the members of his staff but to wait inside and talk about the political situation until dusk, when the call to evening prayer signaled that it was time for the protestors to go home.

As Aji listened to his colleagues rant about the country's chaotic situation—from decisions President Soeharto had made, seemingly without forethought at a time when the value of the rupiah was in free-fall, to the announcement that the president had appointed his cronies and even one of his children to the cabinet—he felt very little except apathy. As bad as the country got, the government wasn't going to change. Despite the perils that the current economic situation foreboded, the government's leaders and their supporters still felt themselves to have the upper hand. One indication of this was that the president was still planning to leave for Cairo the following week—as if the problems at home were going to just vanish.

The strong scent of coffee stimulated his senses. There were times when Aji wanted to step out from the clichéd family portrait of a husband sitting and reading the newspaper as he waited for that morning miracle called coffee to appear, brought to him by his charming wife. Sometimes he wanted to turn the picture around or upside down, with him in the kitchen grinding the beans for coffee, like his brother with his cooking ingredients and spices, and Retno leaving the house to earn their daily bread. But Aji realized that even now as Retno was making cups of Toraja coffee for the two of them, their family was in fact very dissimilar from the one in the clichéd portrait.

While he waited for his wife and their morning coffee, Aji switched on the television and then began to turn the pages of the morning paper. The news in both media was the same: the ongoing demonstrations by students from nine universities in Medan. Finally Retno did appear with the cup of coffee he'd been waiting for, but also with a piece of news that and caused the clichéd structure of their Indonesian family to immediately implode.

"Rama called…"

The morning miracle began to dissipate. Aji tried to enjoy what remained, one small sip at a time.

"Aji…"

Aji was either not listening to his wife or pretending not to hear. His eyes were fixed on the television newscaster, who was reporting details of the demonstration that had ended in mayhem.

"Mas Aji…"

"Yes…?"

"Rama. Your son…"

"What is it? Did you see this? There's rioting in Medan."

"Rama is coming by; he's on the way here now."

This sentence caused Aji to turn and look at his wife. "What for?"

Retno sat down beside her husband and appeared to be searching for the right words, so that her husband's Saturday, the day on which he saved his energy, would not be disturbed.

"Why? What for?" Aji asked again, this time with more stress in his voice in order to force his wife to quickly express whatever disturbing piece of news it was she had to convey. Was there ever any news about Rama that failed to dislodge the clichéd view of their home and family?

"All he said is that he wanted to speak to us."

Aji took a breath and went back to watching television. "Almost four years now he's had little to do with us. Last year he didn't call or come over, just at Lebaran when he showed his face and then vanished like a ghost."

Aji turned off the television with a look of hurt and insult on his face. "Does he even think of us as his parents anymore?"

"Whatever the case, he is our son. We can't just let go of him."

"Didn't he let go of us?"

"No, he didn't. He's just confused is all."

"A teenager having an identity crisis is normal. That's the time when people change. But Rama is an adult, almost thirty years old. Your thinking is too complicated. There's no need to defend him. It's simple: he's ashamed of us and himself!"

The light in Retno's eyes dimmed as she listened to her husband. Although his criticism was justified and he made no false accusations, almost any mother is going to feel a sting when fault is found with her child. A child's umbilical cord with his mother can be severed only by the angel of death. Between Retno and her son there was an everlasting bond, which not even her husband and Rama's father would ever understand.

"Not every child can be as happy-go-lucky as Andini," she said softly to her husband. "Children have their own nature, even when they have the same parents."

Retno tried to be philosophical, even though she, too, felt hurt by the absence of their son in their lives and their home.

Aji took another sip of coffee and then stroked the arms of his wife whose heart and soul were far more noble than his own, this husband who became easily riled when unable to accept things as they were.

"What does he want? He's not coming here just to say hello, for sure."

"Hush…"

With her husband's anger now in abatement, Retno stood to return to the kitchen; but Aji was certain his wife knew the reason for Rama coming to the house.

"Where's Lintang?"

"She's been out with Alam since morning. They went to Bimo's house. Said it had to do with her documentary."

"And Dini?"

"Still sleeping. She was up all night working on her thesis," his wife replied from the kitchen. "I'm making *nasi uduk*, is that all right?"

Aji nodded. While he knew that Retno could not have heard his non-vocal response, it didn't really matter; he wasn't very particular about what he ate for breakfast. Aji guessed that his wife had, if only subconsciously, reverted to being a mother of two children at home in the house. *Nasi uduk* with all the fixings—fried chicken,

chicken livers, and shredded omelet on top of rice that had been cooked in coconut milk—had always been Rama's favorite dish. Andini had never been a picky eater and devoured anything on her plate. She could eat a boiled fence post. But Rama had always been much choosier in his tastes: in his diet and the moods of his heart. This his mother recognized, which is why she tried so hard to make the house a happier place whenever Rama came to visit.

•

The television was now off and the screen mute and dark gray, yet Aji seemed to see in it an electric flashpoint that expanded into a television series about his family—one episode after another telling the story of how his children had been born and raised in a family always haunted by fear. Despite the fact that his family lived in Jakarta and that the hunt for members of the Communist Party and affiliated organizations had waned in the years after 1965, as had the tracking of families and sympathizers of Party members, this did not mean that the Aji Suryo family had ever been able to live in a state of *loh jinawi*, the kind of complete happiness and harmony that marks the end of every *wayang* tale.

Aji was well aware of the paranoia of the New Order government, which issued decrees whose only purpose was to strengthen the regime's hold on power. Given his own experience, with his family's home in Solo having been frequently raided by the military and the interrogations he had been submitted to during their search for his brother, it was natural that Aji chose to keep his head down in later years, both in his career and in his social life.

Unfortunately, his chosen way of life seemed to have had a negative effect on his son Rama, who grew up with an inferiority complex from thinking there was nothing about his family that he could be proud of. His parents rarely held parties or convened large gatherings with relatives or neighbors. Unlike in "normal" families, birthdays, graduations, and even Rama's and Andini's achievements in school competitions were never celebrated in any big way. Unlike many of Rama's classmates, his family didn't live in a palatial home or own an expensive car. Never anything flashy, and not because his family was poor. In fact, they were far from it. With Aji holding a degree in the field of industrial technology from the Bandung Institute of Technology and as head of the materials processing laboratory for research and development at a leading tire manufacturing company, he earned a very reasonable income, even if it was not astronomical.

Ever since Rama was a child, Aji observed, his son had always been good with figures. He paid close attention to everything said to him and was diligent in doing his homework. He was serious in undertaking each task assigned to him—and expected the same degree of fastidiousness on the part of the person giving the assignment. With his family choosing to live outside the radar, as it were, Rama often felt stymied; but he forced himself to hide his frustration—at least until he was a teenager, when it began to burst out of him. At that point he began to complain of how his uncle's political "adventures" had caused such discomfort for his own family's life. In Aji's eyes, however, what his family had had to go through was far from, for instance, what the Hananto Prawiro family had experienced, with their entire life spent beneath the microscopic scrutiny of intelligence agents.

When the government launched its so-called "Personal Hygiene" and "Environmental Cleanliness" programs in 1981, it meant that anyone hoping to become a civil servant or to occupy a public service position—like a teacher or journalist—had to first go through a special background check. Rama, who was in junior high school at the time and beginning to think of his own future, became an ever more tense adolescent. These policies served as a filter and were intended to keep the families of political prisoners from ever playing a significant role in public life. At once, Rama's and Andini's future prospects narrowed.

Rama felt that all his classmates, friends, and neighbors looked down on his family, that they carried a stigma which had best be kept at a safe distance. Rama's paranoia was such that every day he asked his father whether he had been harassed at his office. Rama began to drop his use of the name "Suryo" and, in its place, use his second name instead: "Rama Dahana."

Andini, unlike her older and anxious brother, was born with an easy-going and carefree nature. Whenever she succeeded at something, she never sought to bask in the attention garnered by her achievement. What she liked best was not the end goal—high marks, a trophy, or whatever—but the process leading to that achievement, whether in her education at school or in the stacks of books her father gave her. Without ever having met her cousin Lintang, she had initiated a correspondence, and the two cousins began to send each other books of literature whenever someone their families knew was going to or coming from Paris. The two cousins were equally avid readers who found untold joy in words and their meanings.

Andini never had problems with her homework and never intentionally would do anything to upset her parents. She didn't make an issue of her family's position, which meant always having to keep their heads down as a result of the political views of an uncle she didn't even know. About the only thing that could make Andini lose her control was when her brother unleashed a torrent of complaints or began to shout in anger at their parents—which is something that happened all too often when he was a teenager. Andini was a person who believed that all people had in themselves the strength and ability to overcome and settle their own problems. She didn't believe in weakness and she didn't tolerate whining or sniveling behavior.

Given their two distinct personalities, it wouldn't be difficult to guess how the independent-minded Andini dealt with her shamefaced brother. Although Rama was five years older than Andini, it was he who more frequently pouted and moaned. The result was a never-ending civil war at home between older brother and younger sister.

As children, whenever their family got together with the Hananto family, Rama usually kept to himself. But whenever he and Andini got into a fight, it was her "cousin" Alam who always stepped in to intervene. Because Alam was older, taller, and bigger, with a much dominant personality and the holder of a black belt in karate besides, Rama generally chose to slink away and hide inside himself rather than test his own mettle. The gulf between the children—with Alam, Andini, and also Bimo on the one side and Rama on the other—became even wider as they became adults. Alam and Bimo chose the world of activism and idealism, and Andini set her sights on an academic career. But Rama chose a much more pragmatic career path on which he could keep his distance from them. In the end it happened that Alam and Bimo, who could not abide Rama's attitude, became surrogate brothers for Andini at the Aji Suryo home when Rama was absent. And he was often absent, not just in the physical sense but in the spiritual sense as well.

Seeing such a principal divide within the family, Retno

theorized that Andini had somehow inherited the family's entire reserve of fortitude and resistance while Rama had somehow gotten the short end of the stick, receiving only trepidation, fear, and a sense of inferiority. It was in this state that Rama, with fragile and limited strength of heart, had found friendship with boys from families who seemed to have an abundance of wealth from questionable sources. The more closely involved Rama became with these friends of his, the more impervious he became to his parents' guidance and supervision. In Rama's favor, he had also inherited the height and good looks of his father and the uncle he hated, so that people who weren't aware of his personality defects were attracted to him.

Aji and Retno frequently asked themselves what had become of their son's moral bearings. Aji felt that he had failed in instilling in Rama the understanding that what happens in life to a person or his family is not because of some fault at birth. He had failed in making his son understand that they were not victims; they were survivors. In Aji's mind, the real victims of 1965 were those people who had suffered far more than they: the innocent people who had been murdered, interned, exiled, and disappeared. Aji, like his wife and daughter, too, preferred to look at the challenges they faced as a force for becoming stronger and more resilient people.

Aji sighed sadly. Images from the episodes of the Suryo family drama suddenly vanished with the sound of Rama's voice. The voice he heard was real, not just in his imagination.

"Pak…"

Aji turned his head to see Rama, who appeared to be especially well dressed for a Saturday, in a long-sleeve shirt and black trousers. With his son towering over him, Aji suddenly found himself unable to speak. He felt like he was face to face with a stranger who had no blood relation with him. Or maybe it was because he had buried the hurt he felt so deeply that he felt nothing at all.

Rama looked nervous. Finally, feeling a jolt of pity for his son, standing there anxiously, Aji motioned for Rama to sit down.

"This is a surprise. What's up?" he asked.

"I know it's sudden…"

"Mama made *nasi uduk* for you when she heard that you were coming." Aji looked for the morning paper which he still hadn't read.

"I know, Pak. Pak… Could I bother you with something?"

How respectful! Aji put down his paper and asked, "What is it?"

"I'd like to introduce you to this girl I know. Her name is Rininta."

"Rininta?"

"Yes."

Aji said nothing, waiting for Rama to utter the next sentence. His son was twenty-eight. Was it already that time? Alam and Bimo, who were both around thirty-three, were still single and reveling in their bachelorhood.

"She's my girlfriend, Pak."

"Well then, invite her here. Introduce her to Mama and me. That should be easy enough, right? It's not like we've ever told you not to come home."

Rama said nothing.

Aji felt there was nothing more to be said and he lifted the morning paper to his eyes. He took a sip of his now cold coffee and pretended to immerse himself in the news of the day, even though his ears were twitching to hear what his fickle son would next have to say.

"Actually, I don't want to just introduce you to her, Pak. And she's not just a girlfriend," Rama said cautiously.

"Is anyone saying she's just a girlfriend?" Aji asked rhetorically as he stared at the paper in front of him. "Obviously, if you want to introduce her to your parents, you must already have some kind of special relationship with her. Is that right?"

"Yes, sir."

"So, all right then, tell your mother. I'm sure she'll want to meet this Rininta. And don't forget to tell your sister, too, when it is you intend to bring her here."

Rama looked taken aback. Aji knew that his son wanted to say more, but he was happy to end the conversation and send him off to speak to his mother. Aji concealed a smile. Let Rama know what it feels like, that he can't just come running to his parents when he needs something. If for all this time Rama had been hiding his identity from all those "great" friends of his, then now was the time for Rama to know just how much he had hurt his parents by being ashamed of them.

Aji felt blessed to have been surrounded in his life by good cooks. His mother had been a wonderful cook and she, his brother Dimas who had inherited her culinary skills, and his wife Retno all held the view that well-prepared food, made with good ingredients and careful attention, could be a salve for the soul and even serve as a white flag for the reduction of conflict between two opposing forces. There was no outright war between him and Rama, but there certainly was a degree of conflict that tore at his heart. He was Rama's father, after all.

Knowing what Retno was doing, Aji felt a little sad to see her so busy in the kitchen, shaping portions of the freshly cooked *nasi uduk* on squares of banana leaf and sprinkling on top of each portion crispy slivers of fried shallots and shreds of wafer-thin omelet. Next, she would add to each packet individual portions of *balado teri kacang, ayam goreng kremes,* and *ati ampela.* Proper *nasi uduk* was always served with such side dishes: fried anchovies and peanuts in chili sauce, coconut-coated pieces of chicken, and a mixture of cubed liver and gizzards. When all this was done, she would then wrap the individual portions in their banana leaf squares to create an envelope which she sealed shut with stick pins fashioned from palm stem. Aji again reflected that his wife was confident that good food can ease whatever tension might arise in the house.

Aji looked at Rama, who had a smile on his face as he smacked his lips and swallowed. Then he looked at the wall clock. It was nearly eleven. "Where is Dini?" he asked, even though he knew that if Andini hadn't gotten to sleep until seven that morning, it would be a while before she woke up.

"Let her sleep," Retno advised as she came to the table carrying the last two items to complete the meal: a *sambal bajak* chili sauce and *pete goreng,* fried stink beans whose name did not do justice to their succulent flavor.

"Come on, Rama, go ahead and eat," she said as she took her place at the table.

Aji and Rama each helped themselves to one of the banana leaf packets. Opening the leaves on their plates, they began to use their right hands to mix the foods with the rice. At that moment they heard heavy footsteps dragging themselves across the floor and, looking towards the source of the sound, saw a pillow-wrinkled face.

Andini came forward, her head down and her eyes half shut. "Mama, I could smell your chicken and the chili sauce all the way in the bedroom!" she said with a wide smile and quivering nostrils.

"All this food, Papa... You must have done something right to deserve such special treatment."

Andini plopped on her chair, still oblivious to her surroundings, but then suddenly her eyes opened wide when she realized her brother was there, seated across from her at the table.

"Hey! We've got a guest!" Andini screamed happily as she leaned her head towards her brother.

The word "guest" caused Rama to look down for a moment, but then he raised his head, mouthed the word "Hi" to his sister, and scooped some anchovies and peanuts onto the side of his rice.

When Andini went to pick up some of the shredded omelet with her fingers, her mother patted her on the hand. "Even if you don't want to bathe, Dini, you should at least wash your face and brush your teeth."

Andini grinned, picked herself up from the chair, and traipsed towards the bathroom. Once inside, she stuck her head back out and called to her brother. "Hey, Bro, you're looking real good. All dressed up like that. What's happening? Are you going to propose to a girl or something?"

Rama almost choked on his mouthful of rice. Both his parents noticed and quickly glanced at each other. Rama covered himself by swallowing a glass of water.

Andini could be a wildly wicked tease and had a sharp tongue to match, but this time she was not conscious that with her blithe comments she had set a landmine on the breakfast table. After brushing her teeth, slapping some water on her face, and loosely knotting her hair, she rushed back to the table again, unaware that she might have said anything out of turn. Instead, she started chattering about school; the difficulty she was having in writing her thesis on *The Waste Land*; about Lintang, who just so happened to bring a vintage edition of Eliot's work with her; and about the trouble she was having in tracking down her advisor, who was always out of town, while Lintang, who went to the Sorbonne, was having the opposite problem, with her advisor always getting on her back.

"Lintang? What Lintang are you talking about?" Rama asked, not realizing he was nearing the landmine.

"Our cousin, dummy. Do you know another Lintang?" Andini took a chicken leg and began to nibble on the crispy skin.

Rama looked at his parents and then at his sister who was now engrossed in eating her *nasi uduk.* "Lintang Suryo?" he asked as if befuddled. "Where did you see her?"

"She's here now, visiting," his mother answered.

"Working on her final assignment," Andini immediately corrected, "and she's going to stay for a couple months."

Rama suddenly lost his appetite. His *nasi uduk* on its banana leaf—with its sprinkling of fried shallots and shredded omelet, dressed with chili sauce and anchovies and peanuts—now tasted flat. He found himself unable to raise his head; he couldn't chew his food, much less swallow. Lintang, the daughter of his uncle, Dimas Suryo, the very person who had made his life so difficult, was here in this house?

"Yeah, and tomorrow she's going to interview Tante Surti," Andini went on, either unaware of or not caring about the changed look on her brother's face. "She's even trying to get an interview with Pramoedya Ananta Toer!"

Rama tried to calm his pounding heart. He took another sip of water to clear his throat, but found himself unable to begin a sentence.

"You're not finished already, are you Rama?" his mother asked.

"If you don't eat the food, your sister will," she said, pushing the serving platter with several packets of *nasi uduk* toward him.

Rama nodded weakly. "I still haven't finished my first," he said to his mother as he, pushed his rice around the plate. "So what is Lintang's assignment about, what with her having to interview Tante Surti and all?" he asked his sister with trepidation.

"About the victims of September 30, 1965, and its impact on victims' families. For sure, Tante Surti will be an important source of information on the subject," Andini answered lightly.

Rama tried to force himself to eat. *Nasi uduk* was truly at the top of his list of favorite foods and he did want to show his mother his appreciation for her work, but now he was having difficulty swallowing even a grain of rice. Meanwhile, his sister continued to chatter: about the books that Lintang had brought for her and how happy she was to finally meet this cousin with whom she had traded books and corresponded for so many years, at first through letters but more recently through e-mail.

"Remember how we used to have to wait ten days to two weeks just to receive a letter," she said. "I did love getting all those beautiful French stamps; but now, with e-mail, you can exchange letters in a matter of seconds. Amazing, isn't it!" she prattled on, trying to convince her mother, who had no skill in the use of electronic technology, of the wonder that was the communications systems of today.

Her mother's attention, however, was on Rama, who had already finished his lunch. When offered a second serving, Rama politely refused and took his used plate into the kitchen. Both of his parents were surprised by the sudden change in him: his polite and reticent behavior. Even Andini noticed the change and put a brake on her chatter.

Rama returned to the dining room with a long look on his face.

"Would you like some fruit, Rama?" his mother asked. "There's papaya, bananas, and watermelon in the refrigerator."

"Thank you, Mama, but I think we need to talk."

"All right then, we're here to listen," she said sympathetically.

"Uh-oh, should I make myself scarce?" Andini asked point blank. "This sounds like personal territory."

"No, Dini. You should be here too."

Aji was losing patience with his son's reticence. "OK, Rama, tell us what it is."

"I came here today to tell you that I want to introduce you to Rininta," said Rama slowly.

"This sounds so serious." Andini giggled to hear the formal tone of her brother's voice.

Her mother flashed a look at Andini, indicating the need for her to give her brother time to speak.

Rama looked at his parents. "But this is going to be more than just an introduction. I've actually been seeing Rininta for a long time. More than three years already."

His parents looked at each other in surprise. Aji's heart beat faster.

"Ever since starting to work at Cita Karya..."

"Oh, does she work there too?" Andini asked.

"No. She's Pak Pri's daughter."

"And who is Pak Pri?"

"Pak Priasmoro, the director of the company."

"The director general?"

"No, he's beneath the director general. He's head of the company's construction division. I work for him."

"Ohhh..."

No one seemed to have anything more to say. Aji, Retno, and

Andini of course knew that for the past four years Rama had been working as an accountant at PT Cita Karya, a state-owned construction company, and that his position was one of trust. As such, they were also certain that if Rama had been able to pass the security clearance required to work at a state-owned corporation, then he could only have done so by dropping the use of Suryo as his final name and concealing his family background.

Aji knew that to get a job in a state-owned company, a prospective employee had to go through a barrage of bureaucratic procedures that had been established by the government specifically for the purpose of ascertaining whether the prospective employee was free from the taint of blood relations with a political prisoner or political exile. Suddenly, for Aji too, the *nasi uduk* on its banana leaf lost all appeal, as if it were rancid and left over; as if the fried shallots and shreds of omelet had suddenly turned black. How could the color of food change, chameleon-like, with the mood of one's heart?

No one—not Aji, Retno, nor even Andini—knew how to react to Rama's announcement. Of course they should be happy and proud that he wanted to marry. But he intended to marry the daughter of a director of a state-owned company. What was the implication of this?

"So, Rama, when would you like to bring Rininta here to introduce her to us?" his mother finally asked.

"Anytime, Mama. Anytime the three of you are all here together, I can bring her by."

Aji knew there was a subordinate clause as yet unspoken. "But…?"

"But besides introducing you to Rininta, I'd like you to meet her parents as well."

362

That was it. That was the sentence that had been sticking in Rama's throat. That is what had forced him to come here and to make his mother work so hard preparing *nasi uduk* with all the fixings for him. Rama wanted the family to meet Mr. and Mrs. Priasmoro!

"Ohmygod, ohmygod!" Andini got up to take her plate to the kitchen. "Ohmygod, ohmygod!"

"Shut up, will you!" Rama snapped in irritation.

In the kitchen, Andini cackled as she washed her hands. In the dining room, Aji, Retno, and Rama sat in silence as they listened to her noise. Her voice was a foghorn, loud and shrill.

Aji pushed his chair away from the dining table and stood. Retno called to the back for Mbak Irah, the housemaid and helper, to come help her clear the table and carry the rest of the dirty dishes to the kitchen.

Rama followed his father as he walked towards the living room, his heart beating faster.

Andini grabbed a towel from a stack beside the drying room next to the kitchen and went off towards the bathroom to bathe, even as she continued to intone "Ohmygod, ohmygod, ohmygod!" which was making her brother feel increasingly irritated.

Aji looked at the wall clock. It was now 1:30. Suddenly he felt a throb of pain in his head, as if he had a pinched nerve. He felt his eyeballs being pulled in all directions. This had to be a psychosomatic reaction to Rama's announcement, her realized. Rama's heart must be set on marrying this daughter of the director of a state-owned company. If not, then why did he want to introduce his parents to them?

"Iraaaah!" Aji suddenly shouted.

Mbak Irah, who had just finished putting away the food from their lunch, scurried into the room. She had never heard her Pak

Aji shout so loudly before.

"Please heat me some milk."

"Yes, sir."

For his father to want a glass of warm milk was a sign that he wasn't feeling well—which made Rama feel distinctly ill at ease. Then, as his father kneaded his temples with his fingers, Rama became even more reluctant to continue his unfinished announcement. His mother came into the room carrying a glass of warm milk. The look she gave him told him that he was not to do anything to make his father more upset.

"Would you like to lie down and rest?" Retno asked Aji.

Aji drank the glass of milk, one sip after another. Gradually, the throbbing in his head began to subside and his stomach feel settled and warm again. Retno sat down beside her husband on the couch. Both braced themselves to hear unpleasant news. Finally, Retno nodded towards Rama, who was seated across the coffee table from them.

"I know this is all of a sudden…" Rama began.

"What's all of a sudden?"

"Well, this meeting I mentioned."

"What is it you're saying, Rama? You're just asking us to meet Rininta's parents, aren't you?"

"Well, not just to meet them, Papa. There's also…"

"*Masya Allah!*" Aji quickly gulped the rest of his glass of milk. Milk dripped from the glass and dribbled from his lips.

Retno stared at her son, suddenly finding a headache coming on as well. "So what you're saying is…"

"What I'm saying is that Rininta and I intend to get married, sometime before the end of the year."

"Ohmygod, ohmygod!" came the shriek of Andini's voice from

the bathroom followed by a gale of laughter. How could she hear them speak when she was taking a bath?

"Just a second here…" Retno was becoming upset. "You haven't been to this house in more than a year and now you're telling us that you're going to marry your director's daughter. Am I hearing this right?"

"But it's still a long ways off, Mama. The end of the year."

Aji continued reclining against the back of the couch, a mustache of milk on his upper lip, as he stared forward in a daze. Retno took a tissue from the dispenser on the coffee table and wiped her husband's lip.

"The important thing here is not when you're going to get married," Aji said in a slow and even voice. "If you want to get married tomorrow, that'd be fine with me. What's important is whether or not, when you started to date Rininta and then came to be accepted by the Priasmoro family, they knew who we are."

Rama's face grew pale. He hardly knew what to say next. He was coming to the most difficult part of his mission.

Andini came into the room to join the family circus with a towel wrapped turban-like around her freshly washed hair. She put her hands on her hips as she faced her brother.

"Is she pregnant?"

Andini look very much like their mother, with fair skin, a pointed chin, and small eyes. They also both had long straight hair. But unlike their mother, when Andini spouted those sharp words, she resembled, in Rama's eyes, a she-devil.

"Of course not," Rama growled.

Andini undid her towel and patted her hair, spattering her brother's face with water.

"Well, then, answer Papa's question," she demanded. "Does your girlfriend's family know that ours is categorized by the government as coming from an unclean environment? That we are an E.T. family? And you know I'm not talking about 'extra-terrestrial' or 'entertainment tonight.' E.T.—*Eks Tapol*—former political prisoner! Do you understand? Even though Om Dimas was never arrested and never imprisoned either, his name is the same. He's an E.T. too, a former…"

"Yes, God damn it, I know!" Rama yelled at his sister.

With her wet hair unkempt and in a mess, Andini remained steadfast. Her small eyes bulged, just like their mother's did when she was angry.

"And who the hell are you to shout at me? You disappear for years and now suddenly show up wanting to get married because you feel the need for a family. Where were we all this time!? And now you're swearing at me?!"

Rama said nothing, but he could not check his rising emotion. He too felt like his pride had been stamped on. Rama didn't know how to explain this to his family, but he had never wanted to deceive either his friends or the family of his girlfriend.

Aji guessed what his son was thinking. "So, the problem now is that you've never told them about your family background. For all the years you've dated Rininta, you intentionally hid our identity…"

Rama bowed his head. For Aji and Retno that was the answer: Rama had concealed his family's identity. Even though Rama didn't say it out loud, Aji, knowing his son's character, knew that what Rama most wanted was for his family to bury its history and life story as deeply as possible.

Aji stood and excused himself, saying that he wanted to lie down. Andini looked at her brother like he was a paddy snake, good only for being chopped in two with a machete. Retno stood, her body suddenly stooped with disappointment. She went to the kitchen, her place of consolation.

"Mama…"

Rama's mother shook her head, not wanting to talk any more—or at least for the time being. Andini returned to her bedroom and a few seconds later the combined sound of a hair dryer and the music of Deep Purple bounced off the walls of her room. Rama sat in the living room by himself.

Rama had assumed that there would be some emotional upset and uproar when he made his announcement, but he had never thought that his father would end the meeting in silence. How could he fight back or argue when his conversational opponent wouldn't say a word?

Four years earlier, when Rama decided to take the job at Cita Karya, he knew he would have to erase his family history, at least temporarily. That he was able to get away not using the name Suryo and then pass the security clearance without his family background being looked into too carefully had been a minor miracle. When compared to the situation a decade before, the issue of a "clean environment" had greatly subsided. Nonetheless, the policy was still official and very actively enforced in a number of professional fields, especially public-related work: teachers, government religious officials, journalists, and, of course, the military fields where it was thought that those who were "unclean" might influence the masses. He knew that a number of Alam's friends who worked for the mass media were only able to do so by using pseudonyms.

Rama was just an accountant whose job was dealing with figures. Even so, he didn't want to take the risk. That he had met and fallen in love with the daughter of a company director now presented a large and very personal risk.

Rama closed his eyes and, without knowing it, nodded off for a time on the sofa.

The sun crossed the sky so quickly that it was early evening when Rama awoke. Through partially opened eyes, he could see the blurred form of his father seated before him, staring at him with a look that could have sliced open his heart. Opening his eyes wider, he saw in the light of his father's eyes a combination of sadness, disappointment, and chagrin. Rama slowly pulled his body up and into a sitting position until he was facing his father.

"Rama…" his father began with a tremble in his voice.

"Yes, Papa?"

"I just want to say that I will not stand in the way of you pursuing a future with anyone who is good and loves you. But I will not condone you lying to the world about our family's identity. This means you have two choices…"

Aji intentionally paused to take a breath; he was not used to issuing ultimatums. Rama's entire body went rigid.

"You must either tell Rininta's family about your family or propose to her on your own. If you can't do that, your mother and I will not be involved in your wedding."

Rama looked at his father wordlessly. He'd never thought his father would make such a threat.

"At my age, I'm not willing to be part of your lying games or keeping my head tucked down."

"But that's what we've been doing all our lives!" Rama suddenly shouted, unable to restrain himself any longer. His voice was so loud, Retno rushed into the room and quickly sat down beside her husband.

Now it was Aji who was angry: "Keeping your head down

from the military and the government is one thing, but asking us to keep our head down from your future wife and in-laws is the same as asking us to lie! Do you think that when one day your father-in-law finds out about your family history he's going to respect you? Do you think he'll understand why you concealed your past the entire time you were dating his daughter?"

"He doesn't need to know."

Aji shook his head. "You're so confused, you're not thinking straight. It would be better for you to tell them straight out. I am sure that if Rininta's father, this boss of yours, is a good man, he will not have a problem with it. What's past is past, and this is no longer the time for judging people by their family history but more by their heart and soul and their daily actions."

"But Pak Pri is a stickler for regulations," Rama said in a shrill voice. "I know not much attention is paid anymore to the issue of a 'clean environment,' but some ministries and state companies still require a security clearance. I completely agree that the time has passed for categorizing people like that, but I'm still not comfortable in being frank about it."

"Well then, that's your problem, not ours," Aji said in an equally high voice. "If, from the beginning, you had been open with Rininta and her family, you would have been able to judge whether she and they would be good for you. Whether they could accept you as you are—just as you must accept them for what they are."

"Rama, I'd just like to say…" Retno, who had always tried to be accommodative to Rama, now tried to instill some clear thinking into him. "I think it's normal for a company or institution to check a person's background to ascertain their professional skills or to see if they have a criminal record. And even then, I feel, a person always deserves a second chance. But all this time—and this is what doesn't make any sense—our only fault is our link to Dimas. Isn't that right? And why is it a fault when he didn't even do anything wrong?" She sighed. "Oh, well, maybe we can't do anything about that; but for as long as we live, there is going to be a brand on our forehead: "political prisoner family." And now you are entering a circle of people who view our relationship with Dimas with contempt, as a historical defect. How long will you be able to keep up your act with your future wife and in-laws? If your marriage begins with a lie, what kind of future home will you ever be able to build?"

Aji looked with admiration at his wife. Her argument was brilliant. Rama swallowed. "I've given the matter a lot of thought, Mama. When the time comes, I will open up to Rininta and tell her who I am."

"But Dini is right, Rama. Nobody likes to be deceived."

"I'm not deceiving anyone, Mama. I just don't feel the time is right to tell all. I think you and Papa should be glad that Rininta is able to accept me for…" Rama suddenly stopped speaking.

"Accept you for what, Rama?" Retno demanded. "Finish your sentence! Why do you always insist on thinking of yourself as inferior?"

Rama couldn't continue his sentence. Compared with his father's sharp cry, his mother's roar was that of an angry lion. He had to ease the tension. He had to succeed in his mission of getting his family to accept a dinner invitation at the Priasmoro family home.

"You know that I don't have any problem with our immediate family. The problem is Om Dimas whose wacky politic views put us in this position in the first place…"

"Hello! Anybody home?" came the sound of a voice which caused Rama's heart to jump to his neck. He looked around to see Alam and Bimo coming into the living room. With them was a stiking-looking Eurasian woman. Retno immediately stood up and gave both Alam and Bimo a warm hug. Rama looked on with a sour face but, for the moment, at least, the previous tension had subsided. "Lintang, this is Rama, the cousin you've only ever known by name. Rama, this is Om Dimas's daughter."

Retno put her hand on Rama's shoulder, a signal for him to stand and to shake hands with Lintang.

Rama stood and tried to smile. Lintang shook his hand and then kissed his cheeks three times—first the right, then the left, then the right again.

"That's how we do in Europe!" she said.

Everyone laughed and invited the others to sit down. The ensuing conversation revolved around the subjects of the demonstrations, the price of fuel which was slated to rise the following Monday, and the president's upcoming trip to Cairo.

Retno noticed how flushed Lintang looked. "How have your interviews been going?" she asked her niece. "Have you had any luck?"

"It's been much harder than I thought." Lintang glanced at Alam and Bimo. "It looks like I'll have to follow their advice and try to be more patient."

"I'm sure it will work out," Alam said with a smile. "If it's difficult tying down the others, she can interview my mother first. That will be the easiest."

"Your mother? That will be the hardest one, I bet," Bimo joked. They all laughed, thinking of how prickly Alam's mother could be with the foreign journalists who frequently asked to interview her.

As the others continued their conversation, Rama contributed little, somewhat miffed that his own conversation had been interrupted. Just then, the phone rang, and later Andini came into the living room.

"Hi, Lintang! Did you just get here? Your mother is on the phone," Andini said.

"Is something wrong?" Aji interupted to ask.

Lintang waved her hand dismissively. "I'm sure she just wants to know how I'm doing. Don't worry," she said to her uncle, "Maman is always checking on me."

Lintang stood and went to the telephone stand in the back. Alam and Bimo then began to talk of how all the university student organizations and NGOs in the city were united and ready to move. "Even the private universities have lined up: Trisakti, Indonesian-Christian, and Atmajaya," Alam said, looking at Rama when he said it because Rama was an alumnus of Trisakti. Rama showed no reaction.

"Almost all of the universities are setting up free-speech platforms on their campuses to discuss the increase in fuel prices," Bimo added as he stole a look at Rama as well.

Lintang returned to the room to join the circle with a serious look on her face.

"What is it, Lintang?"

"Maman called to ask about the news, but also to tell me that Ayah is having problems with his liver and that he's refusing to go to the doctor. She wants me to give him a call."

Aji gave Lintang a look of concern. "What's wrong with his liver?"

"A few weeks back, Ayah collapsed at the Metro station," she started to explain. "He went to the hospital for tests and had everything checked out, and they gave him some medicine to take."

"And so?"

"He's in out-patient care for now, but it looks like he needs to go back in again. To tell you the truth, I don't know what's wrong. I never saw the results of the tests, and Ayah refuses to talk about his health." Lintang conveyed this news with a heavy look.

"Still as hardheaded as ever," Aji muttered. "Well, I'll give him a call. You three can have dinner here tonight," he then added, looking at Lintang, Alam, and Bimo in turn. Then he stood and asked Rama to follow him into the dining room.

Once in the dining room, he reminded Rama what he had told him earlier. "Remember this, Rama: you have two choices."

"I want to marry Rininta," Rama said to his father. "And all I want from you and Mama is for you to be my parents."

"And all I want from you is to be my son—to admit to being the son of Aji Suryo and the nephew of Dimas Suryo."

Aji then went to the telephone stand, intending to call his brother.

"Wait, Papa!" Rama said loudly, stopping his father from picking up the telephone receiver.

Aji turned back. "Is there something else?" "I also came here to invite you to a dinner with Rininta's parents."

"When?" Aji asked with a frown.

"Tomorrow, Papa. For the whole family. I'm sorry it's so sudden. They told me last week but I didn't come before because…"

"Because you weren't sure whether you wanted to invite your family," Aji stated. He didn't know whether to be angry, insulted, or disappointed. Maybe it would best if he could feel nothing at all. Wasn't he already immune to emotion? Aji glanced at the calendar but all he could think of was that this was the end of a peaceful weekend. He took a deep breath. He knew that his wife, even if she were angry or upset, would still try her best to accommodate her son's wishes.

"Ask your mother. I have just two requirements: one, that you tell them about us, and two, that Lintang comes along."

"But, Papa..."

"Lintang will come with us. She's family too!" With that said, Aji left Rama standing alone in his confusion. At the moment he felt it far more important to call his brother and persuade him to go to see the doctor than to deal with his son's personal issues.

Rama bowed his head. How was he going to explain his family history to his girlfriend and her family before the next evening?

•

Aji pulled his van to a stop directly in front of a two-story house at the end of a street in the residential area of Lebak Bulus, South Jakarta. He didn't immediately remove the key from the ignition. Retno, who would usually be checking her face in the rearview mirror before getting out of the car, this evening sat silently lost in thought as she twisted her wedding ring round her finger. In the back seat, Andini and Lintang waited for their elders to make a move. Through the front window, Aji and Retno could see Rama's car parked directly in front of their Kijang van. Through the side rear window, Lintang studied the Priasmoro family home, an affluent-looking home with a large front yard, a water fountain, a high protective fence, and a watchman's post on the corner of the street where the house sat.

"Well, are we going to get out?" Andini asked loudly.

Aji took a breath. "Can you see Rama anywhere?"

Andini pointed toward the house where her brother was standing in the front portico.

"Watch your tongue, Dini," Aji said in warning as he turned towards his bright but saucy daughter.

Andini giggled and stuck out her tongue, causing her father to laugh.

The van's occupants opened the doors of the van and got out slowly, as if there were chains on their ankles.

Rama, when seeing his family come up the walk towards the house, almost wanted to fly away, but he made himself stand in place. Next to him was his girlfriend, Rininta, who was dressed that night in long loose black slacks and a white satin blouse—a striking young woman with the beauty and delicacy of a smooth and flawless porcelain vase.

"Mama, Papa, this is Rininta."

Rininta immediately took Rama's parents' right hands and kissed them lightly with her lips.

Andini and Lintang gave each other a questioning glance.

"This is my sister, Andini, and my cousin, Lintang."

"Rama said you just came in from Paris," Rininta said to Lintang.

"That's right," Lintang said, smiling politely.

"I've only been there twice, on trips with my parents to Europe," Rininta said. "I look forward to talking to you," she added amicably. Lintang smiled and nodded.

Once they had been ushered inside, the house, with its high ceilings, seemed even larger and more spacious than it had from the outside. Lintang felt like they were ants trapped at the bottom of a huge and empty upturned bucket. The quartet of guests stood in place, unsure if they'd be able to stop themselves from gaping at the large hanging chandelier overhead, falling over at the sight of the immense display of family photographs covering the room's walls, or sinking into the soft plush carpet beneath their feet. But before Lintang could even to try to guess how rich Rama's future in-laws must be, Mr. and Mrs. Priasmoro appeared before them and greeted them warmly.

Mrs. Priasmoro, with perfectly coiffed hair and emitting the scent of expensive perfume, kissed Tante Retno on her left and right cheeks. They were then led into the living room, which looked to be half the size of a soccer field. Lintang doubted her ability to guess its actual size, but what she really couldn't figure out is why, from the outside, the house hadn't looked to be so immense.

The older couples immediately engaged themselves in friendly conversation. Lintang listened as they talked about topics she found to be on everyone's tongue ever since she had arrived in Jakarta a few days before: the terrible traffic jams caused by the daily demonstrations and the increase in prices for almost everything, even though there still had been no official rise in the price of fuel.

When Rininta began to ask Lintang about Paris, she didn't quite know how to answer her questions and comments. "Why is it so rare in Paris to find discounts on brand-name shoes and purses?" *What?* "How does one get front row seats at the fall fashion shows?" *Are you kidding?* "If I ever go there again, we can go together to see the sights. I don't like the pictures I have of me standing in front of the Eiffel Tower." *Excuse me!*

Lintang feared that she appeared to be stupid, but she really didn't know how to respond. And Andini, not helping in the least to help smooth the crinkles in the conversation, made matters worse by giggling so much that she was soon bowed over with laughter. Andini was obviously thinking to herself how tragic it would be for her to have a sister-in-law whose only concerns were how to pose in front of the Eiffel Tower and where to sit at Paris fashion shows. Meanwhile, as Andini tried to stifle the laughter, Rama looked increasingly irritated. He glared at his sister, his eyes begging for her to be polite; but Andini's wicked streak got the best of her and she kept asking more questions about Europe and pretending to be in awe when Rininta spoke of her shopping sprees and her search for clothing, shoes, and jewelry in the countries she visited.

"So you visited London, Amsterdam, Berlin, Bonn, Paris, Milan, and Brussels and all you did was shop?" Andini asked, as if in wonder of the idea.

"Well, yes, of course," Rininta said with a smile. "I mean it's so cheap over there. The branded items available here are always much more expensive and out of season besides. I mean, take for instance this limited-edition LV purse that Mama bought—it was so much cheaper there. We should have bought two because now I have to borrow it from her. You should the visit the Champs-Élysées. Mama and I just love shopping there!"

Hearing this conversation, Lintang smiled politely, or as best she could, but she was groaning inside. "Branded"? What in the world did she mean? O, *mon Dieu*. And "LV"? Was LV the abbreviation for Louis Vuitton? Champs-Élysées? Was Rininta really talking about brand names of goods that were so expensive only big-name celebrities, children of royalty, and wives of international tycoons could afford to buy them? There was, Lintang realized, a kind of irony—or was it parody?—that was apparent here. She had always thought of Indonesia as a developing country, one trapped in an endless cycle of spiraling debt; yet now she could see that a tiny percentage of people, at the very top of the population pyramid, were able to shop for Louis Vuitton purses and shoes in Paris.

Trying to be polite, Lintang did her best not to judge; but Andini held her eyes wide open in feigned amazement as she listened to Rininta's tale of traveling from one boutique to the next with a group of her friends. Lintang knew her cousin was torturing Rininta without the pretty young woman being aware of it at all. Fortunately, dinner was announced, and Lintang went to the table feeling relieved that the night's circus had come to an end. Or so she thought.

The dining table was immense and the array of dishes fantastic: In addition to two kinds of rice (steamed and fried), four kinds of shrimp crackers (curled, long, brown, and multi-colored), and three different kinds of *sambal*, there were, for the main course, a huge fish—a kind that Lintang didn't recognize—in a turmeric sauce; braised chicken in a chili and shrimp-paste sauce; beef roulade; fried duck in butter sauce; goat satay with soy sauce dressing; stuffed calamari; grilled spiced prawns; and stir-fried mixed vegetables, simmered asparagus, and stink beans… My God, how many cooks and assistants did this family have to prepare all these things? Lintang thought of her father and of Yazir and Bahrum who would have had to jump through hoops in order to prepare a meal as grand as the one this evening.

Mr. Priasmoro invited them to take a seat at the table. As is usually the case in Indonesia, where no matter how official the meal might be, place cards are rarely used, none were on the table that night. This was something Lintang liked; it made meals much more familial—and she didn't feel forced to have to sit beside someone she didn't know. Tonight, on her left was Rininta and on her right was Tante Retno. Across the table in front of her were Rama and her uncle Aji. Meanwhile, at the one end of the table to her far left were Mrs. Priasmoro and Andini. Naturally, Mr. Priasmoro, director of Cita Karya, dressed in a purple silk batik shirt with a bird motif that glowed in the light of the room, sat at the head of the table.

"You first, Lintang. Please go ahead," Mrs. Priasmoro beckoned.

"This isn't like in France, I'm sure; it's just whatever we had on hand. I hope the food's not too hot for you."

Mrs. Priasmoro's lilting voice soothed her guests. They all took turns serving themselves rice as the two kinds went around the table. Then they began to serve themselves the other dishes, taking one and then passing that dish to the person on their left. Lintang complimented herself on her choice of dishes: white rice, some of that fish with the turmeric sauce, green chili *sambal*, stuffed calamari, and simmered asparagus.

As she tried the various foods she'd taken, Lintang politely listened to Rininta chatter on about ever-rainy London and French people who refused to speak English. Lintang paid little attention to this talk, as she was more interested in trying to discern the spicing for the fish. The taste of the yellow sauce was unique: very piquant, a fantastic blend of different spices. She wanted to find out the recipe for her father.

"This fish is wonderful," Lintang enthused, unable to hide her curiosity.

"Oh, that's grouper," Mrs. Priasmoro informed her, "but be careful of those little green chilies. They are very *pedas*."

"Hot, very hot," Rininta said as if Lintang didn't understand Indonesian."

"Oh, I'm used to hot food," Lintang said to Mrs. Priasmoro. "My father likes to cook; in fact, he's a chef." Lintang ate her fish avidly. "I'd love to get the recipe for this fish."

"Your father is a chef? In Paris?" Mrs. Priasmoro remarked in astonishment. "That's amazing! I mean the bistros in Paris are the best in the world. Where is your father's located?"

Unimaginable! Un-fucking-imaginable! Rama suddenly turned pale and stiff. He stopped chewing and looked at Lintang, not quite believing what he'd just heard. Aji and Retno sensed their son's apprehension. But wasn't Rama supposed to have already told the Priasmoros about his own family history—people seen as enemies of the state?

"Oh, it's not a bistro; it's a restaurant, an Indonesian restaurant," Lintang clarified, "but it has a bar in it, too. In Paris, you can't have a place without wine," she emphasized.

"An Indonesian restaurant? Well that's nice, very nice," Mr. Priasmoro said with a nod. "It's nice to know that white people like Indonesian food too, isn't it, dear? It's we Indonesians whose stomachs can't adapt," he stated, and then began to chuckle as he looked at his wife and daughter. "Remember that trip a few years ago—going all the way to Europe for holiday, and still spending half our day looking for rice?!"

Rama felt relieved to see the conversation turning elsewhere.

"You ended up going to Chinatown, isn't that right, sir?" Rama asked, not trusting his own ability to steer the conversation.

Aji was now certain that Rama hadn't said anything to his prospective parents-in-law.

"Yes, yes, that's exactly what we did. Actually there was an Indonesian restaurant in Paris. Where was it, dear? What's the name of the street?"

"Rue de Vaugirard," his wife reminded him while passing a dish of goat satay to Lintang. Lintang took the platter of skewered meat unaware of the unease in the air. She was impressed by the thickness and the marbling of the tender pieces of meat on which was drizzled a soy-based *sambal* and slivers of fried shallots.

"It was Rininta here who always had to have rice. We hadn't been there even a week and she was already whining. But what were we supposed to do? We couldn't go to that restaurant.

It's owned by communists!" Mr. Priasmoro said jocularly, not noticing the change on the faces of his guests. His words so surprised Lintang, she almost dropped the platter of satay. With a trembling hand, she placed the platter on the table.

"So what did we do in the end?" Rininta asked in feigned exasperation. "We ended up going to yet another café for more French food."

"Well, we couldn't go to that commie place. You don't understand politics. And all you cared about was rice," Mr. Priasmoro grumbled at his daughter, as if she were twelve years old. "Funny in a way how those communists became famous for their restaurant, with their names written up everywhere when the food wasn't even special, or so I heard: just fried rice with an egg on top!" He guffawed but then caught himself: "Please, please help yourself to more," he said to Aji and Retno.

"They don't just serve fried rice!" Lintang suddenly exclaimed, her eyes ablaze.

"Ohmygod, ohmygod!" Andini whispered with evident excitement.

"What was that, dear?" Mrs. Priasmoro asked, giving Lintang a chance to clarify.

Rama looked like he wanted to slip from his chair to beneath the table.

"They don't just serve fried rice with an egg on top. They have a complete Indonesian menu and all the dishes taste great. There's Padang-style *rendang*, fried beef lung, shrimp with chili sauce, *nasi kuning* with all the fixings—tempeh, anchovies, and wilted vegetables. There's also *gulai anam* and even *ikan pindang serani*, which are also very good, and the restaurant is always full from afternoon to night. It's full!" Lintang spoke forcefully, her eyes brimming with tears.

Rama didn't know whether to be angry or to crawl inside a hole in the ground to never come out again. Aji and Retno looked at each other—for now it was painfully obvious that their son had not kept his promise to speak to his future in-laws. Andini just smiled, while muttering ohmygod as she nibbled on the satay.

"Oh, is that so?" Mr. Priasmoro asked, giving Lintang a look of surprise. "Have you been there?"

"Yes, I have. I go there a lot. I was at the opening, in fact. My father is one of the founders of and the cook at Tanah Air Restaurant."

Tears now streaming from her eyes, Lintang stood and quickly asked permission to go to the bathroom. Mrs. Priasmoro nodded and shakily pointed her finger in the direction of the bathroom as the tableau at the dining table turned into a scene on television where someone has pushed the pause button. Freeze frame. No one moved. No one spoke.

Lintang rushed to the sink in the bathroom, turned on the water, and washed her face. Tears and tap water turned to one. She scrubbed her face so hard that her cheeks and forehead turned red and puffy. She looked at her image in the mirror. Flaming red, anger-filled, and wild-looking. She didn't recognize herself. And then there flashed on the glass the same blood-filled letters that she had seen in the Marais rising above a pile of fresh overturned red earth: "Dimas Suryo: 1930–1998." Hot tears oozed from her eyes.

"Lintang." Andini tapped the bathroom door.

"Yes." Lintang tried to conceal her hoarse voice.

"Are you OK?"

"*Oui*…Yes."

Lintang coughed to try to clear her throat. Her voice still felt hoarse. Lintang didn't care if someone looked down on her but she couldn't sit still to hear her parents insulted.

"I'm coming in, Lintang. OK…?"

Lintang didn't answer. She heard the sound of the door opening. She'd forgotten to lock the door. Andini was now standing behind her, kneading her shoulders.

"You go, girl!" Andini whispered in English. "I'm proud of you."

Lintang looked at her crazy cousin and suddenly the two of them began to laugh.

"*Mon Dieu,* I can't imagine what your parents must feel. I have to apologize to them for ruining this occasion." Lintang looked around for a tissue to dry her face.

"Don't you worry," Andini advised. "Tonight the guilty party is Rama. You're the hero. Come on, let's go home!" Andini took Lintang's hand, which was still shaking.

•

The Kijang van carrying the Aji Suryo family crossed the streets of Jakarta still thick with people averse to a night at home. Each of the van's occupants drowned themselves in thought.

"Put on some music, Papa," Andini finally said, attempting to break the ice.

Her mother looked through the cassette box and chose a collection of traditional songs.

"Oh, God, Mother, not Waljinah. I can't stand her singing *keroncong.*"

Young Andini had the makings of a dictator.

"Then what do you want?"

Andini leaned over the front seat and rifled through the cassettes. "There! Got one! *Three Little Birds.*" Almost instantly, Bob Marley started rocking the Kijang, shattering the frozen atmosphere.

Aji shook his head. "Waljinah has a golden voice but we can't play *keroncong*. Instead, we've got to hear this bump-bump-bump kind of music," he grumbled but with a smile on his face.

Lintang put her hand on her uncle's shoulder: "*Pardon*, Om Aji…I'm so sorry for ruining tonight's meal."

Om Aji raised his left hand and patted the fingers on his shoulder. The weekend may not have turned out to be as calm and carefree as he might have liked, but his niece's attitude had served to illuminate the dark roads on which they traveled. No doubt, Rama was feeling hurt and troubled right now, but the lesson learned tonight was to be honest and to stand up for what is right. Aji had never felt such relief as he did right now. And he felt an even greater appreciation for his brother, who had raised a daughter who was intelligent and held a firm hand.

"There's no need at all to apologize," he said to Lintang. "You didn't ruin anything. In fact, you've made everything lighter and clearer for us all. Don't ever apologize for standing up for principle."

Lintang smiled as she fought back her tears. She clutched her uncle's hand and squeezed it tightly.

Andini looked out the window as she sang along to Bob Marley's lyrics. "*Don't worry about a thing, 'Cause every little thing gonna be all right!*"

FADED PICTURES

"LE COUP DE FOUDRE..." That's how my mother described the first time she set eyes on my father at the Sorbonne campus in May 1968. Maman and Ayah always spoke of that time full of sentimentality for the revolution, for liberty, justice, and freedom. Although unspoken, yet clearly in the background, I suspect, was the ongoing sexual liberation at that time. (Prior to the May Revolution of 1968, Maman told me, dormitories on the Paris campus were segregated by gender, but not so thereafter.)

History depicts the May 1968 revolution in a heroic light, but when I read historical accounts of the time, I find myself feeling somewhat uneasy; the generation of that time comes across as overly serious and full of themselves. When Maman first used the term *coup de foudre* in a conversation we were having about the May 1968 movement, I almost choked. The water I'd been drinking immediately surged up the wrong pipe and came out of my nose. The literal meaning of *"un coup de foudre"* in French is "lightning," but if used in the context of a meeting between two people which makes their hearts pound, the term is laced with emotion and means "to instantly fall in love."

Whenever Maman told me how romantic her first meeting with Ayah had been, even after their divorce, I could not stop myself from laughing. Like Maman, I guess—before she met Ayah, that is—I simply rejected the possibility of *le coup de foudre*. For me, the road to love is much more simple and predictable: two people meet, get to know each other, and gradually find themselves attuned and comfortable with one another. That is love. Love at first sight is a phrase cooked up by greeting-card companies to sell Valentine's cards and Hollywood, which employs every means to sell love on the big screen. I once suggested to Maman that perhaps she and Ayah thought of May 1968 as such a monumental time for France only because of the meaning it had for them as a couple.

In response to my insolence, she warned me: "Be careful what you say. The time will come when you might have to eat your own words." And now it seems that time has come and I am being forced to eat my own words.

I'd always been sure that I would never experience what my mother did: being struck helpless by a flash of lightning. I already had Narayana, after all, who could never be described as a bolt of lightning. He was a giant umbrella, protecting me from the threat of storms. Having him, why ever would I worry about being struck by lightning?

Yet, the fact is, I was stuck by *le coup de foudre*, in the form of a man named Alam: Segara Alam. Tall, with wavy hair, chocolate-colored skin richly darkened by the sun, and chiseled facial features roughened by the stubble of his beard. The shirt he was wearing could barely conceal the muscles of his arms, the breadth of his chest, and the flatness of his stomach. At first I thought he might be an athlete but that guess made no sense at all. After all, I met him at Satu Bangsa, a political activist organization. He was the son of Hananto Prawiro, my father's friend, but also one of the Jakarta contacts Om Nug had recommended me to meet.

At our initial meeting, Alam didn't appear enthusiastic to see me. It was as if I was an intrusion on his busy schedule. He kept looking, back and forth, at his watch and his cell phone, which wouldn't stop ringing and which he declined to turn off. Maybe it was his flashing black eyes, darting here and there, not looking at me; maybe it was his brisk and clipped way of speaking, as sharp as the knife my father used to slice onions; or, quite possibly, it was his dismissive attitude, which said to me that my presence at his office was a waste of time and space and that he had more important work to do. Whatever, I found myself suddenly nervous in his presence and had difficulty forming complete sentences. I sounded stupid when I spoke, especially with my every phrase being immediately contradicted by this supposedly brilliant and experienced activist.

I became irritated with him for constantly disputing whatever I said, and I began to pout—something I find embarrassing—but he still wasn't in the least bit swayed. With Narayana, I was able to get what I wanted: besting him in arguments (not because I was always right but because he always gave in); the choice of a restaurant; the choice of menu; the choice of where to sleep, at his place or mine; even the choice of position and location when we made love.

Why I suddenly began to think of Nara in the middle of my dialectical duel with this rude individual, I didn't know; but it was clear that Alam couldn't hold his tongue when he was impatient or didn't like the person with whom he was conversing. He refused to let me call him "Mas" even though Ayah had insisted that I was to use this honorific when speaking with Alam and Bimo, because they were ten years older than me.

Initially, at the beginning of our conversation, I thought that

Alam might just be testing my knowledge of Indonesia, as if I were a naïve college student who readily accepted whatever she was told. In the end, however, I finally had to conclude, from both his cynical tone of voice and the anti-government protests that were picking up steam—which he pointed out more than once was making his schedule packed—that he would have no free time to give to me and that I would have to do my work without his assistance. But with him being like that, I thought, who would want his help? Enough was enough, I decided. It was time for me to leave. Taking the Titoni watch from my bag, I rose abruptly, and placed it on the desk before him, causing him to stop mid-sentence and look up at me—finally straight in the eye.

"My father sent you this. It was your father's," I said before turning and walking away.

Marching out of the Satu Bangsa office, I found myself back in the roar of a Jakarta afternoon. The yowling of three-wheeled *bajaj*, like that of lawnmowers; the jumble of cars parked every which way, both beside and on the curb; and the pockmarked sidewalk with loose and missing bricks, made me trip several times and swear out loud. Damn, damn, double damn! Why was I suddenly crying? I wasn't a woman who sniveled. I wanted to walk away from that office with my pride intact. *Merde!*

"Hey, hey, I'm sorry…"

It was Alam's voice, behind me. "I'm sorry," I heard him say again, as he followed at my back along the dusty roadside of Jalan Diponegoro. I did not want to turn around or to look at him. Damn, damn! I was embarrassed by my tears, my runny nose, and the sweat now pouring from my flushed face. I rifled through my bag. God damn it! Why was it was impossible to find my packet of tissues with that snide but attractive man behind me?

That was the moment I felt it. At that moment, he again called my name and put his hand on my arm. What was it called: an electric shock or a bolt of lightning? I didn't know and I'd suddenly forgotten the three languages that I can speak: French, Indonesian, and English. Through his touch, so shocking in sensation, I felt something from inside of him move into my body, which made my blood move faster. My sudden inability to speak in any of those languages—in any language at all—left me paralyzed. Maybe that was the reason he sought a way to make me speak again. He invited me to go with him to Lubang Buaya to visit the museum there: "Museum of the Treachery of the Indonesian Communist Party."

•

The afternoon sun was biting hot and even Alam, who was born and had lived in Jakarta all his life, was constantly having to wipe the sweat from his neck and forehead. And I, being from a country where the sun shone brightly for only four months a year and not nearly as fiercely as it did in Jakarta, could hardly bear the heat. The incredible humidity made me feel like a dampened rag.

In this suffocating weather, with sweat dripping from my brow, I tried to read the booklet which provided explanations about the sites to be found on the museum's nine-hectare plot. I used the booklet's table of contents as a guide to what I then visually recorded with my video camera: each of the thirty-four dioramas portraying acts of heinousness allegedly perpetrated by the Indonesian Communist Party. I then understood why Alam had invited me there. Everything must have a starting point, and President Soeharto's New Order government saw this place and all that was depicted in it as its *raison d'être*, the very basis for its authority.

As if preparing a shooting script for a film, I made notes about each of the dioramas, rooms, and other objects I captured on camera.

"There's a feature film about it, you know," Alam said, as if guessing what I was doing. He stood at a distance, leaning against one of the museum's supporting columns, being careful to not stand too close behind me, so that his reflection wouldn't appear on the protective glass in front of the dioramas.

"I know," I said with an air of authority as I shut off my camera, "a three-hour feature film produced by the government in 1984. I've read about it, but I have yet to see it."

Groups of primary and secondary schoolchildren on a field trip, I guessed, had filled the museum and stood in lines before the displays, listening to explanations from museum guides. Alam studied the children, many of whom were diligently taking notes, and then looked at me and smiled, as if I were a schoolchild too.

I spoke to several of the teachers who were there to chaperone the school groups, recording my interviews on film. Two of the women teachers told me that a visit to the museum was a requirement for history class. They also confirmed what Alam had just told me, that all students were required to watch the film *The Treachery of the September 30 Movement and the Indonesian Communist Party.*

"I really must get hold of a copy of that film," I said to Alam as I approached his side. "Ibu Rahma, one of the teachers I was speaking to, said that the dioramas here are exactly like the scenes from that film."

I put my video camera in my bag and then touched my cheeks and forehead, which were hot to the touch and glistening with perspiration. Because of my fair complexion, I knew they must have turned a bright red. Maybe that was why Alam was staring at me so intensely. Yet he had been looking at me that way ever since he chased me down at the intersection of Jalan Diponegoro. Now as then, I suddenly felt nervous and hesitated to return his gaze, unsure of what would happen if I did. Alam's gaze seemed able to penetrate anyone's body, to infiltrate any defense fort, and with ease his eyes pierced into me. I was bothered and uneasy because I felt that his gaze would leave no shred of privacy in me.

He stepped towards me, took a pack of tissues from his back pocket, and held it out to me. So leery I was of his power, I grabbed the pack from him and sputtered thank you.

"Your face is like boiled crab," he said with a smile, "red but tasty-looking."

Hearing him say this, I laughed. We then left the museum, going down the stairs to the courtyard outside, where I took a number of distant shots for footage of the building from the outside.

"You know, I do think I'm hungry for crab, for chili crab, that is," Alam remarked as if to himself.

Now that was the weirdest non sequitur I'd ever heard, I thought to myself, but then I asked him where one could get good seafood in Jakarta.

He mentioned a number of places, the most popular one being at Ancol Park on the Jakarta bay, but he said that his personal favorite was a place called Kamel in the Kampung Melayu area of South Central Jakarta. The name "Kamel," he informed me, was an acronym from Kampung Melayu, the name of the area in which it was located, and its specialty was boiled shrimp and crabs with pineapple sauce. Then, with evident hyperbole, he asserted that Kamel also served crabs with the best Padang sauce in the world. Despite the exaggeration, my mouth was beginning to water. I hadn't ever tried crabs with Padang sauce, I told him hungrily.

Alam told me that when I got around to going to Roda Restaurant—a stop I had to make at the request of Om Nug—he would take me to Kamel, which was close by. But not today, though, because he had to go directly from Lubang Buaya to the Hotel Indonesia traffic circle, where the demonstration about the government's plan to raise fuel prices was being held. Bimo and Gilang were already waiting for him. Alam's cell phone, which had been ringing regularly every twenty minutes, made me quickly apologize to him for taking his time and upsetting his plan to join the protest.

"No problem," he told me. "The demonstration today is a small one: just a few activist groups and some college students. The big one will be after the government announces the fuel-price increase. When they do that, prices for everything else, staple goods included, are going to follow suit which, at this moment, neither the lower class nor middle classes can afford," he explained while scanning the roadway outside the museum. "But anyway, it's time you met Bimo," he said with a smile. "I'm sure Om Nug is going to demand a full report from you."

"All right, let's go meet him. I've finished my filming here."

Out on the street, Alam hailed a taxi to take us back to the center of the city, where he was to meet his friends at the Hotel Indonesia traffic circle, a favorite site for mass demonstrations. With the traffic so bad that day, it seemed to take forever to get back into town. Even before my arrival in Jakarta, I'd heard of the city's scathing reputation for its traffic problems, but I never imagined that it would be so bad. The only good thing about the lengthy trip was that it gave me the opportunity to speak at length to Alam. We talked about the museum; about how the New Order government, with its solid hold on power, had propagated an image of evil on the part of its historical enemy and successfully cultivated among Indonesians an irrational fear of and hatred towards the specter of communism; and about the many examples of foreign scholarship containing alternative theories on who was in fact behind the events of 1965.

"'Communism,'" Alam said, "is now nothing more than a term used to describe objection to the status quo. Because of the ban on books about communism, Indonesians don't know what communism is. Even university students aren't allowed to read the works of Karl Marx or interpretations of his theories, unless they somehow manage to read them on the sly. What the government fails to see is that its obsessive paranoia about the subject only heightens people's curiosity, especially among younger intellectuals."

Alam took out a pack of cigarettes from his shirt pocket, but then only held it in his hands. I guessed he wanted to smoke but was suppressing the urge. "And if they do learn about Marxian theory, what's the big deal anyway? By and large, it's failed everywhere. Nobody here is interested in trying to put it into practice. I'm not. Bimo isn't either. And this isn't because of what happened to our families; it's because of what we've read and studied on our own and because of reason.

"I'm looking forward to meeting Bimo," I told Alam. "Om Nug is forever talking about him, of course, but his name has been mentioned to me by other people as well. From what I gather, the two of you are real close."

"We've been like brothers ever since we were kids. When dealing with bullies, I was his big brother." Alam glanced at me. "But in terms of girls, he was mine."

I was curious. "Why's that?"

"He always gave in, never had the nerve to face down the bullies," he said.

"No, not that—the second part of your statement. Why was Bimo like your big brother when it came to girls?"

"Oh, that…" he said but then stopped speaking, his hand gripping the pack of cigarettes.

"If you want to smoke, go ahead," I told him, feeling pity for him as he kept turning over the cigarette packet. "Just crack open the window a bit! " I added. "French people smoke a lot." I rolled down the window on my side of the car a bit, then leaned over him to open the window on his side.

He frowned as my body brushed his.

"I'm sorry," I apologized. "Go ahead and smoke. You look nervous."

"I am, but not because I need a cigarette," he said as he shut the windows I had just opened. "I'm nervous because I want to kiss you."

My blood immediately pulsed faster. My head pounded harder. All the organs in my body seemed to shiver with thrill when I heard that sentence spoken—spoken by a man I had met only several hours before yet was able to make my heart tremble. I knew at that moment Bimo was a big brother for Alam in matters of women because Alam was given to the reckless expression of his emotions, of stating things like he had just said.

Oh, Maman, I apologize for having made fun of you.

I noticed in the rear view mirror the taxi driver eyeing the two of us to see what would happen. I said nothing, did nothing. Alam laughed lightly, then touched my lips with his fingers. Even that was electrifying. *Le coup de foudre.*

•

The next few days, as I was trying to set up an appointment to interview Indonesia's most famous former political prisoner, the novelist Pramoedya Ananta Toer, I ran into difficulty because of the author's own busy schedule. Alam promised to help find out the writer's upcoming schedule of activities. "Most of the time, when Pak Pramoedya gives a lecture or a talk, it's possible to ask him for an interview at the location of the talk," Alam said. I had already arranged to meet three other former political prisoners, but those interviews weren't scheduled until two and three days hence. Thus, as my schedule for the next day was free, Alam called me at Om Aji's house and suggested that I use the opportunity to talk to his mother, whom I hadn't yet had the opportunity to meet. Alam wouldn't be able to be with me, however, because the government had just announced an increase in fuel prices and he had to help Bimo and Gilang supervise the demonstrations that were scheduled to take place at several locations in Jakarta the next morning.

"Do you think you can you find my mother's house on your own?" he asked me over the phone, "or do you need me to take you there?"

"Don't be ridiculous. Go off to your demonstration. I can take care of myself," I told him, though secretly I liked his attention, even if only over the telephone.

"Andini told me earlier about what happened last night at the dinner with Rama's fiancée."

"Oh, really, did she?"

"Yup. And are you all right?"

"I'm fine. I'm just worried about Rama and how his job and

his relationship with his fiancée might suffer because of what I said," I answered, thinking of the drama that had taken place the previous night, which was truly embarrassing.

"Don't worry about it," Alam said dismissively. "What with the way he's been and the things that he's done, Rama has hurt his family's feelings a lot," he asserted angrily. "It's time for a little payback."

"Maybe so, but my own behavior last night—that wasn't me either."

"Don't blame yourself," Alam lobbed back, "Rama knew what he'd gotten into."

I didn't reply.

"So, do you want to meet at my mother's house later?" Alam asked in a softer voice. "How long do you think you'll be there? Maybe, when my business is done, I can come to Percetakan Negara to pick you up."

I restrained my glee in hearing that he wanted to see me again the next day. So juvenile, so pubescent I'd suddenly become, like a teenager on the cusp of change. I should have been focusing my thoughts on the questions I would ask in upcoming interviews and the answers my respondents might give, but here I was trying to set my schedule so that it fit in with Alam's. This was ridiculous. What had happened to Nara? I really had to call Nara. It would be expensive, but I knew I had to call him.

"What time do you think you'll be done? I imagine my interview will be two, maybe three hours."

Alam laughed. "You don't know my mother. First, she'll want to get to know you and then she'll invite you to join her for lunch or maybe even to cook a meal with her. Only after that will she let you interview her. I can see it taking most if not all of the day."

"Well then, do you want to meet me at your mother's?"

Alam paused before answering. "Let's play it by ear and call each other in the afternoon. If you finish before I do, maybe we can meet somewhere halfway. You have Andini's extra cell, don't you?"

"Yes, I do, and I have mine, too, but it has my French number." Now, I was feeling disappointed.

"OK then, gotta go. Good luck and take care."

I put down the receiver of the phone in Om Aji's living room and sat down on the couch to reread the notes I had gathered thus far. So, my meeting with Alam tomorrow was still up in the air—or, at best, still uncertain as to when and where. I suddenly felt miserable and upset. But why was a meeting with this tall man, with the almost blue facial skin from having just shaved, so important to me? I had to forget about him—at least for now. I had other business to do, the first of which was to find out where to buy some flowers. My father had specifically requested that when I meet "Tante Surti"—which is how he always referred to her when speaking to me—I was supposed to bring her jasmine flowers.

When Andini came to join me, I asked her, "Din, where can I find jasmine flowers?"

"Jasmine? What? Who's *koit*?"

"'*Koit*'?" I asked, not knowing the word.

Andini laughed. "Yeah, '*koit*.' That's Jakarta slang for dead, as in 'kicked the bucket' or 'bit the dust.' Never heard that one in Paris, huh?"

I took my notebook and wrote down the new word. Though I considered myself fluent in Indonesian, ever since setting foot in Jakarta, I'd been constantly writing down words that were foreign to my ears and not to be found in any dictionary. Andini was constantly chiding me about my obsessive notetaking.

"Are you going to a wake or something?" she then asked. "Or getting married?! Jasmine flowers are for the newly married or nearly buried."

Hmm… Then why had Ayah asked me to take jasmine to Tante Surti?

"Whatever… I just need to know where can I buy some jasmine flowers for tomorrow."

"Well, at the cemetery, for one. Come on, I'll take you. You're the one always touting the charms of graveyards—like a *flâneur*," she said, imitating my expression. Andini smiled and blinked her eyes.

I grabbed one of the extra cushions on the couch and threw it at her, truly pleased at that moment to have a cousin my age.

Om Aji, seated in his lazy chair, looked up and interrupted. "Dini, ask Irah to buy some when she goes to the market tomorrow morning. Are they for Tante Surti?" he then asked me. "I'm sure your father asked you to bring some for her."

I nodded in surprise. How did he know such a thing?

•

The Prawiro family home on Jalan Percetakan Negara in the Salemba area of Jakarta was an older building that looked in need of renovation. Its original white color was now closer to light brown. Even so, the small lawn and garden out front were well maintained, and the house was framed by lantana shrubs with showy heads of purple and yellow flowers. My video camera was in the bag hanging from my shoulder, and in my hand was a clear plastic container with strings of jasmine flowers. (Tante Retno insisted that putting them in the container would help to keep the flowers fresh.) The gate to Tante Surti's home was unlocked and it creaked when I opened it. I looked around at the yard and imagined Kenanga, Bulan, and Alam, who must have spent whole days playing there as children.

I knocked on the door. An older woman, a housemaid, I assumed, opened the door and invited me to come inside, then led me to the living room where she invited me to take a chair. The clackety-clack sound of a foot-driven pedal sewing machine came to me from a side room. Alam had told me that after her husband's death, Tante Surti had supported herself and her family as a seamstress, and that she had two assistants to help with the sewing orders she received.

In the room were a long rattan recliner and a lazy chair that looked to be in need of retirement. Dozens of old and faded photographs in frames filled the bookshelf. A tall vase of white carnations perched on an Indies-style upright stand helped to freshen the room. A large photograph of the Hananto family hung on the living room wall. Om Hananto, still young and good-looking, held a baby in his arms—Alam, for sure. Beside him were two girls: Kenanga and Bulan, of course. And standing next to them was—*mon Dieu!*— Tante Surti? It was no wonder that my father and Om Hananto had once vied for her attention. She looked like a film star the great filmmaker Usmar Ismail might have discovered. She wasn't just pretty, with her thick wavy hair framing her oval face with almond-shaped eyes and finely shaped nose. She was stunning, with a magnetic appeal. Her full lips were a wonderfully natural shape—unlike those of many women today who manipulate their shape with lipstick around the edges to make them appear thinner or transforming thin lips to resemble hunks of steak, like Brigitte Bardot's lips when she was young. No, Tante Surti's lips were natural, perfectly formed, and required no disguise or manipulation. Like Maman, Tante Surti appeared to be a woman who did not depend on cosmetics to enhance her natural beauty. Maybe a light brush of the powder puff or a dab of lipstick on occasion, but that was enough. And certainly no rouge or mascara, either.

Hanging beside this formal photograph was another one that arrested my gaze: Alam dressed in some kind of martial art fighting gear—maybe karate, maybe tae kwon do, I didn't know the difference. He appeared to be of primary school age but even then, next to his teammates, he looked tall and fit for his age. A montage of photographs showed him in action and wearing a black belt. It must have been from those beginnings that he acquired the set of muscles visible beneath his shirt. Alam had his father's face: handsome, stern, and masculine. Both Kenanga and Bulan were blessed with their mother's beauty; but Kenanga, despite her obvious charms, did not smile in any of the photographs on display. She looked serious, almost forlorn. Her sister Bulan, on the other hand, was always posing and staring straight into the camera with a friendly smile.

"Hello. You must be Lintang."

A woman of about sixty years of age stood in front of me: Surti Anandari, who was no less attractive in her later years than she had been as a young woman. What differentiated the present Surti from the one in the faded photograph was that her hair was now silver in color and her skin of a different texture. Nonetheless, for a woman who had suffered so much in life, she remained poised and erect. Alam must have gotten his eagle-like eyes, which had a piercing gleam, from his mother.

I extended my hand and bowed slightly. She took my hand, embraced me warmly, and kissed my cheeks. Her eyes glistened as she stroked my hair.

"Such a beautiful daughter Dimas has," she said, "Please have a seat. Would you like a refreshment?"

I sat down slowly on the sofa, still mesmerized by Tante Surti's aura. She had a presence that filled the room. "Anything's fine. Water would be OK."

"I just split open a young coconut. Would you like some of that, with ice?"

Young coconut with ice on a hot day? A person would have to be crazy to object. *Dingue!* I nodded readily.

Tante Surti went into the kitchen and soon emerged with two bowls of young coconut with shaved ice and flavored syrup. The coconut tasted especially fresh, as if just cut from the tree. As we ate, we began our conversation, first seeking common ground: talking about my father's friendship with Om Nug, Om Hananto, and Om Tjai when they were young; about going to school at the University of Indonesia at the time when Sukarno was president; and about the books they had difficulty in finding but which they usually managed to obtain from Dutch friends of Tante Surti's father. After that, all the classic names emerged: Lord Byron, T.S. Eliot, on up to Walt Whitman and Allen Ginsberg and of course those Indonesian poets whose names were so common on the tongue, such as Chairil Anwar and Rivai Apin. Tante Surti was able to quote these poets' words, and did so with great warmth as she spoke. Her face became overcast, however, when she said that 1965 marked the end of poetry in her life, that at that time poetry had changed it into an alien thing.

"Ever since that time, the only thing I was ever able to think about was how to survive and to protect the children," she said, looking at me as her mind returned to Jakarta today.

I felt it was time to begin to record what Tante Surti was telling me, but then her mood suddenly changed, becoming lighter. Smiling broadly, she announced that it was about time for lunch. Would I like to join? This was an offer I was not about to refuse. Alam was right.

"Kenanga called earlier to tell me that she'd cooked *ikan pindang serani*, and that she would send some over to me. It should be here soon," Tante Surti said as she fetched silverware for the meal.

I helped her set the table as she told me that Kenanga lived with her husband and children nearby. Because Tante Surti now lived alone—her two assistants and the servant went home in the evening—Kenanga often cooked for her mother, even though, Tante Surti insisted, she liked to cook as well. Bulan, Tante Surti said, worked in an advertising agency on Jalan Rasuna Said and lived in a boarding house in the Setiabudi area, which was close to that street, in order to be close to her office. Tante Surti told me that regardless of how busy Alam was, he always visited her on weekends.

Strangely though, after all these years, she remarked with a glance in my direction, he had yet to bring a girlfriend home. Of her three children, Tante Surti said with a smile as she placed water glasses on the table, he was the only one who seemed to have no obvious intention of establishing a permanent relationship with anyone.

I didn't know how I was supposed to react to this information. Wasn't it normal *not* to be married at the age of thirty-three? Or was it that in Indonesia the age of thirty or thereabouts was a demarcation line of sorts, past which one should not wait to get married? I was twenty-three and I didn't know whether I wanted to get married or not.

I was answering one of Tante Surti's questions when a lithe young woman who greatly resembled Tante Surti rushed breathlessly into the house holding a pot in her left arm, a tiffin in her right, and a plastic container beneath her chin. I quickly moved to assist and took the large and hot pot from her.

"You must be Kenanga," I said. "Here, let me help." I extracted the plastic container of fried shallots that was wedged between her chin and neck and then took the tiffin from her hand.

"Thank you," she said, breathing a sigh of relief. "And you must be Lintang. My God, you're beautiful!" she remarked point blank, causing me to blush straightaway. Tante Surti began to remove the food from the tiffin containers and put the various dishes in serving dishes. She shook her head and tisked. "My word, Kenanga, you cooked an entire meal!"

"No extra work, Ibu," Kenanga replied. "It's what we're having at home for dinner tonight." Saying that, she again looked at me, up and down, assessing my features. "I'm not surprised that Alam invited you here," she said to me, then turned to look at her mother: "but I'm guessing that it wasn't just for an interview!"

"I was thinking the same thing," her mother replied. "Earlier, I told Lintang that Alam had never introduced any of his women friends to me. This is the first time."

"You're forgetting Rianti," Kenanga said.

"Oh, Rianti…" Tante Surti said with a flap of her hands. "She only came here because Alam had suddenly vanished like a ghost and she knew that he usually visits me on weekends."

I was strongly tempted to imitate the way Andini said "Ohmygod, ohmygod" whenever she found something to be funny or absurd, but secretly I didn't object to this dialogue between mother and daughter since they had, at that instant, crowned me in my position as "the only girl Alam had ever invited to his mother's home." I didn't know whether to scratch my head or to laugh, the situation was so absurd.

"I came to interview you," I said to Tante Surti, "not because Alam suggested it."

Tante Surti looked me in the eye, gently touched my cheek with her smooth fingers, and turned to Kenanga. "Look how she blushes!"

"It's called the 'Alam effect,'" Kenanga said with a laugh, as she came to the table with a pitcher of water.

Alam was right: when two women were talking, it was always best to listen and to not interrupt—especially when the two were as harmoniously paired as Tante Surti and Kenanga. He was also right that in his home, just as in mine, the family meal occupied an important position in daily life.

The three of us conversed while enjoying our plates of steamed white rice surrounded by tempeh cubes grilled in chili sauce, and stir-fried green beans with shrimp, and portions of milkfish from the soup that Kenanga prepared.

Kenanga seemed surprised to witness my dexterity in using the fingers of my right hand to eat the food she had prepared. When she pushed the bowl of rice towards me, a signal to help myself to a second serving, she asked, "Who taught you to eat with your fingers?"

"My father, of course," I answered. "This *pindang serani* is extraordinary, Kenanga. The milkfish melts in your mouth. My father is the best cook at the Tanah Air Restaurant, and this is one of his favorite dishes."

Kenanga glanced at her mother who was now enjoying the meal in silence.

"The recipe is from your father," Kenanga said.

"Really?"

"Did you know that your father and my mother were once a hot couple?" Kenanga said.

I was glad she'd said that, as it indicated that she and her siblings could look on our parents' former relationship with good humor.

"It's a good thing they never married. If they had, you never would have met Alam!" Kenanga declared as she picked up some of the dishes and began carrying them to the kitchen.

Tante Surti smiled to see her daughter continue to tease me. I brushed off Kenanga's remark.

"Is Alam going to be busy all day?" Tante Surti asked me.

"I think so."

Kenanga quickly cleared the rest of the table and then prepared to leave. She apologized, saying that she had to attend a parent-teachers meeting at the school of her youngest daughter. Kenanga gave her mother a kiss, and then I walked her to the door. Noticing the plastic container of jasmine flowers on the table in the living room, she paused and said, "For most people jasmine is a flower of death, but for my mother..." She pointed at Tante Surti who was preparing coffee for the two of us in the kitchen, "...jasmine is a flower of life."

Her remark implied that she and her mother were so close that she was confidant to her mother's past life. Kenanga leaned towards me, speaking in a lower voice:"I suppose that it's because I came to know of death at a very early age, I am now very short-tempered with people who do not appreciate life. That's also the reason I get angry at Alam when he puts himself close to danger. It was enough that we had to grow up without our father and without a normal social life."

I put my hand on Kenanga's arm. "I hope that you will let me interview you one day."

"Take care of Ibu first. She's the linchpin in our lives. We'll find a chance to speak again," she said, "but now I have to go." She kissed my cheek, then left the house.

We drank our coffee on the back terrace of the house. Tante Surti now seemed to be ready to give her testimony. She positioned herself on a chair facing the camera, a sign that we could begin.

Before starting, I told Tante Surti that if at any point she began to feel uncomfortable, she was to tell me so, and I would stop the camera. But with only one question from me to start, she began speaking to the camera as if it were a long lost friend, someone she had waited for years to meet again…

"I decided to marry Hananto Prawiro in Jakarta in 1953 for reasons of love and conviction. Hananto was a responsible man and I knew that he would love and take care of his family. I knew little about his political aspirations or activities. He worked as a journalist at the Nusantara News Agency where he ran the foreign desk. I knew that, of course, but I knew little of his activities outside office hours. In the numerous times that I was interrogated during the three years that Hananto was on the run, it was always that information my interrogators wanted: what it is that Mas Hananto did, whether he was a member of LEKRA, what meetings he had ever attended, who was present at the meetings, and so on and so forth. These questions were asked repeatedly by different interrogators, and with different tones of voice…"

Tante Surti paused for a moment to take a breath and a sip of coffee.

"Perhaps you could tell me why they detained the entire

family…" I said to her.

"It's not true that they detained our entire family—or at least that hadn't been their original intent. It was my fault that happened. It was just that, with Mas Hananto gone, the kids and I were all so afraid of being separated from each other. But let me go back a bit…

"It all began on the morning of October 2 when Mas Hananto left to go to the office. He said the situation there was very uncertain. He told me not to leave the house unless it was absolutely necessary. Or, if I didn't feel safe, then I was to go to my parents' home in Bogor. But because I had just been at my parents' house for an extended period of time for an entirely different reason—ehem, let's just say that we were having marital problems—I declined his suggestion. I had no inkling of how bad things were to come.

"When Mas Hananto left, he looked worried but he tried to act normal. He reminded me not to be late in feeding Alam. Alam was a fussy child, you see. I reassured him that I would continue breastfeeding Alam as long as possible. Obviously, we didn't know that this would be our last meeting before the day Mas Han was executed a few years later.

"When Mas Han didn't come home that night, I wasn't overly worried and was quite sure that the next morning he would show up at the house complaining about all the unfinished work he had to do. But this time, the situation was different. This wasn't a problem of meeting a deadline, that became clear. When the next day Mas Han still didn't come home, I began to make calls. First I called his office, but no one picked up the line, then the homes of colleagues and friends. I decided I had to go to see for myself. I left Bulan and Alam with neighbors, a kind old couple who lived next door, and then went with Kenanga to the Nusantara News office. Mas Han wasn't there. I wasn't able to meet the editor-in-chief either, who I was told also had stopped coming in to the office.

"The following days, I was tense with worry and paranoia. I tried to be calm so that Kenanga and Bulan could continue to go to school—even though, more often than not, they came home early because they said that class had been 'let out.' My mother called and begged me to bring the children to Bogor, all the while cursing Mas Hananto for being a man who thought nothing of his family's safety. Hearing my mother criticize Mas Han like that, I became defensive and decided to remain at home in Jakarta.

"One night, about three weeks later, I received a visit from Kusno, a journalist who worked with Mas Hananto at Nusantara News. …I suppose your father must have known him as well. Anyway, he told me that the editor-in-chief and a number of other agency employees had been detained. Others had been called in for interrogation, but then allowed to go home. Kusno was one of the latter.

"Kusno told me that coming to my home was risky for him. He quickly conveyed that Mas Han was being pursued by the military and that he was in hiding and could not be contacted but that he wanted me to know that it was urgent I take the children and go to my parents' home. After telling me this, he immediately left, leaving me to wonder whether his message was real or not—which has been a source of anxiety in my life from then on. Where was Mas Han? Where could he hiding? And what was he running from? And why hadn't he called or tried to get in contact with me, if only for a moment?

"These were my questions, those of a wife, a woman, who had

no idea how what had happened would affect the fate of the Indonesian people—not only members of the Communist Party and their friends or colleagues, but anyone who sympathized with the goals of the Party or were involved in its affiliated organizations.

"A few days later, after Kusno's visit, a number of men in civilian clothes came to the house to search through my husband's belongings. They searched our bedroom and then went into the children's room, which made Alam scream. They turned everything upside down, but wouldn't say what they were looking for. They asked the same questions, again and again. Where is Hananto Prawiro? When did he disappear? What did he take with him? Where did he usually hide? Did I know that he had a mistress? Did I know where she lived?"

At this point Tante Surti stopped speaking. Her eyes glistened and her lips trembled with anger. I asked her if she would like to stop and take a break, but she insisted on finishing what she had to say, then and there.

"They didn't take us in that night. That happened a few days later, when a couple of them returned to the house and asked me to come to Guntur—the military detention center on Jalan Guntur—for interrogation. It was difficult for me to leave the children at home because my parents didn't live in Jakarta. Naïve as I was, I took the children with me, assuming that they would let me go home after I answered their questions. And so it was that all of us went to Guntur."

The story Tante Surti then went on to tell about the family's experience at Guntur was the same as the reports in the letters from her and Kenanga that I had found in my father's apartment. She said that they had been allowed to go home, but then had been called in again for interrogation, this time at the detention center on Jalan Budi Kemuliaan. The difference in experience of reading those letters and this interview was that I was now hearing her speak, firsthand and in her own voice, one that had been suppressed for thirty-two years.

Throughout the course of the interview, Tante Surti was able to maintain a calm and even tone of voice, but when she started talking about Kenanga, who first witnessed torture at such a young age, her voice grew raw with emotion. She said, "I could face anything but that: the shouting at me, the lack of food, sleeping on a mat, and being interrogated day after day, but not that. I could not bear the thought of what they might do to my daughter."

Despite the discomfort it might cause, I decided to pursue this avenue of conversation and asked Tante Surti about it indirectly: "During this time of unknowing, the three years in which you didn't know what had happened to your husband, what would you say was the most difficult time for you?"

"The worst time for me was in the last year, before they captured Mas Hananto, when we were transferred to Budi Kemuliaan. I repeat again, I could endure whatever treatment they dished out to me. I did what they asked: I cooked, cleaned the latrines, ironed their clothing, even after being interrogated for hours on end. But the most fearful thing for me as a mother, something that made my soul want to jump out of my body, was a threat to my children's safety.

"One morning, when we were still at the Budi Kemuliaan detention center, I found Kenanga in the hall, massaging the shoulders of one of the interrogators. It was a sight that made my heart shrink. She had such an innocent look on her face, not understanding the evil ways of the world.

"It was one thing if they asked Kenanga to clean up the blood in their torture chamber; but when they brought themselves into bodily contact with her—even if it was 'only' a shoulder massage—the blood rushed to my brain. Kenanga was fourteen years old: a girl on the brink of womanhood, entering puberty in a detention center.

"I looked at her, studying her features more carefully. After all this time at the detention center, her skin no longer had a healthy glow. Her eyes were red and she was thin as a rail. Even so, I could also see that she was an attractive young girl whose breasts were beginning to develop. I wanted to scream at the man and scratch his face. I don't know how but I did somehow restrain myself—even as he and the others undressed Kenanga with their wicked stares.

"Seeing what was happening, I immediately called out for Kenanga to help me with the cooking. The officer nodded his consent and Kenanga went with me back to the kitchen; but then, not more than a few minutes later, one of the man's lackeys came to tell me that I was wanted 'in the middle room.' That was the term they used for the interrogation room.

"In this 'middle room' there was just a table and two chairs. And there was a long neon light overhead that kept flickering.

"When I went into the room I saw two officers there. The one was 'R'—I won't say his real name—but he was the interrogator I hated the most. The other was 'A,' whose skin was as dark as his black eyes.

"Officer R was a man who never shouted. He never beat people, never ripped out fingernails or smashed toes with chair legs, never used electricity to extract information. At first, all of us women who were being held there in 'temporary' detention—that is what they called it—thought that R was more civilized, more humane, especially when compared to Officers A and T, and even more so Officer M, who rarely spoke but had a penchant for cracking the skulls of the male prisoners. It was later we discovered just how wrong we were. Officer R was a different breed of evil altogether…"

At this point I pressed the pause button on my camera. I didn't know if I could bear to record what Tante Surti was about to reveal. I recalled the letter she had sent to my father, the one I read in his apartment. That night in Paris I couldn't sleep. I stayed awake all night, staring at the ceiling and cursing my naïveté. I was foolish to think that I could ever be a documentary filmmaker: I couldn't stand to see a broken heart.

Tante Surti looked at me and nodded. The focused glow of her eyes told me that she needed to continue to tell her dark tale.

"Officer M signaled for me to sit on the chair. So I did sit down, but he remained standing and then began shouting his questions. I tried to answer him, but I could hardly hear my own voice—which made him shout even louder and stick his big, dark, square-featured face into mine. He kept saying, 'What? What? I can't hear you!' He shouted so loud his spittle covered my face. All I could say was I didn't know. It was then that Officer R came up and pushed Officer M aside. He took out a white handkerchief and gave it to me so that I could wipe the spit off my face. As I was doing this, I saw him signal with his eyes for Officer M to leave the room. Maybe he was going to protect me, I thought for a moment. But that was not the case. This was just an introduction to the actual evil."

I grew tense. My heart withered and I had a strong desire to stop the interview, then and there. Suddenly the cell phone I'd borrowed from Andini began to ring. It was Alam calling.

I immediately pushed the off button, because Tante Surti was still telling her story.

"Officer R sat down in front of me. He asked me to unbutton the first two buttons of my blouse. Completely shocked, I had no intention of doing what he asked; but then he smiled, calmly stood, and came over to where I was sitting. When he began to fondle my breasts, I used my feet to push back my chair away from him. It made an awful shrieking sound. Officer R shook his head slowly, waved his index finger at me, and then undid the buttons of my blouse. After that, he went back to his chair. I felt so naked and so exposed, I couldn't regain my composure.

"At first his questions were the same, the ones I'd never been able to answer. ...I tell you, there were times when I was tempted to make up a story about where Mas Hananto was hiding, just to make them stop asking those same questions. But with them holding the three children as a weapon, I didn't dare to act foolishly. So, as usual, I answered that I didn't know.

"But then he asked me, 'What is Hananto like in bed?' and 'What do you like to do?' I was astonished. The man's questions caught me off guard, and my mouth dropped opened in surprise. He repeated his question, all the while staring at my open blouse. He then unfastened his belt and unzipped his trousers. I was silent, despairing. Then he asked in a firmer voice—not shouting or swearing, but more firmly—'What do you two do in bed?'—with a smile on his lips.

"When I still said nothing, Office R began to talk about Kenanga, how pretty and innocent she was; how kind she was to massage his shoulders; how she readily obeyed when he asked her to massage his shoulders; and how, with her now beginning to menstruate, she would very soon be a woman. Horrified to hear him speak of these things, I immediately began to answer his questions. I began to speak, making up things, telling him whatever he wanted to hear, just to have this hell end.

"It didn't stop there or on that day. Thereafter, almost every other day, Officer M would call me into the middle room. Sometimes he just stood there, pointing down at the floor in front of his feet; but more often he sat, leaning back against his chair with his trousers undone, gesturing to tell me what to do. The man had made Kenanga a weapon... Please don't ever ask me how much I regret ever having brought my children to that awful place."

Tante Surti stopped speaking but remained sitting, perfectly erect and glaring at the camera, her eyes shining with anger and tears rolling from them down her cheeks. She was like a woman in a nineteenth-century painting, a woman of almost perfect beauty but whose eyes betrayed sadness and suffering.

I pushed the off button on my camera, then went to the table to get the container with the jasmine flowers I had brought for her. I opened the container and removed from it several strings of flower buds. Kneeling before Tante Surti, I slipped the strands into her hand. She leaned towards me, put her arms around me, and hugged me gently. I returned her embrace.

After some time, with neither of us saying a word, Tante Surti released me and sat back up. Obviously not wanting to dwell on the awful experiences of the past for too long, she took a tissue from the box on the end table and quickly wiped her face. The way she rubbed her eyes, she seemed to want to leave no sign of having cried.

"When I die, I do not want to cry," she said. "I want to die calmly and happily, with my loved ones around me."

For the rest of the afternoon, my conversation with Tante Surti was more about ordinary, everyday concerns: Bulan was a finicky eater and wouldn't eat anything fatty or that had a fishy smell whereas Alam devoured anything and everything set before him, and Kenanga acted more like a mother than a sister towards her younger siblings. Kenanga, she said, had become an adult long before her time. It was she who always reminded her siblings to write to my father and to their other "uncles" in Paris who were so kind to them. It was she who also reminded them to show Om Aji the proper level of thanks and respect for being like a father to the three of them.

Tante Surti laughed when she told me how often Kenanga and Bulan would tease Alam, not for the lack of girls who liked him but for his inability to stick to just one. She spoke more slowly when she told me that what made her most upset when Alam was growing up was the number of times she was forced to go to his school—primary, junior high, and high school—because of his fights with other boys. It was not that Alam couldn't defend himself, especially one on one, she told me, but that they always ganged up on him when he stood up for Bimo, who was a softer target for taunts and harassment.

Alam's name popped up constantly in our conversation, and I became so intrigued to know more that when he suddenly appeared in the house, standing before us drenched with sweat, it was only then I realized that it was growing dark and almost time for the evening call to prayer.

He looked happy to see me sitting on the sofa with his mother. "Give me a minute; I have to shower," he said. "Then I can take you home."

I nodded as he went into the bathroom. When I looked back

at Tante Surti, she took my hands in her own. "Thank you for coming and for bringing me these strands of jasmine flowers," she said. "This is one thing that has always helped me to get by: my children, the scent of jasmine, and *pindang serani*. I know this sounds melancholic, but I see nothing wrong in leaning on something in the past if that is what makes you stronger."

I thanked Tante Surti for her willingness to speak to me and apologized for having had her reveal for me the sad times of her past. I hugged her close and long.

●

"So, how did it go? What was it like?" Alam asked in the back of the taxi. I turned towards him, breathed in his clean, soapy smell, and studied his features, changing with the reflection of light from oncoming cars. "Depressing. You must have guessed that."

I didn't quite know what else to say. The subject of our conversation was not some distant respondent or source. He was asking me to talk about his mother and her family's difficult life story, one whose only silver lining is that it had made them strong and resistant. Unfortunately, it had also instilled in them, or at least in Alam, an anger for forever having to suppress any thought of revenge and any hope of justice.

"I can't imagine the pain my questions must have caused her," I said. "And I can't measure the fortitude your mother must have to be able to revisit that time in her life when her worth as a human had been so degraded. Where did she find the strength? Several times, I offered to stop because I didn't know if I had the strength to continue."

Alam made my heart leap when he took my hand and held it tightly in his own. "Ibu would have refused to stop."

"Yes," I answered while staring at my hand he was holding.

"You must be hungry," he said.

"You're the one who must be hungry," I said. "Your mother told me you can eat anything and everything at any time of the day. What I feel right now is just the need for a bath."

Alam inhaled and said, "You smell just fine!" He then spoke to the driver: "Driver, take us to Kampung Melayu, to the seafood food stalls, the ones near the hospital."

Without even consulting me, Alam had made a decision for the both of us, just like that. And for once, I didn't object, even though I would have preferred to take a bath and refresh myself after another hot and muggy Jakarta day and the interview I had conducted with his mother.

Alam took a notebook from his knapsack and flipped it open. "I don't have much on tomorrow; just a planning session at the office. If you like, I can take you to a book discussion on Jalan Proklamasi where they'll be discussing the books that Pramoedya wrote when he was imprisoned on Buru Island. Pram is supposed to be there. If he is, you might be able to talk to him and get an appointment for a longer interview at his home. Would you like to do that?"

"Of course I would!" One of my goals was to interview Pramoedya and I was so happy I kissed Alam on the cheek. "This is the best news I've had since arriving here. *Merci, merci.*"

Alam's eyes were on the street rushing past the car's side window, but he raised and kissed the back of my hand. Again, I didn't object. At that moment Andini's cell phone rang. What song is that, I wondered, and why had she replaced the normal ringtone with it? No number appeared on the phone screen.

I pushed the answer button and spoke tentatively, "Hello...?"

"*Salut, ma chérie...*"

"Nara!" I looked at Alam and slowly released my hand from his grasp. He continued to stare out of the window, unaffected by my move.

"*Tu me manques*, Nara." Even to my ear, I sounded overly enthusiastic in expressing my longing for him.

He laughed and said, "I miss you too. *Ça va?*"

"A bit tired, actually. Lots going on here."

"How are your interviews going?"

"I just finished one." I glanced at Alam, whose unblinking eyes remained trained on the Jakarta street. Though he showed no outward reaction to my conversation, I sensed that he was listening carefully.

"Have you interviewed Pramoedya or any other writers?"

"Not yet," I told him. "My interview today was with Surti Anandari."

"Ah, Hananto's wife, the friend of your father... Speaking of whom, you've heard about your father, right?"

"Yes, Maman called yesterday to tell me that she would be taking Ayah to the doctor today. I don't know what kind of threat she used, but at least she got him to obey," I laughed.

"I miss your voice so much, and your laughter too," Nara said. "At least now, we might find out what's wrong with your father. I just wanted to call, but now I have to go, Lintang. Be careful, my love."

"*Salut.*"

"*Salut.*"

I shut off the thin cell phone as I tried to think of a way to restart my conversation with Alam and break the uncomfortable silence that had suddenly suffused the taxi. My mind went blank. I didn't know what to say. And Alam continued to torture me with his own silence and by continuing to stare at the passing storefronts as if they were exotic tourist sites.

Suddenly, he turned and looked at me. "So Nara is...?"

"My boyfriend..."

"And this boyfriend of yours is telepathic or has the power to project himself to Jakarta just to remove your hand from mine?"

God, this was confusing. How was I to answer such a question? To talk with my boyfriend on the phone when my hand was being held by another man... How could I do that? Was it even ethical? But hadn't I gone past ethical bounds ever since...ever since *le coup de foudre*?

Alam now gave me a sharp glance. "Don't bother to answer," he said in English. "Do you know why my mother dotes on *ikan pindang serani*, the spicy and sour milkfish soup? And turmeric? And jasmine flowers?"

I nodded my head, unsurely.

He looked at me intensely. "Those three things are symbols of a past love—an intense and deeply felt affection that could never be fulfilled."

"...which is why my father always has a stock of turmeric in his apothecary jars," I replied as if finally inserting the last piece in a jigsaw puzzle.

"I don't want such an ending: to love someone and then to lose that love and only be able to remember from a distance and wonder what might have happened."

"Who are you talking about?"

"Them. Your father and my mother. I don't doubt that my mother loved my father, and I am sure that your father loved your mother, too; but I am also just as sure that they loved each other. Their names, Dimas and Surti, are a symbol of lost hope and a broken love story."

Alam bowed his head, bringing his face very close to my own, but then stopped, not touching me, directly in front of my nose. I could feel his breath, which smelled of menthol and made my blood course faster through my veins.

"I don't want to be like them. I know what I want and now, after thirty-three years, I I've finally found it."

Now it was I who had to look out the window.

Jakarta, May 6, 1998

Ayah Dearest,

I was so happy to hear that you finally let Maman take you to see the doctor. Please ask her to call. I'd like to hear from her what the doctor said, because I know that you don't like talking about your health.

One more request is for you to do whatever the doctor tells you to do. Please do this for me, and for everyone.

Jakarta is not the way I thought it would be. It's so packed and crowded and so hot and humid and so different from how you yourself must imagine it to be. It's a megalopolis now with huge bedroom communities like Bekasi to the east, Tangerang to the west, and Bintaro and Pamulang to the south. The numerous toll roads and flyovers, arranged in pell-mell fashion as they are, make me feel sorry for any cartographer who had to make a map of the city.

Om Aji and Tante Retno have been true saviors for me. They're like my fairy godparents and they treat me like their own child, the same way they treat Alam and Bimo. You are so lucky to have a brother as kind as Om Aji.

During my time here so far, Alam, Bimo, and Andini have

been of great help to me. I regret not having ever met them before. If I had known them since childhood, how very different my life might have been. They are such wonderful cousins to have; they fill my life here with friendship and color. It's only their language I sometimes find difficult to understand. I've been writing down all their favorite swear words. They are very aesthetically challenging.

Please tell Om Nug that I delivered his packet of things for Bimo: the letter, some recent photographs, and the book, Men without Women, by Hemingway. Bimo was very happy to receive them.

My meeting with Tante Rukmini and her husband, the general, was strange and cold. It will take more time than I have now to describe the atmosphere in their home but, suffice it to say, it was so oppressive as to make me feel weary.

If I successfully finish my work here, I will owe it all to the friends I've made at Satu Bangsa, who have been especially accommodating and have helped me to secure interviews with numerous sources. They also let me use their desktop computer to edit the footage from my interviews. Mita, who heads the documentation section, is very good at operating the equipment and has given me a lot of help. Because of all their help, by the time I return home, most of my recordings will have already been neatly indexed and catalogued. I've been trying my best to keep up with my note-keeping, as well, writing up my notes as soon as possible after each interview, because often, outside of the actual interview, my respondents provide me with interesting information and observations that I might be able to use in voice-over narration.

My interviews have, in a sense, taken the form of sporadic

*conversations: the first with Om Aji at his home, followed
by others at the Museum of the Treachery of the Indonesian
Communist Party. After that I filmed one session with Bimo,
and the other day I spent almost an entire day interviewing
Tante Surti at her home in Jalan Percetakan Negara. Before
the interview, we feasted on* ikan pindang serani *that
Kenanga made. She is, I must say, the strongest young woman
I have ever met in my life.*

*Interviewing Tante Surti was the most troubling one for me,
because I've known of her and her family ever since I was a kid.
Someday I'll show you my filmed interview with her—after
it's been edited, of course.*

*I finally managed to get an interview with Pramoedya
Ananta Toer, whose works I had read in English translation.
Now Alam has lent me the original Indonesian versions to
read. I went to a discussion of the Buru Quartet with Alam,
Bimo, and Gilang (the head of Satu Bangsa). In the end,
the discussion got around to his autobiographical work,* The
Mute's Soliloquy, *which made me very happy indeed. I'm
extremely pleased with the footage I captured of Pramoedya
that day. He is so very much alive that I'm sure viewers will
find the material interesting. He didn't just answer previously
scripted questions. He was spontaneous. It was a standing-
room-only crowd, and questions were fired at him from all
directions. There were good questions, clever questions, clichéd
questions, questions from fans, critical questions, blow-mouth
questions (a term I got from Alam meaning talking just to hear
oneself speak). It was a very thorough discussion and I was able
to record everything.*

After the question-answer session, I got the chance to

*interview Pramoedya, though not for very long. He briefly
told me about his imprisonment, his exile on Buru Island,
how he was able to write, and about his family as well. Most
of the information he gave me I already knew from books
and interviews with him I'd read in the press, but it's always
different hearing something for yourself.*

*I think I might have come up with a title for my film: in
Indonesian, "Mendengar Suara dari Seberang" and, in English,
"Voices from the Other Side." (Professor Dupont has insisted
that besides French, I also give the film English subtitles).*

*Just as we were leaving the site of the discussion on Jalan
Proklamasi, Alam and Bimo suddenly told me to get into
Gilang's jeep, fast. After getting in, Gilang took off from the
place like a bat out of hell. Turns out, he had spotted a number
of "flies" at the discussion, that being the term activists use for
undercover military intelligence agents. I myself hadn't noticed
anyone out of the ordinary, because all my attention had been
on Pram.*

*Things are heating up here. After the government raised the
price of fuel, all other prices rose as well, bringing people out to
the street to demonstrate in ever greater numbers. The military
has attempted to engage in "dialogue" the student activists
who are coordinating the demonstration, but the students have
continued to demonstrate. Student demands are not confined
to the price of fuel and the Rp. 100 trillion the government
has provided in subsidies for certain banks (many of them
owned by the president's cronies); they are demanding sweeping
governmental reform, including that President Soeharto step
down. Even with all of this going on, the president has decided
to attend the upcoming High Level G-15 Conference, in*

Cairo—as if the problems affecting this country are minor and will soon blow over and go away.

Alam and Bimo are up to their necks in work, determining strategy, supervising the students, and helping them to unite in a coordinated mass movement. According to Gilang, this is one student movement that both political activists and the mass media are happy to support because their demand is also the same: Reform!

Rama, an alumnus of Trisakti University, found it hard to believe when Alam told him that a free-speech platform had been set up on the campus, where anyone was free to speak, even to criticize the New Order government.

All because of me, I'm afraid to say, Rama was called in by his superiors for an "interview" and subjected to intensive questioning. How was it, his superiors wanted to know, that a person like him from a "tainted background" could get by undiscovered and find a job at a state-owned enterprise? I feel very guilty for what happened, even though Om Aji insists that incident that night was a blessing in disguise.

With Alam and Bimo busy setting up free-speech platforms at campuses and elsewhere, I've had to go to interviews on my own. One was with Djoko Sri Moeljono—a former political prisoner who was exiled to Buru Island because of, he guessed, his activities with SBBT, the Trikora Steel Workers Union. Before being sent to Buru, Pak Djoko was first imprisoned in Serang in 1965. After that, he was held at the Nusakambangan penal island and only after that was he sent to Buru, where he remained until his release in 1978.

Pak Djoko described for me in great detail life on Buru Island, where he served as head of the barracks in which he and other prisoners lived. Until the day of his release, he said, neither the government nor the military authorities ever informed him of his alleged crimes. What I have found to be most tragic—both for him and the other political prisoners I've come in contact with—is the difficulty all of them had had in finding gainful employment after their release because of the stigma of having been a political prisoner.

I'd love to tell you about all the other interviews I've conducted, but there is not enough time for that right now, plus I think it will be more satisfying to watch my documentary film, which will both give a bigger picture and be more in-depth than anything I could put down on paper.

I was happy to hear that you had dinner with Nara at the restaurant. What did you cook for him? I hope it wasn't too spicy. I'm guessing that he will come to the restaurant often now that I'm away.

Give my love to Maman, Om Nug, Om Tjai, and Om Risjaf. Take care of yourself and remember that I always love you.

Your loving daughter,
Lintang Utara

That day was a fateful one. It started in the afternoon when Alam took the time to accompany me to Bekasi, to the east of Jakarta ,and to the home of "Mrs. D," a former member of the Kediri branch of GERWANI, the leftist Indonesian Women's Movement. Although I know the woman's real name, I think it best not to reveal it because of the trauma she continues to feel. Mrs. D is a woman of about sixty, but still in quite good physical shape: she walks erectly, her eyes are clear, and she's able to speak in a clear and crisp voice.

In my interview with Mrs. D, she told me that when she was a member of GERWANI, her job had been to teach village women to read and write. After the events of September 30, she and her husband, who was a member of the Kediri branch of the Indonesian Farmers' Front (BTI), were arrested and imprisoned in separate incarceration facilities for nine years. After their release in 1974, they came to see firsthand the difficulty their entire extended family was having in finding and keeping steady employment, all because they had relatives—Mrs. D and her husband—whose identification cards included a numerical code indicating that they were former political prisoners.

Her father, Mrs. D said, was imprisoned for two years simply because of his relationship to her; her brother, who was also arrested, was sent to Nusakambangan prison and not released until sometime in the early 1970s. (She wasn't sure of the year.) Except for their home, almost all their goods and belongings had been confiscated by the military.

My interview with Mrs. D lasted for almost four hours, after which she invited Alam and me to share a simple meal with her. Finally, when we were ready to go, she gave both Alam and me a hug.

After saying goodbye and leaving her house, Alam and I headed back toward the main street to look for transportation back to Jakarta. Suddenly Alam tapped me on the shoulder and whispered for me to walk faster. Even though I didn't know why, I did just what he said and began to walk at a much faster pace, as if in pursuit of something. Looking around furtively, I saw, next to a cigarette vendor's stall, two men sitting down. Both had crew cuts and were dressed in civilian clothing—obviously undercover military personnel assigned to tail us. Fortunately, they hadn't seen us leave Mrs. D's house. But when we arrived at the intersection that led to the main road and started to hail a taxi that was coming our way, we saw the men suddenly jump to their feet and start walking quickly in our direction. As soon as the taxi stopped in from of us, Alam yanked open the back door, pushed me inside, jumped into the taxi himself, then slapped the driver on the shoulder and ordered him to go and to step on the gas.

For the first few minutes of the ride, neither of us could speak, and Alam kept turning around, looking out of the rear window, until the taxi merged with traffic on the main road. Only then did he start to relax. He took my hand and kneaded it with his.

"Do you think they were watching me?" I asked.

Alam paused before answering. "Jakarta is on the move. Actually, I'm guessing they were watching me."

"But you're going to be OK, aren't you?" I truly was worried about him.

Alam smiled and said, "I'm just fine," then put his arm around my shoulder.

When we arrived at Satu Bangsa, Bimo informed us that three "flies" had come to the office looking for me. I was shocked—I'd never before had dealings with intelligence agents—but the surprising thing was that it didn't disturb me.

"What did they say?" Alam asked.

"Basically, they know who Lintang is," Bimo replied, "and they came here to check her travel documents and to see whether she had obtained official permission to make a film."

Now, I was taken aback. What pesky flies they were! "And so...?"

Bimo spoke as if I wasn't present. "I told them Lintang was just a visitor to this office and that they couldn't meet her here."

I broke into a cold sweat. "How did they find out so fast what I've been doing here?"

"Don't let them get to you," Bimo said to me with a smile. "What do you think flyswatters are for?"

Alam rubbed my shoulders with his hand. "Just be calm. Let them do their own thing. Want to order something to eat?"

Bimo looked at us, shaking his head: "Be careful, Lintang. You've got one rabid and hungry dog on your leash."

Odi then stuck out his head from behind his computer to shout at me: "Yeah, you listen to what Bimo says. Be careful. Alam has an attention span of two weeks. After that, it's *ngehe*. Yup, it's just bye-bye!"

"Or maybe, just maybe," I sparred, "I'm the one who's stringing him along! Ever think of that?"

At this, Bimo, Odi, and Mita clapped their hands and whooped so loudly that Alam started swearing under his breath, "*Bangsat, bangsat, bangsat*—you sons of bitches!" When I took out my notebook to write down this new word for me, Bimo grabbed the pad and began to read out loud all the slang words that were written there: "*Nyokap, bokap, yoi, yoa, nyosor, koit, asoy, bokep, jajaran, ngehe, bangsat…*" Bimo choked with laughter. "These are Alam's words." I grabbed the notebook from his hand.

"As they aren't to be found in the dictionary, I'm interested in looking into their etymology."

"One is pretty and the other one is crazy," Mita said. "No wonder you get along!" She then took the film cassette of my interview with Mrs. D from my hand and returned to her room, where she helped me writing down the time-coding into my

428

footage so we could begin to edit it. From her room, I could hear Alam and Bimo still mocking each other, sounding like high school children.

"You're the one who says '*bokep*' for 'porn flick,'" Alam grumbled at Bimo.

"I say *bokep*, because you act like you're in a blue film," Bimo retorted.

My collection of interviews and notes was growing and beginning to look very well organized—all thanks to Mita, who was an incredibly gifted editor. Even with all the other work she had to do—handling film footage from demonstrations, public rallies, and the free-speech platforms, all of which she had to time-code and index—she kindly took time to help me. She probably felt sorry for me, knowing that in addition to editing the film footage, I also had to transcribe the interviews and translate the written transcripts into French and into English as well, as per the request of Professor Dupont.

That night we worked until late, dining at the work table on *nasi uduk* that Ujang bought for us. By midnight, I was bushed and decided to go home; but, because I still had a lot of work to do, I decided to leave my equipment at the office. I would be back first thing in the morning. Besides, I trusted that when Mita went home, she would lock the cabinets and drawers where I put my things. I simply was too tired to lug all my things back to Om Aji's house.

By the time I arrived home, it was almost midnight, and I was a total wreck. Not even bothering to bathe or change out of my clothes, I plopped my body on the bed and immediately fell asleep.

I couldn't have been asleep for more than a few hours when suddenly Andini's cell phone began to ring with that tone so awful to my ears. I swore that I had to ask her to change the ringtone. I answered the phone quickly, afraid that it would disturb Andini, whose room was next to mine.

"*Oui…*" I said, my eyes still closed.

"Lintang."

Now my eyes opened wide. Alam's voice. Tense and firm.

"What is it?" I asked.

"There was a break-in at our office. I'm coming to pick you up now," was all he said.

I had no idea who broke into the Satu Bangsa office, why they broke in, what was taken, or why he had to call me so early in the morning.

About twenty minutes later, Alam appeared at Om Aji's house in Gilang's jeep, which he had borrowed just a few hours earlier to take me home. On the way to the office, Alam told me that he didn't know all of what had happened, only that Bimo had called him earlier to tell him that the office had been broken into.

"But what happened?" I asked. "Who did this? Was anyone hurt?"

"Odi and Ujang were the only ones there; they sleep there at night. I guess they got a fright but they're all right."

The look on Alam's face said differently—that everything was not all right.

By the time we arrived at Satu Bangsa, most of the staff members had already gathered inside. That's when I experienced my first shock of mental terror: the office looked like a tornado had gone through it. I scanned the room with my eyes. Gilang and Odi were squatting wearily in front of a pile of books and documents as if not knowing how to begin to put things back in order. Agam was righting overturned tables and chairs. Ujang, with a broom in his hand, was sweeping up broken glass, all the while cussing and swearing about the five men in civilian clothes who had broken into the office without him being able to stop them. Mita, meanwhile, was trying not to cry as she attempted to rewind a spool of video tape that now resembled a pile of tossed linguini. And Alam, now back at work, was visibly shaking with anger. In front of him were several computers that looked broken beyond repair. Even as he began to ascertain the damages, he was also on the phone, informing other activists of what had happened. Every room in the office looked like a shipwreck.

It was only then I suddenly remembered my own belongings: my films, video camera, laptop, transcripts, and notes. I rushed to Mita's workroom. Usually tidy and neat, the room was now in complete disarray, and the top of the desk where I had left my things was bare. I yanked open the desk drawers, wildly searching their contents. My hands shook and I sniffled as I tried to chase away the unbidden tears.

Mita stopped what she was doing and came over to me. She looked shocked by my desperate state of confusion. She took me by the shoulders and began to say something but, suddenly feeling my stomach turning, I yanked myself away from her and bolted towards the bathroom.

Everything that had been in my stomach before now filled the porcelain bowl of the office toilet. Partially digested kernels of rice from the *nasi uduk* I had eaten the night before still clung inside of the porcelain bowl. I wearily sat down on the bathroom floor still facing the toilet seat. No more than a second later I heard the sound of someone—I knew it was Alam—bounding through the door. I could feel him gently embrace me from behind but I could do nothing but cry. *Merde, merde.* The tears fell faster.

A half hour later I was still sitting listlessly in a chair in the middle room. On the side table beside me was a glass of warm water Alam had placed there. Ujang had given me some kind of mentholated oil in a small green bottle, which he told me to rub on my temples, but the smell of it almost made me want to retch again.

Mita now looked much calmer and was putting together an inventory of items that had been damaged, stolen, or destroyed. I was continually having to wipe away my tears.

Mita again came to me and put her hand on my shoulder. Her voice was calm and without emotion: "Lintang, listen to me. You have to calm down. The more miserable you are, the happier they'll feel. That's what terrorism is about. We know who did this and we know why. That's how they operate."

All I could think of was my lost work. Monsieur Dupont's comments. "But all my recordings, Mita… All the interviews for my final assignment: Pramoedya, Djoko, Tante Surti, Om Aji, Bimo, and all the other former political prisoners and political observers… All of them are gone, along with my laptop, my notes, my schedule planner."

At that moment, Alam appeared with my video camera in his hand. It was a bit worse for wear, but it hadn't been destroyed.

I yelped with glee and threw my arms around him, but he quickly extricated himself from my embrace. Odi was smiling broadly at the sight—perhaps their first smile since earlier that morning.

"I found your laptop, too," Alam said, "beneath one of the benches. It probably needs a re-boot, but try not to be so down. I'm sure everything will be fine. We'll get everything taken care of, one by one."

I suddenly found myself embarrased. My loss was nothing compared to the damage the office had incurred, much less the suffering of the former political prisoners and the members of their families I had interviewed. What was the value of this material, collected in only a few weeks' time, compared to the lost years of people's lives?

"Thank you," I blurted out, once again about ready to burst into tears, not because of my own predicament but because of the patience and kindness everyone had shown to me. Alam patted my shoulder. "I'm sorry for being so childish and thinking only about myself. Forgive me, please. Did you lose much stuff?"

I felt ashamed for not having asked this question before and for not having immediately pitched in to help them put the office back in order. I took a deep breath and stood up, then began to help Ujang straighten the desks and bookshelves and drawers that were lying about.

"Yeah, we lost some film footage and some document folders," Agam said, but more to Alam than to me.

Alam nodded: "OK, I'll check and see what's missing."

They both seemed calm when they spoke. Though obviously upset, they nonetheless were able to remain calm.

I again offered to help but my mind was going all over the place, thinking about what I would say to Professor Dupont. Suddenly, I began to panic again. "I'm going to need to borrow a computer and get online," I said to Alam. "I have to request an extension from Professor Dupont. And I'll have to repeat all the interviews with my respondents. This is a *force majeure*," I almost shouted. "I have to send an e-mail to Professor Dupont! ...Or maybe I should call him. Yes, that would be better. I should call him!"

Mita stared at me, then said to Alam, "Alam, why don't you take

Lintang to your house and try to get her to calm down. Either that or give the girl a valium."

Alam smiled at Mita and then told Gilang that he was going to take me to his house and that he would be back as soon as he could.

"Good idea," Gilang said. He raised his right thumb in agreement with Alam's suggestion. "Make sure everything's OK." He then glanced at me. "And there's no need to rush back soon."

"Alright, will do. Can I use your jeep again?"

Gilang waved his hand as if to shoo us out the door. "Take it. I'm not going anywhere for a while."

After we got into Gilang's jeep, I asked Alam, "Why are we going to your place?" I was surprised to see the street was quiet—probably the only street in Jakarta that was quiet that early morning.

"You said you wanted to borrow a computer, didn't you? You can use my laptop at home. Besides, I want to show you something," he said with a grin.

I glanced back at my own laptop, resting beaten and forlorn on the back seat. I had to stop myself from swearing. I could only hope the screen wasn't broken. That would be expensive to fix or replace.

•

Alam rented a very small house on a side street in the South Jakarta area of Pondok Pinang. The house was painted white and looked to be well maintained. It was covered with green climbing plants. As the house had no garage, Alam parked Gilang's jeep on the street outside.

When Alam opened the door to his house, I felt like I was entering a large reading room, one both clean and comfortable.

Every wall of the large front room was covered with books, from floor to ceiling. I walked around the room, saying nothing but feeling thrilled to be surrounded by such a large repository of knowledge. At the back of the room were two doorways, one open, one closed. Through the open doorway I could see a small kitchen whose walls and cabinetry were painted entirely red. I guessed that the only thing it was used for was making coffee and instant noodles. The other doorway, whose door was closed, I assumed led to Alam's bedroom.

"You need to rest," Alam said to me. "Why don't you lie down on the sofa there or in my room. My room is also where I work. There's a laptop on the desk. The password is SegaraAlam65 but I change it every week. Make yourself comfortable. I'll put on some water to boil," he said, leaving me.

I entered Alam's bedroom-workroom and was amazed to see how it neat it was: almost too neat for a man living on his own, I thought. He must have a maid coming in regularly to clean up after him…or a girlfriend, I thought. Nara was fairly neat, but I would never have guessed Alam to be as obsessive about orderliness as he apparently was. Beside the closed laptop on Alam's desk were three 2-B pencils and three ballpoint pens, lined up neatly beside one another, like a military defile.

A number of books and piles of stationery were stacked so straight that I hesitated to touch them. There was a door in the wall next to the night table, a closet I guessed. I looked at the bed and the bedside table next to it. The Titoni watch his father had owned was there now. Beside it was a wooden framed photograph. Looking closer, I saw the photograph was of Om Hananto, the same one that my father had in his photo album. The photograph was dated 1965.

I inhaled, wondering if I might catch a scent of perfume, the indication of a woman's presence in the room. I looked around the room: at the bookshelf, the clothes tree, the rack on the back of the door, and the open-sided armoire as well. No photographs of a woman to be seen. No women's T-shirt or a forgotten bra that might have revealed the inhabitant's nocturnal activity. I often left articles of clothing and other items at Nara's apartment—markers of possession, I suppose—but there was nothing like that here, in this room. I suddenly slapped my cheek to stop myself from pondering this issue any longer and sat down at the desk.

Just as I opened the laptop, Alam came into the room carrying two mugs of hot tea and handed one to me. I carefully placed the mug on the desk, far from the laptop, afraid that it might spill. Again I thought the room was too orderly.

"You know, Lintang, this wasn't my first time being terrorized and not the first time for the staff of Satu Bangsa either. Whenever something like this has happened, we've lodged protests through both official and non-official channels and held a press conference; but the news is almost never picked up by the Indonesian media, It's too sycophantic to support an organization like our own."

"I was overly emotional earlier. Forgive me for that," I said. "I was insensitive, thinking only of myself and my own work."

"Listen to me, Lintang," he said as he took my hand. "Mita and Gilang suggested I bring you here for a reason, but first let me tell you that we cannot let ourselves be defeated by terror, can't let ourselves be defeated by evil. And also that because we're now accustomed to being terrorized, we are now always prepared."

I said nothing, waiting for further explanation. To my complete surprise, Alam then opened a door in the wall and motioned for me to look in. What was it? A storeroom? A panic room? A closet for shoes and clothing? Alam switched a knob and a light came on inside. Now my mouth dropped open. The small room, this closet or storeroom or whatever it was, was lined with shelves filled with manila folders and video cassettes.

"What is this?"

"What you see here are copies of documents from Satu Bangsa, our archive, which we move every six months: six months at Gilang's, then to Mita's, and then to my place."

I was astounded. No wonder they appeared to be calm. Too calm, I remember thinking. Obviously they had been angry for the material loss caused by the destruction of their electronic equipment; but they knew at least that their most important documents had been saved.

"Some of the documents we duplicate in the traditional way, in print form; others we save on diskettes. But everything is here. Even all our video recordings."

My eyes opened wide and my heart skipped a beat.

"Alam, are you telling me…"

He smiled and then bent down to pick up a stack of video cassettes all neatly labeled: "Lintang-Pram," "Lintang-Mrs. D," "Lintang-Surti," "Lintang-Djoko," "Lintang-Aji Suryo"…

"Oh my God!" I shrieked. "Is it, it really…?"

"Yes, it really is," he said, placing the stack on the desk. "Mita makes copies of all our visual records and our files."

I don't know how to describe my emotions, but it felt like my heart was ready to jump from my throat. Excited, relieved, happy, and glad, I suddenly threw my arms around Alam and hugged him as tightly as I could. Looking up, my lips searched hungrily for his and, finding them, I pushed him backwards against the wall. He responded in kind, showering my face and neck with kisses as his hands ripped open my blouse, scattering its buttons on the floor.

Whirling our bodies around, he now pressed my bare back against the wall. We didn't even remove the rest of our clothes, so fierce was the desire we had suppressed for reasons of politeness and etiquette.

Just as I had imagined—actually even more than I had imagined every night since our first meeting—Alam possessed an immense and indescribably delicious power. How he so easily pinpointed the sensitive spots of my body, I didn't know and certainly didn't care, but that dark and overcast Jakarta morning was suddenly like the Parisian sky on the fourteenth of July, alight with bursts of fireworks.

Sunlight slipping through the window shades highlighted Alam's features, who was fast asleep beside me. I studied the bridge of his nose and his thick black eyebrows. Pulling my knees up and then hoisting my body into a sitting position, I sat on the bed. Looking down at the buttons of my blouse on the floor, I smiled, remembering the heat of Alam's body as he stripped me of my clothing. Alam's once orderly bedroom now looked like it had been struck by a storm, or lightning, perhaps—by *un coup de foudre*. I had no idea what my next step would be, what I should do, or where I would go. Nara, Alam; Nara, Alam... Such a mad situation this was for me.

I would begin with small steps. First I would tidy Alam's room. It was obvious that Alam was obsessively neat and orderly. Then I would dress, go home, and see about getting my laptop repaired. I would also make sure that my video camera was working properly and then review the work I still had to do to complete my final assignment. That was more important. The question of Nara versus Alam was one that I would put in a drawer in the back of my brain for now.

Alam groaned, then mumbled a question, asking me the time.
"Seven-thirty," I answered, as I wrapped the top sheet around
myself and began to stand. "I have to straighten your room."

Alam threw his right arm around my waist, preventing me
from moving further away from him. "It's still early. Where are
you going?"

His hand slowly removed the sheet that was covering me. He
then began to stroke my breasts. "I want to look at you." He pulled
me around and on top of him, our groins now linked. Was this
un coup de foudre or perhaps a lightning storm? I did not know.
But what I did know is that once again, on that previously quiet
morning, a new storm ravaged Alam's bedroom.

MAY 1998

DEAR AYAH AND MAMAN,

*I don't know if I'll ever be able to answer my own question:
what can I pluck from I-N-D-O-N-E-S-I-A. How can
I even understand this place? Have you seen the news about
the killing of students at Trisakti University yesterday? That
the military could open fire on unarmed students is indefensible.
I was there, at Trisakti yesterday, and didn't get back to the
house until morning, so have slept only a few hours as a result.*

*At breakfast, Om Aji said that after the shootings yesterday,
Jakarta is likely to blow. He and Tante Retno became very
worried when I told them that I had gone to Trisakti campus
and spent part of last night at Sumber Waras Hospital. It's
because I don't want you worrying about me, too, that I'm
writing this e-mail to you now.*

*For the past two days Alam and Bimo have been saying
that the free-speech rallies for students—which have been going
on since May 1—are gathering steam and likely to reach their
peak by May 20. News about this has been circulating among
students on and off campuses—off campus, mostly through
Forkot (an acronym for "City Forum") which was established
to link up students from the various universities around the
city—and among political activist groups and independent*

*journalists as well. I'm sure that the "flies" buzzing around
campus (the term that Alam uses for military intelligence
agents) have already conveyed this news to the campus security,
because security at all of the campuses I've visited since May 9
has been very tight.*

*Even though this is only my second week in Jakarta, I find
myself here when the country is entering an era where the
Indonesian people have found the courage to demand that the
president step down. This is exciting. When I read your e-mail
a few days ago, I couldn't stop laughing, imagining my uncles
placing bets on whether or not Soeharto will step down. Are
Om Nug and Om Risjaf really going to slaughter a goat if
that happens? And are you and Om Tjai still so pessimistic?*

*Please give my thanks to Om Nug, Om Risjaf, and Om
Tjai for all the nights they took turns explaining Indonesian
politics and history to me—even if their own stories of the
country did end in 1965—but also tell them that Indonesia
has changed greatly from the images in the documentary films
I've seen and from the stories I heard from the Four Pillars.
Of course, not all things have changed, as Om Risjaf has
already related. One thing I've noticed is that despite the
extraordinary tragedy they endured, Indonesians are still able
to survive and to forget. (Either that, or they have been forced
to forget? I'm not sure.) They don't seem to put too much
importance on history (or maybe they're trying to forget it).
Something I find strange here is that so few of the young
people I've met are interested in the subject of history. I get the
distinct impression that people like Alam and Bimo are not
representative of the younger Indonesian generation at all.
They are activist-intellectuals who have been formed by history.*

Alam is coming by later to pick me up and take me to Trisakti campus, where we'll meet Bimo and Gilang. This afternoon, we're going to pay our last respects to the students who were shot yesterday—one event I hope that the present-day generation never forgets!

Don't worry about my equipment. My video camera has some dents in it but I was able to fix the lens. Lucky for me, the damage to my laptop was only on the outside. All my files are safe and the LCD screen works fine, which would have been awfully expensive to replace. Bottom line is that my laptop looks pretty bad on the outside but on the inside she's brilliant. I've been going with Alam every day to the Satu Bangsa office, where I'm editing the results of my interviews from the copies of footage that Alam and Mita saved for me.

Rama has spent the past few nights here at Om Aji's instead of at his own place. He was ordered by his office to take "home leave" while they run a background check on him. Alam has tried to be friendly to him and invited Rama to join the protest movement, but he's shown little enthusiasm, almost no response. He stares into space with empty eyes. His girlfriend, Rininta, broke off their relationship. But that's one thing none of the rest of us are mourning because, to quote Andini, "I can't imagine having a sister-in-law who can only talk about the shoes and purses she's bought instead of asking the more appropriate question of where the money for them came from."

Om Aji and Tante Retno haven't said anything, but I think they are secretly thankful for this development. Whatever my personal feelings, I try to show sympathy to Rama. No matter what, I still feel guilty about the entire incident. Heartbreak is not easy to get over.

*Yesterday, like the days before the incident at Trisakti,
I started the day re-compiling and re-editing my footage of
interviews with former political prisoners. Even though it was
a chore to have to repeat all the work, I was relieved to be able
to do it; the most important thing is that my documentation is
still complete. After graduation, when I begin to work, I intend
to imitate Satu Bangsa's standard practice of always keeping
a neat and well-organized duplicate archive.*

*In the afternoon, Alam, Gilang, and Agam went off to meet
some City Forum activists. That evening, I'm not sure what
time it was, Mita dashed into the editing room and started
shouting at me in a loud and dramatic voice. (Usually, Mita is
flat and dry—a young female version of Om Tjai.) She said
that Gilang had called to say that some students had been
shot at Trisakti University and that he, Alam, and Agam were
already on their way to the campus now. Without another word,
Mita and I gathered up our stuff and set off as well. Mita
took her motorbike. This was the first time I had ever ridden
a motorcycle—and in Jakarta, no less. My God! Mita didn't
drive. She flew, dodging in and out of traffic to avoid traffic
congestion.*

*We arrived in Grogol where Trisakti is located at around
8 p.m. The grounds of the campus were dark and the air was
tense, filled with the sound of crying and angry screams. At that
point no one knew for sure how many students had been shot.
There were still lots of students there crying and mourning, but
then one student we spoke to said that most of the student body
had gathered at Sumber Waras Hospital, a couple kilometers
down the road. Mita and I decided to go there.*

At the hospital, Mita ran into some people she knew.

*I tried, as politely as possible, to record the hundreds of students
who were milling around the hospital corridors, sobbing
and screaming hysterically. Everyone was angry. Everyone
was mourning. All were in shock. I didn't know the people
there, but I couldn't help feeling crushed by the sight. It was
heartbreaking.*

*In talking to some of the students, I found out the names
of the known dead: Elang Mulia Lesmana, Hendriawan Sie,
Heri Hartanto, and Hafidin Royan. They said that two other
students had also been killed, but they still didn't know
their names.*

*At around 9 p.m. we finally met up with Alam and Gilang,
just at the same time that a military officer—Alam said he was
a high-level military police officer—appeared at the morgue.
When he showed his face, an argument broke out between him
and the students who were there. They weren't going to let him
in. I recorded this fracas from a safe distance. I know the footage
won't end up being part of my final assignment, but I think
that one day I might be able to use the footage in a different
documentary.*

*I've seen my fair share of protests and demonstrations on the
Sorbonne campus, but now I think that Alam is right in saying
that protests in Europe are mostly polite affairs. I never thought
I'd witness anything as wild and chaotic as what I've seen here.
This is certainly one side of Indonesia I didn't know before.*

*We stayed with the students at the hospital until almost
dawn. Some journalist friends invited us to go with them
to a press conference that had been called by the head of the
Regional Military Command for Greater Jakarta, Major
General Sjafrie Sjamsoeddin. But we decided not to go along*

and stayed with the mourning students instead. We waited with them and their families until the four corpses of the students were taken to lie in state at one of the buildings on the Trisakti campus.

We didn't get back to Om Aji's home until about five in the morning. Then I tried to close my eyes for a while.

I have to stop for now, Ayah. We're going back to Trisakti campus this afternoon.

Take care of yourself, Ayah. In the midst of this heat, I always pray that you are well and taking your medicine. Kisses for you and Maman.

As ever,
Lintang Utara

I didn't think that morning about my sore back or my puffy eyes, which had managed to stay shut for just three hours. I was sure that all of Jakarta, all of Indonesia for that matter, would be all the more on edge because of the killing of those students at Trisakti University the day before. At Om Aji's urging, we used his van this time to go to the campus. He predicted that what with all the universities in the city holding events to show their solidarity, it would be difficult to find a taxi when we needed one.

We arrived at Trisakti a few minutes after 10 a.m. The campus was being guarded by student regiments—*resimen mahasiswa*, shortened to *menwa*—which was another new term for me. Alam grumbled when I took the time to write down the term's acronym in my notebook. The Sorbonne has no such a thing as "student regiments," which is something important to note. These guards were being very selective about whom they allowed to come onto campus.

I don't know how they knew Alam, but they let us enter. Meanwhile, many of the other people who had come to mourn entered through the campus of Tarumanegara University, directly adjacent to Trisakti.

A sea of people dressed in black clothing was evidence of the grief that was in the air. Even though by this time the corpses of the students who had been killed had already been moved to the homes of their families for private rites prior to their burial, the grounds in front of the imposing Syarief Thayeb Academic Building became the center for people to pay their condolences. I recorded people mourning and showing their respects, but I also recorded objects that spoke poignantly to me as well: flower arrangements, the dried pool of blood from Elang Mulia still on the tiles, and thick panes of glass pockmarked with bullet holes. Why were these lifeless things considered to be lifeless? Sometimes such things are more alive and more honest than any living witness.

In addition to the Trisakti students and alumni who had thronged to the campus, I saw numerous public figures participating in this act of public mourning: Amien Rais, leader of Muhammadiyah, one of the two biggest Muslim organizations; Megawati Sukarnoputri, opposition icon and daughter of the former president; Emil Salim, a leading economist and former cabinet minister; Ali Sadikin, former governor of Jakarta; and Adnan Buyung Nasution, a leading human rights lawyer and activist. I tried to make my way close to the center of the crowd, in front of the speakers' podium, to record them as they gave speeches. The feeling in the air was different today. Yesterday, the students had been in grief and shock, but today what I felt was anger and oppression. Aside from that, I felt that the entire country had its eyes on this campus and was sending its sympathy.

"Love live Bang Ali! Long live Bang Ali," the students shouted in greeting at the popular former governor when he was given a microphone to address the crowd. I wedged my way forward in order to be able to better record his image and what he said.

"I helped to establish the New Order government," he said in a loud and clear voice, "but I am disappointed!"

"Long live Bang Ali!" the students shouted again.

The former governor's oration was rousing for me, and I forced myself forward again even though I was being pushed here and there by the crowd.

Suddenly, I found Alam with his hands on my shoulders. "Be careful, baby," he said, "the situation off campus is heating up too. We should probably think about leaving."

Baby?

"That's Amien Rais, isn't it?" I asked to cover the silly thrill I suddenly felt hearing him call me "baby." Damn! Even in a situation as this, I still found time to indulge in pubescent, self-centered fantasies.

"Yes, but I have to find Mas Willy. Gilang said he's here meeting with some of the other big names. I'm going up to the twelfth floor where they're supposed to be meeting." Alam scanned the crowd looking for Gilang.

"'Mas' who, did you say?"

"The poet, Rendra. People call him Mas Willy because his first name used to be Willibrodrus."

"Oh, Rendra! You're going to meet with Rendra? Do you know him? I'm coming with you. I've got to get him on video!" Obviously, I was getting overexcited.

"Better not, babe, this isn't a poetry reading," Alam shouted in my ear to make himself heard over the crowd's continual cry of "Reform!" "I need to talk to him about something."

Giving in, I nodded to Alam; but before he went off to find Rendra he promised that if anything happened, he would come back to look for me around the same spot. After Alam left, I turned my attention back to Amien Rais and his oration. After he had spoken, it was now Adnan Buyung Nasution's turn at the mike. With his thick snow-white mane of hair and because of his frequent interviews with the foreign press, the lawyer was easy to recognize. As soon as he began to speak, he was given a loud and boisterous round of applause and cheers. Suddenly, I saw in the distance a face I recognized. I felt my heart skip a beat.

"Rama!"

Rama turned toward me. I rushed towards him, as best I could, through the pulsing throng. When I finally reached his side, he smiled at me.

"I didn't know you were coming here."

"Yeah, well, I'm here," he said, bowing his head towards mine. "I came straight from my house. Dini called to say that she's coming, too, along with some of her friends."

"Yeah, I know, but I haven't seen them yet."

Rama looked at Adnan Buyung and clapped when the lawyer said that no matter what happened, the process of reform must begin today. I studied Rama's face; his features were twitching with evident emotion. The cause, I guessed, was not because of his breakup with Rininta or the glare he was now under as a result of his family's "political hygiene." I guessed it was because of his sense of belonging with this campus. Maybe.

He looked as if—how can I describe it?—as if he was proud to be part of what was happening. Were my eyes deceiving me?

Rama looked at me as if he wanted to say something but was reluctant to speak. Finally: "Lintang…"

"Yes…"

"Thank you."

That was a true shock.

I sought the meaning for his expression of thanks and I think I found the answer. I nodded and took his arm, then told him that I was going to look for Alam. But just at that moment we heard an announcement roll off the loudspeakers that the people who were now on the campus grounds were not to leave through the main gateway. Apparently, right outside the main gate, a mass of unknown people had gathered and were egging on the students to fight. The students were becoming more restless, moving this way and that. Once again, anxiety suffused the air.

"What's going on?"

"I heard that some people are setting fires."

"Where?"

"Near the overpass."

The speeches continued, but not in as orderly a fashion as before. From a distance I could see campus security officers trying to keep the students away from the main entrance and the unknown people outside. Not knowing Alam's whereabouts, I too began to feel anxious there in the crowd by myself. I tried calling him on my cell phone but he didn't answer. I then called Mita, who did. I was grateful to learn that she was still on campus. We promised to meet me ASAP outside the front door to the Syarief Thayeb Academic Building.

As I made my way there, I saw her coming toward me in the distance. "Mita!" I called out. And somehow, even with her loaded knapsack, she managed to run to me. I was overjoyed to see a face I knew.

"Where's Alam?" she asked.

"I was just going to ask if you'd seen him. He went off earlier to find Rendra."

"Well, most of the big shots just left. I saw them come down the elevator from twelfth floor. Where are Gilang and Agam?" Mita asked, looking at her wristwatch.

The yells of the crowd were growing louder. And then, suddenly, I couldn't hear anything clearly at all; even the loud cries were drowned out by the sound of engines. At first I thought the source of the clamor was from a bulldozer or some other kind of machine outside the campus. But no, the sound was coming from the air. Everyone looked upwards. There were helicopters flying overhead. My God. One, two, three of them, green and dark gray in color. What were they doing, flying so low and circling over the middle of campus like that, as if they were in battle? A shiver went down my spine and my heart beat faster. Were they carrying machine guns? Or were they just showing off, trying to frighten the crowd as they circled around? I started to shake and I could see that Mita was nervous too.

"What's going on?" I shouted at Mita as I grabbed her by the arm. "We have to find Alam and Gilang and the rest of the guys."

As the helicopters continued to circle overhead, the students below grew all the more angry. Even if I could get through to Alam on the phone, I knew I wouldn't be able to hear him over the roar of the helicopters. I concentrated on filming this mysterious incident instead.

When finally the helicopters did begin to leave the area, the students booed and waved their fists in the air. With the choppers' tails still visible, I focused my lens on their identification numbers as they flew away. Who knows, maybe I could use this information at a later date. Just at that moment, we heard the sound of gunfire.

One shot. Two. Then screams of surprise. And wails. Mita sponta-neously pulled me down into a crouch. Everyone covered their heads and ducked. People started running in all directions. We heard some more shots. From the outside, coming in. Members of the student regiment yelled for everyone to move away from the perimeter of the grounds and to go inside the building. Students ran past us, throwing stones. Who knows where they'd found them. I now felt more afraid with that barrage of stones going over our heads towards the outside. Mita clutched my shoulder to prevent me from standing up because I was still trying to see what was going on.

"Don't stand up, you dumbass!" Mita screamed at me while pushing my head down.

"It's stopped, Mita. I want to see."

We slowly stood and I quickly prepared to use my video camera. Mita kept grumbling that I was acting like a damned fool war correspondent. Thankfully, there didn't appear to be anyone who had been hurt or wounded, but the students were swearing and shouting. What had that gunfire been about? Just to make people afraid. *Quel imbécilité!*

"Lintang, turn that thing off and get inside the building!" Mita shouted at me. The shooting had stopped. There was no sound except that of people running. Mita grabbed my hand and pulled me inside the lobby of the building. At that moment I caught sight of Gilang, Bimo, and Alam who were running in our direction. Finding me, Alam immediately embraced me and held me tightly. Suddenly, I felt so safe that I never wanted to part with him.

All together now, we quickly talked about what to do. Alam would drive Om Aji's van. Mita had her motorcycle, but we weren't going to let her go off alone.

"We'll form a convoy," Agam suggested.

"What's the big fuss?" Gilang said. "Bimo comes in my jeep. Agam and Odi can take Mita's bike, and Alam can take the girls in the van!"

Mita had her hands on her hips. "What *girls* are you referring to?"

"Oops, sorry, Mita. I meant 'women.'" Gilang held up his two hands in submission.

As we were making our way to our respective vehicles, something else made us pause: Alam reported that a student guard had told him that hundreds or even thousands of people had congregated at various points along Kyai Tapa, the boulevard adjacent to campus that leads to the center of town. He said they had begun burning cars and were making their way towards the Tomang Plaza shopping center, very close by.

"So what do we do?" Bimo asked. "Wait till they pass or try to make our way through them?"

Not knowing how to read the situation, no one replied. No one knew what to do.

Alam told the rest of us to wait where we were for the moment. He would try to see what the situation was like outside and would be back in five minutes. No! I didn't want to be separated from him again and I ran after him, ignoring Mita's shouts for me not to follow.

"What are you doing coming with me? I'll be right back."

Alam seemed to intentionally pick up his stride.

"No, I'm coming with you!" I answered stubbornly as I struggled with my knapsack.

Alam took my knapsack from me and started to run. Near the front gate, we could see that the crowd of people who had amassed outside the campus gate earlier had begun to drift away.

Alam questioned two student guards. They gave him an answer similar to the news he had heard previously: cars were being set afire and unknown groups of men were commandeering trucks and public mini-vans. The guards pointed towards a cloud of smoke whose source we couldn't see. The situation seemed to be getting out of hand. I squeezed Alam's hand as hard as I could, wanting to sew his hand to mine.

"Thanks!" Alam said as he hugged the younger men who remained standing there steadfast.

He then looked at me and gave me a little smile for having squeezed his hand so tightly.

"Don't be afraid!"

"How can I not be when you disappear like that?"

Now he really did smile. "I didn't disappear. I was just talking to Mas Willy."

We walked back to where Gilang, Mita, Agam, Bimo, and Odi were waiting.

Bimo grinned broadly when he saw us holding hands. Reflexively, I released Alam's grip. This was embarrassing. In Paris, there would be nothing out of the ordinary in such a display. But here, in Jakarta, I was turning into a shamefaced shrinking violet.

We went to our vehicles. Alam called out instructions before we started to go: "The crowd outside the gates has begun to disperse. We'll drive slowly and make our way through. If there are too many of them, don't do anything; just be patient and drive very slowly. But when you get to clear road, step on the gas. Got it?"

Agam and Odi, who were on Mita's cycle, were the first to leave and the first to break free from the crazy mass of people on the street. Now it was our two vehicles that had to pass through the sea of people. It was totally crazy out there. As we made our way towards the intersection, we could see that Tomang Plaza was closed and now surrounded by a huge crowd. I couldn't stand it not being able to record what was happening and I tried to shoot the scene through the van's rear window. God, a crowd of people was breaking into an ATM.

"Are they looting?" I asked, surprised.

"Be careful," Mita said to Alam, pointing to a group of long-haired men. Some were carrying thick wooden clubs which they used to rap the hoods of cards.

"Lintang, put that damn thing away!" she barked at me.

I immediately obeyed her and then was terrified to see that three men from that same group were now approaching our car.

Alam rolled down the window with feigned calm.

"Where are you going?" one of the men immediately asked.

"I'm trying to get home. My wife here is pregnant and I need to get her home," he said as he stroked my cheek.

What!?

The three men stuck their right thumbs in the air.

Across the street, I caught sight of a few soldiers with rifles, sitting idly, watching the scene, and not doing anything at all.

When the men grinned at him and stepped aside for us to pass, Alam slowly stepped on the gas. But then, suddenly Mita screamed, "Watch out, Alam!"

Six or seven men came running towards us from the opposite direction. But their target wasn't us; it was the car behind us, a Mercedes. Why they had chosen to stop the car and prevent it from passing, I could only guess.

"The people in that Mercedes, Alam, what's going to happen to them?" I stupidly asked. Instead of doing nothing, Alam opened the door and got out of the car. Oh my God. He was calling out to the men. Two of the men broke away and came up to Alam. I didn't know what Alam said, but I saw the brutes nod. They then called the other men, who had formed a circle around the Mercedes behind us. Alam got back into the car shaking his head.

"What happened out there?" I asked.

"When I looked inside the car and saw the driver was about the same age as Om Aji, I told the men he was my uncle and they believed me."

He shook his head half hopelessly. Through the rear window we watched as the thugs allowed the Mercedes to pass. Mita tapped Alam on the shoulder and told him to speed up. Alam muttered that it was impossible for us to save everyone and that we couldn't expect any help from security authorities.

On Kyai Tapa we gained a distance from the crowd, and all breathed a sigh of relief. When the van was in the clear, Alam stepped hard on the accelerator, making the vehicle lurch forward.

"So, I'm pregnant am I?"

Alam glanced towards me with a smile. "What did you want me to say? That you were in a hurry to edit your film footage?"

"Who were those men?" I asked. "They definitely weren't students and they didn't look to be people from around here."

Alam shook his head. "I don't know. But it's weird. All the men were about the same age. Some had crew cuts, others had long hair, but all of them looked physically fit and well trained—not like ordinary people. You saw how those soldiers just sat there watching even as those guys were picking and choosing which cars to stop."

"So, who were they then?"

Again, Alam shook his head. I'm sure he had a hunch but didn't want to say.

Mita, who generally had the coolest head and was the most

rational-minded person among us, had just gotten off the phone with her mother and now looked worried as she reported their conversation.

"My mother told me that a group of men in a public transport van came and attacked Bintaro Plaza this morning. She'd gone there to shop at Hero Supermarket. Luckily, she managed to get out of the mall before they started to do anything. Even so, she was still afraid and there was real panic in her voice."

O, mon Dieu.

Mita clutched Alam's shoulder. Mita rented a small house in the Setiabudi area to be close to the office, but on weekends she—like Alam—usually went to see her parents, who lived in the suburb of Bintaro Jaya.

"Is your mother at home now?" Alam asked.

"Yes, but she's in a panic. My father and their neighbors are coordinating efforts to blockade the roads into the area."

"You should go home," Alam advised. "Agam can take you there on your bike."

"That's all right."

"This isn't an offer. It's an order. Hold on tight. I'm going to go fast!" —Alam drove Om Aji's van with the speed of a plane. I was afraid to open my eyes. I was afraid we were going to crash into an electric pole or ram into the curb. But in the end we arrived safely at Satu Bangsa just around dark. Gilang and Bimo still hadn't arrived in the jeep, but Alam felt sure they were safe. I had forgotten to eat all day and immediately stretched out on the sofa. I don't know how long I'd closed my eyes, but suddenly I was awoken by the feel of Alam's hand stroking my cheek. He was seated next to me, on the edge of the sofa. Alone.

"We have to go, Lintang."

"Where is everyone else?"

"They've all gone home to their families, because they're worried about those crowds breaking into the areas where they live. I think this place will be safe. Plus, there are a couple local watchmen outside." I sat up straightaway.

"While you were asleep in here, there were bands of people burning cars and vandalizing stores out there. Agam took Mita to Bintaro. In times of danger like these, it's usually neighborhood associations and their members who come together to prevent anything from happening to their homes and families."

I was perplexed. What kind of mentality was this? What did the people have to protect themselves from?

"What, you mean to protect themselves against the kind of people we saw outside Trisakti?"

"That's right," Alam nodded.

"But why would they attack a neighborhood? What would they do?"

"Almost anything. Rob, steal, vandalize, or worse. Anything that an evil person would do, especially when he finds himself in a crowd of similar-minded people. With any luck, nothing will happen," Alam said as if to calm me, though I felt sure he was trying to calm himself.

"There's something weird about the group psychology in this country. When people are in a group, as soon as one of them screams 'Thief!' or 'Communist!' there's no stopping the rest of the group from attacking the target, whether the target is an individual or a family and regardless if the accusation is right or wrong."

I found this kind of behavior completely outside the norm of rational human behavior. Who could explain this aspect of Indonesia? I came here to study history and hear the stories of the victims of 1965 and now I'd found myself in another mad situation.

I thought of Tante Surti. "How is your mother?" I asked.

"She spent the night in Bogor. Ever since my grandfather died, my aunt Utari and her family have been living with my grandmother at her place in Bogor."

"That's good. So, what do you think we should do?" I asked. "Stay here or go to Om Aji's place?"

"We'll go to my place. I called a neighbor of mine earlier and he said that Pondok Indah and Pondok Pinang are still safe."

I nodded, not inclined to contest his decision.

Once we were in the car, I called Om Aji and Tante Retno, who somehow already knew that I was safe and with Alam and that Andini was with Bimo. *What? How did that happen? Where did they find each other?*

"When you were asleep, I made some calls—to Om Aji, Gilang, and others. Because we were coming to the office anyway, Bimo and Gilang decided not to come back here. Instead, they went and picked up Andini at her place and took her and her friends to Gilang's house."

Even as we were driving from Satu Bangsa to Alam's home, Alam was constantly calling friends to ask what roads were the best to take. Apparently, many main streets in the city had been barricaded or weren't safe for vehicles to pass. Alam took such a circuitous route, through numerous tiny side streets, which he called "rat paths," I could never possibly retrace our journey. And, as was becoming increasingly more common, I left everything in his hands, not even bothering to ask why these rat paths, which were hardly wider than the van itself, should be any safer than the city's main streets. For the time being, I decided, any kind of logical question had best be discarded in the gutter outside.

Or more precisely, anything that might seem logical to "Ms. Sorbonne"—which is how they referred to me when this alien creature began to ask too many questions—had to be put aside.

Jalan Pondok Pinang, where Alam lived, looked quiet and completely dark. I looked at my wristwatch: 11 p.m. With no small amount of trepidation, I picked up my knapsack and got out of the car.

"All the lights are off around here," I whispered to Alam. "Do you think that's intentional?"

Alam said nothing as he unlocked the front gate and herded me inside. After re-locking the gate, he told me to go inside the house. He was going to check the doors and windows outside. The more caution he exercised, the harder my heart beat. Where was I going to hide my video camera and laptop? I didn't want these precious objects defiled again. *O, Sainte Vierge...* Why was I thinking about my belongings again? They weren't important. What if, as Alam had described, a band of marauders had come into the neighborhood and robbed people's homes? Or what if they had injured or harmed the people living there? And what about Mita and her family? Were they safe? I had to call her.

When Alam came into the house, he immediately closed the wooden window blinds of the living room. "All the doors and windows are locked," he told me. "Are you hungry?" he then asked. "Or would you like to take a bath?"

I nodded while I waited for Mita to answer her cell phone.

"Mita, how are you?"

"It's tense here," Mita said slowly, in a half whisper. I wondered why she was speaking that way.

"No one is sleeping. Everyone's awake. We've got *siskamling* outside, but it's dark and scary because we had to shut off the lights. Where are you anyway?"

"I'm at Alam's. It's dark here too. 'Sis' what, Mita? What's that?"

"*Sis-kam-ling*... Alam can tell you all about neighborhood security systems. And tell him to hang a *sajadah* on the fence outside."

"A prayer rug on the fence? Whatever for?"

"Just tell him to do it; he'll know. Bimo and Gilang said there are gangs of men making their way through North and East Jakarta, especially 'non' areas."

"'Non' areas? What are you talking about? I don't understand what you're saying."

I could almost hear Mita struggling to maintain her patience with me for my stupidity.

"To wit, 'non-indigenous Indonesians,' ergo 'ethnic Chinese,' Ms. Sorbonne!" she hissed. "The Chinese are always the first to be hit, their homes attacked and vandalized. But I don't have enough information to say more. Ask Alam about it. I have to get back to watching my mother; she's still in a daze, absolutely *linglung*."

I turned off my cell phone and looked over to see Alam, who was still on his phone. I didn't have even enough energy to write down "*siskamling*" or "*linglung*" in my notebook.

"Alam, Mita said we should hang..."

"...a prayer rug outside. In a minute."

"She said they're attacking ethnic Chinese."

"Yeah, I know, I'm just getting information on that now," he said pointing at his cell phone. "Why don't you take that shower you wanted."

As I hadn't brought a change of clothes, Alam pointed to the armoire, indicating for me to take a towel and choose something of his to wear. I walked lifelessly to the bathroom. I barely remarked to myself about its small size, neatness, and simplicity. I stared at the showerhead with fear and exhaustion. Why did

I feel like I had been betrayed? Why at the time when I had begun to love this country had this feeling been summarily eviscerated? I turned on the water but lacked the energy to take off my clothes. Instead, I walked into the shower cubicle and sat down in the corner, beneath the streaming water from overhead, hoping the water might wash away my fears and sadness. I had just begun to love this place, this place called Jakarta. Maybe I couldn't yet say that I loved Indonesia, because I knew so little of it; but, from day to day, I had somehow begun to feel a bond that was difficult for me to describe. There was this amazing strength and fortitude in the people I interviewed, which I found to be awesome and attractive. How could Indonesians be so strong? What were their bodies and souls made from?

Why did this all this violence have to take place right in front of my eyes, just when I had begun to love this place and its people? The attacks on the homes of Indonesian ethnic Chinese... My God, what year was this? Had we suddenly retreated two centuries into the ignorance of racism? Or, after thirty-three years since 1965, had there been no change? I had to correct what I'd said to my father. There were some things in Indonesia that had not changed.

I heard a soft rapping on the bathroom door. I didn't know how long I had been sitting on the shower floor.

"Lintang?"

I didn't know if the voice was that of Alam or an angel. The warm water now felt more calming and soothing. I folded my body, hugging my knees. Looking up, I saw an image, that of Alam in front of me. He turned off the water, lifted me to my feet, and took a towel. Like a withered stem of celery, I let my body fall onto his shoulder. He led me to the bed and helped me to sit.

I was still crying. He hugged me, then kissed my forehead, and begged me not to cry. I tried as best I could to stop. I was not given to hysterics. Everyone who knew me knew that about me. There were very few films that could bring tears to my eyes or make me unable to sleep from thinking about the fate of their characters, like *Sophie's Choice* and *The Music Box*—or almost any film by Akira Kurosawa. So I didn't understand why I kept crying, with my tears bursting from a dam that had broken open inside me.

I only then realized that Alam was also wet. He gave me a fresh white t-shirt that was much too large for me and a pair of running shorts with a pull tie. He exchanged his own wet T-shirt with an old and faded black one with no elasticity but that was obviously comfortable to wear.

"They might be too big," he said of the clothes I had put on, "but yours are wet."

He handed me a new towel and then helped to wipe my wet face.

"I want the T-shirt that you are wearing," I said hoarsely.

He looked at me in surprise but then took off the shirt and gave it to me without saying anything. Pulling off the white T-shirt he had first given to me, he put that on instead.

"I'm going to make some tea. Want something to eat? I can make some instant noodles."

I shook my head. "Just tea, please."

Alam left the room to boil water. I put on his shirt, which was big enough for two of me to fit inside, but I loved sleeping in T-shirts whose cloth was limp and almost threadbare. And I liked the smell of Alam's body. My own had no energy, not just because I hadn't eaten anything since going to Trisakti earlier that day, but because of my memories of that day's mad events, which I would never forget for the rest of my life. The information Mita had given me was the most disturbing. What was happening in the residential enclaves of ethnic Chinese Indonesians? My God, what about Om Tjai's family? Did he still have close friends in Jakarta? What had those gangs of unknown men done to their homes? Had they raided them, turned them inside out, just as the military had done in 1965 when they set on the homes of Communist Party members, their families, and Party sympathizers? Was this any different? Alam had mentioned to me the wild and angry look he had seen on the faces of the groups of men—"thugs" would be a better word—who had been overturning and burning cars in the street. They had robbed, they had vandalized...

I closed my eyes—damn them—which were still streaming with tears. I heard the door open. Alam came into the room with a cup of tea for me, but I was too tired to even sit up. He stroked my head softly then disappeared into the bathroom. I don't know how long I'd been asleep, but all of a sudden I found him there again, lying on his back beside me. I rolled over and buried my head in his armpit. He stretched out his left arm and held me to him tightly.

"I've got you." He kissed the crown of my head.

"You know, I can take care of myself."

"I'm sure you can."

He turned his body toward mine and stared into my eyes. "But I don't want you ever to be free from me again. I mean it."

And I fell back asleep, a deep sleep.

It felt like I had been asleep for only five minutes, but suddenly the day was bright. I looked at the Titoni wristwatch on the small bedside table. Ten o'clock. The spot where Alam had slept was cold. Apparently, he'd already been up for quite some time. Where was he? My head started to spin. What was happening?

I got out of bed with difficulty, my head pounding ever harder. No one in the living room. The blinds were open. I opened the front door slowly. The street outside was empty. But there was Alam, talking to someone on his cell phone. He waved his hand at me and continued his conversation. Om Aji's van was also there, still parked safely on the street. That's right. I had to call Om Aji and Maman, and Ayah as well, before they started to go crazy watching whatever news was showing on CNN and BBC.

Om Aji and Tante Retno were fine, it turned out. Bimo had brought Andini home safely. (I intended to interrogate her when the situation was calmer.) Maman had called during the night, but Om Aji had managed to calm her worries. That meant I could put off calling France at least for a little while, until things were more settled.

Alam came into the house, plopped down in a chair, and immediately pulled me down onto his lap. He kissed me long, as if he never wanted to let me go.

"I haven't bathed or brushed my teeth."

"I haven't either. Let's take a bath together!"

I laughed. "No wonder Bimo is always telling me to be careful around you. No matter the situation, your hormones are always talking."

Alam smiled but continued to stare at me intensely. "It's exactly in times like these that hormones act up."

"Was that Bimo or Gilang on the phone? What do they have to say?"

Alam took a breath and then exhaled. "It was Bimo. He said that on SCTV they reported that at a meeting with Indonesian people living in Cairo, Soeharto said that he would be willing to step down if that's what the people wanted." He seemed to be thinking of something. "I suspect that he'll still try to hang on."

My head was still pounding.

"What about on the streets? What's happening there?" I asked.

"There's still disorder, everywhere, even near our office… But we can talk about that later," he said. "Right now, you have to eat. Have a headache?"

I nodded. "A little."

"Too little sleep, too much stress," Doctor Alam suggested. "Did you call Om Aji?"

"Yes, everything's OK there. But I do have to go home so that they can stop worrying. Plus, I need to rest." I felt Alam's chin with my fingers, which tingled from the touch of his prickly beard.

"Maybe we should stay put for a while. Might be best not to go out until it's safe, don't you think?"

Alam slipped his hand beneath the loose T-shirt I was wearing. He knew my body too well and what would happen to me as soon as his fingertip touched my nipples. This was wrong. This should be a time of mourning. We needed to grieve for the chaos this country was in. I got up and off his lap, but Alam pulled me back down again—firmly, without hesitation. And the awful thing was, his action made me all the more excited. His hand succeeded in finding my breast. With only the soft touch of his index finger, I had almost surrendered.

"Alam… We should be in mourning."

He didn't answer. Instead, he pulled me to my feet, then removed his shorts, and then mine as well.

"And making love is only permitted in happy and prosperous times?" He smiled. "If that were the case, the population of Indonesia would shrink to a mere percentage of what it is!" He sat down again and pulled me down, facing him, on the center of his lap. "Don't move," he whispered. "Just enjoy. Don't move…"

"But I want to move…"

"Don't, baby… Wait…"

That morning, all the evil in the world was slowly chased away by tender loving I never wanted to end. That morning, all misfortune and catastrophe was cast aside by endless love.

JAKARTA, MAY 16, 1998

Yesterday, when they heard the news that President Soeharto had returned to Jakarta from Cairo, Alam and his friends seemed to become possessed—not because the President wasn't going to be able solve the crisis at hand but because "the time had come for Indonesia to figure out what to do with him."

Gilang and Alam were acting like two generals ready to raise arms even if their weapons were only the toothbrushes they always carried with them. Regardless, there was now hope in the air. According to Gilang, since the previous day numerous important public figures had been calling meetings to discuss the crisis and what to do about it. Several of his sources mentioned that Nurcholish Madjid, the respected Muslim intellectual Gilang referred to as "Cak" Nur—don't ask me what the term of address "Cak" means—had met with several other influential figures at the invitation of one of the senior military leaders at the Indonesian Armed Forces Headquarters. He said that Cak Nur had put together on the spot a concept for the transition of power that was to be delivered to President Soeharto. The plan included several key points, but the most important one, and the one that made Gilang and Alam feel as if they'd won the war, was that Soeharto would not stand as a candidate at the next general election, which was to be held at the soonest possible time.

"But the students, all of them, want him to resign right now," Bimo stated firmly. "No election! No nothing! Just his resignation!"

Hmmm… Ever since he and Andini had gotten closer, Bimo seemed to glow.

"The students are right," Alam agreed. "Soeharto is just trying to buy more time."

While Alam, Gilang, and Bimo were debating and making predictions in overly loud voices, I was reviewing all the footage that Mita and I had collected from May 12 up to this morning. I don't know how to describe my feelings when I saw the series of images we'd shot. Even scenes on streets leading to Jalan Diponegoro—which we shot between yesterday and this morning—showed us to be in the middle of a war zone, on a tour of a slain city that would be difficult to resurrect. A preview of Doomsday. Along the streets, I saw through my eyes and lens storefronts and even large malls now reduced to their basic structures; sidewalks whose brickwork was now piles of rubble; twisted and misshapen fences; traffic signs hanging limply from their poles, some of them even melted; lofty and formerly awe-inspiring buildings now nothing but blackened skeletons. ATM machines that had been broken into and plundered. Supermarkets, banks, and stores devastated. The country's economic and business pulse had been mortally maimed and severed. Even today, several days after the firestorm, there were no other words for it: Jakarta in the morning light was a hell, completely distressed from torture. Television news programs constantly aired horrific images of burned victims—stacked in piles and put into black bags like so much rubbish. And I can't even make myself talk about the attacks on and the rapes of women of ethnic Chinese descent. The stories of perversion were so utterly grotesque they made my head want to explode.

Alam was anxiously waiting for news from his friends in ILUNI, the University of Indonesia Alumni Association. He said that the university's professorial senate, headed by the university rector, had met with President Soeharto earlier that morning at the president's private residence on Jalan Cendana to convey the results of the emergency symposium the university had called on the question of governmental reform. They included a request for the president to resign.

"I want to know Soeharto's answer to that one," Alam said, pacing the floor, phone in hand, grumbling because no one could tell him the president's response.

"Be patient. We'll find out soon enough," Bimo said. "How about getting us some lunch," he then said to Ujang.

As Ujang was writing down our orders, a loud ring was heard. Alam almost jumped from his seat to grab his cell phone on his desk but then suddenly frowned.

"Not mine. Same ring tone."

"Oh, that must be mine…" I said, picking up my phone. I had finally gotten around to changing the irritating ringtone on the cell phone that Andini had lent to me; but the stupid thing was that I had set it with the same ring tone as Alam's. I looked at the screen but saw no number. Was it Maman? Or Ayah?

"*Salut*," came the sound of a familiar voice.

"Oh, Nara… *Salut!*" I glanced at Alam whose hands were now on his hips. I didn't know if he was irritated because the call wasn't the one he'd been waiting for, because our ring tones were the same, or because he heard me say Nara's name.

"Are you all right, *ma chérie*?" Nara asked.

"Yes," I answered. "And you?" My voice sounded stilted even to me. Even though Alam had turned his body away from me and was now busy at the laptop on his desk, I could tell that he and all the other people in the room had suddenly pricked up their ears, even Ujang, who should have been going out to buy our lunches. I heard Mita tell him to get a move on.

"I'm lonely. I miss you. There's only men around here."

"Umm, here too…"

What a stupid answer that was. "Here too?" In a normal situation I would have snapped at such a sexist statement. But I was feeling witless. And in an emergency situation such as this one, the safest thing to do is to repeat or agree to whatever the other person was saying, even if the answer sounds stupid.

"How about your interviews? All finished?"

"Yes, I've finished almost all my interviews. Maybe just one or two more people to do. But you know what's been happening here, don't you?"

"Of course. There's been news of it in *Le Figaro* and *Le Monde*— even though it was on the inside pages. You really must come home, *ma chérie*. As soon as you finish your interviews, come home. I'm worried about you."

"My deadline is still some time away. I've sent a report to Professor Dupont on what I've done," I answered in somewhat of a panic. "And the airport isn't back in full operation yet. Only part of it. The expatriates and some of the diplomatic staff here are preparing to move."

"Well then, I am just going to have to come to see you!"

"Oh…"

Silence.

"Don't you want me to come?"

I could hear the disappointment in Nara's voice. "Of course, Nara."

I felt all eyes looking at me. Alam stepped away from his desk but didn't leave the room.

"It's just that the situation is so bad here. People are trying to leave this place and you want to come?"

"Are you forgetting that I am Indonesian too?!" Nara sounded offended.

"*D'accord*...Of course you are. That's not what I meant."

It was beginning to feel as if I couldn't say anything right.

"Listen, Lintang..." Nara's voice sounded like he wanted to change the subject. "I was actually calling not just to ask about you, but also to tell you the news that I finally got an answer from Cambridge. I've been accepted and will be moving to England at the end of August, because the program starts in September."

"*Félicitations*, Nara!" This time I was speaking honestly. I truly was happy that he was going to realize his ambition of pursuing a higher degree at Cambridge. He had always dreamed of going there.

"*Merci*...But, Lintang, I also wanted to ask you if your mother ever told you what is wrong with your father?"

"Some kind of infection of the liver, she said. Why?"

"Oh, nothing." He seemed to be holding back something. "OK then, finish your work and come home as soon as you can. We all miss you. Not just me, but your parents as well."

I said nothing for a moment, then, "*D'accord*."

"*Salut*, Lintang."

"*Salut*."

When I clicked off my cell phone, all the eyes and ears that had been opened extra wide just a second before suddenly turned their attention back to whatever it was they were supposed to be working on. Alam took the keys to Gilang's jeep and then yelled to Gilang that he was going to take the vehicle.

"But here's the meal you ordered," said Ujang, who was coming towards us with a tray full of our luncheon orders. There was a look of irritation on his face as he watched his "big brother" leave the office with the keys to Gilang's jeep jangling in his hand.

Gilang scurried after Alam, but returned quickly with a confused look on his face. "Earlier he said we'd go to Salemba together after lunch. What got into him?"

Mita, Bimo, and Odi looked at me, as if I could provide the answer. I busied myself with my documentary footage, silently hoping that Alam would sulk for only a few hours.

MAY 18, 1998

For two days now Alam hasn't spoken to me. Hasn't called or stopped by, much less touched me. After the "Nara incident," he's been so busy it seems that I've barely caught sight of him at Satu Bangsa. There's been so much news in the air and rumors flying about meetings of various power holders and interest groups, but their common thread seems to be the same: a request for President Soeharto to resign.

I was sure that Alam was avoiding me so, finally, I decided to interview the last two people on my list of respondents on my own. But while I was conducting the interviews, talk about the hardships of 1965 invariably turned to the recent unrest and ongoing student demonstrations. I had to constantly remind myself of Professor Dupont's message to me: focus. Don't be swayed by news of today. It was fine for me to record the historical events of today out of personal interest, but I had to be able to separate my emotions from the theme of my final assignment.

Then suddenly, after all my interviews were over, I felt relieved. For the first time since my arrival in Jakarta, I really wanted to go home to Paris in order to edit and finish my assignment and turn it in to Professor Dupont. Even more important for me, I wanted to go home to see Ayah and Maman. But just a second. I had just referred to Paris as the place I was "going home to."

Was Paris really my home?

My cell phone rang. Mita. She ordered me to meet her at Parliament where the rest of the staff was heading. The students were on the march and heading to Parliament to occupy the building.

On the way there in a taxi, between urging the driver to get me to Parliament as fast as he could, I kept asking myself why Alam was persisting in his silent treatment towards me. Was it only because of Nara's call?

When I finally made it to the building, its grounds were full of students and public figures—almost a repeat of the scene at Trisakti several days previously. Every speaker was saying the same thing: a demand for *reformasi* and Soeharto's resignation. I wandered the area with a light feeling. It was so odd, the atmosphere that afternoon outside the clam-shaped parliament building seemed almost festive. It was hard to believe that such despicable and widespread horrors had taken place in this country just a few days before.

Free box meals were being handed out. Women in food vans appeared from out of nowhere to give food and beverages to the student orators and their crowd, who were clapping and singing songs I didn't know but whose most oft-repeated phrase was "down with the government." Young couples held hands and hugged each other, as if they were on a date. I thought of my parents' first meeting and imagined the atmosphere here in Jakarta at the moment to be much like it was in Paris at the time of the May Revolution in 1968. There was a heady mixture of politics and arts along with a celebration in the freedom of hormonal urges.

I caught sight of Mita waving her arm in the distance, standing in a group with Alam, Gilang, Andini, and Bimo on the low sloping series of stairs leading to the main entrance of the building. I smiled when I saw Andini.

"Hi…"

Bimo gave me a big hug. "How are you? It's been days since I've seen you." He shot a glance at Alam. "And somebody else has been missing you too."

Alam smiled faintly but didn't greet me. After just a momentary glance at me, he returned his attention to the speakers' stage.

"You owe me a story," I whispered to Andini. As usual, she started laughing. Then she pinched Alam's arm. "Here she is! You've been telling Mita to call her all morning and now that she is here you don't say anything."

Alam looked at Andini with raised eyebrows then turned his gaze back to the students, who were growing ever more wild in their enthusiasm: clapping loudly and shouting "Reform!" time and again. I felt like tinder had set fire to my heart. My blood rushed to my brain. This was terrible. I wasn't a teenager whose emotional state is expected to fluctuate with the temperature of love in the relationship she's in. But the fact was I felt so sad and disappointed whenever Alam kept a distance from me.

"I'm thirsty," I said to Mita. "I'm going to go get something to drink."

"Here, I have a bottle…" she started to say, but I shook my head and turned and walked away as quickly as I could, because I didn't want them to hear the pounding of my heart or see the tears that were welling in my eyes.

Merde! In Jakarta, I had turned into a sniveling adolescent. I swore heartily to myself in three languages—French, English, Indonesian; French, English, Indonesian—expelling all the worst words I could think of and mixing them together while I looked for a spot to be by myself among the students who filled the upper piazza surrounding the building. I had to still my heart and regain my energy.

My work was completed. There was no telling how long the occupation of the parliament building would last. It might be days or even weeks. And I didn't know what was really happening with Ayah. Nara had sounded so strange when he raised the topic of Ayah's illness. And Maman only ever gave the briefest of reports on what the doctors had to say.

How was I going to say goodbye to Alam? How could I even look him in the face if he was going to act cold towards me when I said goodbye? What if he acted snidely and give me the same toss-away smile that he had given me minutes before? Shit!

A hand touched my shoulder. I knew that hand. That smell.

"I thought you said you wanted to get something to drink," Alam said from behind me in a friendly tone of voice.

Now I was angry and turned towards him: "What business is it of yours? And why are you following me anyway?"

Alam looked at me innocently. *Merde!* Men always play so dumb when they hurt a woman. I left him and found a place to sit down on the stairs. As I guessed he would, Alam followed me.

"How are you doing?" he asked politely.

"Fine. Just fine."

Then we were silent. A silence ripe with questions and longing.

Finally, I spoke: "Where have you been? Two days and not

a peep from you," I said in a voice that sounded flat and uncaring.

"I've been busy. Ever since the fourteenth, a lot of public figures and groups have been meeting with the president, and I want to get this down for the record. I've been interviewing the people who have met with the president and documenting what they had to say. ... There's so much I want to tell you."

I did in fact want to hear what Alam had to say; I'm sure the stories would be interesting. But I was still asking myself whether he realized what I had just said and what that implied.

"Mita said you finished your interviews."

I nodded, now feeling slightly warmer towards him. At least he had tried to find out what I was doing. But then suddenly, and for no apparent reason, I started to cry.

Alam was startled and put his arm around my shoulder.

"I have to go home," I sputtered.

"Home, to Paris?"

"Of course. Where else?"

For some time, he said nothing.

"Here, feel this," he said, taking my hand and pressing my palm to his chest. "What is it you feel every time they shout 'Reformasi!'?"

My heart beat faster and I felt my blood speed through my veins.

"Ever since meeting you, Lintang, I've felt that you are part of this place, that you are home here."

A warm feeling spread through my chest.

"Do you think so?"

"I do. Your roots are here."

I paused before speaking again.

"Why didn't you try to call me or contact me?" I snapped at him. My eyes were hot and tears began to fall again. "Why did you just disappear these past two days? I know you were busy, but you could have told me."

Alam looked at me. The light in his eyes was more subdued. "Listen to me, Lintang... Nara had just called you. He wants to see you. He wants to come here. But he could tell there was something different in you from the sound of your voice."

I sensed a tone of sadness in what he said. My tears stopped instantly. I looked into Alam's face. Had he freshly shaved this morning?

"I wanted to give you space, Lintang. I want you to make your life decisions without pressure from anyone."

I couldn't say anything in the face of Alam's explanation. Why did something so simple have to become something difficult?

"I've already told you, I don't want to part from you," Alam said, "despite my bad reputation which Bimo keeps talking about!" He smiled.

The calls for "*Reformasi!*" had turned into a solid scream that was deafening, even though we were seated quite distant from the free-speech platform. The cry of "reform" pounded my eardrums. Meanwhile, from a different direction came the much fainter sound of students singing a ballad whose lyrics I knew well: "*...I can hear voices / wails of the wounded / people shooting arrows at the moon...*"

I was suddenly moved. My heart beat faster.

Alam knew I recognized the words. "Yes, those are the lyrics of one of Rendra's poems set to a song by Iwan Fals."

Alam knew instantly why I was familiar with that poem. The off-key sound of the student voices was beautiful to my ears, even more stirring than a Ravel composition. Now I felt that I knew where my home was. I hugged Alam tightly. I didn't want to ever let go.

"Alam, don't ever again act like you want to give me space. I don't want a space that is empty except for me alone! I don't want distance from you. Not one centimeter. Not one millimeter."

Alam held my face in his hands and kissed me even though my face was smeared with snot and tears.

EPILOGUE

My dearest Lintang,

Listen to these lines: When I die, the cry / that bursts from my heart / will forever be in my poem / that will never die...

Subagio Sastrowardoyo's intimate relationship with death is suggested in his poem, "The Poem That Will Never Die." For me this poem evokes something quite normal. And for that reason, I feel that my own death, which is now very close, is something usual as well—something ordinary for which there is no reason to lament. That said, I do ask your forgiveness for my not allowing your mother to reveal the results of my medical tests to you. The name of the disease alone—cirrhosis of the liver—was enough to make me feel uninterested. The disease has no aesthetic attraction and there is nothing interesting about it to discuss.

Doctors and nurses were created to map the state of our bodily organs. Unfortunately, they often get this authoritarian streak when they do it. As a result, they are often able to influence our actions and emotions by what they say. And I for one would thoroughly object if you (or I) were to peg our lives (or deaths) on a doctor's words.

After a long battle with your mother, who forced me to go

478

*to the doctor to pick up the results from my final examination,
I made a demand: that whatever the results of the tests, you
were not to be told until your visit to Indonesia had ended.
Especially after learning the news of the shootings of those
students at Trisakti and then the horrendous anarchy that
followed, I knew that it would be impossible to extract you from
the midst of the madness the country was going through. This
aside from the fact that the airport had been shut down and
that many expatriates were fleeing Jakarta, at least temporarily.*

*The atmosphere at the restaurant was also tense at that time.
All of us were on tenterhooks as we watched the television,
minute by minute, hour by hour. Even with the delays in news
coverage, quite a lot of information was conveyed. (Apparently,
CNN and other major news outlets deemed other world news
to be far more important so that news about Indonesia was
aired only a few times a day.)*

*On May 21, when President Soeharto made his resignation
speech, the whole lot of us roared aloud. The entire restaurant
erupted in shouting. Our two cynics, Om Nug and Om Risjaf,
yelled that they were going to find a goat to slaughter. (Don't
ask me where they were going to find a goat in the middle of
Paris!) And as if they didn't know better, they also said they
were going to order plane tickets for all of us to come to Jakarta.
Om Nug said that the New Order government had fallen, that
we could at last go home and set foot in our native land.*

*Your mother kept insisting that it was time for you to come
back to Paris to see me but, I'm sorry, I had to forbid her from
telling you so. By this time I was just surviving on medicines,
but you were in the middle of finishing your assignment.*

And now I am surrounded by four white and boring walls

*and a nurse with the look on her face that's likely to hasten
my death. She never seems to smile, but then becomes delighted
when she's sticking a needle in me to extract another blood
sample.*

Oh, my dearest Lintang…

*It's truly ironic that with the fall of Soeharto there is, indeed,
a good possibility that we pillars here will be able to come home
to Indonesia, but that I will be coming home in a coffin (if not
in the open-sided* keranda *we Muslims are supposed to be in).
But that's all right. Didn't I always say that I wanted my final
home to be in Karet cemetery? No need for an expensive plot
for me at Père Lachaise in Paris—and don't dare purchase
a plot at Tanah Kusir or Jeruk Purut cemeteries in Jakarta.
Choose for me a rectangle of earth in Karet. The soil there,
with which my body will fuse, has a smell and texture I know.
Don't cry for me. Don't cry.*

*Scatter cloves and jasmine flowers on my grave so that their
scent reaches my body lying there below, silent and alone.
I am confident of capturing their fragrance through the spaces
in the soil that kindly provide a path for their scent I know so
intimately to reach me.*

*I can picture the ceremony. I can see who will be there to
attend my burial alongside you, my life's most shining star,
and your mother, the most beautiful and strongest woman I've
ever known, who stood at my side through my life's ordeals.
I can see my brother Aji and his fine family; Tante Surti and
her three children; and the remaining three pillars of Tanah Air.
(Try to comfort Om Risjaf, who won't have the strength to hold
back the bitter pain of it all. Of the four pillars, he was always
the most sensitive, and the one the rest of us always thought of*

as a youngest brother. Stay beside him, please.)
I can also see Nara and Alam and all of the friends you made
at Satu Bangsa among the crowd of mourners. Maybe you
will pray for me. Maybe Om Aji will lead the prayer. Maybe
the lot of you will be even so wacky as to play Led Zeppelin's
"Stairway to Heaven." But if you want to help console Om
Risjaf, let him play his harmonica—as long as he doesn't play
"When the Orchids Start to Bloom" because, for me, my orchid
withered long ago. Tell him instead to play John Denver's "Take
Me Home, Country Road." And if that does happen, don't be
surprised if you hear me humming along from my final place
of rest.

There are a few things I need to tell you and I must do
it quickly because that foul-humored nurse of mine will be
back here soon to jab me with her damned needle. But I can't
resist telling you first that a couple of days ago I played a trick
on the nurse that almost drove her crazy. I packed up all my
belongings, then straightened my bed and found a place to hide.
When she came into my room, she must have panicked, because
she pushed the blue emergency call button which brought all
the other nurses and caused the guards to start a manhunt.
Political exile that I am, used to wandering from one country
to the next, hoodwinking my minders was easy for me. I found
myself a place to hide in a storage closet where they keep sheets
and blankets. Even with the commotion in the hallway, it was
so nice and warm and soft in there, I ended up falling asleep.
In the end, they did find me, of course, and with their hands on
their hips marched me back to my room like an apprehended
fugitive.

The price I paid for my insurrection was high: ever since

then, Om Nug and Om Risjaf have been on guard duty,
taking turns to watch over me, day and night, as if I were
a hardcore criminal. And then when your mother comes to see
me in the mornings and evenings, before and after her classes,
she always has this little smirk on her face, like I've finally been
put in my place. Well, just wait! I fully intend to find another
way to make a disturbance.

But, anyway, back to what I was saying. This is the most
important part of what I want to say to you and it has to
do with Alam and Narayana. Though you never said as
much in your e-mails to me, I know that something special
has happened between you and Alam. It's easy to catch the
carefreeness and passion in your words whenever you write
about Alam or quote for me something that he has told you.
You have been struck by lightning. And that's OK. That's
normal. And although I don't know Alam—he was just
a baby when I left—I've seen enough pictures of him to know
that he's gotten the best physical traits of both Om Hananto
and Tante Surti. But I'm sure you're not attracted to him just
because of his height or muscular build; such specimens are
easily available in Europe. There must be something in Alam
that has made you feel at home in Jakarta. It couldn't just be
because of your film assignment.

And then we have Narayana who has the good looks of
a French actor. Again, of course, I know that's not the reason
that you've maintained a relationship with him for several
years. I won't say much about this and I won't try to interfere,
but what I want to tell you is this: don't play with the feelings
of a person until his heart is broken to pieces and scattered
everywhere. Be brave enough to make a choice, even with all the

*risks it might entail. You're still young. Making a choice doesn't
mean having to get married tomorrow. And not choosing either
Nara or Alam is still a choice. Whatever it is, make your own
choice, for yourself and for your peace of heart.*

*I don't want you to be a person like me, who was never able
to choose. I found myself enchanted by so many things, and
wandered from one way of thinking to another without finding
one that was enduring. The only thing I was ever sure of was
myself and my desire to continue my unending voyage. Or, in
your mother's words, to fly like a seagull without ever wanting
to alight. As a result of my indecision, life made its choices for
me and it was not I who determined my life's course.*

*Your mother had the courage to choose. She chose to marry
me, crazy nomad that I am. And then she chose not to marry
again. So, too, Tante Surti, another woman who was brave
enough to make a choice. Believe me, even people like my friend
Hananto and Aji's son, Rama, are people who made choices.
Even if we don't agree with their choices, we must respect their
right to choose.*

*The other thing, Lintang, and this is a question: what did
you in the end finally pluck from I-N-D-O-N-E-S-I-A?
I'm sure that what you found in your time in Jakarta of just
a little more than a month is not enough to explain all of the
factors that have shaped Indonesia. Your final assignment will
help to explain a small part of the country, will reveal a few
of the voices to be found there. I do not use the word "small"
disparagingly, because I am confident that your work will have
an immense impact. Your documentary will be another voice,
a voice from the other side which for thirty-two years has
been silenced.*

After my burial, think long about whether after your
graduation you want to return to Jakarta or to stay in Paris.
I force no choice on you. Both Paris and Jakarta are your home
and each place has special meaning for you. Wherever you
choose to be, you will be close with one part of yourself: with
Maman in Paris and with me in Karet cemetery
in Jakarta.

Uh-oh... I just heard a bell, which means I must get back
to planning some way of tricking my steel-jawed nurse.

"Can death be sleep, when life is but a dream?"
John Keats provides the perfect closure for this letter.
My death, Lintang, will be but a moment of sleep for me,
because when I awake, I will meet you.

Lintang, you gave life to my life and even after I die,
you will continue to live in me.

Your loving father,
Dimas Suryo

●

In Karet, even in Karet (my future abode), the cold wind comes...
In the end, Ayah did come home, to Karet, to finally reunite with
the soil that he said had a different scent from the earth in the
Cimetière du Père Lachaise. The soil of Karet. The land he was
destined to come home to.

At the head of his grave, weighted with commemorative floral
arrangements, was a plain wooden marker on which Om Nug
had written in a simple hand:

For a life full of charm and beauty
For the wanderer now gone forever
For Dimas Suryo: 1930–1998

It was the same image that came to my mind and haunted me the night before I left Paris. It was the image of my father's pending death, the knowledge of which he had persisted in keeping from me.

As my father predicted, Tante Surti, Kenanga, and Bulan scattered jasmine flowers on his grave. Maman sprinkled cloves. Om Aji led the congregation in prayers that sounded to me like music. Tante Retno, Andini, and Rama also scattered jasmine flowers and rose petals too. My father's friend, Bang Amir, and his wife were there. I watched him as he cried silently before the grave. He said a prayer, then covered his face with his hands.

Om Nug and Om Tjai, who represented the larger community of Indonesian exiles in Paris and elsewhere, each gave testimonial speeches. Om Risjaf was too sad to speak; he stood at my left side with a harmonica in his hand, tears falling nonstop from his eyes until finally I took his hand and squeezed it tightly. Pointing with my other hand to the far end of the grave, I whispered: "Look, can you see? Ayah is sitting there laughing at us." Unable to appreciate my dark humor, he cried all the more. Oh, my father was always right in his predictions.

In the distance I could see Alam seated by himself beneath a frangipani tree. His eyes were on me constantly, centered on me alone, binding me with him. Behind me was Narayana. You're right, Ayah. It would be much easier not to choose and to pretend there were no consequences. But, as you said, to choose requires courage; it is what one must do.

As other mourners said their goodbyes and began to leave Karet cemetery, we continued sitting there listening to Om Risjaf play "Take Me Home, Country Road" in a tempo so slow it seemed to shred the red twilight sky. He played with his eyes closed but tears still issued from his eyelids and he would not allow anyone to approach. I could hear Ayah humming along with Maman, who was singing the song. And then, in the distance, I saw a man of about fifty walking through the cemetery with a girl of about seven years. They were holding each other's hands. Softly, I heard the father tell his daughter about an episode in the *Mahabharata*. I heard the name "Bima" and then "Ekalaya." After that, I listened as the little girl pestered the man with questions, sometimes in French, sometimes in Indonesian.

The gloaming came slowly, as if giving us a little extra time to spend with Ayah before complete darkness fell. I didn't know whether I was in Père Lachaise or Karet. But I could see Ayah smiling in the distance, happy to be home and for all of us to be with him.

END NOTES

SOURCES OF LITERARY QUOTES

APIN, RIVAI. Excerpt from his poem "Elegy" (Elegi) in the chapter "Surti Anandari" from *Tiga Menguak Takdir* by Chairil Anwar Asrul Sani and Rivai Apin. Jakarta: Balai Pustaka, 1958. (All translations from the Indonesian, both here and elsewhere, by John H. McGlynn.)

AUDEN, W.H. Excerpt from "On Installing an American Kitchen in Lower Austria" in the chapter "The Four Pillars" from *The Table Comes First* by Adam Gopnik New York: Knopf, 2011.

BYRON, LORD. Excerpt from "She Walks in Beauty" in the chapter "Surti Anandari" from *Lord Byron: An Anthology* by *George Gordon Byron*. Jarod Publishing, 1993.

DE SAINT-EXUPÉRY, ANTOINE. Quotes from *The Little Prince* in the chapters "Ekalaya" and "Flâneurs" from *The Little Prince (Le Petit Prince)*. Harcourt Inc., 1971.

ELIOT, T.S. Excerpt from "The Burial of the Dead" in the chapter "Paris, April 1998" from *The Wasteland: The Complete Poems and Plays*. Faber and Faber, 1969.

JOYCE, JAMES. Excerpt from *A Portrait of the Artist as a Young Man* in the chapter "Hananto Prawiro" from *A Portrait of the Artist as a Young Man*. Dover Publications, 1994.

KEATS, JOHN. Excerpt from "Bright Star Would I Were Steadfast as Thou Art" in the chapter "Surti Anandari" from *John Keats: Selected Poems*. New Jersey: Gramercy Books, 1993.

MENON, RAMESH. Interpretation of the story of Ekalaya in the chapter "Ekalaya" from *The Mahabharata: A Modern Rendering*. New Delhi: Rupa & Co., 2004.

MOHAMAD, GOENAWAN. Excerpt from "Foreword" in the chapter *L'irréparable* from *Goenawan Mohamad: Selected Poems*, Laksmi Pamuntjak, ed. Jakarta: Lontar, 2004.

SASTROWARDOYO, SUBAGIO. Excerpt from "And Death Grows More Intimate" (Kematian Makin Akrab) in the chapter "l'Irréparable" from *Kematian Makin Akrab*. Jakarta: Grasindo, 1995.

SASTROWARDOYO, SUBAGIO. Excerpt from "The Poem that Never Dies" (Sajak yang tak Pernah Mati) in "Epilogue" from *Kematian Makin Akrab*. Jakarta: Grasindo, 1995.

SITUMORANG, SITOR. Description of "The Prodigal Son" (Si Anak Hilang) in the chapter "Paris, April 1998" from *Sitor Situmorang: Kumpulan Sajak 1980–2005*. Jakarta: Komunitas Bambu, 2006.

REFERENCE MATERIALS

AIDIT, SOBRON. *Melawan dengan Restoran.* Jakarta: Mediakita and Penerbit Kukusan, 2007.

ALAM, IBARRURI PUTRI. *Ibarruri Putri Alam* (a biographical novel). Jakarta: Hasta Mitra, 2006.

CASEVECCHIE, JANINE. *Mai 68, en Photos.* Collection Roger-Viollet, Editions du Chene - Hachette Livre, 2008.

HEMINGWAY, ERNEST. *A Moveable Feast: The Restored Edition.* London: Arrow Books, 2011.

ISA, IBRAHIM. *Bui tanpa Jerajak Besi.* Jakarta: Klik Books, 2011.

JUSUF, ESTER; SITOMPUL, HOTMA; ET AL. *Kerusuhan Mei 1998, Fakta, Data dan Analisa.* Jakarta: Solidaritas Nusa Bangsa, 2008.

KUSNI, J.J. *Membela Martabata Diri dan Indonesia, Koperasi Restoran Indonesia di Paris.* Yogyakarta: Penerbit Ombak, 2005.

LUBIS, FIRMAN. *Jakarta 1960an, Kenangan Semasa Mahasiswa.* Jakarta: Masup Jakarta, 2008.

LUHULIMA, JAMES. *Hari-hari Terpanjang: Menjelang Mundurnya Presiden Soeharto.* Jakarta: penerbit buku kompas, 2001.

MCGLYNN, JOHN AND A. KOHAR EBRAHIM, eds. *Menagerie 6.* Jakarta: Lontar, 2004.

REICHL, RUTH, ed. *Remembrance of Things Paris.* New York: Condé Nast Publications, 2004.

ROOSA, JOHN. *Dalih Pembunuhan Massal yang Terlupakan*: *Gerakan 30 September dan Kudeta Suharto*. Jakarta: Institut Sejarah Sosial Indonesia and Hasta Mitra, 2008.

TEMPO. The annual special editions of *Tempo* magazine from the 1980s up until 2009.

ACKNOWLEDGMENTS

I began to write this novel in 2006 but did not finish until 2012. I daresay it still might not be finished without the assistance of numerous friends and informants and the aid of books and music. My greatest thanks go to Indonesia's political exiles, who together served as the inspiration for this novel and who, individually, took the time to answer my questions in meetings with them in Paris and Jakarta. I especially would like to thank the late Umar Said, the late Sobron Aidit, and Kusni Sulang, who revealed in detail to me their life tales, whose combined journey was much more difficult and far more treacherous than is depicted in this novel. Visits to Indonesia Restaurant, which they opened on Rue de Vaugirard in 1982, and walks on the campus of Sorbonne University proved essential for the scenes set in Paris. Amarzan Loebis, my "walking encyclopedia" at *Tempo* magazine, where the two of us work, was kind enough to relate his own personal story to me and to read the initial draft of this novel. His critical eye for detail is much appreciated. Leo Sutanto, who provided moral support for me from the very beginning of the writing process, also gave me his unflagging trust, for which I will always be indebted, as I will be also to my friends at Sinemart: Novi, Mitzy, and Cindy Christina Sutanto. Then there is Mariana Renata Dantec, who helped to bring the character of Lintang Utara to life with her thorough descriptions of student life at the Sorbonne. Other friends in Europe—Ibarruri Sudharsono and Johanna Lederer, in Paris, and Ibrahim Isa in Amsterdam—I owe thanks and many fine meals.

In Jakarta, I am indebted to Dayani Svetlana and Djoko Sri Moeljono, who illuminated for me the dark days that this city went through, and also to Goenawan Mohamad, a co-founder of *Tempo*, who, in 2005, first proposed to me the idea of exploring the lives of the families of former political prisoners for a special edition of the magazine to commemorate the events of September 30, 1965—an idea that then became an annual tradition for the magazine in its quest to make heard the voices that had been suppressed in the decades since that time. I owe much to my fellow employees at *Tempo*, from the library staff up to the editorial board—Arif Zulkifli, Seno Joko Suyono, Hermien Y. Kleden, L.R. Baskoro, Toriq Hadad, and Bambang Harymurti—for their research into and their reports on that seminal time in 1965.

At Kepustakaan Populer Gramedia, the Indonesian publisher of *Pulang*, I must thank Pax Benedanto, Christina M. Udiani, and Candra Gautama, Wendie Arstwenda, Bintang Siahaan, and Esti WW, for the freedom they gave and the forbearance they showed me. To Dian Sastrowardoyo, Wisnu Darmawan, Arifaldi Dasril, and Renny Fernandez, stalwart friends who were always ready to give me a boost when I was flagging, I extend my unending thanks. The same is true for my French language informants—Gracia Asriningish, Winda Fitriastuti, and Noorca Massardi—and for the historians, Bonnie Triyana and Asvi Warman Adam, who believe in historical accuracy and truth.

Additional thanks go to my friends who offered much valuable input during the course of writing this novel: Mira Lesmana,

Riri Riza, Joko Anwar, Arifaldi Dasril; my invaluable research assistant, Ulin Ni'am Yusron; Robertus Robet, a good friend who explained the map of the 1998 student movement; and friends who supplied me with many of the additional resource materials I needed, including Siti Gretiani and Paramita Mohamad. To Todung Mulya Lubis, Rio Lassatrio, and Syarafina Vidyadhana, the words "thank you" is not enough for all the help they gave to me.

To John H. McGlynn of the Lontar Foundation, who published my first collection of stories in English, and who took on the task of translating this novel into English, I have undying respect but also must thank him for introducing my work to Pontas Literary and Film Agency, which now represents me abroad. At the agency, I give special thanks to the Maria Cardona Serra and Marina Penalva, and to Anna Soler Pont, founder of the agency, as well.

I proffer loving thanks to my parents, Willy and Mohammad Chudori, and my older sister and brother, Zuly Chudori and Rizal Bukhari Chudori, for having taught me at a very young age that literature is no less important than food, knowledge, and faith, as a major sustenance of life. And finally and forever, I give my thanks to Rain Chudori-Soerjoatmodjo, the sun that brightens my life, for it was because of her I began to write again.

BIOGRAPHICAL INFORMATION

LEILA S. CHUDORI, was born in Jakarta in December 1962 and began to write at a young age. Her first stories were published when she was just twelve in several children's magazines. She also published several collections of stories when just a teen.

Leila's college education included stints at Lester B. Pearson College of the Pacific (United World Colleges) in Victoria, Canada, and Trent University, also in Canada, where she studied political science and comparative development studies. Even while going to school, however, she continued to write and publish in the Indonesian literary journals, *Zaman*, *Horison*, *Matra*, *Sastra*, and *Menagerie* as well as in *Solidarity* of the Philippines and *Tenggara* from Malaysia.

Her first collection of short stories for adults, *Malam Terakhir*, published by Pustaka Utama Grafiti in 1989, was later translated and published in German, under the title *Die Letzte Nacht* by Horlemman Verlag. Since 1989 she has worked at *Tempo* weekly news magazine, first as a journalist and later as an editor. She is also a film critic and an award-winning screenplay writer.

In 2009, Kepustakaan Populer Gramedia published Leila's most recent collection of stories, this one titled *9 from Nadira*. In 2013, the Lontar Foundation published a collection of translations of her stories under the title *The Longest Kiss*. In 2012, Leila published her first novel, *Pulang* [Home]. A year later, she was awarded the Khatulistiwa Literary prize for best prose work. Since then, between frequent appearances at literary events in Indonesia and abroad (Australia, Holland, France, and Malaysia), she has been working on two novels, one on the young Indonesian activists who "disappeared" in the months leading up to the downfall of President Soeharto in 1998, and the second a prequel to Home titled *Namaku Alam* [My name is Alam].

•

JOHN H. McGLYNN, lives in Jakarta where, in 1987, he co-founded the Lontar Foundation, the only organization in the world devoted to the publication of Indonesian literature in translation. Through Lontar, he has ushered into publication close to two hundred books on Indonesian literature and culture. Also through Lontar, he has produced twenty-four films on Indonesian writers and more than thirty films on Indonesian performance traditions.

McGlynn is the Indonesian country editor for *Manoa*, a literary journal published by the University of Hawaii, and for *Words Without Borders*, a virtual literary journal. He is a member of the International Commission of the Indonesian Publishers Association (IKAPI), PEN International-New York, and the Association of Asian Studies. He is also a trustee of AMINEF, the American Indonesian Exchange Foundation, which oversees the Fulbright and Humphrey scholarship programs in Indonesia.

495

Thank you all
for your support.
We do this for you,
and could not do
it without you.

DEEP
VELLUM

DEAR READERS,

Deep Vellum Publishing is a 501c3 nonprofit literary arts organization founded in 2013 with the threefold mission to publish international literature in English translation; to foster the art and craft of translation; and to build a more vibrant book culture in Dallas and beyond. We seek out literary works of lasting cultural value that both build bridges with foreign cultures and expand our understanding of what literature is and what meaningful impact literature can have in our lives.

Operating as a nonprofit means that we rely on the generosity of tax-deductible donations from individual donors, cultural organizations, government institutions, and foundations to provide a of our operational budget in addition to book sales. Deep Vellum offers multiple donor levels, including the LIGA DE ORO and the LIGA DEL SIGLO. The generosity of donors at every level allows us to pursue an ambitious growth strategy to connect readers with the best works of literature and increase our understanding of the world. Donors at various levels receive customized benefits for their donations, including books and Deep Vellum merchandise, invitations to special events, and named recognition in each book and on our website.

We also rely on subscriptions from readers like you to provide an invaluable ongoing investment in Deep Vellum that demonstrates a commitment to our editorial vision and mission. Subscribers are the bedrock of our support as we grow the readership for these amazing works of literature from every corner of the world. The more subscribers we have, the more we can demonstrate to potential donors and bookstores alike the diverse support we receive and how we use it to grow our mission in ever-new, ever-innovative ways.

From our offices and event space in the historic cultural district of Deep Ellum in central Dallas, we organize and host literary programming such as author readings, translator workshops, creative writing classes, spoken word performances, and interdisciplinary arts events for writers, translators, and artists from across the world. Our goal is to enrich and connect the world through the power of the written and spoken word, and we have been recognized for our efforts by being named one of the "Five Small Presses Changing the Face of the Industry" by Flavorwire and honored as Dallas's Best Publisher by D Magazine.

If you would like to get involved with Deep Vellum as a donor, subscriber, or volunteer, please contact us at deepvellum.org. We would love to hear from you.

Thank you all. Enjoy reading.

Will Evans
Founder & Publisher
Deep Vellum Publishing

LIGA DE ORO ($5,000+)

Anonymous (2)

LIGA DEL SIGLO ($1,000+)

Allred Capital Management
Ben Fountain
Judy Pollock
Life in Deep Ellum
Loretta Siciliano
Lori Feathers
Mary Ann Thompson-Frenk
   & Joshua Frenk
Matthew Rittmayer
Meriwether Evans
Pixel and Texel
Nick Storch
Stephen Bullock

DONORS

Adam Rekerdres
Alan Shockley
Amrit Dhir
Anonymous
Andrew Yorke
Bob Appel
Bob & Katherine Penn
Brandon Childress
Brandon Kennedy
Caroline Casey
Charles Dee Mitchell
Charley Mitcherson

Cheryl Thompson
Christie Tull
Daniel J. Hale
Ed Nawotka
Grace Kenney
Greg McConeghy
Jeff Waxman
JJ Italiano
Kay Cattarulla
Kelly Falconer
Linda Nell Evans
Lissa Dunlay

Mary Cline
Maynard Thomson
Michael Reklis
Mike Kaminsky
Mokhtar Ramadan
Nikki Gibson
Richard Meyer
Steve Bullock
Suejean Kim
Susan Carp
Theater Jones
Tim Perttula

SUBSCRIBERS

Adam Hetherington
Adam Rekerdres
Alan Shockley
Alexa Roman
Amber J. Appel
Amrit Dhir
Andrew Lemon
Anonymous
Antonia Lloyd-Jones
Ariel Saldivar
Balthazar Simões
Barbara Graettinger
Ben Fountain
Ben Nichols
Betsy Morrison
Bill Fisher
Bjorn Beer
Bob & Mona Ball
Bob Appel
Bob Penn
Bradford Pearson
Brandon Kennedy
Brina Palencia
Cayelan & Quinn Thomas
Charles Dee Mitchell
Chase LaFerney
Cheryl Thompson
Chris Sweet
Christie Tull
David Lowery
David Shook
David Wang
David Weinberger
Dennis Humphries
Dr. Colleen Grissom
Ed Nawotka

Ed Tallent
Elisabeth Cook
Fiona Schlachter
Frank Merlino
George Henson
Gino Palencia
Grace Kenney
Greg McConeghy
Guilty Dave Bristow
Heath Dollar
Horatiu Matei
Jacob Siefring
Jacob Silverman
James Crates
Jane Watson
Jeanne Milazzo
Jeff Whittington
Jeremy Hughes
Joe Milazzo
Joel Garza
John Harvell
John Schmerein
Joshua Edwin
Julia Pashin
Julie Janicke Muhsmann
Justin Childress
Kaleigh Emerson
Katherine McGuire
Kenneth McClain
Kimberly Alexander
Lauren Shekari
Lena Saltos
Linda Nell Evans
Lisa Pon Lissa Dunlay
Lissa Dunlay
Liz Ramsburg

Lori Feathers
Lytton Smith
Mac Tull
Mallory Davis
Marcia Lynx Qualey
Margaret Terwey
Mark Larson
Martha Gifford
Mary Ann Thompson-Frenk
& Joshua Frenk
Meaghan Corwin
Michael Holtmann
Mike Kaminsky
Naomi Firestone-Teeter
Neal Chuang
Nicholas Kennedy
Nick Oxford
Nikki Gibson
Owen Rowe
Patrick Brown
Peter McCambridge
Sam Ankenbauer
Scot Roberts
Sean & Karen Fitzgerald
Shelby Vincent
Steven Norton
Susan Ernst
Taylor Zakarin
Tess Lewis
Theater Jones
Tim Kindseth
Todd Mostrog
Tom Bowden
Tony Fleo
Will Morrison
Will Pepple
Will Vanderhyden

AVAILABLE NOW FROM DEEP VELLUM

CARMEN BOULLOSA · *Texas: The Great Theft*
translated by Samantha Schnee · MEXICO

LEILA S. CHUDORI · *Home*
translated by John H. McGlynn · INDONESIA

ALISA GANIEVA · *The Mountain and the Wall*
translated by Carol Apollonio · RUSSIA

ANNE GARRÉTA · *Sphinx*
translated by Emma Ramadan · FRANCE

JÓN GNARR · *The Indian* · *The Pirate*
translated by Lytton Smith· ICELAND

LINA MERUANE · *Seeing Red*
translated by Megan McDowell · CHILE

FISTON MWANZA MUJILA · *Tram 83*
translated by Roland Glasser · DEMOCRATIC REPUBLIC OF CONGO

ILJA LEONARD PFEIJFFER · *La Superba*
translated by Michele Hutchison · NETHERLANDS

RICARDO PIGLIA · *Target in the Night*
translated by Sergio Waisman · ARGENTINA

SERGIO PITOL · *The Art of Flight* · *The Journey*
translated by George Henson · MEXICO

MIKHAIL SHISHKIN · *Calligraphy Lesson: The Collected Stories*
translated by Marian Schwartz, Leo Shtutin,
Mariya Bashkatova, Sylvia Maizell · RUSSIA